COURTING BALANCE

OF ASTRAL AND UMBRAL BOOK TWO

First Edition

ISBNs

E-Book: 978-0-9992067-5-1

Paperback: 978-0-9992067-3-7

Hardback: 978-0-9992067-4-4

TABLE OF CONTENTS

FOREWORD

As with book one, the images above, paired with the voice of the chapter, will be your guide to perspective in this book.

Sections where the narrative are fully italicized indicate that something is a memory in the format of a dream, or purely a dream.

One last thing to keep in mind, is that Devillians are not Human and their behavior will often reflect as such. Their culture is their own, and it is something you will get to learn together with Arianna!

I also want to take a moment to say THANK YOU to everyone who has been patient while waiting for this book to come out. I've finally ironed out my technical issues, so this huge of a delay should not happen again. The number of times that edits were rolled back is painful.

CHAPTER ONE
The Streets of Dauthrmir

The foreign scents and sounds of Dauthrmir assaulted my senses as I followed Darius through the city's streets. Although Devillians were the most prevalent citizens, there were also Humans, Elves, and people of races I didn't recognize. Almost every inch of the streets bustled with people, food carts, or stalls selling every manner of trinket.

Guards sporting Dauthrmiran colors—black, silver, and sapphire—stood at major street corners whilst others patrolled, keeping a vigilant eye on the myriad of people visiting the district.

I found myself overwhelmed by the cacophony of unfamiliar scents and sights. It wasn't until Darius latched onto my left arm that my attention snapped back to the task at hand.

"Ari, we still have time to look around before we go find our house, right?" Darius grinned at me and pointed towards a clock tower with his free hand. "It's still early afternoon regardless of what this crazy-gorgeous sky would have us believe!"

"I…suppose we can look around for a little while." I glanced at our surroundings from within my hood, a knot forming in my stomach. *'I don't like how some of these people are watching us…'*

I wasn't sure if the filthy and disgruntled glares were because we were Human, because of Darius' loud mouth, or because of my hood and mask. A few subtle glances at our surroundings and passing citizens told me that even the Humans were shooting us strange looks—and some of them didn't even look to be locals.

'Ah…. My crest is probably a problem.' I clenched my jaw to suppress a grimace. *'I forgot it's so similar to their oh-so precious general's. Ugh.'*

"What's wrong, Ari? You should be happy!" Darius squeezed my arm and then motioned at our surroundings with his free hand. "It's so beautiful and different here!"

"There's just so much power," I deflected, looking around again. Nalithor's magic ran over my skin like water and made the air tremble in its wake, yet I didn't see him anywhere. Not finding a trace of him was almost worse. It made me bristle, expecting him to pop out of nowhere. "Mrirtec, why didn't you and our parents tell them that I'm—?"

I raised my fingers to my temples and sighed when I spotted

Darius wandering down the street without me.

'Darius seems genuinely happy, for once.' I glanced at my brother's expression when I caught up to him, finding that his usual cheerful façade had been replaced with genuine delight. "Since we have limited time...what do you want to see?"

"Let's go shopping!" Darius hugged my right arm with enough force to pop my elbow.

"Shopping?" I frowned at him. "With what mon—?"

Darius held up a thin crystal with silver etchings on its surface. According to him, it was "linked" to some form of bank account here. One of the "benefits of being a prince," perhaps. The hexagonal rod didn't emit any noticeable aether to speak of, though its entire surface was coated in what looked like nonsensical patterns. How the damned thing was supposed to produce money was beyond me.

"Ari? *Please?*" Darius pouted at me, his eyes wide.

"Fine, as long as you don't overspend, and as long as you don't wander out of my sight." I gave him the firmest look I could muster with half my face being covered. It seemed to have little effect.

'I spoke with Eyrian whilst you slept.' Djialkan nuzzled my cheek and then continued in a matter-of-fact tone, *'Both you and Darius will be working during your stay here—nobility and royalty are not exempt from such things in Dauthrmir, especially not whilst studying.'*

'Darius? Work?' I arched an eyebrow and glanced at Djialkan. A wet nose nudged me from my other cheek, so I reached up to

pet both Alala and Djialkan as we followed my brother.

'Aye. Vorpmasian royals and nobles both work, just as commoners do. They are not pampered like Humans.' Djialkan snorted with laughter. 'Particularly students, of course, as many of them could use a lesson in humility. Your role or job will depend more on who you are partnered with after your tests.'

'Partner?' I frowned. 'I don't much like the sound of that...'

'I will explain it to you later tonight if your brother neglects to do so.' Djialkan nosed my hand once before leaping into the air. 'Fraelfnir, Alala, and I will gather groceries for your new lodgings whilst Darius drags you around. We will await you both at the house.'

Alala leapt from my shoulder and chased after Djialkan. Before they disappeared around a corner, I caught a glimpse of Djialkan taking on the form of a young Devillian boy and hefting the white fox into his arms. The sight of the usually cranky fae-dragon holding or cuddling with something so fluffy made an amused smirk cross my lips.

'A...partner?' I looked down in thought, my heart falling as I contemplated the idea. 'Why does that seem like it should be familiar to me? I work alone. I always have.'

I chose to dwell on it later. Lifting my gaze, I caught up to Darius once more and fell into my role of "silent protector." I chewed on the inside of my lip and swept along after him, stealing the occasional glance at our surroundings before refocusing my attention on the giddy Darius. The way the Devillian and Elven citizens watched my brother stifled my excitement, turning it to unease.

It was clear that I needed to keep a watchful eye on my brother instead of reveling in our new surroundings.

The Merchants' Plaza bustled with even more people than the streets leading to it. I accompanied Darius from store-to-store, soon realizing that "plaza" wasn't quite the correct term for the district. Most of the district we'd seen thus far was a labyrinth of narrow, winding roads lined with both stalls and businesses alike; all of which surrounded the massive plaza the district took its name from.

The *actual* plaza was home to restaurants, cafes, and a few boutiques on the southern end. On the northern end were temples and shrines to many different gods. Judging by the power radiating from that section of the district I could only assume that some of the deities were actually *in* the city today.

'Hmmm… Nalithor is a deity, right? I wonder if he has a temple here as well.' I tilted my head, scanning the eclectic buildings to our north, before turning and catching sight of my brother trying to slip away. The corner of my eye twitched as I shoved my intrigue away and chased after Darius.

Out of habit I remained silent and stayed several paces behind my brother while following him through the city. I watched as he darted from stall to stall and eventually from business to business. He ordered all manner of trinkets, books, and even some artwork and furniture that caught his fancy. As an Astral Mage it would have been very inappropriate for him to buy me, an Umbral Mage, anything...and yet he still offered. Several times.

'Perhaps he's not as "corrupted" by the X'shmirans as I thought?' I shook my head at my brother when he held up a massive gold necklace to me. *'Or is he trying to keep up appearances? I can never tell with this one.'*

When in public places such as this I wasn't allowed to speak with anyone other than "the young master" without his explicit permission. Djialkan usually spoke for me if it was truly necessary to say something. I linked my hands behind my back and clenched them so hard that the leather of my gloves squeaked. I wanted Djialkan and Alala to come back.

Despite the uneasy glances, many of the citizens were quite chatty. It frustrated me to come off as rude or haughty but the pain I'd have to endure for speaking without permission was far worse. Letting myself suffer for the sake of a few words wasn't an option. I wouldn't speak unless absolutely necessary. A few words were all I could get away with.

'Really. Darius is so thick sometimes.' I crossed my arms and watched my brother. *'Does he really wish to keep me silent this badly? He could have given me permission to speak with store owners, at least! I'll be doing most of the cooking and shopping anyway—he'll have to let me at some point! Tch.'*

Ultimately, Darius even moved on to purchasing clothing in

Dauthrmiran, Draemiran, and Suthsul styles. I was forced to decline with a shake of my head every time a store owner inquired if I wished to try anything on, and they were all far too eager to chat with me. Even though I didn't respond, they talked my ear off anyway. However, I did learn from them that Draemir was the territory directly south of Dauthrmir; and thanks to Djialkan's past lessons I knew that it was the homeland of the Adinvyr.

Suthsul was home to Desert Elves—Vunsori in their own tongue—and a Devillian race known as "Sizoul." The Sizoul, apparently, were artisans and scholars. Nomadic Human and Elven tribes were also common in Suthsul, but they disliked the idea of making their home in the stationary capital city V'frul.

The Suthsul Desert was apparently one of the few remaining territories in the known world that wasn't under the reign of the Vorpmasian or Beshulthien Empires. Instead, it retained its independence. The Sizoul, however, were still Vorpmasian citizens. As such, their small province within the desert was also considered part of the empire.

"Ari, what should we go see next?" Darius asked with a cheerful grin as we exited the umpteenth shop.

I paused before answering my twin and glanced around us. An unfamiliar but weak power crept along both of our barriers. It seemed harmless, but… 'Why is someone that weak bothering with us?'

"We should be heading off soon." I sighed before glancing to the side, catching sight of a group of Devillians and the troubled stares they'd fixed on me. "Pick one or two more things to go do. After that, we should leave."

"*Fine*," Darius grumbled, pouting for all of two seconds before perking up and looking around with a curious grin. "What do you think we should get?"

The question must have been rhetorical. Darius' focus shifted instantly, and he wandered down the street once more in search of something interesting. Of course, *everything* interested him, but at least he was being a little choosier since I'd stated only one or two more stops would be acceptable.

I crossed my arms within my sleeves and followed my twin. My back tensed, feeling many pairs of eyes following me down the road. They all seemed more curious than anything, but it still felt strange. In X'shmir, I would have been either ignored or spat at.

"*Those two must be the Human mages from X'shmir, right?*" a female whispered to someone nearby. "*Why is she covered in so much clothing? All the way to her jaw! That can't be comfortable.*"

"*I heard X'shmir follows the Old Ways still,*" another woman stated with clear distaste. "*Poor thing.*"

"Mrirtec, what did I say about wandering off?!" I looked up to see my brother chasing after something. I moved to run after him but making my way through the crowded street proved difficult as it narrowed. "Dehsul! I'll hang him by his ears when I catch him!"

I muttered apologies as I pushed my way through the crowds

of Devillians and Elves. When I came to an intersection, I couldn't spot Darius anywhere. My blood boiled as I tried to decide which way to go. Two of my options led toward the Scarlet District, while the other four streets all led to other parts of the Merchants' Plaza. Darius could have wandered down any one of them.

"Your charge slip away already, my dear?" the powerful, purring voice spoke in Draemiran and was followed by a low chuckle. A large hand came to rest on my right shoulder, causing me to stop and turn abruptly. I would have recognized that voice anywhere.

'Damn it, he's found me already?!'

CHAPTER TWO
Sibling Rivalry

I tilted my head back so that I was no longer staring at the Adinvyr's collarbone. *'Where's Djialkan when I need him? I shouldn't say anything...well...should* say something*...but can't! Was he always this damned tall?'*

As with before, the Devillian deity wore elegant white robes with shimmering embroidery of moons, stars, and dragons. However, this set revealed his throat along with most of his muscular chest and abdomen. Platinum jewelry hung from his pointed ears, throat, and wrists. Similar-colored plates of engraved armor were sewn onto portions of his garments. Now that we were away from X'shmir, the hum of magic from both him and the blue topaz in his attire hummed with strong and unmistakable energy.

His skin was just dark enough to contrast with his long, layered white hair. Platinum trinkets held the hair by his temples in place and several more were entwined with the braid that was draped over his shoulder.

However, it was the Adinvyr's eyes that struck me most. They were the most incredible shade of frosty ice blue I had ever seen. Around his slit pupils, the irises gradated to a rich shade of blue that reminded me of the sky above the Gal'edean Ocean.

The warm smile he'd fixated on me seemed to reach his eyes. I wasn't quite sure how to react to having such a pleasant, seemingly genuine, expression directed toward me. Not at all.

'Tch, his Brands really do mirror mine.' I watched the Adinvyr's eyes narrow slightly as he prodded at my barriers with his magic. *'Oh...? He still can't hear me even though we're away from the Mists? That's interesting. What's changed since Limbo? Hmmm...his frustrated expression is kind of cute too.*

'Shit! I've been staring, haven't I? What was it he asked—ah right. Darius. Slippery little brat.'

"The prince is...a little excitable." I braced myself for the searing reprimand for speaking, but it didn't come. "If you'll excuse me..."

"Here, this will be much quicker. Pardon me," he spoke with a grin that flashed his full set of fangs. Before I could question him, he scooped me up with startling ease and then leapt onto a nearby rooftop. A set of black feathered wings aided his leap but disappeared as quick as they'd come, leaving me wondering if they were magic.

"Your Highness, you know that girl?"

"Isn't she the Lyur'zi from X'shmir?"

"Rely'ric, it's been so long since you've come by the shop! You should come in and take a look!"

"The prince is obviously busy, you can pester him some other time!"

"Mmm…you really are quite tiny," the deity remarked with a chuckle as he stepped over to the edge of another roof. "Well now…he didn't get very far now did he?"

Before I could think of a retort, the pesky Adinvyr dropped from the roof and onto the street below. My brat of a brother seemed oblivious to our presence. The giant of a man set me down carefully but had a mischievous smirk on his face now. His long tail swayed behind him in a way that reminded me of a cat ready to pounce on a toy.

My cheeks burned with a mixture of embarrassment and irritation. I felt a strong urge to pull my hood completely over my face to hide but settled for tugging at it instead while waiting for Darius to notice us. Thankfully, it didn't take much. Another movement from the Devillian deity was enough to startle my airheaded twin, causing him to whirl around with wide eyes.

"Whoa!" Darius yelped and took a few steps back from the much larger Devillian. After a moment he noticed me as well and began glancing between us like he'd been caught doing something bad. "U-uhm, I... Ari—"

'At least I was able to get away with speaking. Briefly.' I chewed on the inside of my bottom lip and looked from Darius to the Adinvyr and back a few times. *'I doubt ignoring a deity would have gone over well, and I get the feeling he noticed me staring. He doesn't seem to have any difficulty discerning where my eyes are, despite my mask. What a pain.'*

"You shouldn't run away from your Umbral Mage like that, Darius-zir." The Adinvyr sounded amused as he crossed his arms over his chest. His magic probed the edges of the barrier that I maintained around my brother, and after a few seconds I caught the glance the Adinvyr shot in my direction. The mixture of intrigue and distrust I sensed from him made me bristle.

"My—?" Darius glanced at me and then at the Adinvyr before stomping his foot in indignation. "She's my *sister*, Nalithor!"

'You still ran off,' I thought as I watched Darius's face grow redder and redder by the second. Clearly, I wasn't the only one that found Nalithor…alluring.

"You really *are* his sister then?" Nalithor smiled when I turned my attention toward him. Looking satisfied with himself, Nalithor bowed and offered me one of his hands. "I hope you will forgive my manners once more, *Your Highness*. I am Nalithor Vraelimir. I serve as a General in the Vorpmasian Imperial Military."

I stayed silent and shot Darius a filthy look from behind my mask. Luckily, although he couldn't see my expression, Darius seemed to get the hint. Nalithor, on the other hand, seemed to pick up my slight shift in attention. His frosty eyes flicked toward my brother in a questioning way. *'Perhaps* that *is what clued Darius in?'*

"Oh, right, woops!" Darius exclaimed. "Sorry, Ari. Of course you can to speak to Nalithor!"

'For now,' he added, causing me to twitch.

"I'm... Arianna Jade Black," I offered after a moment, accepting Nalithor's hand. My face grew warm again when he brought my gloved hand up to his lips and kissed the back of it. He held my hand a little longer than appropriate. "I apologize if I seemed rude, Rely'ric. X'shmiran laws are troublesome and—"

I cut myself off and snatched Darius by the back of his robes with my free hand. Darius wriggled in my grip and tried to slip away even as I turned to glower at him. Though, as usual, my brother seemed immune. He just shot me a sheepish grin and tugged at my wrist in a childlike instead of acting apologetic.

"Come on, Ari!" Darius whined. "I want to explore the city some more! And find some food! And—!"

I just stared at my brother in disbelief for a moment, watching him bounce on the balls of his feet. With each bounce he tugged at my wrist again. My idiot brother was acting like a child in front of a *god* of all people. On our first day in foreign lands to boot!

"*Mrirtec*," I growled in irritation, aware of the slight frown that tugged on Nalithor's face. "You should be *studying*. Furthermore, you put us *both* in danger by running off without me. Kindly control yourself."

"You are required to refer to your *brother* as Mrirtec?" Nalithor looked contemplative. "I didn't think any X'shmirans aside from you knew words in the Draemiran tongue."

"They don't." I released my grip on Darius's robes as my brother's shoulders slumped in defeat. "Djialkan believed it best that I use Draemiran honorifics while in Vorpmasia. He said that the titles I am required to use in our native language have an entirely different connotation here."

I fell silent again and tried not to fidget while Nalithor examined me again. A curious expression had settled onto his handsome face. Earning something *other* than a hate-filled gaze was already strange enough to me, yet Nalithor's oddly penetrating stare made me more on-edge than even those types of looks did. I didn't detect any ill will from him—not yet, at least—but it was still bizarre.

"Ari, why did you call him *that?*" Darius tugged my sleeve again, this time causing me to let out a heavy sigh as I brought my fingers to my temples. "Isn't that honorific only for—?"

"What gave me away as a deity, Arianna-jiss?" Nalithor's purring, playful tone made me cut my eyes to the side at him and ignore Darius' startled yelp.

"I hope you don't mean to say you were trying to *hide* that fact?" I murmured, bringing a knuckle to my lips as I examined Nalithor once more. "Hmmm, to answer your question…

"I'm an instinctual creature at best. Your Brands of Divinity are brighter than any of the mere demigods we have met so far. In addition to that, your presence is many times more potent than anyone else in this city."

A small, self-satisfied smirk surfaced on Nalithor's face and his tail swung playfully again. There was still a glimmer of curiosity in his expression, but it was almost drowned out by that smug playfulness.

"His 'presence?'" Darius questioned, frowning.

"Mrirtec, did you block off your senses *again*?" I chastised Darius, rounding on him.

"Humph, what do you mean my senses?" Darius pouted and crossed his arms, a look of confusion on his face. "I mean, sure he's powerful. A lot of people here are."

I bit back a grimace and shook my head. As frustrating as it was, I knew there was no way to force him to understand his senses, nor could I *make* him learn how to sort through individual presences properly. It was infuriating but, putting my displeasure with the situation aside, there was something else nagging at me.

"Ah…" I murmured, nibbling on one of my knuckles in thought for a moment before lifting my gaze so I could look up at Nalithor. He seemed *terribly* intrigued by my mask and jewelry. "I'm unfamiliar with the proper way of addressing deities, seeing as we have had no contact with such individuals in X'shmir. How would you like me to address you?"

"Ahhh, so *you* are the polite sibling." Nalithor chuckled and tugged my hood over my face with a playful grin. "Arianna-jiss, you should continue referring to me—and any other deities you might meet—as Rely'ric until they specify otherwise.

"You, Darius-zir, should do the same. It is considered terribly inappropriate for you to refer to someone so casually when you have only met them briefly."

"Ral-yeer-eek?" Darius grimaced when he failed to pronounce the title. "Why do *I* have to?"

"*Rehl-eeh-rick,*" Nalithor pronounced it slower this time and then shot me a brief smirk when he caught me pawing my hood back into place. "Rely'ric translates loosely to 'my lord' in the common tongue but it has broader usage. It can be used to address nobility, royalty, or deities.

"There are also more casual uses for it but perhaps that is a lesson for another day."

I gnawed on my lip to stifle my snickering when Darius pouted. He must have been miffed that Nalithor ignored his question entirely. If I knew my brother, a combination of princely and Astral Mage arrogance kept him from understanding.

"Ari, how come *you* can say it so easy?!" Darius whined after several more failed attempts. I tilted my head and glanced toward Nalithor briefly before responding. He looked amused. Nalithor really was much like a cat.

"Do you really think that Djialkan or the Devillians in Sihix would let me get away with botching the pronunciation of *anything*?" I pointed out, shifting my attention back to my twin, only to find myself distracted by Nalithor's rumbling laughter.

"Djialkan has always been quite strict." Nalithor laughed, revealing his fangs again when he grinned in my direction.

"Such matters aside," I shook my head and then rounded on Darius once more, "it's *rehl-eeh-rick*, Darius! You don't *have* to roll your r's, you know. In fact, at this rate, I would prefer if you didn't even *try*."

"Ari! I'm hungry!" Darius declared, causing me to sigh in exasperation, while Nalithor simply chuckled.

"Darius-zir, you will have plenty of time to explore the city without an escort once you've completed your tests," Nalithor reprimanded my twin before making a vague motion in the direction of the districts above us. "However, if you're hungry, the both of you are welcome to join me at the little place I own between the Nobles' District and Sapphire Quarter.

"I was hoping for a chance to speak with you before your tests anyway."

"Oh, of course!" Darius exclaimed a little *too* eagerly. "We'd love to—right, Ari?"

"I'm afraid I must decline," I spoke quietly, linking my hands behind my back. Nalithor shot me a displeased look, so I added, "It wouldn't be appropriate for me to join you and we have yet to purchase groceries to stock the house with."

"Surely that can wait." Nalithor smiled. He turned to me fully and reached for my face, but I turned my head away from his hand with unease. Just his mere presence was making my heart beat faster. This man—rather, this god—made me nervous. I didn't like it.

"I apologize, Rely'ric." I shook my head and took a step away from Nalithor and toward my brother. "Mrirtec, I will finish the shopping while you dine."

'Ari? What's wrong?' Darius frowned at me even as he searched his pockets for the crystal-thing he'd been purchasing items with. *'Sure, he seems powerful, but I've never known you to be skittish. You've fought beasts scarier than him. Hells, you've fought* people *scarier than him.'*

'I'm pretty sure gods are people too,' I commented dryly. *'You didn't lose the damned thing, did you?'*

Darius finally procured the engraved crystal from one of his deep pockets and handed it to me. The suspicious look on Nalithor's face as I turned away from my brother was almost enough to make me break down into tears. However, I had many years of experience with holding back tears and emotions alike. I simply bowed to them before moving to take my leave, but Nalithor caught my wrist and shot me such a warm smile I almost couldn't stand it.

"I insist that you *both* join me," Nalithor spoke firmly but his expression was soft. "You deserve a break and a good meal after your fight against the beasts, Arianna-jiss. Word that you saved Eyrian's men has already begun to spread through the city. I doubt you wish to deal with citizens challenging themselves against your strength at every turn quite yet."

His comment startled me. For a moment, I just looked up at him in surprise. I had thought the Chaos Beasts on the plateau were rather easy kill. Yet, I supposedly *saved* Eyrian's men? It was a strange notion at best. Stranger to me still was the concept that I should be rewarded for my work. *'There's something else he's not saying. What's he trying to hide from us?'*

'He's right, Ari,' Darius added cheerfully when I hesitated. *'It would be* more *inappropriate for you to decline an invitation from a deity, right?'*

"Very well then, Rely'ric, if you insist," I attempted to keep the defeat from my voice as I spoke. *'Damn it. Why did Darius choose now of all times to make sense?'*

The triumphant Adinvyr released my wrist and shot me a boyish grin before beckoning for us to follow him. I fell into step a few paces behind Nalithor and Darius, but I caught the questioning glance the deity shot me. He looked like he was trying to be sneaky about it, but he failed miserably if that was the case. At any rate, his expression said that he didn't approve—but I wasn't quite sure what he found so displeasing.

'He seemed rather adamant that I join them, so I don't think *he's displeased that I'm accompanying them.'* I shelved my mixed feelings

of sadness and confusion for the time being as I walked. *'Bah! Why is this damned Adinvyr—god, whatever—making me so damned nervous? His power doesn't feel threatening. I'm pretty sure I could fight against him just fine.*

'Hells, he can't even break through my shields on myself or on Darius. Is he not a very high-ranking deity?'

As we made our way through the city streets, I noticed a trend among the citizens that bowed to Nalithor; they all addressed him differently. General, prince, archmagus, and professor were just a few of the titles I heard thrown in his direction. None of them seemed concerned or intrigued by his bi-colored Brands, and I didn't hear anyone refer to him as Rely'ric despite the fact he was a god.

"So, Na—*Rely'ric*—you're really a deity?" Darius asked.

I glanced between the two in silence as the handsome Adinvyr chuckled. He didn't seem bothered by Darius' slip up, and my brother's pronunciation was a little better this time at least.

'This is bothersome. Handsome? I can't be thinking like that.' I bit the inside of my cheek hard. *'Just stop, Ari.'*

"Your brother doubts your abilities, Your Highness?" Nalithor stopped walking and motioned toward me as he continued. "Even when your power radiates from you so clearly?"

"Please don't call me 'Your Highness.' I dislike formalities," I muttered as he fell into step with me, much to my brother's displeasure. "In X'shmir we're both required to keep all of our power tucked neatly away behind barriers so that we don't disturb the citizens or attract extra beasts to the city.

"Mrirtec probably isn't even aware that it's my power he's feeling, Rely'ric."

In truth, Darius was just too ignorant in the matters of the arcane and power. However, I wasn't going to just come out and say that in front of my twin. At least not around someone that was effectively a new acquaintance. Despite Darius' arrogance I knew he was at least a little aware of his own shortcomings. I didn't want to rub it in.

"I'm sure you will learn to sort through different auras in time, Darius-zir," Nalithor remarked, contemplative, before directing his attention down at me and speaking in Draemiran. "I get the impression that your brother does not follow Fraelfnir or Djialkan's teachings in the slightest."

"You are correct," I responded after a moment of hesitation, watching a self-satisfied smirk settle across the Adinvyr's masculine features. "My brother values X'shmiran teachings over those of our companions. I hope he has not said anything offensive."

"*Ari*, you're doing that thing again!" Darius balled his fists and stomped his foot heatedly. "Am I going to have forbid you from speaking in other languages?"

"Before he has a *complete* conniption fit," I began dryly as my brother let out an indignant shriek, "I would like to thank you again for the headphones. They have proved to be a welcome distraction and source of entertainment."

"You are quite welcome," Nalithor replied with a warm smile. "There are actually some other matters I wish to discuss with you…but it appears that it must wait. Your brother is quite the impatient one."

"Mrirtec, don't you think you're being overly rude?" I offered innocently in the common tongue as Darius opened his mouth to tell me off. "It's only polite for me to respond in the language I'm addressed in, now isn't it?"

Darius opened and closed his mouth several times, his eyes wide as he attempted to think of a response. After a moment his shoulders slumped, and he let out a heavy sigh. Nalithor chuckled and shot me a knowing look. My brother clearly wanted the Adinvyr's attention all to himself, but he was failing at finding a way to obtain it. Perhaps if Darius wasn't so rude it would have been cute.

I shifted my attention away from them and examined our surroundings. It was now that I realized we were moving at an enhanced pace along the crystalline roads despite the fact we were only walking, and we weren't growing winded.

'Are the roads enchanted somehow?' I glanced down at the translucent material below me, watching the shifting colors and small flecks of light held in stasis within the road's surface. *'With someone as powerful as Nalithor so close… Hmmm. Switching my vision to see magic is probably a bad idea. His power alone should be*

blinding.'

"Even here you're required to wear that mask and veil?" Nalithor reached up, tugged lightly on the front of my hood. He chuckled when I flushed and pulled away from him. "That's a shame. I thought we would have been able to convince the Royal Family to amend their restrictions."

"She's allowed to wear lighter attire while here…and reveal her face to her partner if necessary. That's it." Darius drew Nalithor's attention once more. "Ah! That reminds me, Ari. You're allowed to follow Vorpmasian traditions regarding clothing here as long as you wear your mask, veil, and a hood."

'Partner? What does he mean by partner? *Djialkan said something about that as well.'* I frowned. *'I can wear less heavy attire? That could be a problem with my Brands. I still don't feel comfortable displaying them.'*

That displeased but inquisitive look crossed Nalithor's face again, but he chose not to comment. Instead, his expression shifted to a more pleasant one as he motioned us toward a cute little cafe and informed us that we'd arrived. He opened the door for us and waited patiently for Darius to stop gawking at the exterior.

Pale blue and white flowers that resembled roses covered much of the building's exterior. Many more flowers climbed along trellises and the wrought iron fence that surrounded the brick building. A simple but elegant sign above the dual doors read *'The Little Orchid'.*

Nalithor cast me a surprisingly sultry look as I passed him but, thankfully, it had more of an effect on my brother than it did on me. I, for one, didn't want to do any more blushing for the day. Sure, I wasn't used to attention from…anyone…but I wasn't a young girl anymore either.

Despite the mingling scents of tea, coffee, and all sorts of delicious food baking, *his* scent was still the strongest aroma that my senses could pick out. It nearly overwhelmed everything else. In some strange way he smelled even better than any of the food did.

'Stop it, Ari. Stop, stop, stop it,' I told myself. 'It doesn't matter that he smells like dessert—people aren't food.'

The interior of The Little Orchid was quite posh, sporting tufted leather chairs, barstools, and booths. Blue, white, and cream seemed to be a recurring theme inside the establishment, with occasional splashes of pale pink, lilac, and spring green. There were fresh-cut flowers in vases on tables and on the corners of the large bar that stood at the back of the restaurant. The waiters and waitresses were dressed in formal attire themed on maids and butlers, though their attire colors matched the decor.

"Wow, it's so cute!" Darius exclaimed, oblivious to the questioning glances the other patrons shot our way. It took him a while to realize Nalithor was still walking but, when he did, Darius was quick to follow the Adinvyr toward a plush booth at the back of the establishment. "Hey, Nali… *Rely'ric*, are you going to be administering our tests?"

"Unless more pressing matters arise, I'm sitting in, yes." Nalithor nodded, his tail swaying back and forth as he cast a curious look towards me yet again. "You are taking the tests after all, Your—Arianna? In Eyrian's report he implied that you didn't need to take them."

"Yes I am." I nodded, crossing my arms within my sleeves. "As X'shmir is without the resources to measure power, they will want me to take the tests, so they can confirm once and for all how useless they believe me to be."

Nalithor's expression shifted from intrigue to immense displeasure as I spoke. I watched as he sighed faintly and shook his head. His movements had been subtle enough to slip by Darius unnoticed by the look of things. My brother seemed completely unaware of Nalithor's distaste for the X'shmiran king, queen, and their ways. Even for Darius this was a new level of thick.

To my eyes the Adinvyr looked incredibly unhappy with my statement. His tail's swishing had slowed to a faint sway and he had a sad look in his eyes as he watched me. It was nowhere near as bad as the expression he had on his face when he'd "broken" as a child…yet it still made me want to reach out and comfort him.

Instead, I resigned myself to taking a seat and clutching my gloved hands together in my lap. I refocused my gaze down at the table in front of me so that I wouldn't have to look at them.

There wasn't anything I could do.

If he knew who I was—or who I might be—I was certain it would only serve to put us both in more pain. Two hundred years had passed since that event. There was no denying that even if I *hadn't* lost my memories, we were both very different people now. After all, we were only children back then.

'Assuming those were even my memories to begin with.' I grit my teeth. *'It's…still hard for me to accept.'*

"I *told* you all that she doesn't *need* to take the tests or classes!" Darius let out a disgruntled huff, though his expression cheered up when Nalithor opted to sit beside him.

I looked between them briefly, watching as Darius pondered scooting closer to the deity beside him. Despite what I kept telling myself, and my desire to avoid contact with the people here, I felt terribly jealous that Nalithor chose to sit beside my brother instead of me. Perhaps I really should have denied his request for me to join them. Jealousy was an unpleasant thing and I was angry with myself for feeling it.

"What is this you were saying about partners, Dari—… Mrirtec?" I asked.

Darius' face turned bright red and a sheepish look sprawled across his face. He looked as if he'd realized he'd completely forgotten to tell me something; something important, no doubt.

"Since Vorpmasia, Beshulthien, Suthsul, X'shmir, and several outlying countries are attempting to form a better relationship," Nalithor began as he cast an entertained look at my sulking brother, "it was decided that individuals of similar power, and preferably from different nations, would be paired with each other. According to Vorpmasian traditions. Whether it's for classes and training at the academies, work in the field, or more scholarly pursuits, everyone is required to have a partner they can work with."

"But I wanna work with Ari!" Darius whined, earning a brief but displeased look from Nalithor.

"Do you pair Lyur'zi and Chrot'zi together, or...?" I trailed off when Nalithor shook his head with a small smile.

"We're pairing mages of the same classification with each other. Astral with astral, flame with flame... You get the idea," Nalithor stated, his smile widening when my lips parted in surprise. "You were startled by my white uniform before, yes? Vorpmasia and Beshulthien embrace a more in-depth approach to the concept of Astral and Umbral Mages than most nations do."

"I see," I murmured as Nalithor watched me with an inquisitive expression. "Let me see if I have this right.

"The style of armor and embroidery indicates whether or not an individual is an Astral Mage or an Umbral one, whereas the color of the plate, cloth, or leather indicates whether their masteries are more destruction or healing oriented?"

"You're correct." Nalithor sounded pleased as he tilted his head to the side and gave me another thorough looking-over. "In my case, I'm well-versed in both destructive and healing magics—as well as armed and unarmed combat. I have robes and uniforms in both colors. However, white seems to put the peoples' minds at ease better than black."

"Nalithor-zir, it's unusual for you to bring guests!" A younger male voice with an accent similar to Nalithor's remarked. I glanced to the side to see one of the waiters approaching us, but he stopped to look at me with a startled expression and exclaimed, "By the gods, those lips! How have you not kissed her already?"

I felt my face burn almost as scarlet as my lipstick and Darius erupted into a fit of laughter. Digging my fingers into my forearms didn't seem to help me beat down my blushing, though it did at least help me hold back the slew of sarcastic comments I wanted to make. The look Nalithor shot in my direction was *not* helping. Something about his expression made me feel like food.

'Besides, I definitely don't think I could keep it together if he kissed...' I shoved the thought from my mind as my face grew hotter. *'Fucking hells! I should have stayed in Sihix.'*

"Marius, please," Nalithor began with a laugh, "our X'shmiran friends here have only been in the city for a couple of hours at most. You'd have to give me a few days, at least, to charm her that thoroughly."

"Just a few days?" I arched an eyebrow behind my mask and turned my attention back toward Nalithor. That playful demeanor was back yet again, and his tail was twitching back and forth like a feline stalking prey. I couldn't hold back a quip this time. "I'm rather certain it would take more than a 'few days' to prove to me that you're worth my interest, let alone 'charm' me."

"Ari, *please!*" Darius rolled his eyes and pointed at me. "Nalithor is a general, an archmagus, an Adinvyr, *and* a fucking god! He's got loads more field experience than you!"

"Titles don't—" I started.

"—mean anything, right?" Nalithor finished with a knowing smile. "You may be Human but it would appear that you think more like one of *us*."

"Just another reason our parents want her gone..." Darius muttered before turning to Marius so that he could order from the menu the rusty-haired Devillian had offered him.

I decided to ignore Nalithor's curious glances for now and ordered some dinner and tea before settling back in my seat once more. While listening to the two men in front of me converse I realized that Darius was so giddy that it made it hard for me to think of my twin as a "man" and not as a "boy." Even so, I was content to just sink back into the corner of my half of the booth and pretend I wasn't there.

I'd underestimated how much attention my unusual attire would draw from the Vorpmasian citizens. People who still followed the "Old Ways" appeared to be quite the novelty. For all the attention they were giving me, nothing made me as nervous as the amount of attention the white-haired deity before me seemed eager to bestow.

"So, you took out a Dux-class beast?" Nalithor inquired shortly after my brother excused himself to the restroom.

"Dux-class?" I watched a faint expression of surprise cross Nalithor's face. "Beasts are beasts to me, Rely'ric. If I happen to sense or smell one…I go kill it.

"Alas, Darius exaggerates. General Il'thar helped. A little bit."

"A little bit?" Nalithor shifted in his seat and motioned vaguely with one clawed hand. "*That one* isn't exactly known to hold back."

"A little bit." I nodded. "I had him toss me up into the air above the beast's severed head so that I could rain down magic through the wound and rip the beast apart. Flying magic isn't my forte but I'm capable of floating myself. So, I only needed assistance to get above the damned thing.

"I've heard the Vorpmasians refer to the beasts as 'Dux-class' before but I don't know what, exactly, that means."

"It usually takes a group of demigods to take down a Dux. None of our men have reported encountering anything *other* than a Dux while in X'shmir," Nalithor paused, his mouth curving into an amused smile again, before laughing. "Marius was right, you do have quite lovely lips. Quite expressive too despite that mask of yours."

"Tch. *This* seems to be quite the point of interest Below," I grumbled, pointing with one finger at my veiled mask and then hood in turn. "Why—?"

"Our people are concerned that if X'shmir follows this part of the Old Ways," Nalithor motioned at my attire before settling his elbows on the table, lacing his fingers together, and leaning forward to examine me, "that it means they may follow the Old Ways in full.

"If you give it a few days our people *should* shelve their unease regarding your attire. The descendants of the Humans and Elves who *used* to follow the Old Ways in outlying lands might cause you some trouble...but I would think them to be sympathetic."

"You specified Humans and Elves." I shifted to cross one leg over the other. "Do you mean to say that Devillians never practiced the Old Ways?"

"We have not." Nalithor shook his head before studying me once more. "Perhaps a hundred and fifty years ago, Vorpmasia began conquering a handful of countries that we discovered were practicing what we now call the 'Old Ways.' I think I was about the equivalent of a Human thirteen-year-old at the time and Eyrian would have been eleven or so.

"Draemir, Dauthrmir, and Gron'kial house the majority of the Umbral and Astral Mages that the Vorpmasian forces rescued."

"Yet you didn't conquer X'shmir," I pointed out a little more harshly than I intended, but Nalithor just smiled.

"We have no proof to show to what extent X'shmir follows the Old Ways." Nalithor's eyes drifted down from my mask to my lips again before flicking back upwards. "Despite my role as a deity... There are still laws I must abide by. I'm not permitted to go around poking in peoples' heads for *that* kind of information."

"So, all you know is that I'm required to wear *this*?" I tugged at my veiled mask for emphasis.

"I, for one, wish we could get X'shmir to drop that law of theirs." Nalithor smiled as I shifted again, then glanced to the side at my returning twin. "Which one of you two is the elder sibling, hmmm? I'm disinclined to believe it is you, Darius-zir."

"Oh… Did I forget to mention that as well?" Darius mumbled distractedly, his face flushing under the Adinvyr's gaze. "Arianna and I are twins. She's older than me by half an hour if you want to be *really* technical about it."

"Twins…?" Nalithor glanced curiously at me as he trailed off, then returned his gaze to my brother. "You're the heir because you're male, or because you're an Astral Mage?"

"Because I'm an Umbral Mage," I offered when it was clear Darius didn't know how to reply. "X'shmir has strict laws when it comes to an Umbral Mage's place in society. We may only serve as a bodyguard to our assigned Astral Mage, assist in military matters and, if necessary, carry out judgment on unlawful citizens.

"Once my power as an Umbral Mage was discovered I lost all my value as far as the Royal Family is concerned."

"That is why they didn't attempt to marry you off at any point in the negotiations?" Nalithor sat back in his seat, his tone contemplative. "Humans are notorious for attempting to form political marriages. We were rather surprised, and wary, when the

X'shmirans did not attempt as such."

"X'shmirans believe that offering an Umbral Mage's hand in marriage is the equivalent of declaring war," Darius spoke with clear disdain. "Rely'ric, you saw how insistent they were when it came to making you and the other visiting Umbral Mages follow our laws. It had nothing to do with your foreign origins and *everything* to do with what type of mages you all were."

"*Mrirtec*, I just had an interesting thought." I shifted to look at my brother and crossed my arms, "Since our parents forced the Vorpmasian Umbral Mages to abide by our rules... Why didn't you suggest the same in return?"

"He hasn't...?" Nalithor sighed heavily and then rounded on my brother, his expression firm. "Were you so excited to leave that rock behind that you left your brain somewhere on it?"

Nalithor's blunt question startled me, causing me to bite my cheek to contain my laughter. They seemed oblivious for the moment and my eyes had teared up because I bit myself too hard. I was quite certain that, if it wasn't for my veiled mask, my expression would've been questionable at best.

"I-I just didn't think of that, okay?!" Darius raised his hands in surrender. "I can send word back to them and suggest it. However, it would hold more weight if the Emperor—or at least the Vorpmasian Royal Families—make formal requests. The X'shmirans are still struggling to believe that *gods* exist."

Nalithor pursed his lips and his jaw tensed as he thought. After a few moments he gave my brother a slight nod. Nalithor seemed as though he held strong dislike for the Old Ways. Yet, for some reason, he was incredibly curious about me. I wasn't sure why he kept casting such fascinated glances at me, but I found it more than a little unnerving. I couldn't tell if he was suspicious about who I was, or if he was just intrigued because I was capable of fighting beasts.

All I knew for certain was that it was very strange to receive attention, let alone so much of it, from anyone. But attention from a male? Unheard of.

Soon enough dinner came and saved me from the need to converse. I maintained silence as I ate and settled on listening to Nalithor and Darius discuss a rather narrow range of topics. Darius seemed utterly delighted to have someone to talk with about politics, and yet I got the distinct impression that Nalithor wasn't interested in the slightest when it came to the subject. Nevertheless, he politely indulged my brother and shared some of his knowledge on Vorpmasian politics. It didn't take long for me to grow bored and tune them out.

Nalithor's voice was just as hypnotic as his scent. I found myself having to focus a little harder than usual to keep my barriers tight in their place around my thoughts and around Darius'. To some extent my desire to flee had subsided, but I wasn't sure if the new feeling was any better. Staying around Nalithor seemed just as dangerous as returning to X'shmir without my brother.

"When are the two of you expected to take your tests?" Nalithor inquired some time later, causing me to glance up from my slice of pie. Finally, something other than politics.

"This weekend." Darius summoned a stack of papers from one of his shrizar and rifled through them. "However, Ari's presence has been formally requested at tomorrow's strategy meeting since you're all so eager to pick her brain about the beasts.

"After that we're free until next weekend's tests—though I've been advised that beast activity could put them on hold."

'Oh joy. A meeting my brother neglected to inform me of.' I hid my scowl in a bite of pie.

"Dariu—**Mrirtec.**" I failed to keep the irritated growl from my voice as I pointed my fork at Darius, earning a crooked grin from the Adinvyr beside him. "You and Djialkan meddle more than Oracles do. You could have at least *told* me about—!"

"I'm rather interested in hearing your observations, Arianna." Nalithor shot me an earnest smile when I turned to look at him in surprise. "We were quite startled by your brother's tales of you single-handedly protecting X'shmir from beasts after all."

"They're not tales!" Darius protested, though I just smiled when the deity arched an eyebrow. "Ari's been fighting them since she was five! Or was it six? Djialkan always watched over her to make she didn't bite off more than she could chew, of course, but—"

"He's got the 'adoring little brother' act down quite well,

doesn't he?" I offered with an amused smirk. "I'm happy to lend whatever assistance I can when it comes to dealing with the beasts. The foul-smelling abominations need to die. Their continued existence is wearing on my patience."

I dug my nails into my thigh the best I could through my gloves and raced to rein in my bloodlust. *'Even after killing so many beasts by the ships…it wasn't enough?'*

"If you're truly as familiar with fighting the beasts as Darius claims, then I question the need for you to take classes at the academy." Nalithor stroked his chin in thought, somehow managing *not* to slice his skin with his claws. "If either of you have questions about the tests, now would be a good time to ask. Before I'm officially on duty as an Archmagus."

"I have one question," Darius perked up, his expression and voice filled with confusion as he pulled a single sheet of paper from his stack. "I understand the purpose of most of the tests we've been assigned, but I don't understand *this one* at all. What is a 'DSO Exam'?"

Nalithor's deep laugh sent a shiver down my spine. This man was going to be truly difficult to deal with. He was nice to look at, of course. But his scent, power, and voice were all…intoxicating. I wasn't sure if it was because of the natural magnetism of the Adinvyr race, or if it was his power as a god. Nevertheless, I was starting to understand why my twin seemed so drawn to him. It was difficult *not* to stare.

'Perhaps I can get away with it since I'm wearing a mask?' I wondered, letting my gaze trail down Nalithor's muscular chest. *'Ugh, what is it with the Devillians here and their exposed skin? Do they* want *people to stare?'*

"I wasn't aware we had added this one to the line-up of exams for foreigners." Nalithor sounded highly amused. A smirk remained on his lips as he skimmed the sheet. "This one requires a bit more elaboration. 'DSO' stands for 'Dominant, Submissive, or Other'. We pair off our mages and soldiers based on their personality traits, and some other factors, so that we can keep conflicts of personality to a minimum.

"As you'll soon see for yourself, the theme of dominants and submissives is rather prevalent in our society."

"Oh, so Ari is *totally* going to test as a dominant," Darius spoke slyly. I bit back a grimace when Nalithor cast me his millionth curious glance of the night.

"You think that you will both be assigned all of the same tests?" Nalithor frowned. "Most of Darius' tests are quite…beginner level."

"Yes." I nudged one of the charms on my hood out of view so that I could see better. "As I stated earlier, X'shmir lacks the ability to gauge power and aptitude; our *dear* parents wish to prove once and for all that I'm useless."

"It strikes me as strange that they would want to rid themselves of the one person protecting them from the beasts." Nalithor's frown deepened as he studied me. "I hope you'll forgive me for my endless inquiries. Human mages aren't something we thought we'd ever see again and, compared to the Human mages of old, you two are of an entirely different caliber."

"I'm sure your curiosity about *us* doesn't compare to *this one's* curiosity about all of you," I countered dryly, motioning at Darius. "Besides, it's refreshing. Since you've been to X'shmir yourself I'm sure you can understand at least *some* fraction of the type of attention I'm used to receiving. You did *chase* me for quite some time after all.

"That said, I'm sure Darius and I have already imposed on too much of your time."

"Ari, if you're tired you can go to the house ahead of me," Darius offered, causing me to look at him with unease. "I want to speak with Nali some more about our tests. You'll breeze them easily, but I'm worried about how I'll do...

"Er... I mean 'Rely'ric.'"

"It's quite alright, Arianna-jiss, I assure you." Nalithor smiled when I opened my mouth to protest. "Darius is likely to be one of my students if his tests go the way I believe they will. I'm happy to answer his questions, and *you* are more than welcome to stay if you like.

"If not, I can see him home in your stead."

"I would be a poor excuse for an Umbral Mage if I left my brother on his own here, now wouldn't I?" I countered slyly, glancing to my brother and then back at Nalithor. "If we're truly not imposing, then far be it from me to interfere with my brother's attempts at making friends."

"Oh? You make it sound as though you don't want to make friends as well," Nalithor purred mischievously, a playful glint in his eyes as he directed a roll of immense power at me.

"Tsk, tsk, tsk." I waggled a finger at the Adinvyr. "I do hope you don't think to gain my interest with displays of power alone! Plenty of people in this city are already trying such *simple* methods.

"Granted, in tight quarters such as these, I can't test your worthiness properly, now can I?"

I motioned loosely to my sides, smirked at the playful Adinvyr, and watched as he grinned in response to my question. He looked positively *delighted* by my challenge.

"Ari! He's a *general!* G-e-n-e-r-a-l!" Darius smacked his hands on the table and leaned over it to glare at me. "He—!"

"I'm a general as well. So, what's your point?" I countered, crossing one of my legs over the other and then leaned forward slightly. "Titles are *given*, Darius. They aren't always earned. If I'm going to share knowledge of beasts with the Vorpmasians, and potentially fight alongside them, I reserve the right to challenge their abilities in battle."

"The point of battle is to fight *enemies*, Ari! Not your friends!" Darius argued while Nalithor just chuckled at us; the Adinvyr had that mischievous glint in his eyes again.

"I can't be friends with people who don't share my common interests," I countered once more, watching the corner of Darius' eye twitch. "Nor do I think fighters weaker than myself would be worth my time. If they're weaker than me, they won't be able to put my knowledge to use anyway.

"*General Vraelimir* looks like he desires to get a word in edgewise, **Mrirtec**."

"I agree with *General Black*," Nalithor mirrored my sarcasm and shot me a strangely approving look before turning to my brother. "When it comes to comrades—soldiers or mages—it's important that they are close in strength. They spend most of their time together and often share housing.

"By nature, most Devillians are uninterested in those who are significantly weaker than they are. This is especially true of Adinvyr and Draekin."

'I can't deny that I approve of their beliefs and methods.' I watched Darius mouth a few times as he tried to think of a retort. *'Pairing two strong fighters—or a strong fighter and a healer—makes much more sense than pairing two people of varying strengths. I, for one, would not want to be paired with someone weaker than me.*

'Having to worry about saving their ass instead of killing our target would just serve to piss me off.'

"Bah! What about your title, then!" Darius demanded of the Adinvyr and sat back down with a huff. "It couldn't *possibly* be acceptable for her to challenge your rank so flippantly."

"She wasn't flippant, she was actually quite serious." Nalithor shook his head at my brother and then turned to look at me with an intense but playful expression. "However, I am surprised that you seem to disregard your title so readily, Arianna."

"Can you honestly tell me that you think there's someone in X'shmir who has the experience necessary to receive such a rank?" I asked him and, after a moment of consideration, he shook his head and smiled. "While I *do* oversee the X'shmiran military's training and organization—when my 'services' are 'required'—I was given the title based solely on the fact that I'm an Umbral Mage. I was eleven at the time.

"Titles hold very little weight with me, and I prefer to determine the strength of others by my own hand."

"But if you were given a title, then you earned—" Darius argued, causing me to raise my fingertips to my temples.

"Darius, you treat titles like they're some divine gift upon the world." I withdrew my hand from my hood and pointed at Darius, my tone flat. "Titles just establish the pecking order in society. That's it.

"Ahhh... Speaking of titles, I seem to have slipped, *Mrirtec*."

Before Darius could respond I sensed a wave of power from my right. I made a small motion with my hand and lifted the source of the power by his throat into the air and dangled him several feet off the floor. I turned in my seat and watched the weak Adinvyr's legs swing in the air as he struggled to free himself. *'What possessed him to approach us like* that?'

"I-I-I'm sorry! I just wanted to c-c-c-challenge you!" The young Adinvyr male yelped, dropping his sword carelessly to the floor as he clawed at the shadows around his throat. "I wasn't trying to sneak up on you, I swear!"

For a moment I considered taking out my frustration on the young man by shredding him, quartering him, or perhaps bleeding him dry with his own sword. *'Ah... But, no. That won't do.'*

"Don't you think it's a little inappropriate to challenge someone in tight confines," I began dryly as the Adinvyr kicked at the air desperately even though my shadows weren't choking him, "let alone on someone else's property? I don't know about *you* but I, for one, am quite destructive.

"If you want to challenge me, be a good boy and challenge me in a suitable setting. I'll be in the Sapphire Quarter all week after all."

I released the Adinvyr and watched as he hurriedly reclaimed his weapon and darted out of the cafe. Nalithor was laughing openly with an impish expression on his face, but Darius just looked confused.

"I don't think you'll have to worry about that one coming back to challenge you," Nalithor teased.

"Oh, Nali, I have a question. Er, I mean, Rely'ric," Darius began abruptly, causing me to glance at him when I sensed a faint hint of jealousy coming from him. "If Ari's going to the meeting tomorrow, what am I supposed to do? I'm not supposed to leave her side until we've been assigned partners."

"Some of my men have been assigned to guard you in her stead during the meeting." Nalithor shifted to look at my twin. "However, we've wandered rather far from our original discussion.

"You wanted to speak with me more about your tests did you not?"

I nestled back in my seat and examined the pair in silence. Darius seemed interested in the Adinvyr and was overly eager to draw his attention away from me. Such behavior was unusual for my brother, but at least he appeared to be enjoying himself.

Nalithor was quite proficient at dodging some of my brother's questions, much to my relief. The Adinvyr appeared at least a *little* aware that my brother was a novice in the arcane; much too novice to be asking about the types of magics he kept bringing up, at any rate.

"Mrirtec, you're worried that the tests are something that will be overly strenuous and potentially dangerous, right?" I finally spoke up quite after the umpteenth dodged question. Darius nodded his head in quick succession and his face flushed, so I turned to look at Nalithor. "Rely'ric, we could sit here for the next week and nothing either of us says in that time would put my brother's mind at ease. He would understand better if he could *see* for himself what the tests are—if spectators are allowed."

"That shouldn't be a problem." Nalithor tilted his head in

thought and crossed his arms. "There are several groups of mages taking tests tomorrow. I can instruct my men to escort you to the palace so that you may view them if you wish, Darius."

"Please!" Darius had a bright grin on his face before shooting me a pointed look. "Speaking of tomorrow; Ari, don't you have to be up early?"

'Hmmm… He's trying to get rid of me again.' I clenched my jaw in response to the sinking feeling in my chest. *'You want me gone that badly?'*

Nalithor seemed to pause slightly as he reached for his tea, and I caught the furrowing of his brow when he nudged at my barriers. Clearly, he'd sensed the telepathic reverberations, but it seemed that he still couldn't hear what I had said. After a moment he appeared to grow frustrated and cast me a suspicious, almost pouting, look.

'Don't say it like that, Ari!' Darius whined. I felt the corner of my eye twitch as Nalithor's gaze snapped to the side at my brother—he could certainly hear Darius. My barriers had slipped more than I thought, but Darius was oblivious and continued, *'Nali is hot, and I have more of a chance with him than you do since you're an Umbral Mage. His curiosity about your mask is distracting him from me too much!'*

As usual my brother had no tact and I wished that he could see the filthy glare I shot him from behind my mask. Nalithor looked amused at first…until my brother's comment about me being an

Umbral Mage, that is. Now he just looked like he was trying to hide his distaste for my brother.

"Very well," I began coolly as I slid out of my seat, "I'll go see if your things have arrived, and then I will get some rest."

"Arianna," Nalithor called as I started to move away from the table, so I turned slightly to acknowledge I'd heard him. "I'll meet you at the palace gates in the morning and show you the rest of the way to our meeting."

I nodded once in response and then left the cafe.

Taking a deep breath of air, I closed my eyes for a few seconds to calm my rage and then sighed heavily. Darius really knew just what to say to piss me off, but I would have to save venting my frustration for later. For now, I needed to find my way to our lodgings. After Darius' comment, all I wanted to do was go sulk in a warm bath and then sleep.

I swept along the crystalline roads in silence and made my way through the Nobles' District. Under other circumstances I probably would have taken a more leisurely pace so that I could examine the landscaped estates and the foreign architecture of the mansions themselves. Alas, my mood was too foul to appreciate it, and I had little interest in absorbing my surroundings when angered.

A grimace crossed my face as I pulled the map Eyrian gave me from my pocket. By the looks of things, we'd been assigned our own house somewhere in the Sapphire Quarter instead of rooms in one of the dormitories. Judging by the map, and the occasional glance upwards above my head, the Sapphire Quarter was one of the largest districts in the city. Unfortunately, my map didn't outline the locations of the training areas. I would have to pester someone for that information later.

"Where is Darius?" Djialkan inquired as I approached the cozy-looking two-story house I'd be living in for the foreseeable future. The fae-dragon himself was curled up on the front steps like a scaly cat.

"He's with General Vraelimir, pelting him with questions." I shrugged and then glanced at the numerous boxes lining the porch. "Darius made it rather clear my presence wasn't welcome. As such, I decided to come deal with all of this and then sleep.

"I have some questions for you, but I guess they can wait until I've moved all of *this* inside."

Djialkan released a displeased snarl before flying up to land on my shoulder. I fumbled with a set of keys to open the warm-colored wooden doors to the house and then nudged then open. After locating a series of orbs embedded into one of the walls, I touched them to turn the interior and porch Magelights on so that I could see what I was doing.

Alala warbled happily from somewhere down the hallway and then perched on top of a small table in the foyer to observe us.

"You didn't run into any challengers?" Djialkan asked as I lifted a box off the porch.

"One person tried," I murmured, carrying the box into the house and then setting it down in a large living room. "What is the appropriate way to challenge someone to a fight in Vorpmasian culture?"

"You already found someone you wish to test yourself against?" Djialkan laughed and nuzzled my cheek. *"Ideally you would do it without interrupting their current activity. Voice your desire to spar them, and then permit them to choose whether or not they accept."*

"*Of course* I already found someone to challenge," I grumbled at the laughing dragon. "Ugh. Darius bought so much *stuff.*"

"As we predicted, he forgot about food and drink entirely." Djialkan rubbed his head against my hand when I reached up to scratch his scales. *"Fraelfnir, Alala, and I managed to charm some grocers. They should have started a tab for us."*

I nodded and stifled a yawn. Once I'd finished carrying the boxes into the house, I looked toward the academy's clock tower and grimaced. It was already one in the morning. *'Did we really spend that much time with Nalithor at his cafe?'*

"Djialkan, I'm going to take a bath." I shut the door to the house and then locked it. "Do you know what time my morning meeting is? Darius neglected to inform me."

"One of Eyrian's men came by earlier to inform you that it begins at eight, and Eyrian has already secured access to the academy libraries for you." Djialkan swirled through the air beside me and then floated towards the stairs. *"I will wake you at six.*

"Keep in mind that this house has Draemiran-style baths. The second floor is all yours. Darius is on the main floor, as is your shared study."

I picked Alala off her perch and ruffled the fur on top of her head before making my way up the nearby stairs.

"Draemiran-style?" I asked. "What do you mean?"

"Draemirans oft utilize public baths." Djialkan took on a lecturing tone and flew ahead of me when I opened one of the two doors on the second floor. *"The people of Draemir value a sense of community, and they do not view sexuality in the same way Humans do. Their baths are often public, or at least shared within a house. They do not try to hide their bodies or their desires.*

"Their baths are large enough to swim in and they often treat the water with cleansing oils or herbs. Were you and Darius raised in Vorpmasia, using the same bath would be of no issue."

"So, Darius freaked out and requested lodgings that would keep us separated from each other and from others?" I mused while filling the closets and dressers of my new rooms with clothes and trinkets. "A huge bath all to myself? I can't really complain about that. It could be fun, and much more comfortable than swimming around in X'shmir's lake."

"It is the only other thing on this floor aside from your rooms." Djialkan perched on the stack of blankets I'd set in the corner, and Alala scampered over to join him, *"The door you saw at the end of the hall leads to it. I recommend that you make haste so that you get*

decent sleep."

I smiled at the fae-dragon, nodded, and then finished storing my things in my new rooms. The suite was very small in comparison to my rooms back in the X'shmiran castle, but I didn't mind. A bed, closets, and a washroom were sufficient for me.

'Ugh, can't stop yawning.' I strode down the hallway towards the bath. *'Better make it as fast as possible, don't want to fall sleep in the bath, let alone one this large…'*

CHAPTER THREE
Desire to Fight

The combination of his scent and his sheer power was intoxicating. His hands dwarfed me as they roamed over my body, leaving trails of tingling hot magic in their wake. I should have felt threatened by his power, but I didn't.

I couldn't recall how I came to be in this situation; blindfolded and pinned beneath the Adinvyr, writhing beneath his touch. And I didn't care anymore. So long as he continued, I didn't care. Even if his endless teasing would drive me mad.

"Tsk, tsk, tsk. You're sensitive." He chuckled into my throat, his voice husky with desire. "How am I supposed to take my time when you make such encouraging sounds?"

I couldn't formulate a response, and that seemed to suit him just fine. He pressed me into the bed beneath him and kissed me.

"Perhaps…if you call me 'Master'…I will give you what you so desperately want."

I awoke with a jolt and scrambled out of bed. My entire body was flushed hot, my pulse roaring in my ears. Several firm shakes of my head did little to calm myself, so I stumbled past my sleeping companions and out of my room.

Once the door was shut behind me, I muttered a stream of low curses and stalked towards the bath at the end of the hall. My skin was soaked with sweat, and possibly other things. I would have to bathe before making breakfast.

'What in the infernal hells was that *about?!'* I refrained from slamming the door behind me and, instead, stalked straight into the water.

As I waded toward the deeper end of the bath realization struck me and I came to a halt. That must have been a *dream* I'd experienced. My brow furrowed, and I crossed my arms while nibbling at my knuckles.

I knew I'd never been…*intimate*…with Nalithor before. However, in the past 25 years I'd never experienced an honest-to-gods dream of any kind. The only things I *ever* experienced in my sleep were memories of Limbo and Dauthrmir.

'A dream?' I questioned, moving toward the edge of the bath to retrieve glass bottles of shampoo, conditioner, and soap. *'I haven't even been here for a full day! At the very least I shouldn't be having*

dreams about…'

Burning heat rose to my face again as my thoughts attempted to wander off. I shook my head violently and dunked myself under the surface of the bath. Holding my breath underwater didn't seem to help me refocus my thoughts. Resigned, I redirected my thoughts to my barriers and searched for cracks, holes, or anything else the damned Adinvyr could have slipped through.

I wasn't going to deny that I could be a rather sexual creature at times, but such thoughts only ever occurred while I was *awake.* Perhaps I should have been happy that I hadn't suffered through memories of Limbo or being taken from Dauthrmir again, but I wasn't. The concept of having a dream was so foreign to me that I found myself believing it was more likely that the powers of an Adinvyr were at fault.

While I knew little about the individual types of Devillians, I was aware that dream-walking or taking over the dreams of others was well within an Adinvyr's capabilities. They could use such methods to "hunt" for "food"—that is, sexual energy—if necessary. However, it didn't seem necessary at *all* in his case. We were in a city!

"Humph, he wasn't the only one I would have described as hungry…" I muttered absentmindedly as I shampooed my hair. For once, I made myself twitch. I growled and punched the water hard with one fist. "Gods damn it! This is ridiculous!"

The sensation of fingers trailing down my spine made me

twitch and pivot in the bath. I snarled curses to myself. I was relatively certain that I'd notice if someone or something intruded…but any form of touch was just so foreign to me.

It felt like he was actually *there. Every time.*

A short while later I'd finished angrily scrubbing myself clean and then made my way out of the bath. I couldn't find even a tiny fissure in my barriers. It was strangely infuriating. Dreaming about someone I barely knew was unfathomable to me, let alone for him to take *that* role. Honestly. A *master?* He had a long way to go before I would even *consider* calling him by such a title.

Calling him Rely'ric was already bad enough. He hadn't earned my respect or proven that he was worthy of being called by such an honorific yet.

'Tch, how am I supposed to face him after a dream like that?' I returned to my room and searched for undergarments, shivering as the cool morning air from the nearby window hit my damp skin. *'If Adinvyr can sense these sorts of things I may just go dig my own grave and bury myself alive.'*

"*Awake already, Arianna?*" Djialkan sounded concerned and raised his head from his pile of cushions to look at me. "*I thought Alala and I would have to drag you from your slumber.*"

"Let's not discuss it," I muttered before summoning the pile of trunks Shir and Gari had sent with me. "How formal should I dress for this 'strategy' meeting of theirs?"

"*Mages' robes are formal enough as it is,*" Djialkan spoke dryly as

Alala bounded over to the trunks and rubbed her fluffy cheek against one. *"Alala says to wear the fifth robe in that trunk. It is in X'shmiran style, but lightweight. There are matching gloves, breeches, and an undershirt to accompany it."*

I pulled the clothing from the trunk and then sighed in relief. Thankfully it was thick enough to obscure my filigree-like Brands of Divinity whilst still being light in weight. After dressing I pulled one of my sleeves back and looked at the black patterns encircling my left arm. Despite the thin, delicate design and small dots that bordered portions of the pattern, I still found myself feeling self-conscious about the stark contrast with my skin.

Shaking my head, I yanked on a pair of elbow-length gloves so that I could hide the chaos star designs on the back of my hands. Even with Corentine and Djialkan's warnings I still didn't feel it was appropriate to put my Brands on display. I didn't trust any of these people and, until I was certain that I could reveal them without drawing unnecessary attention to my brother and myself, I would keep the Brands hidden.

"Djialkan, Alala, let's go make breakfast." I pulled my hood over my pinned-up hair and then turned to look at the two Guardians.

With them both in tow we headed through the luxurious house and downstairs in search of the kitchen. I grimaced, looking around at the house's decor. Now that I was more awake, it was clear that Darius shouldn't have purchased so many ridiculous things the prior evening. The house came fully furnished, and with much nicer things than what he had bought.

The light colors and sleek metal fixtures didn't quite suit my tastes, but the glowing blue-white light inside of the fixtures intrigued me. I had expected to find Magelight was the source of light, but instead it appeared to be some type of *flowers*.

'Right… Breakfast,' I reminded myself, moving away from the glowing flowers. *'My meeting is at eight, so I have another two hours before I should head up to the palace. I really don't want to go…but I guess I don't have much choice in the matter.'*

I glanced toward the foyer as I descended the stairs, finding Darius' overrobe from the previous night hanging precariously on the coat rack. Sure enough, Darius had somehow managed to return without waking me. That said, I was a little surprised to find his coat was the only one hanging there. Knowing my brother, I expected him to bring someone back to his bed, be it Nalithor or someone that he met on his way home.

'I guess I should be thankful he didn't bring some random brat off the street back to the house.' I rolled my eyes. *'Not that it will take long. Probably two, maybe three, days tops before he gets too distressed with the lack of men in his bed.*

'He better not expect me to make them *breakfast as well!'*

The kitchen was easy enough to find, so I quickly moved around the kitchen and adjacent pantry in search of ingredients and a way to distract myself. Djialkan and Fraelfnir, unfortunately, had been unable to procure some important items such as flour and sugar. It came as a minor disappointment. I wanted pancakes! But at least I could make do with eggs, sliced ham, and some cinnamon toast.

"Would you two like some as well?" I kept my voice down and then grinned when Alala rubbed the top of her head against my cheek. "I'll make enough for Fraelfnir and Darius for when they wake up…"

"Something is troubling you." Djialkan narrowed his eyes at me, making me sigh. *"Was your dinner last night really so terrible?"*

'Darius was unusually timid and jealous last night,' I replied after strengthening my barriers to make sure Darius couldn't overhear. *'Aside from that, perhaps I'm a bit tetchy because I had an actual* dream *instead of—'*

"Smells good…" Darius grumbled from somewhere behind me, followed by the sound of him flopping into a chair. "Morning…"

"Did I wake you?" I asked, glancing at him before moving to another section of the counter so I could brew my brother some coffee.

"No, I can barely sleep." Darius sighed heavily and crossed his arms on the table, pouting atop them. "I'm too excited about being here. Not only are our tests coming up, but there's too many hot men to choose from!"

"I noticed you seemed rather *interested*." I rolled my eyes. "I was expecting to find you'd brought someone home, but I don't smell any guests."

"I didn't invite Nali to my bed. Nali won't even let me call him Nali!" Darius whined. "There's so many men to choose from that I don't even know where to start! Human, Elf, Adinvyr? Maybe a Vampire or a Rylthra? Sundreht are kind of cute too—their ears look so fluffy!"

"Boy toy confusion?" I laughed and ignored my twin's irritable glare as I carried platters of food to the table. "I'll admit that I didn't pay much attention to the looks of Dauthrmiran men.

"I'm glad you're awake though, there's something we need to discuss."

"What is it?" Darius frowned and then looked down at the platters," Aw, no pancakes?"

"I need to go shopping to get the ingredients for those, and for other dishes." I half-shrugged as both Fraelfnir and Djialkan shifted into their Devillian forms. "And—"

"Well, since I'm going to be watching the tests today and you're going to a military meeting," Darius began scooping copious amounts of food onto his plate, "you can talk to anyone you need to. Did you find out how long your meeting will be?"

"No, just that it starts at eight. I intend to do my shopping before then," I answered as I set a cup of coffee down for him and then took my seat. "Darius, can you shield your own mind while here?"

"You mean you'll let me shield myself?" Darius' eyes lit up. "I've been wanting to do that for ages! Yes, yes I can shield myself!"

"Eesh, calm down!" I sat back with my tea. "You *do* realize you could've just asked me any time you wanted, don't you? Just let me know if you need my help, okay? There's a lot of powerful people on the surface."

"I will!" Darius nodded, still beaming like a child. "I'll be heading out in a few hours to go view the tests. Nalithor's men will pick me up from here and keep an eye on me.

"Ah... Speaking of *Nalithor*, what do you think of him, Ari? You said you didn't pay much attention."

"Being spoken to directly by anyone other than you, Djialkan, and Fraelfnir is a little unnerving." I cut up my food as I spoke. "He seems like he'd be fun to fight, but—"

"Fighting really is all you think about isn't it?" Darius interrupted, pointing his fork at me. "I meant what you think about him *physically*, Ari."

"Physically?" I paused as the sight of Nalithor's exposed chest and abdomen flashed through my mind, and then grimaced. "He's certainly well-built, just like all the other Vorpmasian soldiers we've seen. They seem to train their bodies in a functional way, unlike *our* men."

"I don't think I can go back to X'shmiran men after seeing the ones here." Darius sighed, pouting like he'd lost his favorite toy.

'Your brother is incorrigible.' Djialkan snorted as he turned to

feed Alala some of his leftovers. *'If you intend to bring our purchases back to the house before your meeting we should get going.'*

I glanced toward the clock and then devoured the rest of my food. Darius mumbled his thanks around a large mouthful of egg as I strode past him, and I shrugged in response before making my way down the hall and into the foyer. I wasn't sure what to expect of the Vorpmasian generals, but I decided not to dwell on it quite yet. Instead, I made my way out of the house and into the cool morning air with both my Guardians perched on my shoulders.

The sky was breathtaking. After spending the last twenty years under the sickly violet sky of X'shmir it was difficult for me to accept that the *real* sky was such a beautiful, awe-inspiring sight. It didn't seem real to me, yet there it was in all its glory.

Only one of Avrirsa's three moons hung overhead at the current moment, and it was a mere silver crescent at this stage of its path. Numerous stars and planets hung above us, providing a surprising amount of light. Between the stars, bio-luminescent flora, and the Magelights, Dauthrmir was quite well lit.

I tore my gaze away from the stars and trekked down through the city's districts. At least three districts stood between me and the Merchants' District, assuming I didn't manage to get lost along the way. The granite buildings in this section of the city were adorned with silver inlays and decorations, while many of the larger buildings had aether-bearing crystals set into them. Each of the crystals hummed with faint power but, thankfully, it wasn't quite as intense as the hum the airships produced.

From what I saw, half of the Sapphire Quarter was dedicated to the Mages' Academy, training grounds, and dormitories. The other half housed military-only training areas and varying styles of lodgings. I soon gave up on trying to count how many different training arenas I spotted, and instead quickened my pace on approach to the Nobles' District.

Perhaps if I hurried, I could make it to the Merchants' District and back to the house before I needed to leave for my meeting.

"Alala, wait!" I panicked when the white fox leapt from my shoulder and began running from me.

I chased after the slippery fox, weaving in and out of the throngs of people that were moving to and from and Sapphire Quarter. I'd *finally* built up the courage to wander out of the house, and then Alala had to go and pull this stunt.

My heart stopped for a moment when I rounded the corner to see Nalithor picking up the warbling fox by her scruff. He glanced toward me with a playful smile as he straightened to his full height and then held Alala out to me.

'O-of all the people for her to run into, she had to go find him?!*'* I felt heat rise to my cheeks. *'After that damned dream this morning too! Can I just go find a hole to die in?'*

"This belongs to you, I assume." Nalithor chuckled as I approached him cautiously. "It would appear she shares your brother's habit of running away."

"I apologize, Rely'ric, she's young," I grumbled as I reached out to reclaim the fox. Alala promptly wriggle out of Nalithor's grip and ran up to perch on his shoulder, earning a dejected sigh from me. "Alala, we've already troubled him enough. Come back—"

"I must insist that you dispense with the formalities," Nalithor interrupted me with a warm smile and a brief tug at the front of my hood.

"I'm afraid that wouldn't be appropriate," I muttered, letting my gaze fall to the floor as I pulled away from the deity in front of me. "I'm…just an Umbral Mage, Rely'ric."

"I refuse to let a *fellow Umbral Mage* refer to me in such a stuffy way." Nalithor's voice was firm, making me glance up at him with unease, before shifting my gaze to Alala. She seemed quite content to nuzzle the Adinvyr. "If it is because you dislike me then that is an entirely different matter, of course."

"It's not that!" I responded with an exasperated sigh as Djialkan chuckled at me. "You're a *god*. I'm explicitly forbidden from—"

"I was an Umbral Mage long before I became a god." Nalithor grinned at me and then motioned at the fluffy fox on his shoulder. "Alala here has kindly informed me that you are required to address me however *I* desire *because* I'm a god.

"Please refer to me as General Vraelimir. If you prove yourself worthy…then perhaps I will permit you to call me by name."

"Does Alala intend to stay on *your* shoulder all day, *General Vraelimir*?" I huffed and crossed my arms. The Adinvyr's broadening grin managed, somehow, to frustrate me further.

"Well, I *was* going to invite you to have breakfast with me." Nalithor chuckled, reaching up to scratch Alala's cheek. "However, this one informed me you've already had breakfast, so I suppose that is out of the question.

"Can I convince you to join me for some tea instead before we're expected for our meeting?"

'He's...inviting me?' I just stared at the Adinvyr deity in disbelief. *'Why would he want me to have tea—let alone breakfast—with him? Even if we're both Umbral Mages, he's still a god.'*

"Arianna has important errands to run before the meeting." Djialkan snorted from my shoulder before I could respond, causing Nalithor's expression to fall slightly. *"Alala, we are meant to* protect *Arianna while here, not distract her unnecessarily! She might let you get away with it because you are cute, but I will not!"*

"Did...*Djialkan* just call something *cute?*" Nalithor's disbelieving laugh caused a small smile to twitch across my lips. "Ahhh... Very well. I won't be so selfish as to keep you from your errands.

"Try not to get yourself into *too* much trouble, alright? You are...quite the rare sight."

Nalithor pulled Alala from his shoulder with care and held her out to me again. I felt my face flush slightly as I reclaimed her. I wasn't sure how many of those tender expressions of his I could handle, let alone the occasional sultry or even disappointed tone.

He was far too alluring, far too powerful. Being in the same city as him was already too close. Being within touching distance was worse. Something about his disappointed demeanor made me want to disregard my errands for the day so that I could do as he wished instead.

That was unacceptable.

After a slight bow and a mumbled goodbye, I hurried off through the city streets, aware of my pulse pounding in my ears. Dream or no dream, that man was incredibly difficult for me to face. I was rather curious about what made him tick and, even if I didn't like it, I knew I was physically attracted to him. However, becoming acquainted with him was not conducive to my longevity. Even so, I found myself wanting to challenge him to a sparring match at minimum.

'Should I be concerned as to the contents of this 'dream' you had, Arianna?' Djialkan asked slyly as I rushed through the streets and into the Merchants' District. *'I've never seen you this flustered before.'*

'I don't want to talk about it!' I snapped.

Even at this early hour the Merchants' District bustled with activity. Most of the people were Devillian, but many of them I did not have a name for. I didn't know what to call many of the people I spotted milling about. Many had features that were foreign to me despite my time in the Sihix Forest.

Sprinkled into the mix were a variety of Humans and Elves, many of whom had strange hair or skin colors that I was unfamiliar with. Most striking of the lot were the Dauthrmiran Elves—the Kelsviir. Their skin ranged from pure white to pitch black. The Kelsviir had angular features and oddly colored hair and eyes, while the other types of Elves typically looked more Human.

'Let's make this quick,' I stated, catching a few of the stares and scowls being directed our way. *'I don't like the looks they're giving us.'*

Djialkan muttered his agreement. I strode through the district at a brisk pace in search of places that sold the groceries I was missing. It was much busier this morning than it had been yesterday evening, meaning I had to squeeze my way through the crowds and take care that nothing, and no one, dislodged my hood or mask.

The Devillians and Elves were all much taller than I was, so I found myself having to speak up to get through the crowds more than once. Sundreht women, with their cat-like ears and tails, seemed to be the only particular race close to my height, seeing as they were shorter than I was.

"*Honestly, just who does she think she is?*" I heard a male whispering in Draemiran from somewhere behind me as I browsed a stall of fruits. "*Doesn't she know the Old Ways are over? Is she trying to mock our forefathers?*"

"*Father works with a soldier that was assigned to escort our dignitaries to X'shmir,*" a female began in reply, "*apparently X'shmir still follows the Old Ways. They wouldn't relent and let her follow our customs while here."*

"Just because I am from X'shmir doesn't mean I do not understand what you are saying," I stated coolly in Draemiran, turning slightly to look at the startled group of teen-looking Elves. "What you call the 'Old Ways' are still the way things are run where I am from. If you do not like it, I recommend you take it up with someone that has the power to incite change."

Without a second glance I stalked past the group and down the street. It frustrated me that anyone here just *assumed* I was trying to mock something their ancestors went through. For them, sure, it was the past. However, for me, it was still the present. Maybe one day things in X'shmir would change, but I doubted it would be within my life time.

While I wandered through the streets in search of flour, sugar, and recognizable fruits I found that the Devillians, for the most part, seemed curious about me. At the very least most of them didn't seem to bear any ill will toward me. However, many of them still investigated my barriers or otherwise attempted to sneak through them.

'Honestly! Are all of them Adinvyr or are all Devillians this raunchy?!' My grumpy thoughts earned a snicker from Djialkan. *'Really, Djialkan! Aren't they supposed to pester those who are close to them in power?'*

'You are a Human with power. They are likely curious about you.' Djialkan laughed. *'Alas, we are running out of time. Have you found*

everything you wanted?'

I nodded begrudgingly and made my way upwards to the Sapphire Quarter once more. My discomfort was soothed, to an extent, by my habit of sticking to the shadows as I traveled. The pleasant and curious looks from the Devillians were quite the contrast to the mix of spiteful and hateful looks most of Humans and Elves sent me. At this point I honestly wasn't sure what to think about the people of Dauthrmir.

'The Elves that don't look like they want to shred me—the Kelsviir—why do they seem accepting when the other Elves are not?' I nudged Djialkan's chin.

'Ah, the Kelsviir.' Djialkan took on a lecturing tone, *'They are as native to these lands as the Devillians are.'*

'So, they probably weren't exposed to the Old Ways in the same manner that other Elven races were?' I murmured. *'Ugh, I wish the Devillians would stop tapping on my barriers like this! It's so noisy!'*

Alala let out a small warble and nuzzled me as I pouted. I released a small sigh, pet Alala and Djialkan for a moment, and then pulled my map out in search of a shortcut back to the Sapphire Quarter. I wasn't thrilled about the idea of meeting with the Vorpmasian generals, but it seemed more pleasant than remaining in the lower sections of the city. Perhaps after the meeting I would even be able to find someone to spar, or at least somewhere to work on my training.

Every now and then I was tempted to stop when I spotted

Adinvyr men and women fighting with each other. The spectacle seemed to draw large crowds of cheering spectators and the smell of Devillian blood hung thick in the air. It was a scent that made me even more eager to find a fight for myself.

'Later, Ari, later.' I grit my teeth and dashed along the glowing roads, weaving in and out of the city's shadows. *'It's not like they're going anywhere any time soon. I can take my time to find an appropriate opponent.'*

I was surprised to find Darius reading in the kitchen when I returned to the house, but we barely said anything to each other. My shopping trip took much longer than I expected it to, so by this point I was cutting my timing close.

"*Alala and I will remain here,*" Djialkan informed me as he shifted into his Devillian form and took the bags of groceries from me. "*You should hurry. I will take care of things here while you are gone. Fraelfnir and I will make sure Darius does not leave without his escort. Now, shoo.*"

Nodding, I hurried my way out of the house once more. I readjusted my gloves and hood more out of nervousness than necessity and then headed off for the road leading to the palace district above.

Taking deep breaths of the cool, sweet-smelling air did little to calm my nerves. So much power radiated from the palace that I almost wanted to skip joining their little meeting. I was used to being the strongest person in X'shmir, but I would have been stupid to think that I even came *close* to the source of power that was making my skin crawl.

I hadn't gone very far before noticing that I was being watched. My attention shifted slightly to the side when I caught *his* spicy-sweet scent. *'Does he think he's being sneaky?'*

"There you are." Nalithor's tone was pleasant as he stepped through rippling darkness to my left. A smile spread across his face when I stopped and turned to face him. "No new challengers on your way here, I trust?"

'Does his mere presence count as a challenge, I wonder?' I mused, crossing my arms under my bust as I examined the Adinvyr.

"None." I shook my head and took in the dark Umbral Mages' robes that Nalithor wore. "I hope my brother didn't give you too much trouble last night, General Vraelimir. When he's not speaking endlessly of politics he tends to wander off after every little thing that catches his eye."

Nalithor's warm, welcoming expression was almost enough to brighten my dim mood, but not quite. However, he did seem pleased that I'd addressed him "appropriately." He cast a few glances, and his power, around us for a moment as if searching for something—likely my Guardians—before settling his attention fully on me.

"He lacks discipline and yet he wants to know of the most advanced healing techniques." Nalithor laughed as he motioned for me to follow him. "Darius is a rather perfect example of the stereotypical 'new student.' I'm quite used to it, so don't worry."

I nodded and then followed Nalithor toward the palace. While we walked in silence, I examined him yet again. The dark robes he wore today were much more fitting on his muscular physique, and they contrasted quite nicely with his pale skin and hair. While I hadn't noticed his predatory grace the previous day, I now found myself admiring his movements. Regal, predatory, and graceful were the first words that came to mind when I looked at Nalithor.

Or at least those were the tame words I would've used to describe him.

The crest on the back of his overrobe drew my curiosity. This close it was clear that the dragon's blue topaz eyes were not only the same as the ones that dotted Nalithor's jewelry, but they also matched his eye color perfectly. That frosty color was unmistakable.

"Hmmm, that's neither the Vorpmasian crest nor the Draemiran one," I remarked when my curiosity got the better of me.

Nalithor's scaled tail swayed a little faster when he glanced over his shoulder at me, and then he slowed his pace to fall into step with me. His expression was equal parts curiosity and pleasantness, but I wasn't quite sure how to read the swaying of his tail. His mannerisms and body language were quite different from the handful of Adinvyr I knew in the Sihix Forest.

"Some of the Vorpmasian Archmagi and Generals have earned

the honor of receiving their own personal crest," Nalithor offered with a small smile. "I've earned the nickname 'Black Dragon' over the years. So, when I earned that honor myself, it seemed to fit."

"Ah, so *you're* the 'picky, strict Black Dragon' I've heard the soldiers muttering about." I laughed, earning a mischievous grin from the Adinvyr.

"I would be *very* interested to know who was complaining," Nalithor spoke with mock-innocence.

"Aye, I'm sure you would." I bit back a grin to hide my fangs. "Let me guess, more work as payment for their insubordination?"

Nalithor nodded, still grinning, before assuming a more serious demeanor as we neared the palace gates. Several guards bowed deeply or otherwise saluted him as we made our way through the palace grounds and toward the large ebony twin doors that led into the palace itself.

Much to my surprise many of the guards and servants acknowledged my presence with deep bows as well. It was such a strange occurrence that my first instinct was to hide behind something, but I managed to refrain.

I wanted to run around the palace grounds and examine the unusual architecture, the blooming plants, and any other strange things I could find. However, I knew I shouldn't. I wasn't here for pleasure, and I could explore the rest of the city later if I wanted to. The previous day I'd been too focused on maintaining my brother and thus far this morning I'd been too distracted.

"This way," Nalithor beckoned, leading me down a hallway instead of toward the large doors that must have led to the throne room. "Lucifer hardly ever uses the throne room for anything."

It struck me as interesting that Nalithor referred to the emperor by his first name, but I decided not to question him on it. Instead, I followed him in silence. Nalithor's pleasant scent was distracting me enough already and was strong enough that I couldn't smell anything else in the palace. As I thought, Nalithor was many times more powerful than anyone else I sensed in the city.

'His power and scent alike both surpass the emperor.' I observed, subtly scenting the air. *'Still, I feel like his aura should be stronger. Do the gods hide their power behind barriers? I doubt his power is as close to mine as it feels.'*

"After seeing your crest, I can see why General Il'thar's men were concerned," I spoke up and bit back a grimace when I heard the unease in my voice. "I hope that—"

"I won't pretend that I don't question Aurelian's choice." Nalithor had an amused smile on his face once again. "The fox is certainly fitting though, isn't it?

"I will learn soon enough whether or not his faith in you was misplaced. Don't dwell on it."

'Don't dwell on it?' I tilted my head to the side and examined the Adinvyr's back. *'Easier said than done.'*

Nalithor's long white braid and the platinum ornaments adorning it intrigued me. In X'shmir such a hairstyle would have been mocked as "feminine" just because it was long, let alone the jewelry and clasps used to fasten his hair in place. However, construing *anything* about the man before me as "feminine" was a laughable notion. I couldn't find anything about his physique that fit such a description.

After a moment I turned my attention away from the distracting Adinvyr. Since Darius was so strongly interested in this one, I would be better served to observe the decorations of the palace instead. Fighting my brother for anyone's attentions was a waste of my time, especially since even the most innocent of relationships were forbidden for me.

'Well I suppose that isn't entirely *true,'* I reminded myself while examining a rather macabre painting. *'If I really wanted to risk becoming friends with someone... Bah, no. Not worth it.'*

My attention returned to Nalithor's back when he stopped. His tail swished behind him as he seemed to consider something. His eyes were fiery and his expression intense when he turned to look at me. Both his stance and demeanor were predatory as he studied me before speaking.

"You really are quite different from your brother, aren't you?" Nalithor asked as I looked up at him. "I have a question for you before we join my comrades."

"Ask me anything," I offered as the Adinvyr sized me up with an unreadable expression set on his face.

"Why didn't your brother or your parents inform us that you

are both the X'shmiran princess and their Umbral Mage?" Nalithor's voice was firm and his arms were crossed, but he seemed to sense my confusion despite my obscured features. "When we questioned the King and Queen about the whereabouts of the princess, they claimed you were ill.

"When questioned about the location of their Umbral Mage they claimed you were hunting beasts. Yet our men report that they rarely saw you. In fact, they only ever caught sight of your whenever you brought letters or gifts from the people of Sihix."

"They claimed I was *ill?*" I sighed heavily, shaking my head. "It's true that I wasn't in X'shmir—as you know, seeing as you *followed me* all the way to Sihix.

"It's rather likely they would have poisoned my food to keep me subdued if I had remained. I *was* hunting beasts, just not around the city or the plateau."

"Then you remained near Sihix?" Nalithor muttered, stroking his chin. "Isn't that dangerous? To run the risk of corruption in such a way, I mean."

"It's safer for me in Sihix than it is in X'shmir." I half-shrugged. "To answer your original question... The X'shmiran Royal Family doesn't like to acknowledge I exist, especially not that I am part of that family. While I doubt that Darius hid the matter intentionally, I wouldn't be surprised if our parents were. It is at their behest that I wasn't present for the negotiations."

"I find it strange that your brother, and now Eyrian, both insist you're capable of dealing with beasts stronger than peons." Nalithor's voice carried his unease but his expression was pensive.

"I'm aware that, because I'm Human, my ability to fight Chaos Beasts is in question." The corner of my eye twitched as I curled my hands into fists. "While I'm sure Darius has greatly embellished the tale, actions speak louder than words. There's little point in discussing—"

"I apologize," Nalithor interrupted me with a smile and placed his hand on top of my head. "I didn't mean to wound your pride as a warrior, nor did I mean to insinuate that I look down on you for being Human.

"Whether or not your brother is Human is something we've been questioning for quite some time. And, although most of your appearance is hidden, your ability to fight the beasts is a red flag itself, even *without* those flashes of dainty fangs you've been trying to hide."

"D-dainty? They're not '*dainty*!'" I protested before covering my mouth with my sleeve and looking away from him. "For what it's worth, I think X'shmir's claim that Darius and I are a 'new step in the evolutionary line' is bullshit. Alas, I have no way of proving otherwise, so—"

"Dainty," Nalithor interjected, gripped my chin, and pulled my face up slightly so that I was looking at him again. His mischievous smile sent a shiver down my spine. "It would seem I have misjudged you, however. I thought it was likely you would share your brother's belief in your parents' story. I hope you will forgive me.

"Let's get going, shall we?"

Nalithor released me, shot me a warm smile, and then strode down the hallway once more. I fidgeted with my displaced hood as I followed him, aware my face had probably grown beet red when he pulled my face up. My cheeks felt like they were going to catch fire. Those smiles of his weren't helping either.

'What was that about anyway?' I shot a disgruntled look at Nalithor's back. *'I don't understand this man at all.'*

Several minutes passed in silence before we came to a pair of large doors. Nalithor raised one of his hands to knock but stopped when Eyrian yanked the door open from the other side. The Draekin had a cross expression on his face, his glare set on Nalithor. I stayed silent and glanced between the two of them, watching as they stared defiantly at each other. I got the feeling they were arguing telepathically about something.

A female made an irritated sound and, after a moment, Eyrian moved out of Nalithor's way with a low "humph."

"Arianna-jiss, I hope *this one* hasn't tried to seduce you yet." Eyrian jammed his thumb over his shoulder at Nalithor.

"If he's tried then he's doing a poor job of it, because I haven't noticed," I spoke sarcastically and crossed my arms at the large Draekin. I heard several snickers from within the room and caught a muffled one from Eyrian himself. "Didn't I make it clear that I don't like all this '-jiss' and 'Your Highness' nonsense? Please drop the honorifics when addressing me."

"Contrary to what you might think," Nalithor's tone was dry as he took a seat along the left side of the room's massive table and then shot another glare at Eyrian, "I may be an Adinvyr, but I am quite...particular. I am also a gentleman. It would be rather inappropriate for me to 'seduce' a woman who is still restrained by the Old Ways."

"Like that would stop you from pursuing something you actually wanted," the female voice from before scoffed. I grimaced when I spotted the familiar, scantily-clad Oracle. "Well, you certainly know how to shield your mind at least. I thought your shields would shatter once away from the Mists but, apparently, that wasn't the case.

"How's my hard-headed sister doing?"

"You're *both* hard-headed," I stated flatly, ignoring both Eyrian and Nalithor's muffled snorts of laughter. "Corentine is doing well."

"Most of my generals are away from the capital dealing with other matters." The familiar male voice made me pause and look toward the head of the table with unease. "Feel free to sit anywhere you like. My name is Lucifer, and I would appreciate it if you referred to me as such. I share your distaste for formalities."

Lucifer was undeniably the man I saw arguing with an Elder God in my nightmares for so long. His left eye was brilliant blue like mine, but his right eye was emerald green—yellow around the centers—just like my brother's. His skin was pale and wintry, and his short dark brown curls reminded me of my own, much longer, hair. Of course, the pure white Brands of Divinity, graceful silver horns, and black scaled tail were all things I lacked.

He smelled of leather and old books but Nalithor's scent almost consumed Lucifer's completely.

"A pleasure to meet you, I'm sure." I perched in the nearest empty seat and resisted the urge to pull my legs up beneath me in the massive chair. *'He…looks too much like Darius and me. And he's definitely the same man from those nightmares of Dauthrmir. That…can't be a coincidence, right? Is he…'*

"Normally those who follow the Old Ways are rather devout." Lucifer examined me with an unreadable expression. "However, you and your brother seem quite displeased with X'shmiran law."

"We're the 'young and rebellious' generation, as they put it." I crossed my legs and leaned on the armrest of my chair. "I have a plethora of reasons to be displeased with X'shmiran law as an Umbral Mage, of course. I'm sure General Vraelimir was subjected to some fraction of their treatment while in X'shmir, and General Il'thar most certainly witnessed it at some point in his stay.

"That said…politics and law are not my forte. I believe my presence was requested because you wish to learn more about our beasts, yes?"

"Straight to business, is it?" Nalithor mused with a playful smile before shifting his gaze to the other three people in the room. "Arianna appears less easy to distract than her brother is, at least."

"Have you noticed anything strange about the Chaos Beasts in recent years?" Lucifer settled his gaze on me, brought his fingertips to form a steeple, and leaned forward. His expression was intense, but still unreadable.

"They've been looking for something over the past year," I answered after a moment, motioning with one hand as I spoke. "In the past ten years they've shown signs that they're communicating 'verbally,' so to speak.

"Their attacks have grown more coordinated. The flying ones tend to time their attacks based on the movements of the wingless ones."

"How have the X'shmirans been dealing with them then?" Eyrian frowned, but then his eyes widened slightly. "Wait a minute; the reason the X'shmiran Royal Family demanded troops in exchange for letting you come here was because—?"

"—you've truly been dealing with them yourself?" Nalithor finished Eyrian's sentence, a frown of his own forming on his face.

"Hmmm?" I tilted my head slightly and then nodded, "Yes, I've been killing all of them. The X'shmiran soldiers are too interested in growing muscle mass to impress women. Their focus on *actual* training is, regrettably, as nonexistent as their useful muscle."

"Magic aside, how does a tiny creature like you handle

X'shmir's *entire* beast problem?" Nalithor turned and then leaned over to sniff at me slightly. "Darius is rather insistent that you are both Human. But, unlike them, *your* scent isn't unpleasant…"

"Thanks, I think?" I shook my head at Nalithor as he sat back up, trying to ignore his sultry smirk. "As Darius stated, I've been fighting the beasts for quite some time. They inhabit most of the lands outside of our city and outside of Sihix. I've always thought that X'shmir smells terrible, and the beasts smell a *little* better. So, I spent a great deal of time outside the city walls."

"They don't inhabit the Sihix Forest?" The Oracle narrowed her lime eyes at me, her strawberry blonde tail swished behind her.

"Sihix…?" I shook my head. "No, they're terrified of Sihix. The beasts won't even venture into the fringes of the forest."

"That's unusual." Eyrian's frown grew deep. "Beasts are notorious for hiding within Aledacian Forests. How can you be sure?"

"I'm on relatively good terms with Sihix," I offered after a moment of consideration. All of them aside from the Oracle looked at me with shock plain on their faces. "When I was younger, I found some of their young Guardians—foxes—out on the plateau. They were attempting to flee from a pair of what you lot call 'Dux-class Chaos Beasts.' The beasts had injured the Guardians.

"I took out the pair of beasts and then helped the injured Guardians back to the forest. Once they were inside, I brought them the herbs they'd been searching for."

"She's...not lying." The Oracle sighed heavily and slumped back in her seat. "A *pair* of Duxes, Arianna?! It would take at least twelve demigods an *hour* to deal with two, and they wouldn't come out unscathed!"

"Really?" I tilted my head. "I guess demigods aren't as strong as Human legends make them out to be."

Eyrian choked on the swig of water he'd just taken and began coughing, while Lucifer and Nalithor simply watched me with intrigued expressions. The Oracle, however, was quite amused and was slapping her thigh as she laughed hysterically. I wasn't quite sure why she'd reacted so raucously—or what I should do about it.

"I can show you, if you don't believe me." I looked at the laughing Oracle, but she shook her head.

"Oh, I believe you, cutie." The Oracle giggled, grinning. "You're just damned blunt. I like it! These boys will have plenty of opportunities to see you in action themselves. They can wait!

"Lucifer, add her to the list of reserves—until she has an official partner, anyway."

"You're certain?" Lucifer arched an eyebrow at the still-giggling Oracle, who barely managed to nod her head. "Very well."

"See, I *told* you she kicked those Duxes' asses without Djialkan's help." Eyrian glared at Nalithor. He seemed to notice my attention shift to him, so he added, "They didn't believe me when I told them you did all the work, Arianna-ji... Arianna."

Before the conversation could wander further off-track Lucifer began pelting me with questions again, and I answered them to the best of my ability. Eyrian and the Oracle were both rather vocal about voicing their opinion, surprise, and displeasure throughout the conversation.

Nalithor, on the other hand, sat in silence and observed me with an unreadable expression. I couldn't tell what the Adinvyr was thinking at all but, more than once, he nudged at my barriers as if he was testing me or perhaps looking for a way in. There was something sensual about his power even when it lay dormant around him, and even its passive state put me on edge.

'I get that Human mages are practically nonexistent,' I bit back a shiver, *'but really; if he wants to know something, he should just ask me. Or does he think I haven't noticed his prodding?'*

Several hours later, they seemed satisfied with my observations, for now, and with my suggested strategies for dealing with specific types of beasts. Apparently after whatever barrier once existed around X'shmir disappeared some of our unique Chaos Beasts appeared on the surface, and they were unlike any of the types found natively on the Rilzaan continent.

"Would you like to join me for lunch, Arianna?" Nalithor asked as we made our way through the palace, causing me to look at him in surprise.

"Actually, I was hoping to take a look around the Sapphire Quarter and determine where I can work on my training," I replied after a moment, noting the curious glance he cast at me. "I haven't been able to train properly since—"

"That can wait, can't it?" Nalithor asked in a purr as he rounded on me and backed me into a wall. Power rippled off him in waves as he lifted a hand to my face. "I was hoping that perhaps I could have you to myself for a little while…"

The sheer amount of power startled me and, for a moment, I just blinked behind my mask in surprise before remembering to breathe. His power ripped through me like a storm, making my heart stutter. There wasn't any maliciousness behind the action or his power, but I couldn't identify his intent at all.

'I can't tell if he's testing my resolve or if he's serious…' I grew still as the Adinvyr leaned down with a mischievous smile, his lips hovering just out of reach of mine. *'He really is difficult. I should keep my distance from this one.'*

"Are you suggesting that I should neglect my training, *General* Vraelimir?" I replied with a playful smile. "What happened to 'The Black Dragon' being strict, hmmm?"

"Oh? You won't indulge me?" Nalithor purred, lifting my face a little closer to his. "You really meant it when you said I would have to *prove* I'm worthy of your interest, then?

"You're an odd one…but I'll reward you for your resistance. There are many training areas along the edge of the Sapphire Quarter, several of which are behind your house. If none of those have the equipment you require, any of the guards can point you in the right direction."

Nalithor released me abruptly and moved away, walking down the hallway once more. Perhaps he thought he was hiding it, but I spotted his disappointed expression. The languid swishing of his tail gave him away further. It appeared that he was genuinely displeased that I turned down his offer. However, I didn't plan to relent. *Especially* if he thought he could use his power as an Adinvyr to get his way or seduce me.

"Thanks, I'll try not to break anything." I moved past him and out of the palace, adding to myself. *'I'm considering breaking you after that little display. I think I will make you wait at the very least.'*

I shook my head to clear the lingering sensation of Nalithor's power. I stalked through the palace district and down to the Sapphire Quarter. It was past noon by now and the palace grounds were busy with a variety of servants and members of the Imperial Guard. None of them particularly mattered to me at the given moment. All I wanted was to smash my fist into a training dummy. Or a person.

It pissed me off that Nalithor had tried to use his power against me in such a way. Had he not attempted to *seduce* me into joining him for lunch, I might have relented! Was he testing me in some way? Did he treat all women like that? I sure as hell didn't know, and it was part of what pissed me off so much.

Growling, I yanked my headphones out of my shrizar and slipped them on under my hood. Even after two months Nalithor's scent still clung to the damned things, but I hoped that the music would help me focus on training. At least his directions had been truthful, so I found my way to usable training grounds with ease. To my surprise, and relief, this section of the district was void of people.

After a brief warm-up I squared up with the closest training dummy I could find.

'I would prefer to tear apart some beasts, but this will have to do.' I scowled and twisted into a firm kick. *'Just pretend nothing else exists aside from me, my music, and this stupid fucking dummy.'*

It took longer than I wanted to admit before I was able to focus on training. While the dummy didn't provide me with any challenge per se, it was still satisfying to strike. I decided to make a game out of trying to break the dummy. In the end I discovered that the damned thing was insanely sturdy. As far as I could tell, none of my strikes managed to crack any part of its surface.

'Fuck it. I need something that moves. *That fights back.'* I rested a forearm against the dummy's chest, leaning against it as I caught my breath and thought. *'I want to fight someone...or* something. *This just isn't satisfying! You'd think with all their Magitech trinkets that whey would have something more interesting to fight.'*

I grumbled curses under my breath and then pushed away from the dummy, considering my options as I subtly cast my power through the city. Aside from *him* there were several other interesting presences. Eyrian, for one, but he appeared to be up in the palace district still. In the Sapphire Quarter I sensed a myriad of strong people that might be interesting to fight, and it felt like many of them were already training in various portions of the district.

Even so I was still drawn to fighting Nalithor first over any of the other Devillians I sensed. Reluctant, I turned away from the training dummies and made my way in the direction I felt *his* power radiating from. Before I even *considered* challenging anyone else, I wanted to fight Nalithor first. Starting with the strongest one sounded much more fun that starting with weaker opponents.

This time I took a more leisurely pace across the Sapphire Quarter and let myself admire the scenery since I'd calmed down a bit. Variegated blue grasses covered much of the district when there wasn't a road or walkway in the way. Pale blue veins of bioluminescent material ran through the bark of the trees, and even in the leaves on some bushes.

Plants and trees bloomed everywhere I looked and filled the air with a mixture of sweet scents. Their blooms were all either white or soft pastel shades and gave off a soft glow. Many of the trees looked similar to the cherry, peach, and magnolia trees I was accustomed to in X'shmir—aside from their unusual coloring and glow.

I looked out over the lake below briefly, catching the movements of the large dragons that circled beneath the city. A power spike pulled my attention back to the Sapphire Quarter, so I refocused on where I was going. I wasn't sure what to expect or what I was going to say, but I chose not to dwell on it. Instead, I padded silently through the maze of military buildings that were emblazoned with Nalithor's crest.

His scent permeated the air strongly in this district and I took a deep breath of it despite myself.

'Ari!' Darius called telepathically, causing me to stop mid-step within the shadows. I frowned and quickly re-shielded my twin's thoughts as he continued. *I'm back from observing the tests now! Where are you?'*

'I...was going to see if I could get Nalithor or his men to spar with me. Training dummies are boring...' I grumbled, sinking back into the shadows to watch Nalithor and his men spar in a large sandy training area ahead of me.

'Some of Nalithor's and Eyrian's men are really nice! They invited me to go out to dinner tonight with them!' Darius spoke excitedly. I felt my shoulders slump. *'Can I go with them, Ari?*

'And, really? Challenging them already? Shouldn't you be familiarizing yourself with Vorpmasian ways first?'

'I guess if it's their *men you don't need me to tag along as a bodyguard.'* I felt my expression fall as I watched Nalithor toss one of his men through the air. *'You...are right, though. I forgot that I need to study their ways...'*

Darius' presence faded, and I continued to watch Nalithor spar his men. I knew better than to assume my presence had gone undetected. I could feel them watching me with their senses. It would seem too suspicious if I simply turned and left now. I wasn't sure what to do but I wasn't given much time to dwell on it.

"You didn't lose your nerve, did you?" Nalithor suddenly appeared to my right with a blade leveled at my throat. "Ah…you're quick."

Nalithor glanced down at the gloved hand I'd caught his blade with. He examined my plain gloves with surprising intensity for a moment before lifting his gaze back to my face.

"I apologize, General Vraelimir," I offered as he cautiously withdrew his sword. "Lurking was not my intention. My brother rather suddenly demanded my attention." I motioned loosely at my temples with my other hand.

"Then why are you here, *General Black*?" Nalithor crossed his arms and I tried not to flinch. He looked, and sounded, incredibly displeased.

"I was going to ask you to spar with me…" I muttered quietly, averting my gaze. "However, I can see that I'm interrupting you. If you'll excuse me…"

I turned on my heel and strode away from Nalithor feeling oddly dejected. I couldn't bear that distrusting, suspicious expression on his face. What had changed since this morning? He'd been much warmer and playful then. Had my unwillingness to join him for lunch upset him? He didn't strike me as the sort that would be offended by such a thing. Perhaps I'd misjudged him?

"You don't intend to force a confrontation?" Nalithor inquired from behind me, causing me to turn and glance at him. "Ah… I forget that you're mostly unfamiliar with our ways.

"You have every right to force a fight if your target is unwilling to indulge you."

"It would be rather impolite of me to interrupt you while you're training your men." I motioned behind him. "Perhaps I will challenge you again when you aren't busy, and when I have a better grasp of '*your ways*.'"

Without waiting for a reply, I stalked off and attempted to battle down my displeasure. As tempting as it as to 'force a fight,' as he put it, I didn't intend to interrupt his men's training. One of my own pet peeves was when people interrupted me while training my men in X'shmir. I'd be damned before I did the same thing to someone else. After earning such a reaction from him I didn't intend to see if I could stay and observe either.

"Darius informed you that he's going to dinner with Eyrian, our men, and myself, didn't he?" Nalithor called after me. "You should consider joining us."

'*Tch. Why would I go to dinner with someone that doesn't respect me as a warrior?*' I let both the shadows and my begrudging thoughts consume me. '*At this rate I will have to sneak out of Dauthrmir and find beasts to fight! I just…I just want someone to spar with. Is that so much to ask?*'

I wasn't sure why, but now I was even more pissed off than I'd been earlier. Instead of stalking off to the library to study, I made my way back to the house to sulk and to bake something sweet to comfort myself. Alala and Djialkan noticed my mood instantly and retreated upstairs while I stormed around the kitchen making cookies. Even Darius maintained his distance.

An hour or so later I found myself sulking on the balcony of my room with a tome settled on my lap. I skimmed the contents of the X'shmiran text and flipped the pages with one hand while munching cookies with the other. Neither were helping me much. I needed to fight. Not study.

"Ari, are you sure you don't want to come with us?" Darius called from somewhere below, so I glanced over the railing to look down at him and his entourage.

Several familiar faces and many unfamiliar ones surrounded Darius. Nalithor, Eyrian, a male with spiky black hair, and the Oracle were present along with an assortment of men and women that I assumed were officers of rank in Nalithor and Eyrian's respective forces. I recognized the pink-haired Desert Elf, Aylaena, from my brief stay on the Vorpmasian ship but the rest of their companions were unknown to me.

None of them smelled interesting.

The sight of the Oracle handing on Nalithor's arm made my blood boil. She actively clamored for the Adinvyr's attention, even going as far as to press her cleavage around his arm. However, Nalithor and the others were simply looking up toward my balcony with expectant expressions. For a moment I considered hopping down and shredding the lanky Rylthra woman apart. However, I wasn't quite angry enough to upset Corentine in such a way.

'I'd rather behead myself,' I retorted to my brother and then returned my gaze to the book on my lap.

"Arianna, your jealousy aside," Djialkan spoke quietly but still earned both a twitch and a glare from me. *"You should at least* try *to make some friend—"*

"Come now, there's plenty of fine food and drink to be had!" Eyrian called with a broad grin as I snapped my book shut. "You—! Whoa now, careful!"

'Eyrian's company is tempting…but no.' I suppressed a snort. *'I shouldn't be around anyone while in this mood.'*

I leapt over the balcony and landed in a brief crouch on the grass. The Rylthra Oracle must have sensed some portion of my bloodlust or jealousy as I approached my brother. She shrunk back behind Nalithor slightly as Djialkan perched on my shoulder. Darius had an utterly confused expression on his face as I came to stand before him. I let out a small sigh.

"If you stay out too late, *again*, I will have your head." I pointed a finger against my twin's chest. "Fraelfnir!"

"…what?" The white-scaled dragon shimmered into view on Darius' shoulder and eyed me wearily, using my brother's neck as a shield.

"If Darius misbehaves, bite him or something." I pointed from Fraelfnir to my twin. "Enjoy your 'dinner.'"

I really didn't understand why I felt so gods-damned jealous, but it was even more infuriating than seeing that blonde bitch rubbing herself all over Nalithor's arm. My jealousy fueled my anger, which fueled my jealousy. I hated it. I knew I was being unreasonable and had no right, let alone a good reason, to be jealous. Alas, jealousy seldom made sense to me.

I chose to ignore the rest of my brother's companions completely and turned on my heel to return to the house.

'By the way, Ari,' Darius began and, just from his tone, I knew I wasn't going to like what he had to say, 'now that all the shopping and stuff is done, you're not allowed to speak with anyone outside of combat-oriented encounters. Oh right, you can speak at any more meetings you might be invited to too.'

'Calm down, Arianna.' Djialkan warned as flames threatened to erupt around my feet. 'We knew he was going to pull something like this. You cannot let your anger spiral out of—'

"You won't join us, Arianna?" Nalithor's purring tone made me want to slug him this time. I turned and shot him a murderous glare, noting the Oracle's fearful expression and the color draining from her face—could she see through my mask? "I suppose you really do intend to avoid making friends with—"

"You have made it clear that you do not respect her as a warrior." Djialkan snarled while I considered beheading the lot of them. "And Darius has made it clear she is not permitted to speak with anyone. That in itself is not conducive to her 'making friends' now, is *it?!*

"Kindly refrain from angering my ward father. I am of half a mind to help her punish you all appropriately."

I slammed the door behind me, locked it, and then returned upstairs to read. Tearing those bastards apart seemed like a much better option but, for now, I would refrain.

'He really intends to follow X'shmiran tradition while here?' I grit my teeth in a poor attempt to hold back the tears of anger and frustration. *'Fuck! Why am I so jealous over that cunt Oracle?!'*

Taking several deep breaths did little to help calm me. I shook my head hard and stalked down the upstairs hallway. A long bath and more reading were in order. It upset me that I lost my temper over something so trivial. While I felt I was within my rights to be angry that Nalithor didn't see me as a warrior, I knew my anger toward the Rylthra was unwarranted.

Unfortunately, that just made me angrier.

I was more upset with myself than I was with any of them.

As for my brother... Despite my anger toward him, I was concerned.

Just how much power over him did the X'shmirans have?

CHAPTER FOUR
Proving One's Worth

I strolled through the Vorpmasian Academy's main library and trailed my gloved fingertips along the bindings of the old books. The building was truly massive and housed tomes, scrolls, and even some tablets that were kept in display cases. Many of the people visiting were in the newer sections of the library looking for, or already reading, works of fiction. Others still were studying but, thankfully, there were few people in the same sections as me.

For the past several hours I'd searched for anything that might be of interest to me—tomes regarding the Aledacian Forests, details of foreign customs, or even scrolls pertaining to combat and magical arts were all acceptable subjects.

I'd hoped that a stack of books and music would distract me

from the growing pain in my face.

'Are you sure you're alright, Arianna?' Djialkan shifted back and forth on my shoulder and craned his head around to look at me. *'We should have just destroyed those fools.'*

'I'm fine,' I muttered, lifting a hand to paw at my tender cheek. *'I've taken worse hits from beasts and...putting those bastards in their place would've just made things worse. They were wearing Dauthrmiran uniforms.'*

Over the past few days Darius continued to accompany Eyrian, Nalithor, and their men to dinner. At first, he tried to convince me to join them. That behavior changed the moment the Oracle stopped joining the nightly excursion.

Now, my brother claimed it was a "boy's night out" or some such nonsense. I wasn't allowed to join them even if I wanted to. It was a shame, really. I was beginning to grow bored with staying in the house by myself.

Darius still hadn't loosened his restrictions on me either. As such I was limited in how I could entertain myself. Training, cooking, sleeping, bathing, and reading were my only real options now. I grew bored enough on several occasions to offer Darius help with his own training and studies, but...he was regrettably unfocused. He spent most of his time trying to make friends instead of preparing for the tests we were meant to take a few days from now.

At any rate, Darius seemed like he was making friends at a rapid pace. Even if I didn't approve of his lack of devotion to his studies, it was good to see him getting to know people. Darius seemed to be getting along with everyone he met and was happy to ramble on about that fact for *hours* when he was at the house.

In contrast, I hadn't managed to find anyone that interested me aside from Nalithor, Eyrian, and one of their comrades that had yet to introduce himself to me. The three of them radiated much more power than most people in the city.

On some level I still wanted to challenge Nalithor. However, as he so bluntly pointed out, he'd wounded my pride prior to our meeting several mornings ago—and again later that day. I remained miffed by his behavior and *especially* by the fact he seemed so unwilling to believe that I could fight Chaos Beasts, let alone kill the damned things.

I knew actions spoke louder than words in Vorpmasian culture—and I appreciated that—but I'd hoped that Eyrian's report would have made Nalithor give me the benefit of the doubt.

Even so, I was pissed off enough for the past several days to avoid all of them. Above all else, I was infuriated with myself. I hated my jealousy. I hated how irrational it was. More so, I hated how I was inexplicably relieved when I learned that the Oracle was no longer accompanying Nalithor to dinner. Why was I jealous in the first place? Why was I so relieved by her absence? I didn't understand it at all.

'And then there's his behavior when I did *go challenge him.'* I

sighed in displeasure. *'Humph. I guess the whole "fellow Umbral Mage" thing was just an act after all.'*

"The X'shmiran mage is here again?!" I heard a female huff in irritation on the floor below me. *"Doesn't that filth understand she's not welcome here?!"*

"Rude! She's not wearing attire from the Old Ways just to piss you off, you know!" Another voice reprimanded the first. *"One of my professors said that X'shmir truly practices the Old Ways! She's not making a mockery of what our grandparents went through—she's experiencing the same horrors firsthand!"*

I pursed my lips and tugged my hood a little further over my face before adding more books to my sizable stack. Once the tomes were balanced, I moved deeper into the library and away from the whispering students. I'd claimed a secluded corner of the library for myself over the past few days and, likewise, grown acclimated to the anger that many Human and Elven citizens directed toward me and my attire.

After all, their unease and hatred were nothing compared to the loathing I received from the nobles and royals in X'shmir.

I shook my head and added the newly-selected tomes to my ever-growing pile. After taking my seat once more, I pulled my headphones over my ears and then double-checked to make sure I hadn't displaced my hood.

There were so many things to read in *this* library alone that I could have probably spent several centuries trying to read it all, and it was just *one* of many libraries that were part of the academy. It was a little overwhelming, and I still wasn't used to their organization systems, but I felt like I was making progress.

Despite all my talk of rules and laws, I truly wanted to make friends Below even though there were risks. Lost memories aside, Nalithor, Eyrian, and their Desert Elf friend intrigued me. However, I wasn't sure what to do. Darius was strongly drawn to them as well and, to be honest, I couldn't tell what was on my brother's mind when it came to them. If he was interested in them physically or romantically it would pose a problem. Darius wouldn't let me interact with them at all if that were the case.

'Then again... Darius is interested in almost anything that moves and has a dick.' I shifted to pull my chair closer to the table in front of me. *'Maybe even if they don't move. Can't be too sure with that one.'*

Djialkan snorted and paced along my shoulders for a while until he decided which one to curl up on. I scratched his scales briefly and then pulled a tome toward me. I was struggling to understand Vorpmasian ways through pure observation at this point, so I had selected many tomes on culture and tradition to study. Although it was all interesting, the tomes lacked the kind of helpful descriptions I needed.

They were basically written for people who already had a fundamental grasp of the empire's culture.

In two days, I would accompany my brother to the

Vorpmasian Academy's aptitude tests as a prospective student. There was little time left for me to learn about Vorpmasian, or individual Devillian, ways. Enjoying my solitude wouldn't last much longer either at the rate things were going. At the very least, I would have to deal with my twin. Worst case scenario was that I'd have to deal with both Darius *and* his friends.

The concept of having a partner wasn't something I even wanted to *begin* contemplating either.

'*Student my ass.*' I flicked through the pages of the tome. '*I want to go kill shit. Not sit in a classroom and* learn *how to kill shit I can already kill!*'

"Oh? That's a rather interesting assortment of books." The distinctive Draemiran purr proved my previous thoughts on solitude correct.

I glanced at the white-haired Adinvyr briefly and then pulled down my headphones.

"Djialkan." I nudged the fae-dragon with one finger and then returned my attention to my book. '*What a pain. I was doing so well with avoiding him too.*'

"*Arianna is attempting to learn what she can of Vorpmasian ways.*" Djialkan turned on my shoulder and tracked Nalithor's approach. "*Darius forbade Arianna from speaking to anyone outside of meetings—should she be invited to any—and combat-related communication. You may ask what you like, Nalithor, and I will respond for her.*"

"Most of these books are on *Draemiran* ways or the Aledacian Forests." Nalithor sounded curious as he came to stand to my right. He lifted a book and examined it as he continued, "Isn't this a bit eclectic if learning Vorpmasian ways is your goal?"

I bit back the urge to snatch the book away from Nalithor and instead pouted, tugging my hood further over my face. He made me nervous, and my increased pulse was making my cheeks and lips throb with more pain. I didn't particularly feel like dealing with questions involving *that* right this moment.

"Draemir heavily influenced Vorpmasian culture. As such, I believed it would be a good place for her to start." Djialkan laughed and swished his tail across my back. *"I understand your suspicions regarding Arianna, Nalithor. I can assure you that what Arianna is hiding is not of consequence to the Vorpmasian Empire. Her own vanity is what is in question."*

"Djialkan!" I exclaimed, turning to shrug the cackling dragon off my shoulder. "I'm not *that* vain! It's just—!"

"Arianna, what happened?" Nalithor interjected. A deep frown formed on his face as he perched on the seat beside me and then lifted both his hands to lightly cup my face. "You're bruised."

"Nothing that I'm not used to in X'shmir," I started crossly, but fell silent as Nalithor traced his thumb along my lower lip. Warmth and darkness radiated from his hands as he studied my bruised cheek and lips in turn. His expression was surprisingly soft, but there was fierceness in his eyes. Something about that fire in his gaze made me cautious of protesting further—despite the fact I was still irritated with him.

"Arianna," Djialkan snickered, *"silence, remember?"*

'This one is difficult to deal with.' I huffed.

"They split your lip as well…" Nalithor muttered, letting his magic flow across my skin. His eyes slid from my lips to my cheek and back a few times before he glanced at Djialkan. "Didn't you say she's not allowed to speak?"

"If she says much more, she will be punished for it." Djialkan snorted, earning a brief scowl from the Adinvyr. *"She is permitted speak a few words, if necessary, before the curse punishes her. You could call it a 'safety feature' if you like. It gives her the opportunity to inform people of her restrictions in the event I am not there to speak for her."*

Nalithor fell silent and his expression shifted to one of determination. Despite the intense, almost ferocious, glint in his eyes, his grip and the sensation of his magic was calm and collected. As much as I hated to admit it, his scent and power were still as comforting to me as they'd been when I was in Limbo. Even so, it was still strange to think of the man before me as a god.

"Tell me who did this to your beautiful face," Nalithor demanded abruptly, pulling my face upwards with both hands and studying what was visible of my features with a fiery expression. "I will *gladly* destroy them for their disrespect."

Their disrespect?' I wondered in disbelief, *'He's shown no respect for me as a warrior, yet he thinks he can comment on the disrespect of others?! At the very least he could have asked if it was from sparring, or if—!'*

"*The people of Dauthrmir believe that Arianna is intentionally mocking the past of the Human and Elven refugees.*" Djialkan's hiss interrupted my train of thoughts. "*Apparently 'filth like her' is unwelcome in the training grounds as well.*

"*That said, are you really in the position to be speaking of respect, Nalithor? She's a huntress and a warrior before all else. Yet, you treat her like some fragile doll. Worse still you refuse to let her prove herself.*"

"Is that what you really think?" Nalithor turned to me. His lips parted, a look of surprise crossing his face as he examined my uncomfortable expression. "You know... It would be much simpler if you would permit me to speak with you through telepathy."

"*She is not permitted.*" Djialkan laughed in a rather smug manner, earning a throaty growl from Nalithor. "*Has Darius told you people nothing of X'shmiran custom—?!*"

"Djialkan," I grumbled, reaching up to clamp my hand around his muzzle. "You're supposed to be talking *for* me. Not making me sound like some abrasive, rude little—"

"You really are upset with me, aren't you?" Nalithor chuckled when I flushed. He continued, "I apologize, Arianna. Admittedly, I know very little about X'shmiran ways. Likely less than you know of the Draemiran or Vorpmasian equivalents.

"I was looking for you so that I could request you *teach* me about X'shmir and the Chaos Beasts you've fought there. Alas, with these two problems…" Nalithor frowned and ran a finger over my lips before shifting his attention to the dragon on my shoulder. "Djialkan, I have two questions for you to answer. First, who is responsible for striking Arianna? Second, why has Darius forbidden Arianna from speaking with anyone?"

"Several soldiers chased her out of the training grounds she was using," Djialkan snarled once I released his snout. He gave me a firm smack on the back with his tail before continuing, *"I do not know which general they serve under. Their attire bore only the Vorpmasian crest. However, they seemed quite smug about being capable of knocking Arianna off her feet with a punch.*

"Arianna would quite like to skin them alive, but she restrained herself. Barely."

"Skin them alive?" Nalithor tilted his head slightly, a crooked grin stretching across his face. "You're a Devillian under there somewhere, aren't you?"

"As for your second question, Darius believes that he is protecting Arianna by forbidding her from speaking," Djialkan's voice was venomous, earning an uneasy but brief glance from Nalithor. *"If she cannot speak, then she cannot make friends. If she cannot make friends, then she cannot make allies or find a lover.*

"If she has no friends and no lover, then she will not be forced to slay them before returning to X'shmir."

"Slay…?" Nalithor trailed off and stared at Djialkan in disbelief for a moment before turning to me. "You are required to murder anyone that gets close to you?"

"If she does not, then, she will be executed herself upon returning to X'shmir," Djialkan spat as I made a sour face. *"The X'shmirans have no need for an emotionally-compromised mage. Does that answer your—?"*

"Wait here," Nalithor commanded, finally releasing my face. He rose to his feet with his tail thrashing behind him. "I am going to deal with the fools that harmed you. And then… We are going to have a *chat* with that brother of yours."

Before I could even attempt to form a protest, the infuriated deity disappeared in a whirlwind of shadows and blue-white flames. I blinked after him in stunned silence while Djialkan chortled. The fae-dragon seemed far too amused. I, on the other hand, was just confused by Nalithor's words and actions alike.

'He looked like he wanted to kiss me… Why?' I stared blankly at where Nalithor had been sitting. It took most of my self-control to keep from touching my fingers to my lips. *'I wonder what he tastes— Damn it all! I can't be thinking like that!'*

I gave my head a firm shake and then shifted my attention to the tome once more. Books were my only chance for distraction at this point. The lingering sensations of Nalithor's hands and magic on my face were terribly distracting but, after a few minutes, I managed to regain some semblance of composure. Nalithor, admittedly, was much more interesting than the book I'd chosen.

Draemir from a Human's Perspective was just as boring and analytical as it sounded.

It wasn't much longer before I caught Nalithor's scent mingled with blood. I didn't even get a chance to shift to look at him before his arm draped around my shoulders from behind. I glanced back at him and examined the mixture of red and blue-black blood dripping from his other hand and its claws. His robes and exposed chest were partially covered too. Despite the mess, he had a contented manner about him. That playful smirk was still there though.

"Oh? I didn't startle you?" Nalithor inquired, leaning down further so he could nuzzle the top of my head, laughing. "I thought I was being quite sneaky."

"You can hide your presence all you like but you did not hide your scent or the scent of the blood that coats you," Djialkan replied for me as I motioned with one finger toward the bloodied hand that had come to rest on my right shoulder. *"By the smell we are assuming that none of the blood is yours."*

"The fools who thought it appropriate to attack Arianna believed that getting into a fight with *me* would get them out of trouble," Nalithor spoke with a mischievous grin before releasing me and sitting beside me once. He began cleaning himself with magic as he continued, "Eyrian and the other commanding officers are laying into our men and the academy staff as we speak.

"Now then, Arianna, we should speak with your brother. I wish to learn of both X'shmir and your beasts. There are no books for me to peruse on such subjects and, as such, it would be much easier for us to learn from each other, would it not?"

"You could just as easily learn of X'shmiran ways from Darius," Djialkan huffed, causing Nalithor to scowl briefly.

"Darius is horribly focused on politics, healing, and *peace*," Nalithor spat with so much disdain that he was *just* short of haughty. "Understanding such a person is beyond my capabilities. I would prefer to speak with Arianna as she seems to think more similarly to my kind."

"I cannot deny that Arianna is more agreeable to work with." Djialkan cackled.

"Do you mind if I ask you a rather blunt and potentially inappropriate question, Arianna?" Nalithor took on a more serious tone after a moment of contemplation, a strange look forming on his face.

I shook my head in response before Djialkan could spit out a snide remark.

"Their Majesties are siblings, aren't they?" Nalithor's expression was uneasy as he crossed his arms and looked down at me. "Are you and Darius—"

"Gods no!" I yelped in disgust before Djialkan could even open his maw to speak. "I won't deny that they've attempted to practice what they call 'family purity' for *many* generations, but—!"

The sensation of molten hot metal wrapping around and filling my throat made me cut myself off with a slew of internal curses. I winced and rose a hand to my throat, blinking back the tears as the pain threatened to worsen. The intensity took my breath away. I shot Djialkan a look, hoping he would get the point and explain to Nalithor for me.

However, Nalithor's undivided attention was focused on me. A look of concern dominated his features. He hesitated and then lifted a hand towards my throat. I caught him by his wrist and tried to pull his hand away from my throat, but he wasn't having any of that. Darkness seeped from his fingertips and slid along my skin in search of injuries. Of course, he found nothing.

"Dilonu and Tyana are barren. Darius and Arianna are children which they adopted," Djialkan began, attempting to draw Nalithor's attention. *"They did intend to have the twins wed but, thankfully, their power as mages put an end to that."*

"That was Angelic magic I smelled," Nalithor spoke with distaste, tugging gently at the collar of my robes. "Will you let me heal—?"

"The pain you sensed was not from physical wounds. There is nothing to heal." Djialkan hopped onto Nalithor's forearm and shot him a firm look, preventing the Adinvyr from pulling the collar of my robes down. *"Before we attempt to continue this conversation… You wished to confront Darius, did you not?"*

"You're alright?" Nalithor frowned at me, earning him a brief nod in reply. "Arianna… The amount of pain I sensed from you should have had you screaming in agony."

Djialkan seemed unsure how to respond, so I grabbed one of my notebooks and scribbled a response on one of the back pages. Once finished, I held it up for Nalithor to read. I wasn't sure if my writing was illegible or if he was simply dumbfounded because he read my reply at least five times before looking at me again.

"You're *used* to it?" Nalithor sighed and ran a hand through his hair, an almost defeated expression forming on his face. "Very well. I will save my prying for later. Let us go speak with your brother.

"Darius should be at the house since he is not with you, yes?"

I nodded, watching Nalithor rise to his feet. He offered me a hand up from my seat and I hesitated briefly before accepting it. Once standing, I turned to the table and gathered my belongings. I pursed my lips and glanced to the side at him. He dwarfed me. My hand almost seemed fragile in his. *'We were so close in height in the dream of Dauthrmir. Was it because we were children back then? Or…did growing up as a Human make me short?'*

After securing my belongings I followed Nalithor through the library in silence and watched the mismatched swaying of his braid and his tail. He kept glancing over his shoulder at me with a concerned look, but I couldn't quite tell what he was thinking beyond that. Was he checking to make sure I was still following him, or was he worried that my "curse" would kick in again?

"Professor Vraelimir!" A voice exclaimed as we descended to the ground level. "Is this bitch bothering you? I'll happily get rid of her for you!"

"Kindly watch your mouth in Her Highness' presence!" Djialkan growled as I snapped tendrils of darkness out toward the rude Devillian girl. I lifted her off the floor by her throat and tilted my head, examining her, as Djialkan continued, *"While normally her prey consists of Chaos Beasts, I am certain she would not mind adding a whelp such as you to her list of targets to hunt."*

I considered quartering her but instead chose to wait. Despite her whispering earlier I wasn't quite angry enough to stain the library with her blood. However, had she waited until we were away from the books, it would have been another matter entirely.

"Now, now," Nalithor purred, slipping both arms around my waist and then leaning down to chuckle by my ear. "Let me take care of this, *Arianna-jiss.*

"Sophia."

I examined the girl with my lips parted slightly, running scenarios through my head on how I could kill her while inflicting the most pain. Taking her outside of the library wouldn't be hard since she couldn't seem to struggle beneath my shadows at all.

"Y-yes, Professor?" Sophia whimpered with wide eyes. "I-I swear, under there somewhere, I think s-s-she's looking at me like I'm…"

"Correct. You are nothing more than prey to her," Nalithor interjected as he straightened. He kept an arm around my waist as he motioned to Sophia with his other hand. "Your grandfather was an Umbral Mage bound by the Old Ways, was he not?

"That you would treat someone who is similarly bound this way disgusts me. I'm of half a mind to let the X'shmiran princess here hunt you in the way she seems to be contemplating…but it seems that you wouldn't provide her with much challenge."

"I could simply devour her instead." Djialkan shifted into the form of a biast and hissed a Sophia, causing her to shriek.

"I may not be able to hear your thoughts, Arianna, but I know that sort of expression well." Nalithor looked down at me, his face and eyes unreadable. "Am I going to have to restrain you, my dear?"

"She's seriously a *princess?*" Sophia exclaimed as I shook my head at Nalithor.

I sighed irritably and flipped open my notebook once more, scribbling a few sentences while Djialkan continued to make threatening noises at the girl. Finally, I turned the notebook to Nalithor so that he could read what I'd written. After all, I had my doubts about whether the girl could read Draemiran.

"She was the heiress to the throne until her powers as an Umbral Mage surfaced. Now she is the 'princess' in title only," Nalithor spoke after reading my message a few times, a small frown tugging at his mouth. "Umbral Mages in X'shmir are… Arianna, is this *really*—?"

Nalithor sighed heavily and his shoulders slumped when I nodded at him. He continued, "Umbral Mages in X'shmir are considered lower than rats. I would rather not repeat the rest of what she wrote, Sophia. Suffice to say that X'shmir's treatment is worse, in some ways, than what your grandfather experienced."

"Why is she required to dress like *that* in Vorpmasia?! *We* don't follow the Old Ways!" Sophia protested, causing me to sigh in frustration, roll my eyes, and then begin scribbling in my notebook again. "And why won't she talk?!"

"She isn't allowed to speak without the permission of the X'shmiran Chrot'zi," Nalithor spoke with distaste. "As far as her attire is concerned, I was under the impression that Darius-zir had convinced their parents to relent to some extent. However…"

I held up the notebook to Nalithor again and felt my face grow hot with embarrassment. Nalithor read it and then shot me a crooked grin. Although I didn't mention my Brands of Divinity, what I wrote was still true—I was so accustomed to covering myself that I'd grown self-conscious about whether I was nice to look at. My clothes had become my security blanket.

"Is this what Djialkan meant when he referred to your 'vanity?'" Nalithor chuckled when my face flushed darker, then turned his attention back to Sophia. "Sophia, I'm assigning you extra classes. You seem as though you could use more education regarding the events your grandfather, and many others, experienced.

"Arianna, dear, be a good girl and release her. Or…do you still wish to tear her apart for her lack of manners?"

With an indignant huff I released Sophia and dropped her unceremoniously on the floor. After, I scribbled a new note to Nalithor to inform him that the bitch wasn't interesting enough to hunt *or* torture.

"You're adorable." Nalithor grinned, laughing when I snapped the notebook shut. "I must say, I'm impressed by your control over your darkness. Most Shadow or Umbral Mages would have torn her apart in the instant they lifted her."

Nalithor smiled, released me, and then motioned for me to accompany him out of the library. Sophia shot me a filthy glare when I walked past her, but I just smirked and then picked up my pace. Nalithor clearly didn't intend to slow his pace to match my shorter stride, and that was fine by me. I might have turned my darkness against him next if he assumed I was unable to keep up.

"Arianna is quite accepting of her darker desires," Djialkan chortled after shifting back to his cat-sized form and coiled himself around my shoulders. *"It does not hold the same sway over her that it does over most mages. The choice of whether or not to act on her desires is comparable to choosing which tea she would like to drink with her breakfast."*

'I guess I can't deny that,' I mused, examining Nalithor's back once more and then glancing down at his tail. Although most of his outward appearance seemed composed, his tail lashed back and forth. Several times it gouged the dirt beneath him as he walked. *'Djialkan, why is he so pissed off by that girl's behavior?'*

"Arianna does not understand why you are so pissed off," Djialkan spoke bluntly, causing the corner of my eye to twitch.

"I have *plenty* of reasons to be angry." Nalithor glanced over his shoulder, displacing his braid, and then beckoned to me. "I would appreciate it if you did not linger several paces behind me. *That*, at least, is part of the Old Ways I am familiar with. I am not a Chrot'zi, nor am I arrogant enough a god to expect you to treat me with the same subservience.

"As for my anger... I thought I was hiding it quite well. It infuriates me that our own soldiers, rookie or not, would go as far as to strike you outside a sparring match—let alone speak so rudely to you. As with Sophia they are young, but that is no excuse for their behavior."

'Sophia was Devillian, wasn't she? I thought he said Vorpmasia never followed the Old Ways?' My thoughts elicited a snort from Djialkan.

'She is half Elf.' Djialkan answered telepathically, causing Nalithor to look between us with that curious-yet-frustrated look on his face again. *"Ah good, you cannot hear her thoughts at all, Nalithor?"*

"I wouldn't say that's a *good* thing," Nalithor protested with a subtle pout, causing Djialkan and I to both snicker at his expression.

"Arianna, I have some matters I wish to attend to." Djialkan leapt from my shoulders and hovered nearby for a moment. *"Do at least*

try *not to kill anything while I'm gone? I should not be long.*"

I pursed my lips and watched the fae-dragon fly away. I felt like skinning him for leaving me alone with Nalithor, but he'd already flown out of reach. The Adinvyr, however, looked quite satisfied with the situation. Nalithor offered me his arm as I tugged at my hood in slight discomfort. His expression was warm, but insistent. It was tempting to decline for the sole reason that his behavior the other day had pissed me off…and because it reminded me of the sight of the Oracle on his arm.

Finally, I relented. Just this once. *'He did heal me, after all.'*

"I want you to know that I'm very sorry for the behavior of both my countrymen and my students," Nalithor offered after several minutes of silence, causing me to glance up at him once more. "It sickens me to know they've treated you this way.

"I…am curious, however. About the matter of you requiring permission to speak—is that why you simply ran from me in X'shmir and didn't bother to stop?"

'Ahhh, I "ran from him" did I?' I attempted to hide my amusement and just nodded my head. *'He's miffed! He's trying to hide it but it's so obvious.'*

"You look amused." Nalithor arched an eyebrow at me, which just made my smirk broaden. "Ahhh… I do hope we find your brother in an agreeable mood. I really do wish to speak with you properly. Furthermore, we still need to spar as well."

'Spar?' I thought in surprise. My expression earned a warm

smile from Nalithor.

"Come now, did you really think that I was going to reject a challenge from such an interesting woman?" Nalithor chuckled and tugged at the front of my hood. "I still have to prove that I'm *'worth your interest,'* remember?"

I contemplated his statement for a moment, but my thoughts were interrupted when I caught my brother's cloying floral scent. Darius was perched on the front steps of our shared house and looked *incredibly* bored. That bored demeanor gave way to one of immense displeasure when he caught sight of Nalithor and me. His chartreuse eyes fixated on our linked arms and then back up to our faces. The jealousy radiating from him was so suffocating that it made me wonder about his true motives for sealing my ability to speak.

"Ari...don't you think you've wasted enough of Nalithor's time?" Darius inquired coolly, causing me to flinch involuntarily. It was obvious to me that Nalithor noticed my reaction, because I felt his muscles tense and I heard a low, subtle growl rumble within his chest.

I froze mid-step and stared at my brother in disbelief. Nalithor growled again but I barely heard it over my own whirlwind of thoughts. Nalithor seemed like he *wanted* my help! Not like he'd asked me out of common courtesy. Why would he lie about wanting me, *specifically me*, to help him? Nalithor could have come to either of us for information about X'shmir but he chose *me*.

'Was it...was it just because I'm a "fellow Lyur'zi" and he wanted to make amends for the actions of...' My thoughts trailed off as the severity of Darius' glare worsened. I felt my heart sink and I dropped my gaze to the ground. *'Oh... Right. Because I'm an Umbral Mage, I...'*

"Arianna, apologize to Nalithor and—" Darius trailed off into a flinch of his own when Nalithor openly growled and settled his own threatening glare upon him.

"I-I apologize, Rely'ric. I... I won't inconvenience you again," I stuttered quickly and then pulled my arm from Nalithor's so that I could flee into the house.

Shimmering particles of frost swirled around Nalithor's hands, legs, horns, and tail as he glowered at my twin. His shadow rippled and churned beneath him, matching the waves of power radiating from the infuriated deity. The Adinvyr beside me was incredibly pissed—pissed enough to give me pause. It took me a moment to realize *I* wasn't the target of his anger. Every single ounce of his power, his anger, and his indignation was channeled toward my brother.

Even so...disobeying my brother's direct order was not conducive to my health.

"I see. So, you are part of the problem as well aren't you, Darius?" Nalithor's frigid tone contrasted with the warm and protective embrace he pulled me into. His chest rumbled against my back with poorly-contained growls. "I was going to ask you, *nicely*, to release the restrictions on your sister whilst the two of you remain on the surface. But... You are going to make me use my authority as a deity, aren't you?"

'His authority as a deity?' I resisted the urge to look up at him and instead kept my eyes on my fuming twin brother. Darius' face and neck were crimson. His body shook, and his fists were clenched so tight that his knuckles had turned white. However, his rage was nothing compared to what emanated from Nalithor. If the Adinvyr wasn't so adept at directing his power, it would probably have suffocated me to be so close.

"What do you mean 'I'm part of the problem?!'" Darius stomped in outrage and then motioned at the arms Nalithor had fastened around me. "I've decided that I won't let her wind up in a situation that requires her to murder our hosts, or one that causes our parents to execute her! I'm sure Djialkan already told you of—"

"I require Arianna's assistance with several matters. Being unable to converse with her directly is troublesome." Nalithor growled at my twin again, his grip tensing enough that I felt his claws digging into my sides. "Furthermore... How do you expect your sister to work *anywhere* if you force her to follow these outdated laws? You have been informed time and again that you must both work during your stay.

"You stated yourself, when we spoke in X'shmir, that you loathe the way your people treat Umbral Mages. So, why are you being such an *ass* to Arianna? Were you lying?"

'He can be really blunt when he wants to be.' I glanced upwards at Nalithor and then back to my brother. *'It's...kind of a nice change of pace to have someone act protective over me. But am I...am I really not being an inconvenience?'*

"Allow Arianna to speak freely with *anyone* 'Below,'" Nalithor's commanding, magic-infused, voice caused my skin to prickle, "and allow Arianna to speak without being forced to refer to *you* and *others* with honorifics.

"Our culture is vastly different than what you are used to, Darius-zir. If you force your sister to abide by X'shmiran ways it will only cause more problems for her—and for us. I, for one, am of half a mind to eviscerate anyone else that tries to harm her."

"Harm her?" Darius' confusion was plain on his face, "What do you mean *harm* her? 'Anyone else?' What are you talking about?"

"Many people have taken offense to Arianna's attire," Nalithor lifted one hand to motion at my mask and hood, but quickly returned it to my waist when I tried to wriggle away. "They do not realize she is genuinely bound by the Old Ways. Instead, they believe that she is mocking them.

"You put her in danger by taking away her ability to speak freely, and she has already been attacked for it."

"Ari?" Darius questioned as if to confirm whether Nalithor was telling the truth, so I nodded in reply. "What if I allow her to speak with military parties? Will that be sufficient?"

Nalithor's fingers twitched and I felt a rumble against my back yet again. I was a little sad that I couldn't see his expression. Whatever look it was, it caused my brother to turn pale. However, Darius wasn't willing to give in yet. His weak magic attempted to push back against the free-flowing torrent of Nalithor's power, but it just blew away in seconds.

"You will allow her to speak to everyone or I will have you sent back to X'shmir." Nalithor's voice was like a honed edge of ice and sent a shiver down my spine. That calm but murderous tone was...impressively intimidating.

"Honorifics, then. Using '-tyir' should be acceptable, yes?" Darius crossed his arms.

"Are you going to make me repeat myself, boy?" Nalithor asked as frost crawled up his hands and forearms, soon joined by twisting tendrils of shadow. "You wear on my patience. Either you will accept my demands, or you will return to X'shmir. You, *boy*, are an Astral Mage. You are not above even a Lesser God, *let alone me*. I would be well within my rights to execute you for your insubordination...but I am not so cruel as to slay you in front of Arianna.

"Though, with your behavior, I question whether or not she would mind... Arianna?"

I knew Nalithor must have felt me tense or heard my pulse raise to a panicked level since he paused, but I whipped out my notebook and hurriedly scribbled a message to him anyway. Even if I hated Darius more than anything in Avrirsa—which I didn't— I couldn't let Nalithor kill him. Nalithor was a god. I knew I couldn't fight back. But he seemed open to discussion, at least.

Darius, on the other hand, still seemed like he wanted to argue.

"I see..." Nalithor murmured in Draemiran near my ear, lowering his voice to a mere whisper. "If one of you dies...you *both* die? You are trusting me with this knowledge? This is not typical to the Old Ways."

"*Fine!*" Darius' shoulders slumped but his eyes were glazed-over as if he was under the influence of something. "I'm not in the mood to argue with a deity about what is or isn't best for my sister. Ari, you're allowed to speak freely and drop the honorifics while Below... Adhere to the Vorpmasians' customs instead of X'shmiran ones. Well, aside from the hood and mask of course. You know as well as I do that *I* am not in control of *that* problem.

"Nalithor, do you really have to hold her like that?! It's not like I'm going to attack her!"

"You've already attacked Arianna with something much worse than a blade, Darius-zir," Nalithor stated with distaste as he placed a hand over my heart, startling both Darius and I for *very* different reasons. "I may not be able to read your thoughts directly, Arianna, but I am a minor empath. Your physical pain from earlier is not the only kind of pain I've sensed from you."

"You're *really* tall, you know," I deflected in a flat tone, tilting my head back so that I could look up at him. A brief expression of surprise crossed his face, but he smoothed it over, so I continued, "Pain is pain. I'm accustomed to it. However, I am not accustomed to…this."

"Do you find it objectionable?" Nalithor tilted his head and smirked, giving my waist a firm squeeze.

"Your height, my pain, or *this*?" I nudged his arms, causing him to grin.

"Can you at least tell me what you need her for?" Darius interrupted, bringing my attention back to him and his stifling air of jealousy.

"I'm not obligated to share my reasons with you," Nalithor replied with a half-shrug. He chuckled when Darius scowled in response and then turned me away from the house and my brother. "Let's go, Arianna. I should indulge your sparring request before we see to the matters I mentioned earlier."

Nalithor steered me toward the maze of military buildings without giving my brother a chance to comment. Once we'd disappeared into the web of walkways and buildings, Nalithor released me and fell into step beside me. It was now that I realized just how angry he was with Darius.

The Adinvyr's tail thrashed behind him as he walked, occasionally slamming into the path beneath us, and his muscles visibly tensed. By the look of his shoulders I estimated that he'd clenched his hands against his forearms within his long sleeves.

Frost still swirled around a few sections of his body but his shadow, at least, had stabilized.

"X'shmiran laws regarding Lyur'zi are more strict than the Old Ways you're familiar with?" I questioned after a moment, causing Nalithor to stop and turn to look down at me.

"Speaking of which, I would like to ask you something while we're still on the subject of X'shmir." Nalithor frowned and kept his arms crossed. "What is it they require you to call Darius whilst on X'shmiran soil? It struck me as strange that Djialkan would recommend you switch to Draemiran honorifics."

"Ah... How to explain it..." I murmured, linking my hands behind my back. "You weren't in X'shmir for very long, I take it?"

"Less than a day." A scowl crossed his face.

"While most people in X'shmir may simply call Darius 'Your Highness,'" I began, "servants and so-called 'lesser' mages are required to address him as 'Young Master.' I'm sure you've heard at least *someone* refer to him as 'Astral Master'...

"One could say that X'shmirans have an unhealthy 'appreciation' for Astral Mages. In X'shmir the term 'Master' is interchangeable with both 'Lord' and 'Prince.' From what I understand, 'Master' means something entirely different here."

"I can see why Djialkan was concerned." Nalithor's frown deepened. "If anyone heard you call Darius 'Young Master' they would assume both that he is underage, and that the two of you are engaged in a sexual relationship.

"Both matters are illegal and subject to the appropriate punishments."

'Appropriate punishments?' I tilted my head to the side and contemplated the notion. *'That's quite the contrast to what the X'shmirans believe about Devillians. According to them, the Devillians condone and encourage such behavior. Just how far have the X'shmirans twisted the truth, I wonder?'*

I shifted my gaze back to Nalithor after a moment, having sensed him skulking around the edges of my barriers again. The angry thrashing of his tail had changed to a frustrated twitch and his face showed immense, almost boyish, displeasure. I found it strange that Nalithor, a *deity*, was incapable of listening to my thoughts. He quite clearly had access to them when I was trapped in Limbo, and his power didn't feel much different, so I didn't know what had changed. *'Perhaps I'll ask Djialkan later—if he's in a good mood.'*

"I still don't fully understand what 'Master' means here." I unlinked my hands and raised them into the air with a shrug. "However, I intend to avoid conflict with things and people that don't *need* to die...and I actually prefer the system you all use for honorifics."

"If seems as though we both have a lot to learn," Nalithor mused as he offered me his arm. "If you are unfamiliar with what 'Master' means in Vorpmasia... What do submissives refer to dominants as in X'shmir?"

'Submissives? Dominants—? O-oh. So that *is why...'* I knew exactly what Nalithor was implying and the thought made my face grow hot—something that the Adinvyr seemed to notice, given the low chuckle I heard. *'So...it's a term used in that kind of relationship, then. No wonder Djialkan insisted on using Mrirtec instead.'*

"You're much quicker than your brother." Nalithor chuckled again and tugged at my hood.

"I'm not sure if I should repeat what submissives and their owners call each other," I replied humorlessly, shaking my head. "X'shmir is a decidedly fucked-up society. They look down on sexuality almost as much as they look down on 'Evil Mages' such as you and me.

"Suffice to say their chosen terminology is quite vile."

"Ahhh yes, 'Evil Mages.'" Nalithor laughed, shook his head, and then guided me in the direction of a large sparring ring. "I take it they believe Chrot'zi are 'Holy Mages' then?"

"Yes, basically." I nodded, "Their concept of 'good' and 'evil' is not only screwed up, but also blatantly incorrect. They fail to understand that such concepts are subjective at best."

"Yet you understand?" Nalithor paused by a bench and removed his outer layers of robes, draped them over the back rest, and then removed his shoes to reveal clawed toes. "Give me an example then. I'll be the judge of your understanding."

"An example?" I examined Nalithor's now-bare torso, arms, throat, and the Brands of Divinity that covered him. "War is a simple enough illustration. Both sides of a conflict believe that theirs is the just cause, and, both sides believe what they're doing is for the good of their people."

"You seem amused." Nalithor smiled and placed a hand on his hip as he studied me, his tail swaying behind him once more.

"It's just comical to me." I grinned, motioning with my hands. "While I do prefer to solve conflicts with my fists instead of through politics and negotiation, it still tickles me that countries will war over resources, women, hurt egos, religion…anything, really. Even the most trivial matter can be fuel for war.

"Yet they all still pray to the same gods. I've read about several different wars and it's always the same thing; they fight over resources, power, and religion. Then they pray for the gods to aid their victory. They are fools who over-complicate everything."

"You really *are* adorable." Nalithor grinned and placed a hand on top of my head, causing me to shoot him a glaring pout. "Don't give me that look—I don't mean it in a condescending way at all! There's something quite endearing about a dainty little Human that acts like a Devillian warrior."

"General Vraelimir," a gruff-voiced soldier called from nearby. "I can only assume that if you're stripping in front of a fine young woman, here, that you must intend to spar her?"

"*Spar her?*" Another soldier snorted. "Look at how small she is compared to the general! He'll break her!"

"Not if I break him first!" I snapped at the soldier, wishing he could see my glare.

"You intend to fight in such cumbersome attire?" Nalithor motioned at my robes. "Arianna, I'm quite aware you have armor and weaponry forged by Aurelian. His handiwork is unmistakable. I know you're hiding more beneath your robes as well. You jingle when you walk."

"Hmmm, you're right. I do still jingle," I murmured, shaking my wrist slightly. Shrugging, I reached behind my back and unlaced my armored corset. "I don't feel the need to wear armor in a sparring match. Aurelian's 'gifts' are a relatively new addition and I'm not accustomed to wearing armor in fights quite yet."

"Yet you've been fighting beasts." Nalithor examined me a little more intently than I thought necessary. "Surely you wore some sort of armor while dealing with the creatures?"

"None." I shrugged, earning startled looks and murmurs from Nalithor and his nearby soldiers. "Outfitting me with armor and weapons is considered a waste of resources. I had to rely on my ability to react, dodge, and occasionally augment myself with my elements."

"Who taught you?" Nalithor questioned as I tugged off my robes to reveal a hooded, high-collared blouse and skin-tight black breeches. "*Honestly*! Even your shirts have a hood?!"

"Even though I'm not *officially* a princess, I'm still required to cover my skin and hair as if I were," I replied dryly. "Although, I am supposedly allowed to wear Vorpmasian attire while here, aren't I? I should find out the specifics for that."

"Thus, the gloves?" Nalithor caught one of my hands, lifted it, and studied my black leather gloves. "Why, exactly, are princesses required to hide so much? Is it because you're the Lyur'zi?"

"It's a long, boring story." I reclaimed my hand and turned to face him. "As for who taught me, the answer is simple. No one." Nalithor opened his mouth to protest my claim, so I raised a finger into the air and shushed him so I could continue, "*People* aren't the only ones threatened by Chaos Beasts. The forest creatures are just as desperate to protect their homes as we are.

"Remember how I said that I spent much of my time in the forest surrounding the city? I observed the forest creatures. How they protect their homes, how they move through the underbrush or the branches, and so on."

"Yet you have clear mastery of your darkness." Nalithor frowned but I just grinned crookedly. "Most Umbral or Shadow Mages will never reach such a level of mastery in *any* lifetime."

"You haven't even fought me yet and you're saying I have mastery over darkness?" I teased, earning a chuckle.

"It was obvious when I chased you from X'shmir to Sihix. You proved it further with your treatment of Sophia earlier." Nalithor smirked before continuing, "However, you seem eager to spar. What would you prefer; armed or unarmed?"

"Your turf, your choice," I offered sweetly.

The nearby soldiers had looks of concern on their faces.

Nalithor, however, seemed delighted as his smirk shifted into a broad, boyish grin. His expression was infectious. I found myself biting back an amused laugh as I sat on the bench and removed my boots. However, my socks stayed on. Displaying my Brands *now* would only serve to delay our match further.

"Oliver, let us have the pit," Nalithor called to one of the soldiers before turning back to me. "Let's see if Eyrian's praise of you is well-placed shall we, Arianna? Attack me however you like, with anything you like.

'*Anything goes, huh?*' I ignored the protesting soldiers and followed Nalithor towards the pit. '*Interesting. Is he confident because Human women are weaker than Human men, or does he mean to lure me into revealing something?*'

Instead of admiring the sparring pit, I stepped to the side and snapped out with a roundhouse kick across Nalithor's ribs when he turned to strike me. My shin landed square across his abdomen but he just grinned. His tail swayed back and forth like that of a cat stalking prey, even as he took a few steps back and adopted an offensive stance.

"What gave me away?" Nalithor purred as I tuned out his soldiers' whisperings.

"I sensed your movements." I shifted into an offensive stance of my own. "Let's start out unarmed and see how long it takes for you to make me draw a weapon, hmmm?"

"Is that a challenge?" Nalithor smirked crookedly.

"Always." I shot him a small smile.

Nalithor must have approved of my answer because his response was to dart toward me again. I blocked, deflected, and countered most of his strikes but let a select few hit me. I wanted to determine whether he was boosting his strikes with magic, and if he was pulling his strength against me. Nalithor didn't appear to be using magic—not yet, anyway.

'Let's see if I can change that.' I bit back a grin and then lunged for the Adinvyr.

Several minutes of cat and mouse passed before I managed to duck under one of Nalithor's kicks. I slammed my foot upwards beneath his jaw. The blow knocked him clean off his feet and onto his back. He must not have expected me to be capable of kicking so high, if his laughter was anything to judge by, anyway.

"That actually *hurt* you know!" Nalithor exclaimed, pulling himself to his feet. "You're flexible though. Good. You will be at least a little difficult to break then."

Nalithor disappeared in an implosion of shadows before I got the chance to question his word choice. I sensed his strike and brought up my forearms just in time to block his kick. A brief look of approval crossed his face and then he disappeared again. And again, and again, and again. It was like he was testing how fast I could sense and avoid his strikes. He just kept getting faster and faster.

However, something changed about what I sensed from the

Adinvyr deity. The hum of magic pricked along my skin and made me tense. I summoned a large platinum scythe and blocked Nalithor's strike with its staff section.

His bladed spear looked like a cousin to my scythe. It boasted the same pale metal, intricate designs, and the same deceptively decorative appearance. The base of his spear's blade had several large blue topazes set in it, with several more gracing the shaft. It was a perfect match to the jewelry that was ever-present on Nalithor's form.

Furthermore, the designs and materials were a match for *my* jewelry.

'Aurelian's handiwork?' I pushed back against Nalithor as he bore down on my scythe. *'Pale blue topaz and platinum for Nalithor, sapphires and platinum for me. Pale green crystals and pewter for Eyrian. Does Aurelian match the stones to the eye color of the person he's making a set for? Why?'*

"An interesting choice." Nalithor studied the blade of my scythe for a moment before flicking his icy eyes back to my face. "Let's see how well such a petite woman can wield such a hefty weapon.

"I do believe that I'm at least *slightly* more difficult to land a strike against when compared to the beasts you're accustomed to."

We broke away from each other but the moment Nalithor's feet hit the ground he shifted and lunged toward me with his spear. I jumped and landed with my feet on the shaft of the weapon, rested my scythe on my shoulder, and grinned down at Nalithor. He laughed and sliced upwards in an attempt to dislodge me. I simply kicked off his spear and shoved it back toward the sand beneath us. Using my momentum, I twisted in the air and swung my scythe down at Nalithor's shoulder from overhead. As expected, he leapt away with ease.

'Hmmm. We've drawn an audience.' I glanced at our surroundings as I arced through the air away from Nalithor. A mix of both uniformed and plainclothes Devillians had surrounded our sparring arena.

I landed in a crouch and extended my weapon behind me before launching myself across the sand at Nalithor. I chased him across the arena and sought to sink my blade into him. A slight shift in Nalithor's stance made me plant the butt of my scythe into the ground. I used my weapon as leverage and spun myself into a kick. My foot connected with the flat of Nalithor's blade and sent it hurtling out of his grip.

Before Nalithor could attempt to summon it back to hand I continued my spinning motion and swung my scythe towards his stomach. The scent of blood caught my attention, making me glance over my shoulder at him. Several of our spectators began cursing at me for marring the Adinvyr's pale flesh, but the man himself seemed amused rather than angered or pained.

'Why does his blood smell so...sweet?' I shifted my gait and circled Nalithor, watching for an opening. *'He smells like food. Dessert,*

perhaps. Does Devillian blood not carry the same metallic tang of Human blood? Or is it because he is a deity?'

"You're stronger than you look." Nalithor touched his fingertips to the wound and then brought them to his mouth, lapping the blood from them in a rather...*erotic*...manner. "I should make you use that pretty mouth of yours to clean this up, you know."

"Na-Nalithor-zir!" Several male and female spectators shrieked from the audience, sharing my astonishment. *"She's only Human! I'd be much better suited to do that for you!"*

I knew damn well my face must've been red. It'd have been a minor miracle for my face to be that hot and *not* flushed with color. However, Nalithor wasn't going to give me time to be flustered— let alone recover. Pale blue-white flames sprung into existence around his fists as he renewed his attack on me.

His forearm grazed past my hood as I dodged. A kick followed but I danced out of reach. When he lunged for me again, I swung my scythe's blade towards his legs, but he slammed his heel down against the flat of the blade. He closed the distance, grabbed one of my wrists, and twisted my arm until I was forced to let go of the weapon. I jabbed him in the ribs, hard, with my other elbow.

Nalithor still didn't let go of my wrist, so I raised my leg and kicked to the side. The ridge of my foot connected just above where my scythe had cut him open and he released me. He stumbled back a few feet and I pursued him. I needed to end this. Something about the smell of his blood was blurring my thoughts.

Once I was close, Nalithor attempted to grab me with his tail, causing me to leap out of the way and eye him wearily.

"You can use your tail like that too?" I asked as we circled each other. *'His movements are smooth. Predatory. It suits him...'*

"Oh, my dear, there are all *kinds* of things my tail can do to you." Nalithor's sultry purr sent shivers down my spine.

I couldn't come up with a witty retort, so I sprung towards him with a kick aimed at his throat instead and followed up with a second kick to his ribs when he dodged the first. Black blood still dripped down his lower abs, but he didn't seem concerned. Instead his attention seemed solely on our fight. We matched and returned each other's attacks with a fluidity that surprised me. It was refreshing to spar against a *person* instead of a damned beast, but I wanted more.

Our game continued for a while longer, until Nalithor vanished without a trace. I cursed when I realized that his presence was just...gone. I couldn't sense him at all.

I let out a startled yelp when Nalithor's arm came to rest between my breasts and his hand wrapped around part of my throat and jaw. He lifted me off the ground and pulled me back against his chest, keeping my jaw gripped between his thumb and index finger.

Nalithor's other arm wrapped around my hips. He let out a playful chuckle. I had to bite back a purr when he squeezed my throat briefly, but I had a feeling that the rumbling of my throat didn't go unnoticed.

"Ahhh, I've caught myself a rather slippery vixen," Nalithor teased, and then chuckled when I brought my hands up to pry his fingers from my throat. "I must say; I'm impressed you can keep up with me, Arianna. I'm glad there was no need for me to go easy on you."

"If you went easy on me, I would've taken your head!" I snapped, earning a deep laugh from the playful Adinvyr. He carried me out of the sparring pit with ease as I struggled and walked past several chuckling soldiers. "P-put me down!"

'Quite the feisty one, aren't you?' Nalithor nudged through my barriers with startling ease.

'And it seems that you *finally found a way through my shields.'* I huffed.

'I hope you don't mind.' Nalithor sounded amused and gave me a brief squeeze around the waist before sitting on the bench we'd placed our overrobes on. For some unfathomable reason he pulled me onto his lap with him. *'It is much simpler to converse with you through telepathy. I do have some orders I must give my men, after all. Carrying on two conversations is much easier when one is nonverbal.'*

"Oliver, Maric," Nalithor's voice was firm as he addressed two nearby Adinvyr. "Pair off with M'reltar and Raejir, respectively. They both need to practice their footwork."

'I'm just curious how you managed to slip through so easily,' I

BONNIE L PRICE

began, my tone dry. *'You've been so frustrated with my barriers for the past few days. It's a little strange you found it so easy* now.'

'You were having so much fun that they weakened.' Nalithor laughed. *'It's rare to find someone who enjoys fighting so much. I do hope this wasn't a one-time indulgence. Although... Didn't Djialkan say you're not permitted to speak telepathically with others?'*

'He lied.' I rolled my eyes behind my mask. *'It seems like he enjoys getting a rise out of you.'*

'Humph. He hasn't changed much,' Nalithor muttered.

"General, it is rather inappropriate of you to hold the princess captive—at least like that," one of the nearest soldiers spoke dryly but shrunk back in response to whatever look the deity shot him.

"Oh? I was considering making a snack out of her in return for the wound she inflicted," Nalithor purred, leaning down to nuzzle the crook of my neck. His lips parted against the underside of my jaw and his fangs slid across my skin, making me bristle. "What do you think, Arianna? Does that sound 'inappropriate?'"

"Y-you haven't earned it!" I retorted and crossed my arms, eliciting snorts of laughter from the soldiers.

"I have to earn it, do I?" Nalithor sounded thoughtful as he grabbed my chin and shifted me sideways in his lap. He tilted my head slightly so that I had to look up at him. His eyes ran down the front of my throat as if he were contemplating undoing the buttons that hid it from him. "Not going to let me conquer you so easily?"

"Of course not!" I countered, baring my fangs at him. "I don't know what sort of strumpets you're used to, but *I* have at least *some* class.

"Don't you Devillians know what 'personal space' is? Unhand me, before I decide—"

"Then I will just have to earn it, won't I?" Nalithor murmured quietly before leaning down. He planted a soft but brief kiss on my lips and then smiled when he saw the shade of scarlet I'd turned. "You've eased my boredom, that's for certain. I'm sure our rather vocal audience learned a thing or two from watching us. Well, assuming they were capable of paying attention to our fight instead of your...*assets*."

Nalithor smirked but finally released me. I scrambled off his lap with a sense of relief. That spicy-sweet scent of his was driving me crazy and, at this point, it would take a very long walk to get it out of my mind—if I even could.

However, before I could walk away, Nalithor caught my hand and brought it to his lips. That playful smirk was still on his face and only seemed to grow as more members of our "audience" shrieked their protests.

"You are welcome to stay and observe if you like," Nalithor offered, lowering my hand from his lips. "Although... You look like something else is on your mind. I'll indulge you. What would you like to ask?"

"I...was just going to ask if I overdid it," I grumbled in

embarrassment before sitting down to tug my boots back on. "I've only ever fought beasts, so—"

"You do not have sparring partners in X'shmir? I thought you said one of your roles is to oversee military operations and training?" Nalithor's expression was unreadable. "No, I don't think you overdid it. That said, I am now a firm believer that you are *not* Human…but that's another matter entirely, isn't it?

"If you find the free time you should you should spar with me more often. It's rare to find someone who can keep up with my full strength."

'Full strength? I doubt it. I shouldn't be able to keep up with a Devillian—let alone a deity.' I sat up and shifted to look at him. "Is that an invitation?"

"Most definitely." Nalithor grinned. "Unfortunately, I have duties to tend to for the rest of the afternoon but, as I stated, you are welcome to observe.

"Can I convince you to join us for dinner tonight? I would like to speak with you at length about our differing cultures and the beasts."

"That'll have to wait, Nali," a voice called from behind us. I looked over my shoulder to find Eyrian approaching us, his expression grim. "You and I are to leave as soon as you've finishing issuing orders for your men's training."

"A beast to deal with?" Nalithor's tone was surprisingly eager. I glanced back to him when I sensed a small spike of bloodlust. He looked ready to spring from his seat.

"That's right. One wandered too close to the barriers and we need to take care of it." Eyrian grimaced. "My partner is still off visiting her family, so Lucifer-y'ric has order you and I to go stamp the beast out."

'Well, I guess I'll be tolerating my brother tonight then,' I mused as I rose to my feet and pulled on my overrobes.

"Arianna, Nalithor wasn't too rough with you, was he?" Eyrian turned and shot me a concerned look.

"*Too* rough?" I asked innocently, fastening my armored corset into place. "I'm afraid I'm unfamiliar with such a concept."

"You're..." Eyrian's face flushed slightly. I grinned when I heard Nalithor's rumbling chuckle; Nalithor grasped my sarcasm much faster than his friend had. "You're a difficult woman to deal with, aren't you?"

"Maric!" Nalithor called to the battle-scarred Devillian nearby. "See to it that *anyone* foolish to mistreat Arianna-jiss is imprisoned until I can deal with them personally. I will not tolerate any further hostility towards her. The X'shmirans may not consider her to be a true princess but, by our laws, she is still a visiting royal. See to it that she's treated as such.

"Arianna, might I impose upon you to lend Maric and Oliver a hand with my men?"

"What...? You're sure?" I looked up at him as he rose to his feet. He gave me a broad grin and then nodded his affirmation. "I certainly wouldn't mind the entertainment. I'll try not to make them cry *too* much.

"You owe me another sparring match, later, as payment."

"*Just* a sparring match?" Nalithor teased in a mock-hurt tone and then tugged my hood as he passed me. "I'll happily make it up to you *any way you like*, 'Your Highness'."

"I'm not picky." I pivoted to track him. "A sparring match should serve to make amends for leaving me out of a hunt."

"You *like* hunting beasts?" Eyrian asked in disbelief.

"You'd better get going." I grinned and crossed my arms at the Devillian pair. "Preferably *before* I change my mind and decide to follow the both of you to your mark."

"She's quite serious, Eyrian." Nalithor chuckled, shooting his friend a look. "Let's go."

'Are Devillians always so handsy, General Vraelimir?' My question caused Nalithor to shoot me a smirk over his shoulder as he walked away.

'Only when it comes to interesting morsels like yourself.' Nalithor's tail swished once as he focused his attention forward once more. *'However, it's clear I underestimated you. Human or otherwise you are a talented warrior. I hope you will accept my apologies for my prior behavior.'*

'I'll consider it,' I spoke dryly. *'Now then... Out of my thoughts you go.'*

Nalithor's back stiffened and his tail jerked to the side when I slammed my barriers back into place. His head shifted as if he might look back and comment but, after a moment, he shook his head, sending his long white hair scattering across his back.

I watched the pair walk away for a moment and admired their physiques. They were both attractive but there was something about Nalithor in particular that drew me. I wondered if it was the fault of some fragment of the past that lingered on the fringes of my memory, or if it was because of the natural allure of Adinvyr.

At any rate, Nalithor's magnetism made me hesitant to let him communicate with me telepathically. There were few people I was willing to let in my mind, and I was concerned that as a god—or even as an Adinvyr—he'd be able to detect things I didn't want him to know.

Choosing not to dwell on the matter just yet, I turned to look at Maric, Oliver, and the rest of Nalithor's men.

'Training his men, huh? What a strange request. Is he testing me further by giving his men a chance to judge me?' I sized-up the variety of armored and half-armored male Devillians. *'Adinvyr, Akor, snake-people…I should really learn the names of the other races.*

'All men, though? I've seen plenty of female soldiers and guards in Dauthrmir.'

"Would you like me to brief you on our usual training regimen, Arianna-jiss?" Maric offered, settling his grey-green eyes on me. I shifted and examined the older-looking Devillian for a moment, noting that he was the only one with scars.

"Please; I would prefer it if you all refer to me by name—without honorifics." I placed a hand on my hip. "If you insist on being formal, General Black will suffice.

"As for your standard regimen… Let's shake it up a bit, shall we? I'd prefer to get a grasp of everyone's ability for myself. I'll spar each of you individually to gauge your strengths and weakness. Afterwards we can go from there."

"Each of us?" Oliver sounded suspicious. "There's easily fifty of us present, General. You'll tire long before—"

"There's no way she's a Human if she can keep up with Nalithor." Maric laughed, cutting off the younger soldier with a firm slap on the back. "Nalithor seems to trust you, girlie. We'll do things your way. It's been too long since we've had an interesting training session and, if your sparring match with our general was any indication, this should prove *real* interesting."

"Let's start with the lowest ranks and move up from there then." I grinned and punched my right hand into my left palm. "I want to see how much information the higher ranks take in from watching the fights leading up to theirs."

"You think like an Adinvyr! Good!" Maric laughed heartily, pulling himself out of the sparring pit. He motioned to several of the younger Devillians nearby and barked, "You heard General Black! Get your asses lined up!"

CHAPTER FIVE
An Allusion to the Truth

'I should have remained in Dauthrmir to test Arianna further.' I mused, striding through the streets in silence. My arms remained crossed within my robes, but I stayed alert for anything "off" that could have occurred at this time of night. This portion of the city never slept. *'Bah, the beast was such a disappointment. Eyrian could have handled it on his own.'*

I glanced at the Merchants' District's central clock tower and sighed. It was far too late to seek out the X'shmiran princess for another sparring match now. A mere day had passed since our first clash and I already found myself eager to spar with her again. Despite her mostly Human appearance her movements, speed, and control gave her away as anything but. It was foolish of me to insist that she was a mere Human, and that was not a mistake I planned to repeat.

'Hmmm. Their tests should take place tomorrow.' I wandered along the street that would take me from the Nobles' District up to the Sapphire Quarter. *'Perhaps if I snatch her away from her brother I can...'*

My thoughts trailed off and I frowned, surprised with myself. I still believed that Arianna, most likely, was a fake created by the Elder Gods. Why was I still drawn to her despite that? Sparring with her or getting to know her should have been the last thing on my mind. If she was truly a fake it was *my* responsibility to destroy her, no matter whose form she appeared in.

Grimacing, I glanced to the left and watched the shifting shadows. Two familiar goddesses appeared and were accompanied by a single god; Sebastian, the God of Chaos. The three of them looked uneasy and, for them to approach me in the open streets of Dauthrmir, something heavy must have weighed on their minds.

My duties as a deity were of little interest to me at the given moment but I chose to give them a chance to explain themselves.

The first woman had pewter-colored hair and brilliant amber eyes. Her appearance was like an Elf's aside from her diamond-shaped pupils. She was tall, spindly, and carried herself with arrogance. Her name was Llrissa, the Goddess of Justice. Despite her important role, she had been one of the neglectful deities prior to my "promotion."

As a child, Llrissa had intimidated me. However, now, my feelings were of disgust and contempt. Such an important role should never have been approached so lightly.

The second woman, Ceres, was far more pleasant. Ceres was the Goddess of Nature and looked much like what I imagined a half-Elf, half-Dryad would look like. She was a strange fusion of flesh, roots, leaves, and flowers. Her hair was brilliant spring green. Horn-like protrusions from her skull looked like branches and had lavender-colored flowers sprouting along them. Thankfully Ceres had not shirked her duties during the Elders' years of quarreling.

"Have you discovered something useful?" I questioned. Sebastian's violet eyes flicked around with unease, but his two companions stood in place, calm.

"Llrissa and I have been questioning the Lesser Gods, as you requested," Ceres spoke with a bright smile. "None of them have had contact with X'shmir since the country disappeared centuries ago. Not even the God and Goddess of Humans knew it existed. Even now they find their access is limited."

"They're struggling to See anything going on in X'shmir, just as the rest of us are." Llrissa scowled. "You know how Hadyn and Edan are; they didn't want to discuss *that* country much. However, Edan did state that the prince and princess are not one of 'his.'"

"Not his?" I arched an eyebrow. "Meaning that they are not directly descended from him?"

"Meaning they aren't *Human*." Sebastian shook his head and

then pushed his displaced hair out of his eyes. "Have you been able to turn up anything on your end? The Lesser and Middle Gods are being even less helpful than usual."

"Darius is less than forthcoming with information. I sense that we may have problems with him down the line," I answered, recalling my confrontation with the boy. "Arianna is going to be...difficult. Until I earn her trust, I don't believe she will be of much help. She thinks too similarly to my kind."

"What do you want us to do then?" Ceres frowned at me, her faintly glowing white eyes showing concern. "If you can't charm her... Then you have more reason to believe she's a fake, yes?"

"The *Elders* still claim to have reincarnated the twins, right?" Sebastian interrupted, "Don't you think it's possible that *this* Arianna and Darius are the result?"

"The time table doesn't match." I shook my head. "They are twenty-five years of age. As you know, it was twenty years ago that I ventured into Limbo. I've already confirmed for myself that the God of Time hasn't intervened in some way.

"The Exiled Gods have been known to play cruel tricks. Until we have proof regarding the twins' identities, I'm going to operate on the assumption that we're dealing with fakes."

"Because the other option is that the Elders are lying through their teeth?" Sebastian offered, earning a brief glare from me. "You know as well as we do that the Elders are a mess right now, Nalithor."

"Until the Elders settle matters amongst themselves, it's best we act with caution." Llrissa tossed her hands into the air. "If the twins are replicas then this poses all manner of problems."

"Yes. The Exiles shouldn't be able to make something that's so convincing even a fae-dragon would fall for it," Ceres murmured. "The fae-dragons could be fakes as well... However, we know that the Exiles failed to replicate such creatures in the past. Whichever it is, it means the Exiled Gods have improved their technique...or that they're not the ones making 'fakes.'"

"Djialkan and Fraelfnir are not fakes," I muttered. "They've been consulting Onyre and Aleri since returning to Dauthrmir. I don't believe the city's Guardians would be fooled by the Exiles' creations."

"Nalithor, are you alright to handle this on your own?" Ceres inquired, her face full of worry. "Arianna was—"

"If she is a fake then it's my responsibility to destroy her," I interrupted, my tail snapping behind me. "I won't allow a mockery of *her* to live."

"Still, I find it unlikely that she's a fake." Sebastian crossed his arms. "The Exiled Gods could have chosen any country to deposit a 'fake,' and they wouldn't have needed to recreate both twins. We know for a fact that the Lesser, Middle, Upper, and Exiled Gods have not had access to X'shmir since its disappearance.

"Why would the Exiles send fakes to X'shmir? Who would they be trying to fool? It would have made more sense to plop fakes in

Vorpmasian or Beshulthien territory."

"We know that there are remnants of Angelic items and magic in X'shmir," Llrissa pointed out. "For all we know there could be Angels or even Exiles hiding in the Sihix Forest."

"Sebastian, I want you and Ceres to investigate the Exiled Gods. We need more information on their replication techniques and how they create the Chaos Beasts," I gave the order with a small frown and then turned to the Goddess of Justice. "Llrissa, I want you to contact Aurelian, Elise, Erist'il, and Arom'il. The five of you are to investigate X'shmir. We need to discover how and why they disappeared in the first place. It strikes me as strange that their culture changed so drastically since their disappearance.

"Of course, the presence of Angelic magic and tools is a problem as well."

"What do you plan to do?" Ceres furrowed her brow at me.

"I still have duties to tend to in Vorpmasia." I sighed. "I'm stuck here for the foreseeable future, so, I will take the opportunity to learn what I can from Darius-zir and Arianna-jiss. If I can I will determine just who or *what* they are."

"We'll contact you if we find anything else." Sebastian nodded as both women hooked arms with him.

The three of them disappeared into Sebastian's darkness and their presences faded from Dauthrmir entirely. It was unfortunate that they had so little information to share, but the confirmation that Arianna and Darius weren't Human would still be useful to me. I now had more direction for which way to focus my research and questions alike.

Once satisfied the three deities were gone, I began my journey to the palace once more. I glanced up at the stars briefly, thinking back to the previous day's events. After fighting Arianna, and then tasting her, it was difficult to keep telling myself she was a fake. Her fighting style, her scent, her taste, and even the feel of her power was identical to what I remembered from my childhood friend—and from what remained of her in Limbo.

The rage I felt towards Darius was the same as if it were *my* Arianna was who had been hurt.

'I miss her…' I sighed and shoved loose hair out of my eyes. *'Two hundred years and I still can't accept that she's…gone. Or perhaps seeing her in Limbo ripped the wound open anew. Yes, that would make more—'*

I paused when I reached the Sapphire Quarter and scented the air with a frown. Arianna's alluring scent hung in the air, but the house she shared with her twin was on the opposite side of the district. There was no reason for her to be so far from the house so late at night. I nestled my hands in my pockets and turned to my right to follow her scent.

It wasn't long before I found myself staring at a small gap in the walls. I clenched my fists and grit my teeth. This was *her* hiding place. Arianna—my Arianna—had always gone there to read, hide, or take naps along the district's outer wall. No one aside from myself and a handful of others who knew the princess ever ventured there.

I stepped through the gap in the wall and found a surprising sight just a few feet away. Arianna was curled up on her side in the grass with a messy pile of books surrounding her. Her back was nestled against the granite wall as she slept, but, she still dozed dangerously close to the precipice. One or two rolls in the wrong direction would send her tumbling over the edge and into the lake below.

'Djialkan?' I cut my eyes to the side at the fae-dragon. Djialkan looked unworried and was lounging on a boulder near his ward.

'Darius will not leave her be,' Djialkan stated dryly as he lifted his head and blinked his deep purple eyes a few times in silence, examining me. *'Might I impose on you? Carrying her back to the house myself is difficult at best.'*

'Darius is still causing problems?' I bit back a growl as the slumbering princess shifted, then glanced down at her peaceful but mostly obscured face. My chest clenched as I looked between Arianna and the precipice. *'I'm of half a mind to bring her to the palace instead if that is the case.'*

'That should not be necessary.' Djialkan snorted, shifting to the form of a small boy so that he could pick up Arianna's mess of books. *'Darius is concerned that Arianna will be executed for consorting with you. He may not be going about it in the best, most mature way possible...but his concerns are based in fact. This time.'*

'*Ah yes... You did mention something about that.*' I muttered, studying the petite woman at my feet. '*What do* you *believe will happen?*'

'*Obeying a deity trumps almost every restriction that she and her brother suffer.*' Djialkan grimaced and shook his head. '*Despite the fact that Darius is meant to be responsible for his sister, he has not educated himself regarding the laws and restrictions surrounding her status as a Lyur'zi.*

'*If consorting with her is your will then there should be no issue.*'

'*My will?*' I wondered in private, tracing the intricate designs of Arianna's mask, '*Not even the smallest hint of her hair frees itself of her hood. Does she keep it pinned, or is she forced to keep it short?*'

I shelved my curiosity for the moment and knelt beside the princess. Taking great care not to wake her, I hefted Arianna into my arms and cradled her head against my chest. I was stricken by her slumbering expression and its similarity to the Arianna of my past. My heart threatened to beat out of control as *hers* flared hot within my chest. '*Can...can the Exiles truly recreate someone down to the minutest of details like this? The Elders, perhaps, would make sense. But the Exiles?*'

"Warm..." Arianna purred and shifted in my arms to nuzzle into my chest, startling me.

'*She is still asleep, fear not,*' Djialkan assured me humorlessly before shifting back to his draconic form. '*Come. Let us return her to bed, where she belongs.*'

'*Have there been any more incidents since yesterday?*' I walked with care as I followed Djialkan, often glancing down at Arianna's slumbering form to make certain she was alright, and that she was still asleep.

'*None to worry about.*' Djialkan's simple answer made me breathe a sigh of relief.

It was almost comical that such a tiny woman could fight me so close to evenly. She looked, and felt, so delicate in my arms and yet she had already proved to be anything but. My instincts screamed at me that this was truly *my* Arianna, that I was a fool for telling myself she was a fake, but I couldn't accept that notion. Not yet. Aside from her ability in combat, her scent, and her aura… I had no reason to believe she was the same girl. I needed to test her further.

'*Djialkan aren't you at least a* little *concerned that she's a fake?*' I finally questioned the fae-dragon, causing him to freeze mid-air and almost fall from the sky. '*You and I both saw her die. The Elders—*'

'*You were never one to believe the Elders when you were a child.*' Djialkan huffed, beating his wings to regain altitude. '*I have the proof that I need to believe she is the real one, Nalithor. If you are unable to accept that…then there is nothing I can do for you. You will just have to wait until she proves it to you herself.*'

I shot Djialkan a glare and then looked down at Arianna once more, feeling her stir in my grip. Her expression had grown less peaceful and the beating of her heart was growing ever more frantic. A small tremble had entered her petite form, and I got the distinct feeling that it was fear, not shivers from the cool night air.

'The chains the Oracle and her sister removed from Arianna's back...did you know they are of Angelic construction?' I inquired, catching the disapproving look Djialkan shot me. *'Ah... Did the Oracle not inform you that she was bringing them to me?'*

'She did not.' Djialkan snorted. *'You have been studying them then?'*

'If they're forged of a naturally-occurring metal it isn't one found on—or under—the Rilzaan Continent.' I ascended the steps of the twins' house and grimaced when I caught Darius' lingering stench. *'I'm more curious as to how she survived the torture. Unless you and Fraelfnir have seen a drastic improvement in your healing abilities, Arianna should have—'*

"Djialkan? Nali?" Darius opened the door and peered out of the crack at us, then looked down at Arianna with a startled expression. "Is she alright? No one hurt her, right?"

"She's sleeping." I kept my answer low. Arianna grumbled something incoherent while turning her face toward my chest and away from the light. Her pulse quickened in fear once more, taking on an erratic pace. "Her perch was precarious at best. It seemed prudent to return her here."

"I can take her upstairs—" Darius flinched and went silent when Djialkan hissed at him.

"I doubt you have the strength for the task." I shook my head at the pouting prince.

"Fine… Djialkan, *you* show him where her room is," Darius muttered, turning on his heel. "I'm going to bed."

Without another word Darius stalked off and disappeared toward the back of the house. The moment Darius was out of sight Djialkan moved to the controls for the lights and turned them off. Arianna's pulse slowed to a calmer pace once the light was gone and I felt her relax into my arms once more. *'Light was the problem…?'*

'You should be able to use your flames to light the way without disturbing her.' Djialkan perched on my left shoulder and looked down at Arianna. *'Up the stairs, first door on the left. Keep the lights off.'*

I remained silent and summoned several orbs of pale fire around me. They floated to the stairs and staggered themselves every few steps to light my way. Satisfied, I made my way upstairs at a slow pace as to not wake Arianna. Once there, I found that her room was surprisingly plain. I chose not to question it and, instead, moved to the bed so that I could place her upon it. If I were to be truthful, her room was more suitable for a commoner—not a princess or mage.

My musings, however, were interrupted when I attempted to lay Arianna on the mattress. Her heartbeat became frantic when I attempted to move away, and her hands latched onto my robes.

The small, fearful whimper that escaped her made me freeze in place.

"N-no, don't leave me a-a-lone...don't..." Arianna whimpered. Something about her frightened voice tore my heart in half and made me stop completely. I couldn't possibly leave her. Not after hearing that, and not after feeling the aura of fear that consumed her.

"*Alala!*" Djialkan called the fox, his voice firm.

I watched the fluffy fox's head peek out of a nearby drawer before she leapt from it and onto the bed. Alala released a soft warble and nuzzled Arianna's cheek, tilting her head. Arianna's pulse didn't calm, but her grip on my robes loosened enough that I was able to place her on the bed and take a step back. Alala curled up against the princess' chest and nosed her again, attempting to calm her, but it didn't appear to be working.

'*Will she be alright, Djialkan?*' I looked to the fae-dragon, my chest tightening with worry.

"*She is no stranger to nightmares.*" Djialkan sighed, drifting to a stack of cushions by Arianna's bed. "*Thank you for your assistance, Nalithor. I will see to it that she knows you are the one overseeing the research on the chains taken from her flesh. I imagine that you will need to discuss such matters with her. It is best we do not catch her unawares.*"

'*What of the twins' medical examinations?*' I asked, cupping Arianna's face in one hand and running my thumb over her plush lips. Her head shifted so she could nuzzle into my hand and her expression relaxed slightly.

"They received their initial examinations this morning." Djialkan narrowed his eyes at me. *"You still insist she is Human?"*

'She couldn't possibly be Human.' I hesitated to release Arianna's face and then rose to my feet. *'I have reports I must make before I sleep. You're...certain that she's alright?'*

For just a moment, I could have sworn that I saw glowing white markings alongside the princess' throat when her head lolled to the side. Were those Brands of Divinity I had seen, or was it simply her pale skin reflecting the light of the moons? It had been so brief that I couldn't be sure, but I still found myself staring at her covered throat. *'Brands would certainly help explain how she's so powerful. However, if she's a fake, that should be impossible...'*

"You believe she is a fake and yet you are still concerned about her?" Djialkan spoke dryly, drawing my attention away from my thoughts.

'The Exiled Gods aren't known for abandoning their creations or subjecting them to torture.' I grimaced at the snickering fae-dragon. *'Fake or not she is a victim of the Old Ways. If she is a cruel joke planned by the Exiles, as I think she is, that still raises questions that I must find answers to. It is part of my role as a god.'*

"Tread carefully, Nalithor, lest you find yourself Exiled." Djialkan's strange tone elicited a frown from me. *"Have you forgotten already that it is the Elders who were involved with her*

'death' to begin with?"

'I haven't forgotten...' I glanced at the slumbering princess once more and then shut the door behind me, escaping into the hallway beyond. 'I couldn't possibly forget such a thing. But...it was only a particular group of Elders that deviated from their "plan" and executed children like Arianna...right?'

"Nali!" Darius called in a low tone as I descended the staircase. "Er... Rely'ric, rather. Did I say that right? I have something I want to discuss with you."

I considered refusing the boy's request as I studied the nervous shifting of his feet and wringing of his hands. He had a pleading expression on his face as he looked up at me and even Fraelfnir looked uneasy. Despite my proximity to the male half of the twins I couldn't detect his scent or power through that of his sister.

Arianna's darkness coated every nook and cranny of the house like a thick, ever-shifting blanket. It seemed like it was watching me and yet I hadn't sensed the initial spread of her power through the house.

'I should keep this short, before I feel any more drawn to feed from her.' I crossed my arms and grit my teeth, my tail swaying with agitation. "Yes, you pronounced it correctly. Your accent could do with some work but that's a matter of practice. Let's step outside. It's much too hot in here."

"Hot?" Darius sounded confused, and rightly so, as I turned to leave the house.

'Undoubtedly she's trapped inside of a Human body. For now.' I thought distractedly, inhaling deeply of the cold spring air. *'I don't even* need *to feed and yet I want to devour every inch of...'*

"Do you really require Arianna's help over mine?" Darius latched onto my right arm and looked up with what he likely believed was a sultry expression. "I'd be *much* better suited to help you, don't you think? Unlike her I won't try to kill you, and you can feed from me, and—"

"I have no interest in you." I reclaimed my arm with ease and took a step away from the boy. "If that's what you wanted to discuss I will be leaving. I have reports to write."

"I heard about you kissing my sister." Darius' voice was flat as I walked away from the house. "Don't you think it's unfair of you to lead her on when she's explicitly forbidden from—?"

"Darius, stop interfering with laws you do not understand." Fraelfnir snarled at Darius, causing me to glance at him. *"Nalithor-y'ric needs to learn of beasts and you are the* last *person to go to for such knowledge."*

"But, Fraelfnir," Darius protested, "if the noble or royal families find out they'll think she's emotionally compromised, and then they'll—!"

"Arianna tastes very sweet," I teased, raising my fingertips to my lips and half turning to shoot Darius a look. As expected, the boy flushed bright red and went silent. "What makes you think I'll let her return to X'shmir to begin with?"

"Let…her…?" Darius blinked at me, his face growing a darker shade of red. "F-Fraelfnir, what does he—?"

I shook my head and resumed my walk toward the palace district, smirking to myself as I shoved my hands into the pockets of my robes. No matter who Arianna turned out to be, it was unlikely she would be allowed to return to X'shmir. If she was a fake, she would be executed. If, by some miracle, she was the real Arianna…I would protect her no matter the cost.

A strong spike of fear from the princess in the district below made me pause in the palace gardens. I wanted to know what struck fear into a woman like her but, after a moment of hesitation, I chose not to pry and instead hastened my pace toward the nearest door. It was well past midnight and I needed to write my reports before resting. I didn't have the luxury of investigating that woman.

'Still, I can't in good conscience just leave her in a terrified state…' I considered, striding through the silent palace and ascending the stairs. *'Perhaps I can alleviate at least* some *of her suffering…'*

Nodding to myself, I reached out to Arianna's with my mind and took care as I searched for a way through her barriers. Changing the tide of her dreams would be simple…if I could find my way in. To my surprise I was met with barriers just as firm as if she was still awake. I could feel the raging storm of emotions and power trembling just on the other side and yet I couldn't find my way in. There wasn't even the slightest hint of Djialkan or Alala reinforcing her barriers.

'*Countering me even in her sleep, is she?*' I smiled, shook my head, and began to withdraw my power. '*She really is a cautious one isn't—*'

My mind went blank for a moment. I staggered, catching myself against the wall when Arianna's power rushed along mine and slammed into my barriers with enough force to knock the air from my lungs. Her presence wrapped around me and my barriers so snuggly that I found myself checking to make sure she hadn't *physically* wrapped her arms around my torso. Fear, panic, rage, hunger, the desire to kill, and *lust* were intertwined inseparably with her power. I found it impossible to sort through her emotions let alone determine whom they were directed towards.

'*Quickly, Nalithor! Cut yourself from Arianna's thoughts!*' Djialkan's voice burst into my mind, distracting me from the maelstrom that was the princess' presence. '*Tch, reckless as always! Have you learned nothing in the past two hundred years?!*'

"General Vraelimir, are you alright?" A voice filled with concern questioned. I glanced up to find one of the male servants watching me wearily from over the stack of firewood he carried. "You're…"

"I'm fine," I spat before straightening and then storming past the servant.

Growling, I stalked through my wing of the palace, pawing at my eyes and cheeks as I went. If that woman could reach my mind in her sleep, of all things, I would have to be more careful than I first thought. For her to use the door *I* opened as a two-way path…just what was she? Who was she? Her emotions, her pain, and her terror had been genuine and pure enough to bring *me* to tears. It was as if she was desperate to escape her own mind, even if it meant entering another's.

'Yet her hunger and varied lusts…' I bit back a groan and shivered, slumping back against the doors to my suite. *'What is she? I almost lost myself to her hunger and lust. Even now, I just want to…'*

I shook my head hard and attempted to dismiss the lingering sensation of Arianna's power caressing me. Despite myself, I seriously considered using my power as an Adinvyr to slip into her dreams and make use of that delicious, unadulterated lust she seemed to be hiding. Her lips had tasted so sweet in the brief taste I took, and now I found myself wondering if the rest of her was just as enticing.

If she was truly stuck in the body of a Human, I might very well break her…and that had its own appeal.

CHAPTER SIX
Slip

'It smells like Nalithor here still...' I frowned and pulled on my elbow-length gloves, scanning the room for any sign that the Adinvyr had intruded. "Djialkan, what happened last night?"

"You fell asleep in a precarious position. I had Nalithor carry you back to the house. It gave me a chance to discuss important matters with him, at least," Djialkan answered with a dragon's version of a shrug. *"Your fool of a brother thought to carry you to your rooms himself...but we both know he is not strong enough for such a task."*

"Important matters?" I sat down on the edge of my bed and summoned an array of weapons from within my jewelry. "What sort of 'important matters'?"

Djialkan let out a huff and curled up on his stack of pillows to watch me. His gaze was wary as he tracked my movements. My weaponry was overdue for cleaning and polishing, and I wasn't quite awake enough to tolerate my twin's presence yet. There was one weapon in my collection that I didn't look forward to caring for, and it was the one unlike the rest.

It was a blade from my past and it made my blood run cold whenever I looked at it. Djialkan and Corentine had insisted, numerous times, that I needed to keep the *"Godslayer"* in my possession. However, I wanted nothing to do with the blade.

'Why would I keep the blade that someone attempted to kill me with? Why should I?' I hefted the large silver sword and examined its gilt decorations and the large gems set within its hilt. *'Hells, why did those bastards try to kill me with a weapon meant for destroying gods? I don't understand. It can't harm mortals but...*

'Humph. If those even are my *memories.'*

I dismissed the offensive sword with a click of my tongue and then glanced over at Djialkan. I was growing impatient waiting for him to respond.

"The Oracle entrusted Nalithor with the chains removed from your back." Djialkan shifted, bristling. *"He has been studying them in order to learn their composition, origin, and—"*

"What a pain." I sighed, chose a dagger from my collection, and began cleaning it. "What of our tests? Darius and I need to arrive in a little less than two hours, right?"

"Nay." Djialkan shook his head and then rested it on the

cushions again. *"All examinations have been delayed. Multiple threats were detected near several of Vorpmasia's barriers. The majority of the city's resident Archmagi and military have been deployed to deal with it.*

"Nalithor, Eyrian, their men, and a handful of others remained here to protect the city."

I frowned at Djialkan and then reached for another blade. There were few things I could think of that would elicit such a large movement from the Vorpmasian military; beasts, or war.

I wanted my share of the fun. Beasts—especially ones I'd never seen before—seemed like an excellent way to relieve my boredom and satisfy my desire to hunt.

Nalithor's men were entertaining but they didn't provide me with the challenge I craved. I wanted to challenge the Adinvyr himself again. But…I wasn't sure how to deal with him. Not after he kissed me, and certainly not after he claimed he wanted to earn the right to make a snack out of me. I figured he must have been joking but there was a small part of me that didn't think that was the case—and perhaps even hoped it wasn't.

'I don't understand that man…' I shook my head and grimaced before looking over at Djialkan. "Darius has more time to study then?"

"Aye. Fraelfnir and I will be instructing the boy for the remainder of the day." Djialkan laughed, stretching his wings. *"Darius already committed himself to staying home and catching up on his studies in*

preparation. What will you do for the day, Arianna?"

"I'm going to work on my training." I dismissed my weapons into their homes within my jewelry and then rose to my feet. "Nalithor bested me with some technique I'm unfamiliar with. It made me panic and, because of that, I lost. That's unacceptable."

"So, you are going to make sure it does not happen again?" Djialkan cocked his head.

"If something like *that* causes me to panic then I still have a lot of room for improvement." I motioned with one hand as I walked to the door. "Had that happened on the battlefield… I would be dead."

I summoned my headphones and cranked up the volume as I left the house. Something grated against my nerves, but I couldn't quite place it, so I adopted a brisk pace. I wanted to get to the training areas as soon as possible. At first, I thought perhaps Nalithor's lingering scent in the house was the cause of my agitation. However, even though I was now away from it, my irritation kept rising.

My dreams hadn't been anything out of the ordinary the prior night, and I'd even found Nalithor's scent…comforting. Of course, his scent's presence in *my* house startled me at first, but I got over it.

'Some music and training will soothe me. I hope.' I sighed.

When I arrived at a secluded training area, I kicked off my boots and then strode across the sand in my socks. I wanted nothing more than to beat the living hells out of Chaos Beasts right now, but that obviously wasn't an option. The sturdy-yet-boring training dummies would have to suffice. I didn't feel like seeking out Nalithor's men this morning. Once I'd relaxed some, I would reconsider it.

'Hunting would provide me with a better distraction.' I slumped and looked at the ground for a moment before straightening and squaring off with a dummy. Feeling sorry for myself would just make me angry. *'Are the Devillians* ever *going to stop tapping on my barriers? Haven't they gotten the hint that I'm not interested? They have no chance with me!'*

I scowled and struck the dummy once, hard. It didn't make me feel better. I took a deep breath, trying to steady myself, and then moved through a fluid set of strikes. I moved in time with the fast-pace music I'd selected and attempted to focus solely on my exercises, the dummy, and the music blasting in my ears. However, I was having more difficulty than normal focusing.

None of the Dauthrmirans even came close to breaking through my barriers and yet their endless knocking and prodding annoyed me. Very few of them felt their way around my barriers in the careful, examining way Nalithor had. The few that shared his more measured method weren't even worth my time. Their auras were even weaker than my brother's.

As far as I knew, Nalithor should have been able to break through my barriers with ease. He was a god and there was no denying that he was insanely powerful. I knew I shouldn't have been able to fight him so evenly, and it seemed strange that he couldn't listen to my thoughts at will.

'Just…just what am I?' I slammed my shin into the dummy's head and then sighed in exasperation. *'I grew up as a Human and have a Human body—I think. Before I was taken from Dauthrmir— if that really was me—I was a Devillian of some kind. So, what does that make me* now?

'Are my capabilities really beyond that of a Human? Or…did Nalithor go easy on me?'

Spitting curses, I struck the dummy several times in rapid succession with as much strength as I could muster. No matter what I did it seemed as if my thoughts always circled back to Nalithor or the fact I was potentially not a Human.

To make things worse, something about Nalithor's disappointed expression the other day bothered me. It didn't make sense to me for him to look *that* disappointed when I declined his lunch invitation. After all, he tried to use his power to seduce me. Since then our interactions had been limited. However, our meeting in the library, and subsequent sparring match, were startling at best.

'Did he really have to kiss me?' The corner of my eye twitched as I continued my assault on the dummy. *'I don't get why he was so angry with my brother and that girl. What does he care?'*

At first, I thought my rejection of his lunch invitation had hurt his feelings. However, even after everything that happened in the past few days, he still hadn't asked me to stop addressing him as "General Vraelimir". To me, that meant he wasn't interested enough in me to be genuinely hurt. But I wasn't sure why he would fake it, either.

'*Ugh I should have followed them to the beasts after all!*' I spun and slammed my shin into the dummy's throat. '*I just want to kill something! Is that really too much to ask for? I'm sure there's plenty of prey to choose from. I know Lucifer and the Oracle said they'd call me if my help was "needed" but...*'

I pouted, took several deep breaths, and shut my eyes. I needed to focus on my training; that, at least, was one thing I could control and influence. Anything else would come with time.

Once I'd calmed, I squared off with the dummy once more and resumed my training. I rotated through a series of rhythmic strikes and repeated them. Eventually my mind and eyes both unfocused and my breathing relaxed. Nothing but the feel of my skin striking the dummy and the scent of nearby grass filled my senses. There were no unusual presences, noises, scents, or blatant threats within my range of detection. No beasts for me to hunt, no criminals for me to massacre. It was almost a disappointment.

I wasn't sure how much time passed before I sensed a change in my surroundings but, soon enough, I caught Nalithor's scent growing closer. His jewelry jingled faintly as he walked but his feet made no noise. I decided to ignore him for now and continued to smack the dummy. There was no guarantee Nalithor was coming here and, if he was, he could talk while I practiced.

"Training in solitude once more?" Nalithor spoke by my ear and plucked my headphones from my ears, startling me. "My men didn't—?"

"They behaved themselves." I twisted into a kick and broke the dummy in half. "Oops… Well. At the very least I promise I didn't do *that* to any of your subordinates."

"How about sparring with me instead?" Nalithor grinned broadly and offered me my headphones, but I just examined his bare torso and low-rise pants for a moment. "I won't break as easily."

"Well… I did say you owe me a sparring match." I paused, my eyes running down the v-lines that disappeared into his dark trousers. The Adinvyr wore nothing else aside from his dangerously low pants and it was…quite a sight. I could only hope that my mask hid the fact I was staring. "How shall we spar this time? Ah…and, how was your hunt?"

"Disappointingly *easy*," Nalithor informed me with an amused smile. "It would appear that our scouts were overly panicked. Eyrian could have dispatched the beast on his own."

"I'll try not to be as 'disappointingly easy'," I commented, dismissing my headphones into a shrizar.

We walked a few yards away from the training dummies and over to a proper sparring pit. Once there we faced each other, and

I adopted an offensive stance. It would take a minor miracle for me to keep my concentration on the fight itself when Nalithor was dressed like *that*.

"Let's see how you fare without the use of magic, shall we?" Nalithor stretched his arms over his head and then took on an offensive stance of his own. "As far as 'easy'… that is the last word I would use to describe you."

Nalithor leapt forward with a roundhouse kick aimed at my head. I grinned and blocked his shin with my forearms, briefly studying his focused expression and the tension in his body. It seemed like today he intended to start at full strength instead of taking it slow at the start. Good.

'If he's going to come at me like this, I don't have time to be distracted by his scent or physique.' I settled into a rhythm of countering Nalithor's strikes and danced out of his tail's reach. *'Though…he's fast. Just a blur.'*

I would already have been on the ground if it weren't for my instincts. His strikes disturbed the wind just enough for me to sense them beforehand.

"You're more focused today," Nalithor remarked thoughtfully as he caught my ankle in one hand and held my leg in place by his head. "It's such a shame you've retreated behind those shields of yours again."

"With the incessant knocking, prodding, and rolls of power people keep sending my way, layers of shields seem prudent," I pointed out as the Adinvyr examined my leg. His expression was unreadable now, but his grip was just firm enough to keep me from pulling my leg free.

"The weak ones are still pestering you?" Nalithor arched an eyebrow and shifted his gaze back to my face. "Isn't it uncomfortable for you to have your leg this high for this long?"

"Discomfort is a wasted sensation in both battle and sparring." My flat statement making Nalithor break into a broad grin. "And yes the 'weak ones,' as you called them, are still bothering me. Their thoughts are quite pornographic, you know. I'm not sure whether to be flattered or insulted anymore."

"They…" Nalithor's brow furrowed and his eyes flashed with anger. A hint of jealousy leaked out from behind his barriers before he tightened them further. His hand twitched around my ankle. "Fools. They must be weaker than I thought if their attempts have had so little effect on you. Regardless of their power—or lack thereof—they should have had at least a *little*—"

"This isn't very conducive to sparring," I commented as Nalithor's gaze flicked up from my lips. "You'll have plenty of time to be frustrated with your countrymen later."

"If only you were as eager to get to know me as you are to spar me." Nalithor shook his head and released my ankle.

"I consider this 'getting to know you'," I countered with a laugh, causing him to tilt his head and look at me with that unreadable expression again. "I told you before that I have to determine if you're *worthy* of my interest, remember? Sparring is my prime method of gauging that since I haven't had the opportunity to see how you perform against beasts."

"Ahhh... You know, if you continue talking like an Adinvyr I'm going to have to kiss you again," Nalithor teased, a playful smirk forming on his face as his tail swished.

Nalithor disappeared into a blur again, forcing me to refocus my instincts on our match. Even though I couldn't follow him with my eyes my other senses more than made up for it. For now. However, if he was hiding more power and speed somewhere, I wasn't sure how much longer I could keep up with him. As it stood, I was already going to have some nasty bruises, both from blocking strikes and from weathering others.

I let my vision unfocus and continued to fend off Nalithor's flurry of strikes. It was easier to deal with him once I couldn't "see" him anymore. With the distraction of my vision gone I grew faster and began attacking and countering. Now I could sense his movements as he went to make them, instead of when he was already partway through the motion.

It wasn't long before Nalithor drew a weapon, but I didn't let him maintain his grip on it for long. Disarming him was a surprisingly simple matter and I heard his weapon resound as it collided with something. He was struggling now. His breathing was heavier, and I felt his magic rippling behind his shields. *'If I can just—'*

"Do you…intend to kill me, Arianna?"

"Do I—?" I froze as an unwelcome spike of fear shot through me.

Nalithor was beneath me in the dirt and I was straddling him. I held the *Godslayer* poised over the left side of his chest. Blue-black welled up around the silver blade's point and trickled freely down his pale skin. Under other circumstances, I would have found the scent of his blood alluring. Now, however, I knew I was in a dangerous situation.

"W-what…" I started, dumbfounded, trying to recall what I'd done in our fight once my mind had unfocused. "I-I'm so sorry, I—"

I moved to pull the sword away but Nalithor reached up and gripped the blade, drawing it deeper into his chest. His expression was wistful as he looked up at me, and he seemed oblivious to the sword's edge biting into his hand. The flow of blood from his chest hastened, causing me to grow still so I wouldn't make it worse. I opened my mouth to protest but Nalithor instantly shushed me.

"That fear you just felt was directed at the sword, not at me." Nalithor's voice was calm as he studied me. "Can you dismiss it? Or…must I take it from you by force?"

'I-it's a sword meant to slay deities, isn't it?' I tried to swallow my panic, my eyes flicking from the blade and Nalithor's wounds in rapid succession. *'He seems unaffected by it. Did the blade stop short of his heart? Why did he pull it deeper?* **When in the infernal hells**

did I draw it?!'

"Your hands are—" I started to protest. Nalithor just chuckled and lifted one of his bloodied fingers to my lips once I dismissed the *Godslayer* into the accursed jewel it came from. "What are you doi—?"

"You're genuinely concerned?" Nalithor sounded curious but his eyes were on my lips as he painted them with his blood. "You've displayed excellent control up until this point, Arianna. What made you slip?"

'What made me slip?' The question surprised me enough to distract me from the temptation to taste his intoxicating-smelling blood. "There's very few things that can make me slip like that, that I know of. Hmmm…"

"If you keep making a habit of injuring me like this," Nalithor suddenly gripped my hands and placed them over his chest, "I really will make you clean it up with those lips of yours. My blood on your mouth certainly suits you. And…the sight of you straddling me is certainly pleasant as well."

'Don't…tempt me.' I felt my face growing hot as I glanced down at his bloodied skin. "You seem unconcerned that I—"

"The *Godslayer* can't harm a deity of my rank. Not permanently, at least." Nalithor shot me an amused smile. "Aside from that, your emotions and the sound of your heartbeat were plenty to convince me that you didn't intend *me* harm. If you felt bloodlust during our fight it was directed elsewhere. So, I will ask you again; what made your control slip?"

Before I could answer Nalithor flipped me onto my back and pinned me to the sand beneath him. He smirked, his lips hovering just out of reach of mine. I heard his heart pounding almost as fast as mine was and, after a moment, I realized his presence was slinking along my barriers once more. The damned Adinvyr didn't seem like he was ever going to give up on finding a way through.

"Only things like being kept from killing something that *needs* to die can make me slip like that," I muttered, unsure of whether Nalithor was listening. He'd resumed tracing my lower lip with his bloody thumb. His pale eyes shone with a surprising amount of desire and made me question what he was thinking. It seemed prudent to distract him from whatever those thoughts were. "Did…did you bring a piece of the beast back with you? My focus shouldn't have been drawn to *you* instead of—"

"How did you come into possession of *that* blade, Arianna?" Nalithor gripped my chin, his eyes wandering from my lips and down to my covered throat. "For the sword to have dispersed into the shadows like that I must assume you dismissed it into one of your pieces of jewelry. Did Aurelian give you the blade for some reason?"

"The God of Chaos." I spoke with unease as Nalithor's frosty eyes snapped back up to my face. "I-I'm really sorry, I didn't mean to—"

"I'm not angry with you." Nalithor chuckled, sliding his hand from my chin and down to my throat. "Mmm... This is an exceptional view as well.

"Alas, I did not bring a piece of the beast back with me. You seem almost like you are in pain, Arianna, but I was quite careful with how I chose to pin you."

"Pain?" I blinked behind my mask a few times, attempting to think of what Nalithor might have been sensing. "The presence of anything that needs to die is...straining. At best. My ability to sense beasts, and particularly filthy criminals, is closely connected to my role in X'shmir. If I sense either, I—"

"Let me feel it," Nalithor interjected, causing me to look at him in confusion. After a moment he rested his elbows in the sand and brought both hands to my face. "I will understand better if you let me feel this 'strain' instead of trying to describe it to me. There shouldn't be anything close enough to Dauthrmir to affect you. So, as much as I would like to make a snack out of you, I suppose it should wait."

I wanted to make a snarky reply but Nalithor closed his eyes and let his warm power spread through me before I could. It wasn't long before he flinched, and his eyes snapped open to reveal his surprise. He looked down at me in silence for a moment. The back-and-forth snapping of his tail was the only indication of his irritation.

"You...are more in-control than I thought. How have you not run off to kill the damned thing already?" Nalithor studied me with clear curiosity, looking as if he wanted to dislodge my mask. "It's strangely refreshing to find someone that has the same reaction to beasts as I do, but…you seem to have sensed it from much farther away than I am capable of."

"Are you ever going to let me up?" I demanded, watching a mischievous grin spread across his face. "You're bleeding all over us both, we're covered in sand, and—"

"Then heal me." Nalithor chuckled and brought my hands over his heart. "Afterwards, I suppose we should find this beast that so strongly stole your attentions."

'I never told him that I can heal.' I looked at Nalithor warily as he watched me in a predatory manner, his eyes kept tracking my movements and his muscles seemed coiled to pounce. "Wouldn't your goddess be rather miffed by this situation?"

"Goddess…?" Nalithor asked with a crooked grin. "I'm a solitary deity, my dear. You have nothing to worry about."

"Oh? I suppose Darius was making up stories then," I murmured distractedly, letting my darkness flow into Nalithor's deep wound. "Well, that or he was more drunk than I thought."

"What did he say?" Nalithor tugged at the front of my hood. "You know, this view would be much more pleasant without *this* and your mask in the way."

"Hmmm?" I paused, surprised, when I sensed the two crystalline hearts in his chest. However, I quickly smoothed my expression, resumed healing him, and hoped that he hadn't noticed. *'He...he keeps his* and *mine here...?'*

"Darius said that the Oracle and Eyrian are both your lovers and prospective 'fellow deities'."

"He...*what?*" Nalithor bristled, his tail smashed into the ground and his chest rumbled with a poorly-contained growl beneath my hands. "I would sooner bed a male horse before I would bed either—!"

"There's a fetish for everything," I muttered with a half shrug as I finished healing his chest and then looked up at him again. "Hmmm, I didn't realize that I'd cut you so deeply. I...? What's that look for?"

"You let your 'innocent little princess' act slip." Nalithor grinned and lowered his face toward mine, his tail swishing playfully behind him once again. "Should I be worried about what goes on behind those shields of yours, *Your Highness?*"

"You *are* an Adinvyr, aren't you?" I countered dryly. "I know that shields do nothing against your ability to sense inappropriate thoughts. I have done *some* reading you know! That said, I wouldn't claim that I've been pretending to be an 'innocent little princess.'"

"True; you did appear rather comfortable whilst *straddling* me." Nalithor's tone was conversational as he stood and then pulled me to my feet alongside him. "I will go see if our scouts have spotted any Chaos Beasts nearby. You should finish your morning training, Arianna. I'll return to fetch you shortly."

Nalithor and that playful smirk of his disappeared in an implosion of shadows. I let out a heavy sigh and staggered back, raising a hand to cover my face. I took a few deep, steadying breaths and tried to clear my mind. The smell of Nalithor's blood was maddening. It was a minor miracle that, with what little remained of my self-control, I was able to keep myself from tasting the blood he'd smeared across my lips. Even keeping myself from following his casual suggestion to clean up his blood with my mouth was difficult.

'This isn't good at all,' I complained, touching a finger to my lips. Gritting my teeth, I summoned magic around my fingers and cleansed the blood and sand from both my skin and clothes. *'I shouldn't want to taste his blood so badly if I'm still mostly Human, right? Although…that is probably the* last *thing I should worry about right now.'*

I stalked towards the training dummies once more and smashed my fist into the closest one, cursing. Nalithor had obviously recognized that specific *Godslayer*. The look on his face when he asked if I wanted to kill him, and then the expression when he pulled the blade deeper into his chest, both tore at me in a way I didn't think I was still capable of feeling. His pain, and his distress, shouldn't have affected me.

Deep breaths didn't help me calm myself at all, so I tore into the dummies with reckless abandon. In a strange way I regretted that I hadn't taken a taste of Nalithor's blood, and that regret only served to infuriate me further. Just as my lapse in control did, Nalithor would have been well within his rights to turn a blade against me for what I'd done and yet he seemed to approve.

'Damnit!' I kicked another dummy in half. *'That fucking beast needs to die before I do something else stupid!'*

"I expected you to calm down, not grow worse." Nalithor's arms wrapped around my waist and he nuzzled into the crook of my neck, chuckling, "Oh? I was able to sneak up on you this time? Tsk, tsk, tsk."

"I assume the beast is close? When do we—" I trailed off and just stared at both Nalithor and Eyrian once the Adinvyr released me. "You call *that* armor?"

"The crystals provide us with more protection than the armor itself does. You should know this." Eyrian grinned at me as I examined their bare chests with a flushed face. "You can do your sightseeing as you accompany us to deal with the beast."

"*Sightseeing?*" I stalked past them to fetch my boots. "I wasn't staring *that* much!"

"I'm pretty sure he's inviting you to stare." Nalithor laughed, tracking my movements as I sat to pull on my boots. "Arianna, is it true that you've been avoiding accompanying your brother to dinner this past week? After what you told me... I'm not certain I can believe him anymore."

"Avoiding?" I looked up in surprise. "Darius made it very clear that I wasn't invited at all. 'Boys only' and such."

"When I inquired about your whereabouts, he stated that you were avoiding people entirely," Nalithor stated in distaste before offering me a hand. "Does Darius make a habit of lying often?"

"Well," I began as Nalithor pulled me to my feet, "Darius hates the fact he has to have an escort and he hates the fact that I'm forced to fulfill that role. I know he hasn't made the best impression, but he does genuinely detest the way mages of our ilk are treated in X'shmir."

"He's selfish." Eyrian shook his head. "Enough of that. This way. We're taking the lift down. There's a boat waiting for us along with the others."

"Others?" I followed the two tall Devillian generals, examining the plate armor that encased their backs and conformed to their muscles like a second skin. "Just how many beasts are there?"

"One." Nalithor glanced over his shoulder at me with a curious expression. "Come now, have you fallen back into your habit of trailing behind once more? That won't do. I, for one, would much prefer you stay in step with us."

"I agree." Eyrian nodded, his much thicker tail snapping behind him in rhythm with his stride.

Instead of speaking I caught up and fell into step between them. It was rather unusual to me, but I certainly wasn't going to complain about being treated as a person instead of a "thing" or outcast. That said, Nalithor's strangely favorable reaction to me trying to *kill him* bothered me. However, Djialkan didn't seem willing to respond to my prodding. I would have to remain in the dark.

The "lift," as Eyrian called it, was a large crystalline platform. After Eyrian stuck something into the control panel the platform descended through the city and toward the surface of the lake. The quick descent made me want to cling to something or someone, so I linked my hands behind my back and wriggled my toes in my boots. I almost would have preferred to take flight in an airship instead of riding this stupid contraption.

"May I ask you a personal question, Arianna?" Nalithor asked after a prolonged silence, so I nodded my head and looked toward him. "Why is it you're so uninterested in making friends here? Do you really believe that Vorpmasia can't convince X'shmir to change its ways?"

"If you think that Vorpmasia can change things in my lifetime you have underestimated how twisted X'shmir has become," I answered, eliciting a frown from them. "What of this beast we're hunting, hmmm? Why have so many people been called for one Chaos Beast?"

"It's a Dux-class." Eyrian started, but then he frowned again and glanced down at me. "That's right...you kill Duxes by yourself."

"A group of six demigods can kill a beast, but," Nalithor turned to face me fully with his arms crossed, "the only demigod currently in the city—that is capable of fighting Chaos Beasts—is Eyrian.

My power as a deity doesn't make up for the missing numbers since I am expected to show a certain degree of restraint. Because of this we are bringing mages and archers to support us while we wear the creature down."

"Speaking of mages and archers…" Eyrian frowned and motioned to my attire, "Will you be alright without your armor? We didn't give you a chance to retrieve the rest of your jewelry."

"I'll be quite alright," I answered with an amused smirk and lifted one arm, jingling my jewelry for emphasis. "I *have* all my jewelry. Most of it is beneath my robes. It simply won't fit over-top."

'Darius, what are the restrictions regarding my clothing and armor while here?' I called to my twin, noting that Nalithor's eyes snapped toward me with that half-curious, half-frustrated expression in them again.

'What? Why?' Darius' voice trembled.

'I'm about the help the Vorpmasians with a beast problem. It's much too warm for my full plate armor,' I answered plainly, sensing Darius sigh in response.

'You're required to hide your face and hair, but you can show everything else,' Darius answered, reluctant. I was satisfied with that response, so I cut off the connection once more and looked down at the island below Dauthrmir that we were fast approaching.

"General Vraelimir, General Il'thar!" An unfamiliar soldier acknowledged the Devillians with a sharp salute once the crystalline lift came to a stop, "The beast is currently on the northwestern shore. It will take an hour for the boats to draw into range. Who—?"

"Arianna-jiss is the X'shmiran Lyur'zi that will be accompanying us." Nalithor's Draemiran purr grew stronger after speaking the honorific, giving his voice a warmer timbre. "Arianna, you will join Eyrian and I in the assault against the beast. We'll take the primary boat."

"I hope you have some way of entertaining yourself for the next hour." Eyrian grimaced and then nodded his approval when I summoned my headphones. "Good choice."

I followed Nalithor and Eyrian onto one of the waiting ebony boats and glanced around at the myriad of soldiers and mages present. Across all the boats there must have been at least a hundred people. It truly surprised me that so many people were necessary for taking down a single beast and, with how intently Nalithor was watching me, I figured my surprise hadn't gone unnoticed. Somehow his gaze had managed to grow in its intensity.

"Is the beast X'shmiran?" I asked, twirling my headphones around one finger as I examined our surroundings.

"Yes. That is *one of* the reasons your presence is desired," Nalithor confirmed and came to stand beside me, but I kept my eyes on the surface of the lake as the boats sped along. "At first, I thought that perhaps you were just arrogant...but you truly don't understand why we require so many people to fight against the beasts, do you?"

"I've been fighting alone all my life." I pointed out with a slight shrug. "Since I've never needed assistance, I can't understand why people—who are stronger than me—would need to swarm a single target."

"And yet you didn't learn from anyone," Nalithor stated just as pointedly. This time I glanced up at him. He looked almost as if he was trying to hide his curiosity, for once.

"As I told you, I learned through observation and action." I stopped spinning my headphones, gripped the band, and placed a hand on my hip.

"Instincts, huh?" Nalithor mused with a small smile as he looked down at me. "You seem displeased. Are you still concerned about our match?"

"It isn't that." I shook my head. "The closer we get to the beast the more impatient I become. I haven't had the opportunity to fight a beast in a while, so I'm eager to arrive."

"I'll leave you to your music then." Nalithor smiled as he turned to walk away from me, but he paused to shoot me a sultry smirk over his shoulder. "I'll try to let you get at least one or two hits in."

I scoffed in reply and pulled my headphones on. Nalithor's scent was still distracting me but the beast's presence now distracted me more. As far as I was concerned, the damned thing was weak. The fact we were bringing so many people to fight it made my blood boil. I wished that I could run across the surface of the lake. That way I could behead the creature and end its miserable existence before the boats even arrived.

Alas, the power of water was Darius' forte. Not mine.

'I should contain my bloodlust.' I shut my eyes, bit my lower lip, and shifted from one leg to the other. *'Too many of them noticed that spike.'*

I ignored the mixture of wary and intrigued glances and focused on my music instead. I looked over the boat's railing and watched the gargantuan forms of the lake's Guardians twist along the water just below us. None of the Vorpmasians seemed concerned by Onyre and Aleri's proximity to the boat. It was quite obvious that they were following us, and I wasn't sure how I felt about that.

Thanks to my music it didn't seem like much time had passed before I was able to spot the beast making its way along the shore. It tore at trees and farms alike with its many arms, leaving a trail of debris in its path as it wandered along. It didn't seem like it had any specific target, simply destroying whatever was directly in front of it. I fixed my gaze on the monstrosity and examined its movements as I flipped through my memories of X'shmiran Chaos Beasts. Was this one poisonous? Did it have acidic blood? Where were its organs located?

I sensed Nalithor and Eyrian watching me expectantly as we drew within a hundred yards of the beast. The boats slowed to a more cautious pace as we approached even though the beast seemed oblivious to our presence. Nalithor, in particular, was watching me with unreadable intensity once more. For some reason the Adinvyr investigated my shields even more thoroughly than previous times, but he was still unable to breach them. However, the tendrils of his power sliding over me, and my shields were terribly distracting. *'Is he* purposely *making it erotic?'*

"Humph. It's weak," I muttered mostly to myself, crossing my arms as I studied the beast. "Not poisonous, no 'special features'… Just brute strength and very little speed. Tch. Still smells bad though."

Once we were within fifty yards of the shore I'd had enough. I stretched a hand toward Nalithor and Eyrian without even bothering to remove my headphones.

"Toss me." I glanced at the Devillian pair when I sensed their hesitation. "Bringing this many people was a waste, like I thought, so toss—"

Both of them shook their heads, making the corner of my eye twitch. I attempted to beat my bloodlust down, but it was pointless. With an aggravated sigh I called my scythe from within one of my rings, swung it behind me in an offensive stance, crouched, and then summoned my light armor and let it replace my robes entirely. The armor was admittedly scanty, little more than a dancer's outfit as far as I was concerned, and revealed all my jewelry. However, I didn't care anymore. There was a beast to kill and I needed to be able to *move*.

My bi-colored Brands of Divinity shimmered into place along my skin when I summoned darkness around my scythe's blade. I bit back a smirk when I saw the beast on the shore pause and flinch in response. Its reaction was one of fear but the men and women on the boats seemed too startled by *me* to react. Clearly my Brands were unexpected.

"Onyre, Aleri!" I yelled, springing over the side of the boat. I landed on Aleri's black scales in a crouch as she burst through the surface of the water. I waited a moment for her to settle.

"Arianna, what are you doing?!" Eyrian and Nalithor both yelled after me, but I just laughed in response as adrenaline flooded my system. Finally, there was a beast for me to kill!

I sprang into a run along Aleri's scales and let my scythe trail behind me. Onyre rose out of the lake by the shore and roared at the Chaos Beast that had turned to make its way toward us. The white dragon's deafening roar paused the beast long enough for me to close the distance. With a gleeful grin I leapt from Aleri's back and raked my scythe through one of the beast's arms, cutting it off entirely as the Guardian dragons sunk back into the lake.

'Mmm... Right. Contain my bloodlust.' I bit my lower lip and held back a giggle as I spun my scythe into a new stance, tapping my foot in time with the music that was blasting within my ears. "Hmmm, so you're *that* type, are you? Well, this may take a *little* longer than expected. Try not to wail too terribly much while I tear

you to bits."

I dodged to the side of the beast when it swung an arm down at me, sighing disappointment. The beast's bones crunched under my bare foot when I kicked its wrist. *'Really! This one is that weak?'*

Glancing to the side, I found that the Vorpmasians just offshore seemed unsure of whether to provide me with assistance. Severing another arm from the beast sounded like an *excellent* way to make up their minds.

Smirking, I leapt upwards and extended darkness from my scythe. The beast's second arm fell, leaving eight remaining. This time the creature screamed loud enough that I heard it over my music, causing me to grin crookedly in response. I managed, at least, to withhold my pleased purr. Perhaps destroying filth like beasts really did excite me too much.

However, I didn't have much time to ponder the notion. I sensed Nalithor and Eyrian approaching, cautiously, from somewhere behind me. That they hadn't opted to remain on the boats impressed me a little, so I pulled off my headphones and dismissed them into my shrizar.

"You could have stayed on the boat," I offered without turning to look at them, instead choosing to lop off several of the beast's fingers. *'Even though the beasts are easy... This one shouldn't be quite so easy. It should be able to get a few hits off against me—what's wrong with it?'*

"You would have had no respect left for us if we remained on the boat." Nalithor leapt past me, a platinum spear clutched in his left hand. "Anything we should know about this kind of beast, *Princess?*"

"The location of its vital organs is always different," I offered as Eyrian dashed past me to join Nalithor. "It's similar to the kinds Eyrian saw me kill in X'shmir, except slower."

I observed in silence for a moment as Nalithor slipped through the beast's strikes like liquid. His long white hair and platinum-adorned braid streaked behind him like a blur as he launched himself toward the beast's throat. He slashed the long blade of his spear through the creature's neck, decapitating it with ease, but it didn't matter. As usual this type of beast had no vital organs in its head aside from its eyes.

Nalithor's graceful, predatory movements and intense focus were strangely pleasing to watch. The fire in his eyes made it clear that he had been serious this morning when he'd suggested my reaction to beasts was similar to his. However, he was more controlled than I was. Despite whatever similarities he'd sensed between us I couldn't tell if he was actually *enjoying* the fight. *'Is he bored already because it's too easy? Or did he lose his drive at some point?'*

"Ideas?" Eyrian called conversationally as he kicked the beast, shattering several of its ribs.

"Mmm..." I tilted my head, observing the beast for a moment. "Sure... Get back."

"Get back?" Nalithor arched an eyebrow at me, drawing my attention with his tone. "I was half-expecting another 'toss me' request."

"I can't make it too easy for you to claim you've tossed me around, now can I?" I countered sweetly, smirking when the Adinvyr's face turned slightly pink. "If you would like me to end the beast quickly, I can. I was just having some fun with it."

"*Fun?*" Eyrian demanded even as he obliged me and retreated. "You're a real piece of work, you know that?"

"You have no idea." I laughed and dismissed my scythe. "Well, *General Vraelimir?* What will it be?"

"I'm not afraid of your darkness," Nalithor stated, leaning against the shaft of his spear. "I'll stay here."

The beast swung down at Nalithor and, in a lazy motion, the deity shifted and sliced the creature's hand from its wrist. I bit my lower lip when the beast yowled in pain and wobbled around, grasping its wrist. At least I couldn't accuse Nalithor of being weak, unprepared, or unaware—even if his refusal *did* irritate me.

"Have it your way." I shrugged, making a small upwards motion with my index finger.

The ground beneath the beast grew pitch black, causing the monster to start screaming in terror. I smiled in response, making a point to shield my own bloodlust even as the beast's screams egged me on. Instead of letting my darker inclinations control me, this time, I remained calculated and focused. After enough darkness had gathered, I summoned large hands of shadow from the pool beneath the beast.

"They're afraid of darkness?" Eyrian's confused mutter caught my attention.

"I'm not sure if they're afraid of darkness in general, or just mine." I made another motion, letting the shadowy hands pull the beast's limbs in different directions. "Didn't you want a piece or two of the beast, General Vraelimir?"

"You aren't concerned that my darkness might overtake yours?" Nalithor countered, earning a crooked smirk from me.

"I'm rather confident that I can confine my darkness to itself, if that's what you're concerned about." I laughed, shaking my head. "Please, don't hold back on *my* account."

The Adinvyr smirked, but I was prepared for the massive burst of darkness he summoned around us and the beast. Nalithor's darkness blotted out our surroundings and the moons-lit sky above, plunging everything into inky blackness. That smirk of his and the playful switching of his tail gave him away completely. I just laughed in response even as the beast's gurgling screams worsened.

Nalithor's darkness was warm and carried his scent. It wasn't unpleasant at all, let alone something to be frightened of.

'Still, it's a good thing I healed him.' I thought, briefly. *'If he was still wounded, I don't know if I could keep myself from—'*

"He's right, you know. You really are a piece of work."

Nalithor purred into the side of my throat. My breath caught in my throat as his lips brushed against my exposed skin and his hands gripped my hips firmly. "That said… You've more than earned the right to call me by name. Consider me impressed."

The Adinvyr shadow-stepped away from me but the sensation of his mouth against my throat lingered. I bit back another amused laugh when his darkness imploded around the beast and me alike. Using that much of his power was sheer overkill and, surely, he knew it. *I wonder. Is he trying to test my comfort with darkness? Are there more cultural differences I'm missing here? Or is he trying to show off?'*

"I don't think you have room to comment about *our* armor being revealing," Eyrian informed me as I turned to stride over to him and Nalithor. The large Draekin pointed at my chest, continuing. "Aren't you not supposed to show—?"

"Don't worry. I have permission," I replied dryly, tugging at my hood to make sure Nalithor hadn't dislodged it. Satisfied, I glanced down at my cleavage, bare abdomen, and mostly exposed legs. "As long as I have free range of movement, I don't particularly care how much skin I show. Are you complaining?"

"N-no, that's not what I—!" Eyrian began hurriedly, his face reddening as he shook his head hard. Nalithor snickered at him. "I-in all seriousness, Arianna, how did you come into possession of items forged by Aurelian? I was under the impression that none of the gods had contact with X'shmir."

"They suit her." Nalithor examined me, his arms crossed as he stroked his chin with one hand. His piercing gaze trailed over my curves in a way that made me want to squirm. "Her Brands *and* her jewelry alike, that is. Those robes of yours were hiding quite the *exceptional* figure, Arianna.

"Womanly charms aside, we should return to Dauthrmir. I think your sudden cooperation with Dauthrmir's Guardians gave everyone a heart attack, Arianna. Your shift in attire assuredly gave several more."

"My jewelry is a relatively new addition," I offered in response to Eyrian's question. "Djialkan was given them for safekeeping until I was ready to wield them or found myself in severe danger. I'm not sure *when* he was entrusted with them, mind you... Djialkan isn't exactly forthcoming."

"He never has been." Eyrian grimaced.

I shrugged and let my armor disappear into my jewelry once more, returning to the heavier robes I'd been wearing previously. Neither of them had commented about my bloodlust, so I hoped that I'd hidden it sufficiently. However, they both looked disappointed by my return to thick clothing. The Vorpmasian soldiers, on the other hand, still looked stunned by what they had witnessed.

It took me a little longer than it should have to realize it wasn't Nalithor's display that had grabbed their attention. It was mine.

"Arianna-jiss, how did you get the Guardians to cooperate?" A soldier asked of me as I walked up the boat's ramp. Nalithor's head turned slightly, but his hair still obscured his face.

"I noticed they'd been following us since we left the city." I tucked my hands into my pockets. "They seemed as though they were just as displeased with the beast as I was. Though, that could just be an assumption on my part."

"Leaping off the boat like that was terribly reckless." Nalithor looked down at me with an unreadable expression as I perched on a bench, keeping my back to the water. "You really are a creature of instinct, aren't you?"

"My instincts are the only reason I'm still alive, you know." I shrugged, watching the Adinvyr take a seat to my right, "I apologize if my lack of patience troubled you, Nalithor, Eyrian. Seeing so many people brought to fight such a weak beast frustrated me."

"*Weak*?" Eyrian exclaimed. "You consider *that* weak?"

"Oh yes. Most definitely." I nodded, crossed one leg over the other, and folded my hands in my lap. "Although it can be annoying to locate its heart or brain, it's still the easiest type of beast to deal with in X'shmir. Unlike most of the others, these don't have an exoskeleton or otherwise thick hide. As such, they're quite easy to rip apart with magic, weapons, or even your hands. There is one other type of 'squishy' beast in X'shmir but they're much more dangerous to fight."

"Nali, she thinks that was *easy*." Eyrian looked at the chuckling

Adinvyr in disbelief. "Just...just what kind of beasts do you *have* up there?!"

I grinned at Eyrian. "I would argue that they're more pleasant than the X'shmirans at least."

"You handled your darkness quite fluidly." Nalithor's remark made me turn to look at him in surprise. "Despite bring a mage you opted for more physical attacks. Yet you have at least three elements within your control, that I'm aware of, and you only utilized one of them."

"I have to leave *some* surprises." I laughed, shaking my head. "You may have seen three quarters of my repertoire, in limited usage, but you have yet to learn how I typically wield them in combat."

"Now I really *am* curious." Nalithor smiled. "I really must take the time to sit in on your test of power."

"You told Darius that you were already assigned to preside over our tests." I motioned at him, my tone sly.

"I may have stretched the truth a little." Nalithor chuckled and caught my hand, bringing it up to his lips with a playful glint in his eyes. "I'm not entirely certain which of you it is...but one of you will most likely break the testing equipment. Judging by the power you two released when you removed your seals, anyway."

"Well, Darius has no control." I attempted to reclaim my hand, gently, as my pulse sped up. Nalithor just smirked at me and tightened his grip. "I take it we have no other beasts to kill?"

"That wasn't enough?" Nalithor lowered my hand from his lips and then turned his head to look at Eyrian. "I think it's high time we put an end to Darius' selfishness, don't you?"

"You think he'd try to keep her from joining the celebration of a successful hunt?" Eyrian made a sour face and motioned at the hand Nalithor was still gripping. "Are you ever going to let her go?"

"I'm not inclined to." Nalithor chuckled.

"What celebration?" I looked between the two Devillian men. "And why should I go?"

"Our hunt was successful, and no one was injured or killed." Nalithor smiled, finally letting me retrieve my hand. "Such occasions are always celebrated in some form. It's a part of my culture that has rubbed off on the rest of Vorpmasia."

"You did most of the work, Arianna." Eyrian added, motioning at me before sitting to my left, "Although you're not *required* to attend...we would like you to."

"I'm not going to accept your brother's excuses anymore," Nalithor added haughtily as I fidgeted with my hood. "When we arrive tonight, if he is still pulling his selfish shenanigans, I will come find you and you can tell me yourself if you don't wish to join us."

"But—" I started to protest, looking up at Nalithor, but he just looked down at me with another of his warm smiles.

"Think about it," Nalithor offered. "I'd imagine you're quite bored. This would be an excellent chance for you to alleviate your boredom *and* learn about the culture of your potential comrades."

'Potential comrades huh?' I looked away from Nalithor and stared blankly at my hands. *'What a strange notion. I almost forgot that if I'm not assigned classes I'll have to work with a partner. Still, why would he speak of me as a "potential comrade" after I tried to…'*

I shut my eyes and tried to still my thoughts as they circled back to this morning's events. Nalithor had, at first, looked so hurt by my attempt to slay him. That expression of hurt had turned to one of approval, and I just couldn't wrap my head around it. Did he *want* me to kill him? That was even worse. But it didn't seem like that was case.

Perhaps Djialkan would know.

CHAPTER SEVEN
A Surprising Loan

I stared up at the starry sky from where I lay in the grass, too irritated to appreciate what would have been a lovely scene on any other occasion. Darius really knew how to be an asshole. After returning from slaying the beast I had bathed and then found proper clothing to wear to dinner tonight. However, my brother hadn't hesitated in the slightest to make me feel utterly unwanted once he realized I didn't intend to stay at the house for the evening.

"I can devour him for you," Djialkan offered from his perch on my stomach.

"That's alright. He probably tastes terrible." I reached out and stroked Djialkan's scales. "Really though… It's obvious now why Darius is acting like this, isn't it?"

Djialkan snorted, nodded, then laid his head down on my stomach. It was annoying, but Darius was clearly trying to keep me away because of his own interest in Nalithor. Darius had been enraged when I returned to the house with Nalithor's scent clinging to me. I'd never seen him enter such a jealous fit before, let alone accuse me of encroaching on "his territory".

I just wanted to get out of the house and enjoy our new surroundings for once. Despite all my tough talk I did want to at least *attempt* making some friends here. Perhaps I was a bit pickier than my brother was. Nevertheless, in a country where Humans were the minority, it wasn't difficult for me to find interesting opponents if I paid attention. Aside from Nalithor and Eyrian there were plenty of strong individuals in Dauthrmir that could be interesting.

'I wonder why he blew his lid.' I stared up at the twinkling stars and tapped my foot against the air. *'Is it because I chose one of my prettier sets of robes? Does he really believe I'm trying to fight him for Nalithor's attention?'*

The clothing I wore was elegant, not revealing. It was still technically Umbral Mage attire, but it was more like a dress than robes. My usual vulpine embroidery was still prevalent along the hems of the sleeves and skirt. However, unlike my X'shmiran style robes, my throat and cleavage were revealed by a tasteful but deep neckline.

Even though Darius threw a tantrum, he hadn't ordered me to

hide my skin again. Perhaps he had taken Nalithor's demands more seriously than I thought. That, at least, was an improvement.

'It's a shame I still have to hide my hair in these gods-damned hoods… At least the gloves are gone?' I sighed, reaching up to fidget with my mask and hood alike. *'Djialkan, you sensed what happened this morning between Nalithor and I, right? Why wasn't he enraged?'*

'Adinvyr nearly kill each other all the time whilst sparring.' Djialkan cackled. *'Nalithor is one of the oldest Adinvyr, after his parents. There are few close enough in power to prove him with such a challenge. Once he was satisfied you did not truly wish to slay him it is likely he approved of your display of combat prowess. That he painted your lips with his own blood is another sign of his approval…amongst other things.'*

'So that *wasn't just some strange whim?'* I arched an eyebrow. *'"Other things?"'*

'That and the fact he trusted you to heal the wound you inflicted.' Djialkan gave me a brief nod. *'Perhaps he is still testing you. I am unsure. Since he has given you permission to address him by his given name it is difficult to determine his intentions.'*

I paused my fidgeting and listened for footsteps when I detected Nalithor's scent nearby. While I wasn't exactly *trying* to hide, I did choose a rather secluded area of the district to sulk in. There was a gap in one of the walls that surrounded the Sapphire Quarter, and I had slipped through it, so I could look out across the lake and at the sky with an unobscured view. I wasn't too terribly close to the drop off, at least.

'Ah, but this is where I fell asleep last night.' I pouted when realization hit me. *'He must've known exactly where to look for me.'*

"So, this *is* where you were hiding." Nalithor spoke in Draemiran, causing me to glance to my right and watch his approach. "The boy claimed he didn't know where you had run off to but, judging by Djialkan's expression, that is not the case."

Nalithor wore black Umbral Mages' robes again instead of his white ones. These were in the Draemiran-style, consisting of loose layers of embroidered kimono, and were clearly meant for nobility or royalty. I was beginning to get the feeling he disliked covering his torso because even the regal set gaped open to reveal a considerable amount of his muscular body. The inner layer of fabric was a near-perfect match to his eye color.

"Humph. I will be back at the house, Arianna." Djialkan snorted and disappeared in a puff of violet smoke.

"Yes, well, I decided that cool air *might* help me refrain from slugging my brother in the face." I looked back up at the sky for a moment before sitting up and shifting my attention fully to the Adinvyr. "However, I was not *hiding*."

"I would certainly hope not. You didn't even cover up your scent. You really do speak Draemiran well, don't you?" Nalithor chuckled, shifting back to the common tongue and offering me his hand. "Looking like *that*... I hope you don't intend to remain reclusive."

"I can't promise that I won't knock my brother on his ass." I accepted Nalithor's hand, noticing that he seemed to relax slightly in response. "However, I *did* decide I'm sick of him acting like a spoiled brat."

"As distressing as his 'spoiled prince' act is," Nalithor pulled me to my feet with a smile and then raised a hand to cup my face, "I would say you've more than earned the right to some good food, good drink, and a friendlier atmosphere. They've all gone on ahead. We can take our time joining them if you prefer, or I can carry you if you want to catch up to them."

"Are...you looking for an excuse to carry me again?" I asked, surprised, as a playful smirk stretched across his mouth. "Really! Is my height, or lack thereof, really so fascinating?"

"It's quite strange to see such a tiny woman fight a beast in the way you do." Nalithor grinned and withdrew his hand, offering me his arm instead. "You may be around the average height for a female Human, but Adinvyr women are half a foot taller than you on average...and fight much less aggressively than what you've displayed."

"So, I'm an oddity," I spoke sarcastically, accepted his arm, and then let him lead me back to the Sapphire Quarter proper.

"I prefer the term 'rarity,'" Nalithor countered. "I must admit I'm curious—you had to ask your brother for permission to show skin even after my...*confrontation* with him? What of your hair?"

"As far as my hair is concerned, that's a rule for a X'shmiran princess." I shook my head. "Princesses aren't supposed to show any skin from the jaw down and are required to keep their hair covered. Since that isn't possible with most armor sets, for obvious reasons, I'm required to ask my brother for permission since he's the 'Holy Mage.'

"In regard to my clothing... He neglected to tell me the specifics regarding what I could wear. I wasn't asking for his permission this time, I was asking for elaboration."

"Ahhh... It's so strange to me that X'shmiran law requires such an obviously beautiful woman to cover herself in such a way." Nalithor sighed. I felt my face ignite. "In Draemir we celebrate the male and female physique, yet X'shmir seems to be the exact opposite."

"Aye, X'shmiran laws are prudish." I laughed, looking up at Nalithor. Hopefully I could turn our conversation away from flattery, I wasn't sure how to handle his attention. "If you would like a better understanding of our laws and customs, I have plenty of books on the matter. I know you said that you would like to *discuss* such matters with me but reading first might be faster."

"Oh?" Nalithor tilted his head, his expression intrigued. "From what I saw in my short time there, books seem uncommon in X'shmir."

"Most of them were locked away in the palace vaults so that poor, innocent citizens wouldn't be corrupted," I spoke in a mock-innocent tone and then grinned slyly. "I assure you that I acquired them through entirely innocent means."

Nalithor grinned, laughing, and flashed his full set of fangs. His genuine amusement, perhaps even delight, came as a surprise to me. Nalithor seemed oblivious to everyone we passed, and I had no idea how to feel or react to having *anyone's* undivided attention, but especially his. Not only was my brother lusting after him, but Nalithor was a deity of high enough rank that he wasn't even fazed by a *Godslayer*. After all, how was that even possible? Was the name of the weapon inaccurate?

'Perhaps I'm a little oblivious to our surroundings as well.' I realized, glancing around briefly to find that we'd already arrived in the Merchants' District. *'Well I do consider him "distracting" for a reason...'*

"You wouldn't mind lending them to me?" Nalithor asked with a smile. "I would certainly welcome a chance to better understand what makes X'shmir tick."

"I don't mind." I shook my head. "I'm not very good at explaining X'shmiran ways from scratch. So, I'm sure the books will be more informative than me. At minimum it should help you ask me the right questions. That aside... Aren't we a little close to the 'Scarlet District?'"

"That's right." Nalithor shot me an entertained look. "The restaurant we're going to is between the Scarlet and Merchants' Districts. Establishments with lavender lanterns are the ones that provide innocent entertainment, arts, and good food. The ones with the scarlet lanterns are the ones you want to avoid if you're not looking for…company."

I fell silent and let the Adinvyr lead me to a rather large establishment with tiers of enameled architecture that I didn't recognize. We were greeted by several kimono-clad men and women who shooed us upstairs to the top floor where everyone else was waiting for us. Nalithor seemed to notice my nervousness and shot me another smile before politely asking an employee to slide the door open for us.

"Ah, Rely'ric!" Darius called cheerfully. I bit back the urge to hide behind Nalithor when Darius spotted me. My brother's expression fell slightly as he narrowed his eyes at me. "Ari? You didn't trouble Nalithor, did you?"

"What are you talking about, boy?!" Eyrian asked with a raucous laugh, smacking Darius on the back. "This wouldn't be a celebration without the star of the party here!"

Nalithor had twitched slightly in response to Darius' rather rude question but, instead of commenting, he led me to the large low table that Eyrian, Darius, and several men I didn't know were seated around. I ended up situated between Nalithor and Eyrian, much to Darius' clear displeasure. However, I couldn't tell which of the Devillians my brother was more jealous over.

"Isn't this place pretty, Ari?" Darius adopted his bright, cheerful facade once more. "It's one of the best Draemiran-style establishments in the city!"

"Darius-zir, please, you flatter us!" A waitress exclaimed, blushing brightly. Somehow, she must have *intentionally* blushed, as her words were an exaggeration at best. "Please, let us know if there is anything we can get you or your guests."

"Ari, tea?" Darius inquired.

"That would be a good start, yes." I clasped my hands together in my lap and tried to compact myself between the two large Devillian men as best I could.

"Don't drink?" Eyrian asked, causing me to glance up at him.

"Only *with* or *after* food," I answered dryly as the Draekin reached for his own glass of strong-smelling liquor.

"A proper lady at the dinner table and a predatory beast in battle?" Nalithor asked slyly.

"Something like that," I answered with a small smirk, ignoring my twin's glare.

I fell silent and listened to the men around me talk, choosing to remain quiet and absorb information instead of attempting to chime in. Soon enough tea was brought to me and I sipped it while studying the eclectic gathering. Nalithor and Eyrian's company was decidedly pleasant, though I still wasn't entirely comfortable with sitting between them. The rest of Darius' friends, however, appeared uninterested in even introducing themselves to me.

'Didn't their families every teach them manners?' I buried my grimace in my cup, then glanced to the side. *'Is it my imagination, or is Nalithor getting closer?'*

Listening to the motley group made me realize just how strong Nalithor's accent was compared to the others. Everyone present had their own unique accent but, aside from Nalithor, everyone else's was diluted and only present on certain words or syllables.

Nalithor was easy to understand, at least, but his accent combined with his deep, purring voice was both distracting and alluring. Something about the way he sounded gave off a sensual impression. I couldn't determine if it was due to his aura as an Adinvyr or if it was some nuance to his articulation. *'Or maybe I'm losing my mind.'*

"Ari, are you *ever* going to eat your vegetables?" Darius demanded, pointing at my pile of assorted meats.

"Do I *look* like a rabbit to you?" I tugged my bowl of rice closer and shot Darius a glare.

"This is probably why you're so short, you know!" Darius exclaimed, pointing a pair of chopsticks at me.

"What's your excuse then?" I asked with a sly grin. "You're the same height as me."

"At least I'm the better-looking twin!" Darius retorted, his face reddening.

"Well we can't actually prove that, now can we?" I motioned at my veiled mask. "That said, I'm content with my ability to kill things. It's much more satisfying than having a beauty contest with my *brother* of all people."

Darius turned away from me with a shrill huff and returned to conversing with the small group of men to either side of him. The two Devillians beside me, however, seemed like they were struggling to contain their laughter.

Something about Darius' new friends struck me as strange. I couldn't quite place it, but they felt "off." Not like they meant ill, but like they were just...different. For example, the man that I once thought to be a Desert Elf had a different aura compared to the other Elves present. He seemed as if he knew Nalithor and Eyrian quite well, if their banter was anything to judge by, but he didn't *feel* like an Elf, a Devillian, or any other race I was familiar with.

Another male Elf sat between the black-haired not-Elf and my brother. He felt just as strange as the first one did. This paler not-Elf had waist length cherry red hair and pupil-less violet eyes. The rest of the Elves and Devillians near my brother felt normal, and far less powerful.

'What are they?' I studied the not-Elves and then the Elves in turn. Everyone else seemed at ease with the unusual pair so I chose not to pry. Yet.

Once I had my fill of meat and rice, I excused myself from the main table and drifted out onto the balcony adjacent to our room. I set my tea down on the balcony's single, small table and then walked over to the railing, resting my palms against it. Avrirsa's three moons hung high overhead, their soft light illuminating even the narrow pathways of the Scarlet District. It was beautiful, but…it was a bit lonely.

After a few minutes feeling returned to my legs again and I took a seat at the small table. It was much better than kneeling at the table inside, and cooler too. Here, I could cross my legs and look out at the district below, or at the sky above. The Scarlet District didn't seem so bad from my perch.

Better still, I was no longer sandwiched between *those two*. Eyrian turned out to be a rather loud drunk—and highly susceptible to liquor—while Nalithor was quite the opposite. The Adinvyr seemed almost reserved in comparison. *Almost.*

I had noticed the curious glances he kept sending my way throughout dinner, and his disinterest in conversing with my brother or the other guests. Nalithor had kept his hands and tail to himself but there was a glimmer of something like desire in his eyes whenever his attention turned to me. It had been there since our fight this morning and, for the life of me, I couldn't fathom it.

Unlike Nalithor, Eyrian seemed at ease with Darius and his circle of friends. Though, I wasn't sure if that was because of the liquor or not. I would need a lot more alcohol than what the Draekin had consumed before I could be even *half* as friendly with my brother's friends.

"Care to have a drink with me?" Nalithor asked.

I glanced over my shoulder, curiosity getting the better of me. Nalithor held a bottle of bright blue liquid in one hand, and two glasses, similar to wine glasses, in the other. He didn't look at all concerned that I might decline or shoo him away. Quite the opposite.

"Sure, why not." I nodded and then shifted in my seat, watching him sit across from me. Once he was situated, I glanced to my left at the group of Devillians, Elves, and my brother. They were all still inside and raucously drunk. It looked like they were oblivious to the towering Adinvyr's absence.

"You seem confused by your brother's demeanor," Nalithor remarked as he poured us each a copious amount of the bright liquid.

"You determined that despite my mask?" I turned my attention back to the smiling Adinvyr.

"Aside from the fact that you're quite expressive," Nalithor began, offering me one of the glasses, "I can sense your mood to an extent, and I can read your body language. I'm sure we can both agree that I'd be a poor excuse for a warrior, let alone a general, if I couldn't."

"Fair enough." I smiled, nodded, then accepted the glass from him. "My brother's recent bouts of jealousy are unusual. When he wants something, he is usually very straightforward in his attempts to acquire it. He also tends to be quite dependent on me despite his complaints about having me as his escort."

"Yet he's been nothing but jealous since arriving here." Nalithor grimaced, settling back in his seat. "He's gotten upset if a waiter or waitress so much as looks at any of us and gets rather huffy if they draw our attention away from him. Were he an Adinvyr, he would simply solve the matter through combat. However…that clearly isn't in his forte, nor is it his interest."

"He can't let his precious harem be compromised, now can he?" I smirked, my tone dripping with sarcasm.

"Harem…? Gods, I hope not." Nalithor shook his head but he was grinning. "Another thing that separates him from many of my kind if *that* sort of thing intrigues him."

"If that's the case you really will find my books amusing!" I laughed. After watching Nalithor take a swig of his own drink I lifted my glass to my lips and took a small sip. "Oh? It's good…"

"It's a Draemiran spirit," Nalithor offered with a smile, "I had a feeling you liked sweet things. We call it 'mri'lec.' Don't let the sweetness fool you—it is quite strong."

He "had a feeling I liked sweet things?" I wondered before taking another taste of the sweet, citrusy liquor. The beverage didn't bear the familiar sting of alcohol, and it tasted quite light. It was hard to believe that it was strong, but he seemed quite serious. "Well if it ends up being *too* strong, I'll just have to have you take responsibility and carry me home, won't I?"

"Yours or mine?" Nalithor countered with a mischievous smirk, earning a laugh from me. "In all seriousness, may I ask you a personal question?"

"Ask me anything you like," I replied, shifting to switch which legs I had crossed. "I'm rather difficult to offend and I don't mind personal questions."

"I was wondering why you seem so...uneasy would be the word I suppose, in response to being noticed," Nalithor spoke after a moment of contemplation, studying me. "You have the same reaction to being treated like a *person*."

"Oh, that's quite simple." I motioned loosely at my mask and hood, a small smile on my face. "I was expecting *these* to be problematic here. I know that *I* wouldn't trust someone who hides their face all the time. Especially not in battle. Yet most of the people here seem more curious than anything. Well, aside from the handful of rude individuals, anyway."

"I'll admit that I'm suspicious of you on some level, but it isn't because of your mask," Nalithor mused as he swirled his drink around in his glass. Something about the look in his eyes gave me the sense his mind was elsewhere. It was like he was looking through me or past me, not at me.

"Frustrated because you can't nose your way past my barriers anymore?" I smirked at him, watching the look of surprise that crossed his face. "Oh? Did you think you were being sneaky, Nalithor?"

"Actually, yes, I did," Nalithor replied dryly before taking a large gulp of his drink. "What gave me away?"

"I'm on rather high alert thanks to the number of people attempting to brute force their way through." I snorted, causing Nalithor to arch an eyebrow. "They've been trying non-stop since

Darius and I released the seals on our abilities."

"Well," Nalithor chuckled, "aside from *that* problem you...simply don't smell or taste Human. Your brother could pass for one despite his fangs and ears. Humans seem fond of modifying their bodies. Since he smells Human, most of us assumed that was the case. He smells Human enough that we were even willing to dismiss his unusual eyes...but then there's you."

"So, my scent, jewelry, power, what you can see of my appearance," I counted off on my fingers, "combat prowess, my dismissal of Dux-class beasts, and the fact you can't sneak through my barriers? I suppose I can see how that would outweigh mask-driven suspicions."

"You also think like a Devillian, not like a Human," Nalithor added with a small smile, "Well, I should probably say that you think like an Adinvyr, actually. You seem to have a better grasp on instincts, combat, and honor than most of the Devillian species do. Draekin women are close. However, you seem feistier than most of them."

"And less scaly," I offered, earning another laugh from Nalithor. "You've seen that for yourself at least. Ah, but that reminds me. I suppose my Brands are a major red flag too, aren't they?"

"Brands aren't an unusual occurrence here." Nalithor shook his head slightly and then motioned at the glowing marks visible from his throat down. "You must realize there are *many* gods and goddesses, and they have had *many* children. Demigods are not uncommon.

"Aside from them, there are mortals that the Elder Gods have marked as 'candidates' for new roles. The fact that your Brands are bi-colored is what's strange. Brands like ours are anything but common."

"I would hate to be accused of being common." I grinned crookedly. "As much as I would like to claim that I know why I have Brands, let alone bi-colored ones, I really don't know.

"Seeing yours startled me. The X'shmiran tomes and scrolls all claim that Brands of Divinity are *only* white. Other colors are meant to imply corruption."

"I get the feeling that your tomes have a great deal of misinformation in them," Nalithor remarked thoughtfully, refilling both our glasses. "I wonder if they are responsible for some of your brother's more *offensive* offhand comments."

"Quite likely." I nodded. "Aside from that, Darius was raised on a pedestal. Although he's aware of his limitations, he was raised to act and think as if he's better than everyone else. X'shmirans have a rather silly belief that their Astral Mage's purpose is to conquer Avrirsa for them. The fact that we're a city-state aside, Darius is a *healer* not a fighter, and certainly not a conquerer."

"You, however, would make a fine conquerer." Nalithor purred, his tail switching behind him, but I couldn't help but laugh in response.

"Perhaps if I had something or someone worthy of conquering *for*." I shook my head. "As interesting of a concept as it is, that isn't my goal or my purpose."

"You do have a goal, then." Nalithor smiled, that mischievous sparkle in his eyes again. "It must not be something that would harm Vorpmasia if you're willing to mention it so casually. I don't think you've had *that* much mri'lec yet, anyway."

"Until I know who I can trust..." I began thoughtfully, considering what to say. The Adinvyr just looked amused, so I continued, "All I can say is that it has to do with why the sky around X'shmir is violet."

"You're cautious." Nalithor looked approving, but his voice belied his curiosity. "But you're also confident enough in either your ability or your goal that you don't feel the need to hide."

"Both." I grinned. "I may not seem like the bookworm type, at times, but I'm a firm believer that knowledge is power. One of the reasons I came Below with Darius is because I knew I'd exhausted what could be learned in X'shmir, and I knew it was likely that the academy would have books to assist me."

"Speaking of your brother," Nalithor glanced sideways at the room we had come from. "I'm not sure who is more drunk: Eyrian or Darius."

"Darius has little tolerance. Eyrian is just very...loud. I would say my brother is more drunk," I replied, following Nalithor's gaze. "I hope he doesn't intend to carry on like this all the way until our tests."

"You think he will continue with this behavior until the night before the examination?" Nalithor asked, a small frown tugging at his lips.

"Most likely." I nodded. "On some level he believes he's as great as the X'shmirans tell him he is, and that means he thinks a hangover won't affect his results. He's in for a rude awakening once he's actually there."

"And what of *your* tests?" Nalithor inquired with a playful smirk as he motioned toward me, his tail twitching again in that catlike manner of his. "Classes or partner? Dominant, submissive, or 'other?'"

"Although I'm certain there are things for me to work on or learn, I would say partner," I answered with a shrug. "As for the latter, I suppose we'll just have to wait and see, won't we? There's so many differences between Vorpmasia and X'shmir that I'm half expecting to find their views on such personality types differ as well."

"Not going to indulge me?" Nalithor teased, leaning forward on his elbows.

"You haven't earned *that* much indulgence yet," I answered dryly.

"Ahhh... You really do intend to be difficult, don't you?" Nalithor smiled, studying me once more. "I can't say that's a bad thing."

I glanced away from Nalithor instead of responding to him. My rather drunk brother stumbled through the doorway to the balcony and stopped beside our table, resting his palms on it. I stifled a snort and the rest of my irritation by taking another sip of my second glass of mri'lec.

Darius smelled like cheap booze and sweat.

Nalithor nudged me under the table, causing me to glance to the side at him. An amused smirk settled onto his face as he gestured for me to put my glass down. He refilled my drink like the "gentleman" he was, then turned to look at Darius when he made a disgruntled sound.

"Nali!" Darius spoke in a loud, whiny voice. "I need new stuff! Where's—*hic*—good place?"

"'Stuff?'" Nalithor arched an eyebrow.

"He probably means clothes," I offered as my twin nodded furiously. "The climate in X'shmir doesn't get very warm. The current temperature *here* is about as warm as it gets during X'shmiran summers."

"In that case… It depends on what sort of attire you're looking for, Darius." Nalithor turned to look at my brother again. "While I get the distinct impression your sister will look excellent in anything she wears, I get the feeling *you* are terribly particular."

'*Is he* trying *to make Darius more jealous?*' I glanced at the Adinvyr briefly before taking another sip of my drink. '*Or is he attempting to flatter me? I really can't tell with this one.*'

"Sexy stuff!" Darius answered all-too seriously, making me gnaw on the inside of my cheek to keep from laughing. "Tired of all this stupid cloth, and these stupid sleeves, and these stupid layers! But I can't be naked. That'd be too sexy. So—"

"I'm afraid I can't claim to be familiar with what makes a man 'sexy,'" Nalithor interjected dryly, shooting me an amused smirk as I attempted to hide my laughter. "I can certainly recommend some tailors to you and leave instructions with your considerably more sober sister."

"How—*hic*—the hells are *either* of you sober drinking that...that...*stuff?*" Darius demanded, wobbling as he pointed at the bottle of mri'lec. "Besides, Ari looks like she's actually h—*hic*—happy or enjoying herself. She *must* be drunk if th—*hic*—the case! Or did you manage to kill a beast on the balcony without destroying half the—*hic*—building in the process?"

"I think it's time for you to go sleep it off, Darius." I shook my head at my brother. "I'm sure one of your nameless *friends* over there can see you back to the house while I finish up business with Nalithor, hmmm?"

"Don't you dare sleep with him!" Darius stated firmly but his wobbling made it more comical than threatening, causing me to start laughing again. "You're—"

"That's enough out of you, Darius." One of the men from before shook his head and grabbed hold of my brother. "Come on, you *definitely* need to sleep it off."

"Business is it?" Nalithor inquired in a strange tone. I turned toward him as my brother and the other men disappeared through the doorway. He'd suddenly become difficult to read again. I couldn't tell if Nalithor was insulted, hurt, or if it was something else.

"Well, you seemed interested in my books," I began in a conversational tone, "so I thought perhaps this would be a good opportunity to loan them to you. Besides, if I told Darius I wanted to stay at least a little longer he would throw a fit like you wouldn't believe."

"Don't want to make your precious brother angry?" Nalithor scoffed.

I paused and looked at Nalithor again, examining his expression—or lack thereof—and his posture. *'Is that...is that jealousy I'm sensing?'*

"Considering the way Darius has been acting, I don't want any further headache from him." I turned to fully face the Adinvyr. "Your company is significantly more enjoyable than his. It seems like he desperately wants you to himself, though. Getting rid of him peacefully seemed like the better option."

"Getting rid of him, hmmm?" Nalithor smirked at me and leaned forward to tug my hood further over my flushed face. "Tsk, tsk, tsk. If you really wanted to fight Darius for my attention, I'm sure you wouldn't have any qualms about putting him in his place. Mmm... What's holding you back?"

"First of all, *if* I wanted to compete with my brother for something there would be no contest," I replied pointedly, ignoring Nalithor's victorious smirk. "Secondly, Darius may not have realized it, but *I* have noticed that you're simply tolerating his presence for the most part. Therefore, if I *do* decide you're worth my interest, I… What? What's *that* look for?"

"You really do think like one of us," Nalithor replied. "It's amusing that you notice things so clearly when your brother does not. I thought I was hiding my displeasure quite well."

"I try to make up for Darius' lack of observation skills." I shook my head. "It seems he certainly has a way of invading conversation even without being here himself."

"You're right about that." Nalithor laughed. "Tell me, then. These books of yours. Are they all of X'shmiran publication?"

"That's just it, no one knows who penned them." I settled back in my seat and swirled my drink around its glass. "Yes, I said *penned*. They're all hand-written books and scrolls. Even though there's no indication as to who wrote them, the X'shmiran people believe everything the books teach until proved otherwise.

"A prime example of this would be how terrified and antagonistic our people were when we first came into contact with the Vorpmasian cartographers."

"I hear they were petrified." Nalithor watched me, his expression still unreadable. "From what I heard they were frightened of the Elves as well."

"That's correct." I grinned, tilting my head as I examined Nalithor in turn. "It's one of the few cases where the citizens were desperate enough to come beg me to kill something."

"And yet you didn't." Nalithor narrowed his eyes at me. "Why?"

"They weren't interesting enough for me to bother with," I replied, crossing my arms. Nalithor's expression relaxed as he laughed.

"And yet you challenged *me*." A sly grin settled on Nalithor's face. "I hope I'm not too much for you. I would rather like to spar you again."

"Honestly? I haven't decided what to think of you yet." I let my eyes wander down the Adinvyr's exposed chest, lingering on where I'd injured him in our previous fight. "I've had little interaction with you since arriving... So, I suppose you could say I'm still sizing you up."

"Or rather you 'haven't decided my worthiness' yet?" Nalithor smirked, and I grinned back at him. "Are you sure you just haven't been dealing with too many challengers yourself?"

"No challengers." I shook my head. "I haven't exactly been out of the house much aside from training and a few trips to the library. Thus far no one has been foolish enough to interrupt me."

"Oh? You haven't been making yourself available?" Nalithor chuckled. "I suppose I can see that."

"I have to admit that I'm surprised you want to spar with me again after what happened this morning." I frowned but Nalithor grinned again, this time broad enough to show his full sets of fangs. "You would have been well within your rights to execute me—"

"Had you actually intended to kill me... I might have," Nalithor interjected, amused. "However, your desire for slaughter was clearly directed elsewhere. I am familiar with such slips and the fact you reined yourself in with such ease is admirable.

"That you were able to get the upper hand against me in a purely physical match is reason enough for me to wish for more sparring matches with you."

"Still..." I trailed off as Nalithor shook his head at me. *'He's male, and Devillian. I shouldn't have been able to get the best of him. How in the hells did I manage to pin him?!'*

"I really am going to have to teach you Draemiran ways," Nalithor remarked. "You think so much like one of us that I keep forgetting you're not. For now...suffice to say that I don't intend to abandon such an interesting sparring partner."

"At least I can't accuse you of running from a challenge," I commented, watching as the playful swishing of his tail hastened. "Rather, you look as if you'd like to challenge me to another sparring match *now*."

"That is one of the many options I've considered, yes." Nalithor purred. He set his empty glass down on the table and then rose to his feet before continuing, "It is getting late, however. I assume you keep your texts at your house?"

"Actually, no." I accepted the hand Nalithor offered me and let him pull me to my feet. "I keep all of them in my shrizar. I'll give you three guesses as to why."

"Mmm…" Nalithor pulled me close to his chest. "You…really aren't frightened by me in the slightest, are you?"

"Why would I be—?" I attempted to pull away from him, but he just chuckled and slid an arm behind my back, pressing me tighter against his torso.

"I thought perhaps you were intimidated by me and *that* was why you've shown so little interest. It isn't uncommon," Nalithor replied. Something about his amused smirk made me fidget more than his proximity did. "But no…you are genuinely attempting to judge if I'm worth your attentions aren't you, Arianna?"

Nalithor chuckled to himself and released me so that he could head for the door. I watched the sway of his long hair and tail for a moment while trying to think of a response. He wasn't wrong, but he wasn't quite right either. It wasn't that simple.

"Does *that* frustrate you too?" I shook my head and then moved to follow him.

"Perhaps." Nalithor offered me his arm once I caught up to him. The mischievous glint in his eyes and the swaying of his tail made me hesitate. "Shall we? I would hate to be accused of keeping a lady out longer than appropriate."

"With a smirk like that I doubt you're worried about what's 'appropriate,'" I countered, accepting his arm. "Nevertheless…

Thank you for the drinks and the pleasant company, Nalithor. Where to now?"

"My rooms and my study are both in the palace," Nalithor offered as he led me downstairs and out into the brisk night air. "You've implied that you have quite a large collection. It would probably be best if you brought them to my rooms yourself. If you're feeling tipsy, I can carry you, of course."

"It takes more than a few drinks to get me tipsy!" I retorted, bristling when Nalithor chuckled. "But yes—my collection isn't small by any means."

"To my study then." Nalithor nodded before proceeding to guide me through the city. "Afterward I will see you home as a *proper* gentleman should."

'A proper gentleman my ass.' I stole a glance at the self-satisfied Adinvyr. *'Ahhh well… He's certainly not boring, at the very least.'*

Most of our walk through the Merchants' District was done in a comfortable silence. However, when we passed several groups of men and women I couldn't identify the species of, Nalithor pulled his arm from mine and slid it behind my back instead. His claws dug into my hip as he pulled me tight against his side, keeping a firm, protective grip on me.

The people we passed seemed to be something "other," but they didn't strike me as Elven or Human either. Like two of Darius' "friends" these people were just…different. I couldn't place it, and it annoyed me. Nalithor released a low growl as we passed more of them, but he offered no explanation for his sudden and protective behavior.

'Is there something I should know about those people?' I asked, my curiosity finally getting the better of me. Nalithor's grip on my hip twitched. I glanced up to find an expression of surprise on his face, but he was quick to hide it.

'They are Vampires.' Nalithor refocused his gaze forward and away from me. *'Although we are currently allied with the Beshulthiens, our relationship with their empire is strained at best. Like Adinvyr, Vampires must feed to survive. However, they can only feed on blood, and their practices are not as disciplined as ours. They have no qualms about using their power to force their prey into submission.'*

'And your kind takes a different approach?' I probed, arching an eyebrow when Nalithor's grip twitched again.

Nalithor glanced down at me, looking as if he was about to ask if I was serious, but instead closed his mouth and sighed. *'That's right...until we came along, you'd never seen or heard of Vampires in X'shmir. Come. This way, they shouldn't follow us through the District's main streets.'*

'So, they are hunting us.' I looked over my shoulder and then up at Nalithor as he hastened his pace.

'Adinvyr prefer genuinely willing *partners.'* Nalithor's voice was much firmer than his grip. *'If we are in dire need we are permitted to use our power to draw in prey. However, we can absorb the energy*

we require from the atmosphere that surrounds places such as the Scarlet District.'

'The Vampires are required to always feed on blood?' I asked, watching Nalithor nod in confirmation.

'Vampires were created by the former God of Chaos, Kalenek. The First Exile.' Nalithor's grip relaxed a little as we moved onto the main thoroughfare. 'Due to the Elders' own convoluted laws, Vampires were accepted as a legitimate species instead of being slaughtered as abominations. Unlike the Chaos Beasts. My role as a deity makes it difficult to accept the Vampires regardless of the Elders' claims.'

'Well Devillians smell better than Vampires do at any rate,' I observed dryly, earning a rumbling chuckle from the Adinvyr. "What? It's true! They smell like—'

'You smell far better than either,' Nalithor teased, smirking, before turning his attention upwards. 'Do you sense it?'

'We're being followed again,' I acknowledged with a slight nod as Nalithor's tail coiled around my waist and hips several times over. 'They don't appear very friendly.'

'Will you permit me to carry you to the palace now?' Nalithor's tone and expression were both serious when he looked down at me.

'Oh? I thought it would be more interesting to put them in their place...' I murmured distractedly, slipping a few tendrils of my power into the deep shadows behind us. 'Or... Ah. Beshulthiens, right? Should we not kill them?'

'I can't let you ruin such a wonderful dress, now can I?' Nalithor laughed and squeezed me with his tail, but I sensed his bloodlust rising. *'They do appear to be particularly vile ones, don't they?'*

'They're like the criminals I sought out and executed in X'shmir,' I stated, earning a startled look from the Adinvyr. *'If you're not going to kill them, I will* gladly—'

'And let you have all the fun, my dear?' Nalithor purred and slipped both of his arms around me, pulling me back against his chest. He tightened his grip when I tried to squirm away. Once I gave up, he turned to face the encroaching Vampires.

"Do you have a good reason for tailing a god and his *prey?*" Nalithor's dangerous tone made me shiver.

'Prey huh?' I glanced up at Nalithor briefly before fixing my gaze on the startled Vampires. They looked as if they hadn't expected us to notice their presence.

"We just want the woman," one of the Vampires snarled. "With a scent like that... She's wasted on a pampered little demigo—"

The Vampire must have struck a nerve because, quicker than I could blink, his head had been removed with a single stroke of darkness. I wrinkled my nose in displeasure when the scent of blood reached my nose. The growing pool of dark red liquid blotted out the faint glow of the crystalline road beneath the now-lifeless corpse. I could only describe the scent as "wrong." Unlike the scent of Nalithor's blood, there wasn't anything alluring or appetizing to me about *this* scent. Nor did it have the metallic tang of Human blood. It reminded me vaguely of the blood of beasts.

"I really can't stand filth like you." Nalithor growled over my head and pulled me tighter against him. "All you *creatures* care about is your next *meal* isn't it?"

Instead of responding, the remaining Vampires released feral screeches and rushed us. Nalithor remained icy and calm. Before I could make a move to destroy them myself, Nalithor's power rushed past me and tore each of the Vampires asunder. He didn't even give them a chance to draw near enough for the blood spatter to reach us. I blinked a few times, staring at the corpses, and then sighed. No matter how I tried, I couldn't place what was so *wrong* about them. And now I didn't get to play with them, either.

'Not even a little fear?' Nalithor's question made me shift my attention upwards at him. *'Most people would be at least a* little *adverse to such bloodshed…and to the power of a god.'*

'I see nothing to be averse to now that they're dead—though you could have left me one.*'* I shrugged and moved to free myself from Nalithor's grip. *'With them gone, we can now head—?'*

I yelped, startled, when Nalithor suddenly dipped down and scooped me into his arms. Six pairs of black feathered wings sprouted from his back mere moments before he sprung into the air. Clearly whatever patience he'd had left was gone after the Vampires' antics. I turned my face into his chest and pulled my hood into place with my free hand, hiding from the wind while also trying not to inhale too much of his scent. He was far, far too distracting, especially after drinks.

"You're so easy to tote around," Nalithor teased, landing on one of the palace's balconies. He set me down with care, shot me a cheerful smile, and then strode toward the sliding doors nearby. "I'm going to have to make sure no one else carries you off, aren't I?"

"I still can't decide which one of us those creatures actually wanted a taste of," I deflected with a huff, crossing my arms. "I'm not the only one they were examining like meat.

"Does their blood always smell so vile?"

"You noticed as well?" Nalithor questioned as he unlocked the doors. After sliding them open he pivoted and offered me a hand. "In short, they were likely drugged on something. They usually aren't so barbaric unless starved. That they would consider taking a bite out of a deity—let alone a Devillian one—is stranger still."

Nalithor escorted me into the warmth of what was quite obviously his rooms. I tried to hide my curiosity as I glanced around the suite, taking in the varied black, sapphire, and sky-blue décor. The styling of his furniture, the fixtures, and even the decorations were all much different from what I'd seen in other parts of the palace.

Orbs of pale blue-white Magefire hovered in the room, casting a cool glow across everything. It struck me as strange that Nalithor chose to light the room with his magic instead of relying on the

Magitech fixtures, but I certainly wasn't complaining.

"This is part of my study." Nalithor strode through the large room, motioning around us at the floor-to-ceiling bookshelves. "I have some free space along the shelves over here. Just how large is your collection?"

"You have your own library." I arched an eyebrow, following the Adinvyr. "I think 'study' is a little too humble—especially if this is only a 'part' of it."

"I spend a lot of time reading." Nalithor smiled and moved out of my way, leaning back against a chair. He watched my approach before continuing, "Unfortunately there is little else that holds my interest when I'm not training my men or hunting."

"I can relate." I opened my shrizar and summoned just over three dozen books. "Even before I was recognized officially as an Umbral Mage there was very little that could keep me entertained. The piano and reading were just about the only things that could hold my attention."

"You play?" Nalithor's strange tone made me glance at him as he moved to stand beside me. His expression was passive as he snatched one of the books out of the air. "Ah… That's right. You *did* mention music in a rather eloquent manner in your letter."

"I'd recommend starting with this book, not that one." I pulled down another tome and offered it to the Adinvyr. "Most of them are dated and should be read in chronological order. I've slipped notes with date estimates into the covers of the few that are lacking identifiers."

"This…isn't paper." Nalithor frowned, flipping through the first book for a moment before setting it down and accepting the one I'd offered him. "The scent is reminiscent of…"

"Beast hide," I confirmed, watching Nalithor's eyes widen slightly. "The few books that have been reproduced from these are transcribed by hand onto paper. However, these—"

"You're loaning me the originals?" Nalithor asked in disbelief. I simply looked up at him with slight surprise in response to his tone. "Aren't you concerned that—?"

"Only the more recently penned tomes are actually in circulation to the public." I shook my head. "The rest of them are the ones I mentioned *acquiring* from the castle vaults."

"One moment you sound like an Adinvyr, the next you sound like a tricksy Rylthra," Nalithor spoke dryly, snapping the book shut. He set the book down and then braced an arm on the shelves above my head, leaning down to examine me. "Can I convince you to stay and speak with me for a little longer before I see you home? I would like to make certain that there aren't any other Vampires searching for you…and I'm sure you would rather wait until Darius has passed out in a drunken stupor."

"No convincing required." I laughed. "As long as I'm not imposing or keeping you from your work. I certainly wouldn't mind your company for a while longer."

Nalithor shot me a small smile as he moved away and toward

a large desk at one end of the room. "In that case, would you like some tea, or more mri'lec? Either way, I insist on escorting you home myself, so pick whichever you like."

'The Vampires are that big of a concern?' I perched on a nearby chair and watched the Adinvyr carefully. *'Still, I can't claim that I mind his company…quite the opposite.'*

CHAPTER EIGHT
Annoyances

'I should have known Vampires would take interest in Arianna. Are they watching Darius as well?' I stalked through the palace's corridors at a brisk pace. My tail thrashed behind me as I thought on the previous night. Although I hadn't sensed more Vampires when I escorted the princess back to her residence, that they had shown themselves at all troubled me.

'Rabere isn't bold enough to send them. He may be a bastard, but the Alliance is as necessary to him as it is to us. He wouldn't jeopardize his empire's relations.' I grimaced, hurrying down the palace stairs and towards Lucifer's throne room. *'Nor should they have been interested in* my *blood—unless they were genuinely suicidal—but that didn't seem to be the case.'*

When I came to the grand entry hall I paused for a moment, surveying my surroundings. *Her* scent lingered there, and it was recent. As pleasant as her company was, and grateful as I was for the books she had lent me, I wasn't certain why she was there so early in the morning. Darius' scent was nonexistent beneath that of his sister's, but I knew he was there. He, at least, was scheduled to be.

'Who lured the vixen from her den?' I reached out to Eyrian and picked up my pace. *'And who convinced the brat to allow his sister to join him?'*

'She's difficult to deal with and isn't here by choice.' Eyrian snorted. *'Lucifer had me fetch her when our men went to escort Darius-zir to the palace for our meeting. He was quite insistent that she needed to be here to meet with the Families as well.*

'I think he suspects, Nalithor.'

I frowned. *'Lucifer called for her?'*

"General Vraelimir," a guard called as I neared the throne room doors. "Lucifer-y'ric moved the meeting to the Mrifon Chamber at the Oracles' behest. The boy is not prepared for His Excellency's...ah...*trophies*."

"Of course he's not." I sighed, bringing my fingers to my temples. "Have Archmagus Leukos contact me as soon as he's able. There are important matters I need to discuss with him after todays' meeting is over.

"Send someone to triple the city's patrols while you're at it."

"Sir?" The guard just looked at me for a moment before saluting me again. "As you command, General."

I nodded to the guard before taking off through the halls of the palace once more. It didn't surprise me in the least that the Oracles had the meeting moved from the throne room. Darius was opposite enough to his sister that, even without poking around in the brat's head, I assumed he likely had an aversion to blood and gore.

Lucifer's trophies were like to make the boy ill.

'If the Oracles are sitting in, I may take a head or two as trophies for myself.' I snorted and shook my head before crossing my arms in my sleeves.

'It isn't like you to be late, Nalithor.' Eyrian coughed as if it would make his point clearer.

'The princess kept me up late,' I retorted, smirking when my friend snarled in response. *'Not in the way you are thinking, I assure you. Her Highness attracted some rather nasty creatures on our way back from dinner last night.*

'I will be speaking with Xander about them as soon as possible.'

'Vampires?' Eyrian questioned, unease filling his presence. *'While you were with her?'*

'She wasn't the only one they wanted a taste of,' I answered.

A grimace settled on my face as I neared the Mrifon Chamber. Arianna's scent hung so thick in the air that I couldn't even smell the emperor anymore. Her power clung to the shadows in the hallway, giving them life and making them ripple and shift like water. It was as if she noticed my presence before anyone else did.

'What—?' I began.

'Difficult to deal with,' Eyrian reiterated, his tone dry.

I smoothed my expression before pushing open the doors to the Mrifon Chamber. The thick smoke from the Oracles' incense coiled out of the room and drifted past me into the hallway but, for once, I could barely discern its cloying scent. How Arianna's scent managed to drown out that of Lucifer, the Oracles and their incense, and the representatives from the Vorpmasian Royal Families was beyond me.

To my dismay, my arrival went unnoticed by those present—except for *her*. I grew still when Arianna's attention and power shifted to me. The almost imperceptible shift of her head let me know that her gaze had focused on me. It was as if a great beast was stalking me, yet it was just the petite woman before me.

The petite woman who was sitting on *my* chair.

"I don't understand why you requested my sister's presence, Your Excellency," Darius' statement made me glance at him with distaste. The boy wrung his hands and shifted from foot to foot as he looked from Arianna and to the Vorpmasian representatives. I wasn't even close to him, yet I could still hear the frantic racing of his heart from across the room.

"For once, I agree with my brother." Arianna shifted her attention away from me but not before shooting me a small smirk.

"Politics aren't my strong suit. *Killing things* is. Unless you want me to tear something to shreds for you, I'm not quite sure why you asked me to join you."

"There's always something or someone we need dead," Lucifer answered dryly. After a moment he cut his eyes to the side at me in a way that almost made me flinch. *'If you try to say they are "fakes" created by the Exiles, I will see to it that you rot somewhere for the rest of time.'*

'I wasn't going to…' I released a small sigh in response to the emperor's firm glare. *'We just need to be careful, regardless of their origins.'*

'You are only fooling yourself at this point.' Lucifer turned in his seat to face Arianna in full. "Your knowledge of, and experience with, the Chaos Beasts is one of the reasons we are willing to work with X'shmir. For us, anything that helps us understand the beasts and get an upper hand against them is a political matter."

"Surely there is some other way to deal with the beasts?" Darius looked a touch green as he ran a hand through his curls. "There must be something—"

"Do *you* want to try talking to one?" Arianna crossed one leg over the other with a flourish and then motioned at her brother. "They breed like rabbits and the Duxes are the size of a commoner's house. What they *want* is *food* and we are the perfect size for them to gobble up.

"They are *creatures*, Darius. Not *people*. Would you be saying the same thing if a pack of wolves overran the city and ate half our population?"

"No, of course not, but they seem intelligent!" Darius protested, stomping his foot. "Fae-dragons and dragons are 'creatures' too, but they're intelligent like you or I!"

"I see beings like Fraelfnir and Djialkan as people *because* they're intelligent like we are." Arianna tilted her head to the side and pursed her lips for a moment. "Besides, you are talking about trying to cooperate with creatures created by *the Exiled Gods*. While *in front of gods*.

"Even if the beasts *are* as intelligent as…say…a Human child. They were created by, and serve, beings who are meant to be punished. Beings who were cast out for neglecting their duties or acting against the Elder Gods."

'She looks like some sort of evil queen, sitting there like that,' I commented, eliciting a snort from Eyrian. *'Whose idea was it to let her take* my *seat? And why is no one protesting her proximity to Lucifer?'*

'Arianna-jiss took one sniff of the room and went for your seat once invited to be seated,' Eyrian answered, rolling his eyes from where he stood behind Lucifer. *'You are right though. She looks like she's just waiting for an opportunity to start ordering executions. That, or make everyone in the room her slave. I'm really not sure which at this point.'*

Darius returned to arguing over something trivial with Lucifer and the other representatives, and I returned my attention to the deadly princess. A small, lopsided smirk settled on Arianna's mouth as she watched me approach. Her full attention returned to me and sent a shiver run down my spine and through my tail. I didn't know what to make of her.

Arianna wasn't even *trying* to be threatening, let alone sensual, yet that was precisely what this woman was. I knew many people who could direct their power as they saw fit, but none of them shared Arianna's effortless aura of bloodlust and sensuality.

'Well, at least someone interesting finally arrived.' Arianna's smirk turned into a smile as she nudged at my thoughts. *'I figured you would be studying the books I lent you.'*

"That is *my* seat, Arianna." I placed one hand on the back of the chair and leaned over her. She didn't look intimidated in the slightest. Instead, her posture remained relaxed as she leaned on one of the armrests. Her legs stayed crossed and the corner of her mouth curled back into a smirk when I growled at her.

"It's quite comfortable," Arianna spoke with mock-innocence.

"While I appreciate you keeping it warm for me, it's high time you vacated it." I narrowed my eyes at her.

"Make me." Arianna grinned and cocked her head. I felt her studying me from somewhere behind that mask of hers.

'Make her...?' My tail snapped behind me as I attempted to read her intentions. "Are you challenging me, *Your Highness?*"

"If the two of you make a mess of the Mrifon Chamber, it is

the Oracles you will have to deal with." Lucifer's amused but dry comment made me shoot him a sideways glance. *'A bit tetchy this morning are you, Nalithor?'*

'You should have sent me *to fetch her,'* I retorted.

'I'm quite capable of handling the princess myself.' Eyrian shot me a strange look. *'What happened to thinking she's a "fake," Nalithor? You were only ever so territorial over the* real *Arianna.'*

'Aye. Acting like that*, you can't truly expect us to believe it isn't her.'* Lucifer's voice took on a dangerous tone once more, even as he returned his attention to the X'shmiran prince.

'I'm...not sure.' I hesitated to answer. *'If the Elders—'*

'To the hells with the Elders.' Eyrian snorted. *'You've never believed them before, so why start now? And, if it* is *her... Don't expect me to just let you have Arianna without a fight.'*

"'Let" me—' I started to snarl at the Draekin, but a sharp yank on my braid made me return my gaze to the small woman that was *still* occupying my chair. She was like a cat that had discovered a most interesting toy. I wasn't going to become her prey. "Humph. 'Make you,' you say?"

Without further warning I lifted the princess into the air with vines of darkness. Arianna's power pushed back against mine with full force, earning her a chuckle. I perched on my now-liberated chair and took my time making myself comfortable. The princess growled at me and squirmed within my darkness, but I wasn't ready to free her quite yet.

"Are you really so bored that you would challenge me here?" I asked, directing a roll of power at the princess. It only came as a mild surprise to me now that the action seemed to not have the desired effect. Instead, she seemed more eager to free herself from my darkness and likely challenge me. *'I want to fight her, but… It wouldn't be appropriate for me to challenge her. Not after the manner in which she bested me.'*

'She probably thinks it isn't right for her *to challenge* you *either,'* Eyrian commented. *'Lucifer has a point though. I don't think any of us want to deal with the Oracles' wrath.'*

"There's room enough for two," I stated, watching as Arianna stopped wriggling and looked to me with parted lips. "Lucifer is right. We shouldn't fight here. However, our antics are disrupting the meeting. *If* you want to challenge me properly, it can wait until after."

"Share? Two? But—" What was visible of Arianna's face reddened when I placed her on the chair beside me. Her legs twitched when I let them rest over my lap. She looked like she wanted to say something but after a moment she turned away from me with a grumble.

"Yrlseyr, please fetch the princess some tea." I looked to the nearby Rylthra servant.

"Of course." The man bowed to me and then looked to the princess. "Black or sweet, Your Highness?"

"Ah. Sweet, please…" Arianna grumbled, lacing her gloved

fingers on her lap. *'Is this position really necessary?'*

'Of course not.' I shot her an amused look. *'However, I'm quite certain you could resituate yourself if you wish. Yet you haven't.'*

'I don't want to accidentally kick you…you know.' Arianna shook her head at me.

"Now then, what have I missed?" I turned to look at Lucifer and the other Devillian dignitaries.

I felt Arianna flinch when Darius pivoted to look at us. The pure contempt on his face gave me pause, causing me to glance to Lucifer and Eyrian. All I received from them was a small shrug in response. They looked as uneasy as I felt. Before I could question the boy, Arianna withdrew her legs from my lap and scooted away from me and as close to the left armrest as she could.

"The X'shmirans are being difficult about repairs and additions to their city." Lucifer made a vague motion with one hand, pulling up an aetheric overview of the crumbling Human city. "The temples, libraries, and schools have long since been dismantled in order to rebuild other sections of X'shmir."

"The king and queen are reluctant to revitalize the city's Magitech." Darius sighed, turning his attention away from his sister. "I won't pretend that their reasoning makes any sense. It's born of ignorance and superstition. The same goes for their concerns with erecting new temples and schools."

"They don't believe gods exist," Arianna added, motioning at me. "To them, temples will be considered a waste of resources and a pandering to ego. As far as schools…the more stupid the populace, the more likely they are to put up with the Royal Family's antics."

'And what do you *believe?'* I hesitated to reach out to her, but the subtle tilt of her head indicated she had heard me. It surprised me that she hadn't shut me out of her thoughts yet. However, I wasn't going to waste the opportunity. *'You have been taught differently than your brother—let alone the rest of the X'shmirans— but you haven't made it quite clear what your thoughts on the matter are.'*

'My thoughts are irrelevant.' Arianna shook her head. *'The king and queen are less than eager to cooperate with non-Humans. Perhaps I shouldn't say this, but it wouldn't surprise me in the slightest if they continue to refuse both temples and schools. I doubt they intend to remain associated with the Rilzaan Alliance for long.'*

'They subscribe to the notion that a highborn Astral Mage is a conquerer?' I chuckled, watching the princess nod. *'X'shmir only ever tolerated us in the past as well. It would seem that they haven't changed much in that regard.'*

"What *I* want to know, is which of the Families is the princess marrying into?" One of the Imviir representatives spoke up.

Arianna twitched hard enough for me to feel it. I caught a small, contained growl from the princess but her brother beat her to speaking.

"I'm afraid Arianna will not be marrying into *any* families, my lord." Darius flourished with one hand and continued. "We've already gone over the way Umbral Mages are treated in X'shmir, but I will expand further: Offering my sister's hand to anyone in the alliance would be our way of declaring war."

"I can't claim I'm adverse to the notion," I commented, feeling Arianna freeze beside me. "Conquering X'shmir seems like a small price to pay for—"

"I agree," Eyrian interrupted, causing me to cut my eyes to the side at him. "Arianna's abilities are wasted on the X'shmirans. We can treat her much better and find interesting challenges to keep her entertained. What does X'shmir provide her with?"

"We…" Darius went pale, his eyes flicking back and forth.

'Honestly. Both *of you?'* Lucifer sighed at us. *'Nalithor,* you *are the one who insisted we shouldn't—'*

"I'm afraid it doesn't work that way." Arianna's voice cut through the air like a blade. "Darius and I are bound to X'shmir in a way that 'conquering' simply can't break. If those bonds are threatened, I will be forced to act."

"Surely you do not *wish*—?" The Akor woman flinched when Arianna shifted her attention toward her.

"I did just *say* I would be *forced* to act, didn't I?" Arianna's tone dripped with venom.

"That's a shame." The Imviir from before shook his head. "I'm quite certain that any one of the Families would be more than happy to welcome you in. Someone so capable of slaying beasts would be—"

"Do you really think the princess is physically capable of bearing your brood?" I growled at the Imviir. "We have been over this time and again with you. Arranged marriages are not condoned in the Empire. The discovery of X'shmir, and this dangerous little one here, does not change that."

"I am not little!" Arianna whirled around with a growl, undoubtedly glaring at me from somewhere beneath her mask. She looked like she was going to say something, or perhaps punch me, but instead she crossed her arms and settled back with a low "humph."

"Back to the temples and schools," Darius said, clearing his throat before continuing, "I'm more than happy to work with you to convince my parents of their importance. That said, repairs to the existing buildings take precedence in my mind. Our remaining Magitech hardly functions, and many of the buildings—"

"Of course, of course," Lucifer spoke, waving his hand. "We don't expect X'shmir to prioritize temples and schools over repairing the city itself. Making the city more habitable comes first."

"Then why the focus on—?" Darius glanced at his sister when she sighed.

"Darius, cities take *planning*." Arianna propped her elbow on the armrest and settled her cheek against her fist. "Repairs and expansion will have to consider both existing architecture and any later additions, such as temples or schools.

"X'shmir has no semblance of districts anymore due to disrepair."

"Ah... I see." Darius frowned, visibly sinking into thought for a moment. "I will do what I can. Unfortunately, I can't think of a way to *prove* to the X'shmiran Court that both schools and temples are a necessity."

'Did you really have to sit me to your left?' Arianna's question surprised me into glancing down at her.

'Is there a problem with sitting to my left?' I frowned at her, perplexed.

Arianna opened her mouth as if to speak but sighed instead, what was visible of her face flushed pink. She looked away from me and nestled her cheek on her fist again. For a moment, I didn't think she was going to answer me.

'Never mind. If you don't know what I'm talking about, ways here are likely different,' Arianna mumbled.

'What is it?' I sighed at her. *'Another X'shmiran quirk that will make me want to rip that rock from the sky, perhaps?'*

'Is there anything about X'shmir that doesn't *make you want to rip it from the sky?'* A small smile twitched across Arianna's lips. *'In X'shmir, whoever sits to the left of royalty is considered... Mmm, how should I put this...'* She tilted her head and drilled the fingertips of her free hand against her thigh for a moment before continuing, *'Perhaps I should start with the right. Whoever sits to the right of*

royalty is someone respected, in a great position of power, or second-in-command. Whoever sits on the left is…the opposite. Disliked at best.'

'Your people truly frustrate me.' I huffed, settling my arm behind the princess' back. *'I allowed you to sit to my left as a show of respect. It seems X'shmiran ways are eager to follow the opposite of our ways…though the right is also a place of power. Just less so.*

'If it bothers you that much, we can switch. However, it may raise questions among the Families.'

'Respect…?' Arianna's attention shifted to me and then back to her lap. *'Didn't I try to kill you?'*

'You're still worried about that?' I arched an eyebrow at her.

"Arianna-jiss, given last night's events, I believe it would be prudent to assign you an escort," Lucifer spoke, shifting Arianna's attention toward him and earning a confused look from Darius. "Although you have proved you're a capable warrior, I do not trust those—"

"An escort? Last night's events?" Darius interrupted, frowning at Lucifer and Arianna in turn. He appeared to miss the aggravated look the emperor shot him.

"Nalithor, you explain. I wish for the Families to hear this as well." Lucifer settled back in his seat and lifted a long pipe to his lips.

"I really don't need—" Arianna began to protest but fell silent when Yrlseyr returned with her tea. The princess accepted it with a quiet "thank you" and remained silent.

I spent the next short while explaining to the families and to Lucifer about the Vampires we had found hunting Arianna and myself. The princess didn't seem concerned about the matter in the slightest, but the same couldn't be said for her brother or for the Families.

If Rabere was behind the Vampires' actions, it would mean war.

"Arianna-jiss, I insist you permit me to assign you and your brother each a personal escort," Lucifer said, his expression one of concern. "Those *creatures* aren't to be trifled with. That something was wrong about them only makes them more dangerous."

"An escort will just get in my way." Arianna shook her head and then rested her cup of tea on her lap. "Darius could use an escort, of course. He's a healer and can't fight."

'Keep an eye on her. Both of you.' Lucifer's firm tone made me bristle. Enough so that the princess seemed to notice it and shifted her attention toward me briefly.

'I will do what I can, Your Excellency,' Eyrian answered with a slight bow. *'Our spies stated that she doesn't often venture far from her residence, but if she does…I will be among the first to know. You wish us to tail her?'*

'If she lets us,' I pointed out with a small sigh, nestling back in my seat. *'I still have a great deal of studying to do. Arianna's collection of X'shmiran texts is much larger than I anticipated. Can you handle her on your own for a time, Eyrian?'*

'I'd be a failure of a hunter if I couldn't find that darkness lurking in the city.' Eyrian motioned subtly at the princess herself. *'Our spies said that Arianna is well-aware of their presence but has made no attempt to conceal herself from them. As long as that continues—'*

"Ari, didn't you say you have a lot of work to do?" Darius turned to look at his sister. "Isn't this eating into your time?"

"Are you saying I should have ignored the *emperor's* summons?" Arianna smirked at her brother as his face reddened. "I'll admit, watching you flounder around does have its own appeal."

"I will not take offense if you wish to return to your work." Lucifer chuckled, a warm smile on his face as he looked at Arianna. "You both have much to do in order to prepare for your entrance exams. Eyrian will see you back to the Sapphire Quarter when you are ready.

"I will call on you again when we have need of something more in your realm of expertise."

'But I *can—'* I tensed and shot Lucifer a glare.

'I need you here *to keep the Families and the boy in check,'* Lucifer spoke dismissively.

"Arianna-jiss?" Eyrian came to stand next to my seat and shot the princess a questioning look.

"I'd rather fight something—or *someone*—but I suppose reading has its own appeal," Arianna answered, her tone dry as she rose to her feet. "It was a pleasure meeting all of you. Do see to it that I'm not left out of any interesting hunts in the near future, alright?"

"*Ari*," Darius groaned.

'The one beast truly wasn't enough?' I prodded Arianna's thoughts, causing her to smirk over her shoulder at me as she followed Eyrian out.

'You underestimate my boredom and *my nature if you think one was* anywhere near *enough,'* Arianna answered. Something about her almost sing-song tone made me tense and shoot her a wary look. She said nothing more and simply pulled all her darkness back to her, leaving the room surprisingly cold.

I went to question her again and was met with the void-like wall she normally kept around her thoughts. I sighed and slumped back in my chair, watching her disappear out of the room with Eyrian.

'Don't worry, I'll make sure the Vampires aren't lurking around their house,' Eyrian answered before I could even speak. *'They were really that "off," Nali?'*

'If they really were sent by my brother, we have more to worry about than his loyalties,' I picked up Arianna's cup and handed it to Yrlseyr. *'Speak to the patrols and academy staff as soon as you're able. I will speak with Xander as soon as I'm free of this meeting.'*

"Rely'ric, will you be sitting in on the exams still?" Darius attempted to sound sultry, but it did absolutely nothing for me.

"Unlikely. It appears that I have much work to do in other

parts of Dauthrmir on that day," I answered with the most bored-sounding tone I could muster. "As much as I hoped to learn more of that delicious sister of yours, I will be unable to. For now."

'Nalithor.' Lucifer shot me a warning look.

'Do you honestly expect me tolerate the boy's futile attempts?' I countered.

'Must you take everything as some form of challenge? The girl isn't even here now!' Lucifer shook his head and then sighed. *'Have you learned anything useful from the X'shmiran texts?'*

'Only that we will have to work harder than originally believed to gain their trust,' I answered, pulling notes from my shrizar. *'These are just some of their misguided beliefs about our kind. It's a minor miracle they're working with us in the first place.'*

'I see...' Lucifer frowned at the paper. *'Compile a list of pertinent information and have copies sent to the ambassadors, scholars, and myself. We need to come up with a way to quell the X'shmiran commoner's unease and reeducate them. Or are you still considering making good on your threat from earlier?'*

'I know better. Arianna has given us some hints of what binds her and her brother to that rock, after all.' I shifted my gaze to Darius, tracking his mannerisms as he spoke with the Family representatives. *'You're certain you need me to remain for this?'*

'You are the Vraelimir representative.' Lucifer reminded me.

I suppressed a sigh. That, at least, was something I couldn't argue with.

CHAPTER NINE
Examinations

The sensation of hands dancing up my inner thighs and fangs buried deep in my throat awoke me with a start, sending me tumbling out of bed in my haste to draw a blade. I looked around the room, my vision still bleary with sleep, then paused. There was no one there. Just me, my nerves, and the distinct sensation of arousal. I took a moment to refocus both my thoughts and vision on reality.

'Really... This again?!'

With a few short curses I rose to my feet, stalked out of my bedroom, and headed for the bath. A scowl crossed my face when I glanced at the clock. I had little time to prepare myself for the day, and no time to work out my near-overwhelming lust.

Today, finally, we would take our tests. Assuming they didn't get pushed back. *Again.*

'How am I supposed to focus on my tests when all I can think about is...?' I let out a shaky sigh and slumped back against the door as fragments of my erotic dream came back to me. My entire body felt like it would ignite, and I wasn't sure if it was from embarrassment, arousal, or both. *'I haven't even seen him naked yet! What am I doing having dreams like* that *about* anyone *here?! Is all this prodding from the city's Adinvyr wearing down my sanity?*

'I shouldn't be thinking of him *doing things like* that *to me... Let alone drinking his blood... I don't know which is worse!'*

I bit my lip hard and shoved the thoughts from my mind to the best of my ability. After a quick bath I hurried back to my room to dress myself.

No matter how I tried, or how hard, I couldn't clear my thoughts. The now-fuzzy image of *his* nude body refused to leave me alone, and my mind kept trying to find ways to see the few parts of him that my imagination hadn't filled in.

I didn't think I was *that* attracted to Nalithor...but my mind clearly begged to differ.

"You are running out of time to find breakfast, you know," Djialkan informed me. *"You enjoyed your date with Nalithor, did you not? Why have you not sought him out for another spar—?"*

"T-that wasn't a date!" I yelped, tripped, and fell on my ass in my haste to glare at both the cackling fae-dragon and the warbling fox.

"You should challenge him again since you have only seen him once since loaning him your books. A sparring match between the two of you will mean more if you initiate it instead," Djialkan continued as if I hadn't said anything. *"I know that today you have your tests to contend with—"*

"Djialkan, I'm still worried about X'shmiran laws." I gave him a pointed look and picked myself off the floor to resume dressing. "I know Corentine said that I shouldn't avoid 'old acquaintances'…but you know as well as I do how harsh those bastards in X'shmir can be."

"Are you avoiding challenging him again because you are concerned that he will misconstrue it as another *form of interest?"* Djialkan's blunt question earned him a brief glare. *"You are drawn to him, are you not? Stop worrying about what your damnable brother and the X'shmirans think. Nalithor has no interest in Darius. That much is certain. You, however, have grabbed his attentions quite thoroughly."*

"That I have his attention means nothing," I retorted, pinning up the rest of my curls. "He's just curious about what I am, and what my motives are. That's it I'm sure. **Ow!**"

Djialkan snarled at me around the mouthful of my arm he'd bitten. After a moment he released me, but his tail continued thrashing behind him in anger. Darkness poured from the sides of his maw as he let out another feral snarl.

"You hate it when others make assumptions, so stop making assumptions of your own!" Djialkan chastised me, baring his fangs when I opened my mouth to argue. *"X'shmiran laws are of no concern. Stop worrying about them.*

"You lent him your books so that you would have more to talk about, did you not?"

"What...? No! I lent him my books so that our contact would be as minimal as possible!" I shook my head vehemently. "The more he learns about X'shmir from books, the less reason he has to talk to *me!* And then, even if he does need to speak with me, his questions will be more focused and won't take too long! The less time we spend near each other, the better. Besides, he's probably just using me for information. I won't risk—"

"I did not raise you to be such a fool!" Djialkan arched his long neck and shot me a haughty look. *"Alas, you are running late. You had best hurry. Alala and I are remaining here to watch the house whilst you and Darius are gone."*

I shot the irritable fae-dragon a grimace before fetching a veiled mask and leaving my room. As I walked, I bit the hem of my gloves and pulled on the mask, yanked up my hood, and then pulled back my sleeve to check if Djialkan had broken skin when he bit me.

Although it still stung, he hadn't drawn blood. I breathed a small sigh of relief. I wasn't in the mood for any of the unwanted attention the scent of blood could bring me.

'Especially not with how "hungry" Nalithor seemed in that

dream... Ugh.' I shook my head hard, hoping it would push away the recollection. Of course, it did nothing. *'If that's the kind of place my mind goes after not seeing him for several days, I'm not sure how long my sanity—or my dignity—will hold out! Hells, I'm starting to wish I'd stayed in X'shmir. That'd certainly be easier...kind of.'*

A few quick glances around the main floor of the house was all it took to reveal Darius had already run off without me. I muttered curses under my breath and stalked over to the front door. Neither the foyer nor the front porch held the scent of anyone that might have escorted Darius in my stead.

'Just how much worse can my morning get?' I sighed and brought my fingers up to my temples. *'How am I supposed to do my job if he's always running off without me?'*

I yanked my gloves on as I walked through the Sapphire Quarter and attempted to quell my displeasure. Perhaps four days had passed since I left my books with Nalithor. Since then, Darius had flip-flopped between reasonable and irrational on an hourly basis. It was like my brother couldn't decide between his jealousy and keeping up his "holy" appearances.

Despite Nalithor's mischievous demeanor that night, he had behaved himself. Aside from a few sultry glances here and there, at any rate. We had drunk another two bottles of mri'lec by the time he escorted me back to the house.

Admittedly, I was surprised that he stayed true to his word and conducted himself like a gentleman. I was further impressed that neither of us had grown tipsy after so many drinks.

I bit my lower lip hard and stifled an annoyed growl. It infuriated me that Nalithor managed to be on my mind so often. As far as I was concerned, I had barely interacted with the damn Adinvyr yet! Yet, my thoughts always circled back to him. Even while training.

Nalithor's power wrapped lazily around everything in Dauthrmir. It was impossible for me to tune the hum of his power out of my mind, so steeped the city was in his power. Then there was the Adinvyr's scent, which seemed like it still clung to me even though Darius and I hadn't seen Nalithor since meeting with the representatives from the Vorpmasian Royal Families.

'A fact I should be happy about.' I rolled my eyes at myself.

Unfortunately, I hadn't learned much about Vampires since I last encountered Nalithor, either. Something still struck me as strange about them, but I couldn't quite identify what. Another infuriating nuisance. Since that incident, my studies had shifted toward the races of Avrirsa and tomes regarding Avrirsa's deities. That I knew too little of the world "Below" had become glaringly obvious, and I intended to change that. Learning about the races and their deities seemed of utmost importance.

For the life of me, I still couldn't figure out what kind of magic Nalithor had used to slay the Vampires. It didn't feel like any type of power I'd encountered before. Whatever it was, I couldn't deny that it was effective. Not as fun as ripping the creatures apart by hand, perhaps, but it got the job done. I would have rather done the job myself or, better yet, gotten to see Nalithor truly at work.

'Tch. Maybe I should skin Djialkan later.' I released an irritable sigh and fidgeted with my hood. *'What does he mean I'm "drawn" to that Adinvyr? I'm not here to make friends, and I'm certainly not here to—'*

I caught that damned delicious spicy scent in the air and let my thoughts trail off into silence. Glancing upwards from the road, I attempted to determine where Nalithor was. For a brief moment, I wondered if he had passed through recently. However, a ripple in the shadows to my right made it clear that wasn't the case. Moments later the Adinvyr himself emerged from the shadows and fell into step with me. He had a rather amused, self-satisfied expression on his face.

"You seem irritated," Nalithor spoke in an observing manner as I tugged at my hood. "Isn't it a little early in the morning for you to be so agitated?"

"Darius ran off without his escort," I replied with a grimace, deciding that my brother's actions would be a better explanation for my mood. After all, there was no way in the hells I would admit to Nalithor's face the *actual* source of my irritation. He didn't seem satisfied with my short answer, so I continued, "Didn't you tell Darius you would be working elsewhere today? He's been complaining for *days* that you wouldn't be able to 'watch him beat his tests.'"

"I am, but I'm sitting in on your first test." Nalithor offered me his arm and shot me a sly grin. "Afterward, I have to test an endless parade of recruits. They all want to join the Vorpmasian Imperial Military for one reason or another. Most of them are untrained men and women who believe a sharp uniform will get them laid."

"I can see you're just *dying* to get to work," I commented, accepting his arm. "You still think one of us is going to break the testing equipment then, hmmm?"

'Ugh. Just how does he manage to smell like food?*'* I bit the inside of my cheek, hard.

"Yes, I do think so," Nalithor replied with a smile. "Were you not planning on getting yourself more suitable attire? You can't possibly be comfortable in such heavy robes."

"I have plenty of attire to choose from. Old habits die hard." I shook my head and then sighed. "Darius apparently wants to drag me shopping with him, anyway. He's been researching various styles of clothing in an *attempt* to determine what he wants. If he spent this much time on his arcane studies, he wouldn't need classes so damn badly!"

"You're feisty this morning," Nalithor teased. His amused tone made the corner of my eye twitch. "Do I need to help you settle down before your tests, *Your Highness*?"

"I'll be fine," I answered dryly. Nalithor just chuckled, snuck his tail around my waist, and gave me a brief squeeze. "Is it really appropriate for someone of your rank to escort a *potential student* in such a way, *General Vraelimir?*"

'Really? Squeezing me with his tail now?' I questioned privately. *'Just what is he up to?'*

"Considering you were so kind as to lend me such an impressive collection of books... The least I can do is show you to your tests." Nalithor kept his voice innocent, but I glanced up at him with curiosity anyway. He looked like he had something else to say.

"You have that inquisitive look on your face again." I nudged him in the ribs with my elbow. "I assume you found something that piqued your interest?"

"Aside from this little vixen here," Nalithor began, nudging me back as he smirked. "Yes, I do have some questions regarding the texts you lent me. We have some time before your group is expected in the first testing hall...if you do not mind being pestered with questions so early."

"I did tell you before that you can ask me anything," I pointed out, earning a moderately surprised look from the Adinvyr. "That wasn't a one-time invitation. What would you like to know?"

"This way." Nalithor gave me a light tug and pulled me into the palace. He escorted me along the main floor and into a room with plush chairs and sofas. After a glance around the room, he motioned toward one of the sofas and spoke again, "I took particular interest in the tomes that speak of the species from

'Below.' That said… I would be lying if I claimed to expect what the series on *'Demons'* states."

"Yes, the X'shmiran texts can be rather offensive," I agreed, perching on the sofa. Nalithor wasted no time in sitting down directly to my right. He shot me an unreadable glance and then summoned one of the books I'd lent him.

"I want to know if this book in particular is among those that are public to the people in X'shmir." Nalithor tapped his claws against the cover of the book and then turned it so that I could see the cover. "Or is this one of the 'forbidden' ones you 'acquired' from the vaults?"

"Ah, I had a feeling that one would grab your attention," I remarked with a crooked grin, crossing one leg over the other. "That one, and the series it's part of, are all things that are taught to the X'shmiran public."

I glanced up to the side at Nalithor, curious, as he released a feral growl. He looked displeased, bordering on enraged, but I rather liked the sound of his deep, bestial growl. There was something strangely attractive about the sound, as well as the vehement anger in his eyes.

"Do you…?" Nalithor trailed off as he looked down at me. His lips parted slightly as a more relaxed, surprised expression overtook his angry one. "You look extremely amused. Sitting hip-to-hip with an angered deity and you're *amused* instead of frightened? That alone should answer my question."

"You were going to ask if I believe this nonsense?" I offered, motioning to the book. Once he nodded, I continued, "The entire basis of X'shmiran beliefs is that each species represents a particular sin or virtue. Which is ridiculous if you consider that most of their basic beliefs on what sins and virtues even *are* is incorrect.

"In short, I don't agree with *any* of the X'shmiran texts or beliefs. However, I can understand why you are so angry with this one in particular. Djialkan and the people of Auvry'e informed me of Draemiran ways to some extent. So, I'm aware that X'shmiran teachings regarding Adinvyr are as close to opposite from actuality as possible."

"Their accusations of what we do *aside.*" Nalithor grimaced, his voice still little more than a growl. "It is ludicrous to me that they consider sex and sexuality a *sin*! More pleasurable aspects aside, how do they expect to *breed* if they consider such things a sin?"

"They punish themselves and each other for it." I shrugged, raising my left hand into the air as Nalithor shot me an incredulous look. "It isn't uncommon for X'shmirans to mutilate themselves— and each other—as punishment for committing something they consider a sin. Even sex for reproduction is a sin to them. A weakness of flesh. To convolute matters, not carrying on one's line is also a sin.

"Ah, and before you ask, no, the Royal Family isn't taking action to change X'shmiran beliefs regarding Devillian races. They genuinely believe that the individual Devillian races exist for the sole purpose of luring Humans into one sin or another. Adinvyr represent the 'sin' of lust, Rylthra represent greed, Akor represent wrath—'the list goes on,' as they say."

"Yet they allowed their only prince and princess to come to the capital of the very beings they seem to despise," Nalithor murmured, and I felt a small, sad smile creep across my face. "Why would they let—?"

"I think you underestimate just how badly they want me to die," I interrupted Nalithor, not even bothering to look at him since my mask was in the way. Instead, I motioned with my hands as I spoke, "They see no value in Umbral Mages. That their 'precious princess' was born as one is a disgrace to the family. Even more so than Darius being born *after* a girl.

"X'shmiran law is self-contradictory. They despise Lyur'zi, but we are still assigned to protect our Chrot'zi. They want their Lyur'zi dead, but their laws state that they can't execute me unless I break very specific laws—else they will find themselves without protection. Astral Mages are considered holy existences, above all else in the kingdom, and yet there are many times when Darius must ask *me* for permission to do something. *Especially* when his safety is involved, since I am responsible for him."

"They also don't appear to worship *any* of the gods, despite the fact that whoever penned these tomes knew of our existence." Nalithor frowned and summoned another book. Although he kept his expression passive, I could hear in his voice and see in the twitching of his tail that he was angrier now than before. "I'm almost certain I saw shrines to some of the deities whilst in X'shmir, but..."

"I'm not sure when X'shmir originally lost contact with the outside world," I offered as Nalithor flipped through the book, his eyes scanning the pages at a startling speed. "There are quite a few hidden 'cults' that still worship the Upper Gods. However, they appear uninterested in Lesser, Middle, and Elder Gods.

"They're among the few X'shmirans willing to speak with me. I was able to confirm that whatever keeps X'shmir hidden from you all seems to have also kept the 'faithful' from contacting their gods. That changed around the same time the Alliance's scouts found us."

"Sounds like *meddling*." Nalithor grimaced as I examined his irritated expression. "If this is the sort of drivel you've been taught all your life, why don't you believe any of it?"

"That's a secret." I smirked when he looked down at me with a questioning expression.

"If you decide I'm 'worthy' will it still be a secret?" Nalithor countered in a teasing tone, and this time I couldn't help but smile.

"A different type of worthiness is needed for that!" I replied with a laugh. "Proving you're worthy of my interest is a start but proving you're worthy of my trust is another matter entirely. I'm sure I don't need to explain to you why the latter is considerably more difficult than the former."

"I must admit that I am relieved you don't believe in this nonsense." Nalithor sighed as he slipped an arm around my waist and pulled me closer. "What of this book, then?"

Nalithor dismissed the first two books into a shrizar and spread a larger tome across his lap. I felt my face grow hot as he squeezed my waist, but I did my best to ignore it and focus on the enormous tome instead. The proximity of Nalithor's presence was strangely comforting, as was his scent. At the same time, it was highly distracting, almost dizzyingly so.

"Ah, this book," I murmured, watching him flip through the pages in search of something. "What would you like—?"

"Ari, there you are!" Darius exclaimed from the doorway. I looked up from the book and to my twin, surprised to find him still by himself. "It's almost time for our first test! What are…?"

Darius trailed off with a frustrated scowl when he spotted Nalithor's arm around my waist. I glanced up at Nalithor when I felt his grip tighten and found quite the self-satisfied smirk settled on the Adinvyr's features. He looked incredibly pleased with himself. It was difficult for me to not fidget when he started stroking my side through my robes.

"I'm *so* sorry, Darius-zir," Nalithor purred in a tone laden with sarcasm. "I needed to borrow your sister. Arianna was kind enough to lend me some of her books so that I might better understand X'shmiran culture. As you can imagine, I have many questions for her."

"But *I'm*—!" Darius started in frustration before sighing. I arched an eyebrow behind my mask as Darius' shoulders slumped and I felt the jealousy coming off him in waves. "Whatever. Come on, Ari. Our group is about to—"

"I'll bring her along shortly," Nalithor interrupted my brother, his voice chill. He tightened his group on my waist before continuing, "I'm not quite done with her yet. We'll join you in the testing hall once we're finished."

For a moment I thought Darius was going to burst a blood vessel. Finally, Darius made a frustrated sound and stormed off. I blinked after my twin for a moment. However, Nalithor brought my attention back to *him* when he abruptly pulled me closer. I had to brace myself against his chest to keep myself from toppling across his lap.

"You really are *much* cuter than that brother of yours," Nalithor commented with a chuckle, bringing a hand up to cover the one I'd used to brace myself. My face grew hotter when I glanced up to shoot him a questioning look. The sultry expression of his really didn't help matters. "I was wondering if you had found any other tomes that delved so deeply into the matter of the Aledacian Forests, Arianna. Such detailed information on them is unusual."

"I think that's the only one," I replied after a moment of thought, and then attempted to reclaim my hand. "I lent you *all* of the books in my collection, after all. If there's more, they'd be amongst the others."

"*All* of them?" Nalithor inquired, causing me to look up at him again in response to his firm tone. "You're certain you didn't leave anything out?"

"Yes, all of them." I pouted, irritated. "I did say that—"

"You're right, you did say you were lending me all of them." Nalithor chuckled, tightened his grip on my hand, and looked down at me with a mischievous twinkle in his eyes. "I'll just have to take you out for another drink as an apology for doubting you.

"For now, I suppose I should show you to your first test, now shouldn't I? As *cozy* as this is, I'm starting to understand why you attempt to avoid pissing off your brother altogether."

Before I could articulate a retort, Nalithor pulled me to my feet alongside him. Once again, I felt dwarfed when standing beside the Adinvyr, and the fact he kept one arm wrapped around my side only served to make it more apparent. He released me with a playful chuckle and then motioned for me to follow him through the palace once more. His gait was more playful now, as was the swishing of his tail. Although he'd been so displeased, it appeared as though my answers to his questions were what he was looking for. He was much more relaxed now.

It wasn't long before Nalithor led me into a large granite room with sparse decorations. The room could have fit a hundred people, perhaps more, and I got the feeling that under normal circumstances there would have more furnishings. There were fifty or so mages awaiting testing but none of them struck me as interesting. I found my brother quickly and strode over to his side, taking note of the faint tremble that had entered his limbs.

Alas, most of my attention was still on Nalithor. I watched as he joined the Vorpmasian and Beshulthien Archmagi at the back of the room. Although he didn't take a seat, he leaned back against a pillar near the Archmagi and crossed his arms. He already looked bored as his pale eyes flicked across the mixed group of Elves, Devillians, and the handful of Vampires that made up the crowd of potential students.

'At least I think they're Vampires...' I cast a subtle glance at the small group. *'They're wearing those gaudy Beshulthien robes at any rate. Burgundy and gold. And what is that, velvet? Do their mages not participate in battles? That would be atrocious to fight in!'*

Holding back a snort of displeasure, I shifted my attention toward the equipment laid out at the end of the room between us and the boring-looking Archmagi behind it. The tanned not-Desert Elf who seemed to be friends with Nalithor and Eyrian sat among the Archmagi. He looked to be the youngest present. There was an assortment of different races represented amongst the men and women tasked with testing us. Several different types of Elves, and at least five separate races of Devillians were present.

This specific test, as I was led to believe, appeared to be a measure of individual power. A large series of crystalline cylinders sat between the Archmagi and us. The mages were instructed to come up, one at a time, and fill the cylinders with as much power as they could. The catch? They had to keep each element separate in the event they had multiple elements at their disposal.

Darius and I were both quick to notice that all the people present had two elements at most, and we exchanged a look as the low hum of magic filled the room.

'Nali looks bored,' Darius remarked as he turned to face me fully. *'What'd you do?'*

'I'm bored too. Their powers seem so…watered down.' I kept my eyes trained on the slow procession of mages. After a brief pause and some exchanged looks of confusion, one of the Archmagi called Darius' name. *'Your turn already, looks like.'*

Darius froze and flicked his eyes from me to the Archmagi and back. His face grew pale and a tad green as he audibly gulped. He was so nervous that he didn't seem to notice Nalithor watching him with faint interest, or the pale shimmer of magic that left the deity to reinforce the cylinders in front of my brother.

After a moment of hesitation, Darius lifted his hands and summoned his unwieldy, unrefined power to fill the cylinders. However, he lacked the control to separate the mixture of water, light, earth, and lightning magics. Soon he fizzled out and staggered back with a heavy sigh. Despite the poor display, and the fact that Nalithor had to use his own power to buffer my brother's elements, the appearance of *four* seemed to be plenty to startle those present.

Nalithor tracked my brother with narrowed eyes as Darius returned to my side.

Judging by the curious glance he flicked my way, it appeared that Nalithor was still in the dark about my elements and my capacity as a mage. I had a feeling that he knew I had four elements at my disposal as well, and it struck me as strange that Eyrian hadn't disclosed more information to his friend. Or, if he had, I wasn't sure why Nalithor would be so intrigued still.

'Gods, they're all so powerful!' Darius slumped in defeat as he looked toward me. *'How are you not a nervous wreck? There's so much incredible power just…just* wafting *off them all! Especially Nali… He's the scariest out of all of them.'*

'Fighting Chaos Beasts means I have to be able to keep calm,' I answered with a dismissive shrug, watching as more mages were called up to perform their tests. *'You noticed, right? Less than a quarter of these mages have any semblance of control of their power.'*

'Are you trying to make me feel better?' Darius inquired with a grumpy huff, before looking toward the mage currently being tested as well. *'Okay…tell me I didn't do that bad at least!'*

'You have little-to-no control, but you still filled all of the cylinders to the brim,' I offered in response. *'Once you've received training… Just think how great of a healer you'll be with that much raw power at your fingertips.'*

I shot a brief smirk at Nalithor when I sensed his power

slipping along my barriers and spotted the frustrated look on his face. Something about my expression must have pleased him, because he broke into a brief grin and his tail swished a few times before he smoothed his demeanor over. Nalithor nudged at my barriers again with his power and I shoved back in kind, earning an amused grin.

'More cat than dragon,' I thought to myself dryly as I shifted my attention away from the Adinvyr and back to the mages.

"Arianna Jade Black?" One of the Archmagi called. I stepped forward and ignored the strange looks I received from the other mages. The Archmagus addressed me again, "Whenever you're ready fill the central cylinder with your element. Depending on your control we'll have further instructions."

"How much?" I asked with a small tilt of my head. Several of the Archmagi paused and stared at me in confusion, but Nalithor just smirked.

"How much...?" A female Imviir blinked at me before shaking her head. "All of your power. Don't hold anything back."

I glanced toward Nalithor briefly as I caught a glimpse of magic leaving him to reinforce the cylinders again. His smirk shifted to a more approving expression when he noticed my attention shift.

Shrugging to myself, I didn't even bother to pull my hands out of my pockets when I summoned fire, wind, ice, and shadow into the largest of the eleven cylinders. I watched in silence as the writhing elements twisted and warped in their desperation to break free from their confines.

"Bloody hells!" A student behind me yelped. I heard several of them scramble backwards away from me and the cylinders, but I just continued to release all my power. I tapped my right foot against the granite floor, bored.

'Why are there eleven?' I wondered, listening to the sound of scattering and panicked mages. *'There are only ten elements—at least two of which can't be wielded. At least not in the same manner as fire, ice, or darkness...'*

Nalithor was now more active in his attempts to reinforce the cylinders but it seemed the other Archmagi were oblivious to that fact. Even as the glowing Brands of Divinity on Nalithor's exposed skin shone brighter in response to his magical exertion the others remained ignorant. I wasn't impressed with the Archmagi in the slightest. They should have noticed the deity's usage of magic and the strain it was causing him.

"Very well," muttered another Archmagi, his voice filled with unease as he stared at the writhing cobalt flames. "Are you capable of intermingling them whilst they move?"

In response, I willed the elements to spread out through the eleven cylinders. Deciding to make a point, I separated all four into separate cylinders for a moment before swirling them all together. They mixed with ease and expanded to fill all eleven of the crystal contraptions to the brim, continuing to writhe in protest. After a few seconds I heard a cracking sound.

I was fast to react and formed four large orbs out of my four elements as the cylinders shattered into tiny pieces, ignoring the few shards that nicked my face in their path through the air.

"Well then, my hunch was right," Nalithor remarked with a triumphant smirk as he approached me. He motioned up at the four orbs I was maintaining in the air and then glanced at his fellow Archmagi. "I think Arianna-jiss can dismiss *those* now, don't you?"

The group of Archmagi nodded, their mouths still agape. I willed the elements away as Nalithor came to a stop in front of me. He reached up, startling me, with faint traces of shadows around his fingertips. He cupped my face in both hands and ran his thumb over my lower lip, then swiped his other thumb over my cheek. I felt the cuts from the shards of crystal heal in response to his touch, but something about his rather alluring expression gave me the impression that healing me wasn't the only option he'd considered.

"Can't have those lovely features of yours being scarred, now can we?" Nalithor purred with amusement, before leaning down to speak quietly by my ear, "These poor bastards may be oblivious, but that little display of yours just now... You're quite the interesting little morsel, aren't you?

"You should be careful about who else you let see such a display."

'Display...?' I wondered as I looked up at him. *'That sounded more like a warning than a threat. Just what does he mean by that?'*

After a moment, Nalithor shot me another smirk, released me, then left the room. Flustered, I returned to my brother's side and found he was still too startled by my display of power to inquire about much else.

With the equipment broken, the Archmagi dismissed those of us that were finished so we could continue to our next tests. I mumbled a few apologies for breaking their equipment, but it didn't seem like they were having any of that.

"We have a little while before we're expected at the next test. Want to go get breakfast?" Darius inquired after I dragged him out into the hallway. His voice held a cheerful lilt to it, but when he latched onto my arm, I felt that his entire body was trembling. "One of the rooms is set up with food and stuff. So, if you haven't had breakfast yet we can go get some."

"What's our next test?" I asked, letting Darius drag me down the hallway. "That one appeared to address amount of power, control, element, and aptitude...plus whatever the machines I broke measured."

"Let's see..." Darius murmured, pulling a piece of paper from his robes. "Physical fortitude, mental fortitude, followed by that BDSM test, and then—"

"BDSM test?" I laughed when Darius pouted and nodded his head furiously. "Unless you know something I don't, that sounds terribly offensive, Darius."

"Those kinds of relationships are really common here!" Darius protested as I laughed at him again. "Particularly among Adinvyr,

I'll have you know! They're known as being the most possessive and jealous of the Devillian species, so they usually have at least *light* BDSM relationships! They believe they mutually *own* each other, so—!"

"It still isn't a 'BDSM test,'" Eyrian interrupted, placing a hand on top of each of our heads and startling a squeak out of my brother. "Our Oracles are quite good but even *they* aren't matchmakers. While they do look into your romantic inclinations—as women their age are wont to do—we're more concerned with what your predispositions in the workplace are."

"So you can avoid the 'two cooks in the same kitchen' scenario?" I offered, earning a nod and a grin from the Draekin. He was quick to return to a more serious air as he turned fully to me though.

"Arianna, can I convince you to seek Nalithor out for another sparring match?" Eyrian asked with a small frown. "After your rather…*intense*…second match, it's considered inappropriate for him to challenge you. He's been sulking for *days* because he doesn't wish to be rude. He will be in the Sapphire Quarter all day dealing with new recruits, so—"

'It's considered inappropriate for him *to challenge* me *after I tried to kill him?'* I arched an eyebrow behind my mask. *'I see why Djialkan struggles to understand Devillians. At least now I know why Nalithor hasn't sought me out…'*

"I was already planning on asking him to spar me later today,"

I replied, tilting my head to the side as I examined Eyrian and watching as he breathed a sigh of relief. "Despite his shadowy display when the three of us fought that beast, Nalithor hasn't actually let himself reveal much of his fighting style. I can't deny it's made me curious."

Eyrian grinned broadly before excusing himself, leaving my twin and I to our breakfast and tests. I shot a frown at Eyrian's back and then shook my head. I didn't like it, but I was a little miffed that Eyrian hadn't shown any indication of wanting to spar with me. He seemed concerned only with the state of his friend. Perhaps Draekin were less battle-oriented than Adinvyr were, or perhaps their friendship was just that important to him. At any rate, it wasn't a concept I could grasp.

'Maybe I'll ask Eyrian to spar later once I've dealt with the mischievous one.' I watched Eyrian disappear around a corner, then turned to look at Darius.

"Let's go!" Darius beamed at me.

After breakfasting my brother and I parted ways. As expected, I aced my fortitude tests to both the dismay and discomfort of the mages that administered them. Darius, unfortunately, failed both of his. Miserably.

I glanced to my right at him and watched as he wrung his hands. We were both late to the Oracles' DSO test due to how long it had taken me to help calm my brother. The other mages and I had managed to prevent him from vomiting all over his robes, at least.

The mental fortitude test utilized illusionary magic to make us see and experience things that, in theory, should unnerve us based on our roles. However, I'd already seen and experienced enough death and suffering. It didn't faze me in the slightest. As for Darius...he didn't cope with things as well as I did.

I was concerned that the test might have drudged up memories that would make Darius break. But aside from the vomit and tears he seemed mostly fine. For now.

'I'm pretty sure at least half the palace would be gone now if they made him experience memories of his past,' I considered, shooting a wary glance at my unusually pale twin. *'Just what did they show him?'*

The Oracles shot us a displeased look the moment we entered their gathering place. Darius flinched and ducked behind my arm, trembling. I glanced over my shoulder at him and then returned my attention to the Oracles. Corentine's sister was present, but she was the only one I recognized. The others were new to me, but they were all visibly irritated.

"I apologize for our lateness," I offered, motioning with one hand at my brother. "I couldn't just leave my brother alone, you *See.*"

The Oracles seemed to take the hint and shifted their attention to Darius for a moment. They seemed to look right through him for a few seconds, and then nodded their understanding in silence.

Corentine's sister motioned for us to join the rest of the waiting mages, so I tugged my nervous twin over to the small group.

As Eyrian told us, the Oracles really did investigate both work and romantic inclinations. I had to stifle my laughter in response to how many of the mages were frustrated with the readings they received from the Oracles. It was almost entertaining enough to distract me from the presence of Corentine's sister. Something about that woman still irritated me.

Although the Oracles didn't announce the results to the room, we still learned a great deal about our fellow mages. Almost every single one shouted their protests and disbeliefs at the dismissive Oracles. The few members of the Imperial Guard that were present seemed accustomed to this behavior. I caught several poorly-covered snickers and a few other guards rolled their eyes.

"Hmmm, so what do you think?" Darius motioned at me. "Alpha female?"

"I guess we'll see, won't we?" I replied dryly. "You really are adamant that I'm dominant, aren't you?"

"Absolutely." Darius nodded. "If you are, I can have Nali all to myself. He's a dominant, not a submissive or whatever the hell 'other' is. So, he totally wouldn't want you anymore if you're a dominant, right?"

"So *that's* your motive." I rolled my eyes and shook my head. "You're incorrigible."

'Wouldn't want me "anymore?" I doubt he actually wants me to

begin with!' I bit back an irritated scowl. *'Nalithor's an Adinvyr—couldn't he just use his powers to seduce me if he "wanted" me? Tch.*

'Unless… If that bastard is responsible for those damned dreams, I'll skin him!'

Darius stiffened next to me, and a moment later hurried to kneel before the Oracles. His struggle to speak with the Oracles through telepathy was clear on his face.

Soon enough, Darius' face turned a special shade of tomato red. I tilted my head to the side, wondering what the Oracles had said to make him turn that color. He seemed so flustered that he couldn't even begin to protest. Instead, he simply returned to my side in silence once dismissed. He was so red that several mages around us cast him curious and concerned glances.

I settled with my back against a pillar and watched the slow procession of mages, noting that most of them didn't seem to take kindly to whatever the Oracles Saw about them. Some went as far as to scream profanities at the Oracles for their results. The Devillian mages, for the most part, were the calmest of the lot. For whatever reason, the Elves seemed most prone to becoming enraged. It struck me as strange.

Eventually, the Oracles called upon me as one of the last to be tested. I begrudgingly strode up to the dais and then kneeled on the pillows before the Oracles. They examined me with curious expressions but remained silent. Unlike the Archmagi from our previous tests, these women were all Devillians. The central one,

Corentine's strawberry blonde sister, seemed to be in charge. Wonderful.

'You're the one that caused the disturbance during the test of power earlier.' An Imviir Oracle spoke, shifting the serpentine half of her body so she could lean forward. *'I wasn't expecting someone who looks so Human yet smells so Devillian.'*

'You and your brother have the most peculiar eyes. For Humans,' a woman with deeply tanned skin and quartz-like horns added, smiling when my gaze flicked toward her. *'We can See through your mask and veil, the same way we can See through your mind.'*

'Hmmm. What do you think, ladies?' Corentine's sister tilted her head as she thought, her tail waving up and down beside her. *'Alpha female most definitely, but...'*

'A submissive, absolutely,' a molten-haired Akor woman stated with a sharp nod. *'And she doesn't look surprised in the least.'*

'You must be very picky about men.' The annoying Rylthra pointed her pipe at me.

'If a man can't earn my submission, then what's the point in being submissive to him?' I countered, shooting a glare at her even as she beamed at me in delight. *'I'm not inclined to submit to* anyone *that hasn't earned my full respect.'*

'It's interesting, however, that you are the same both in and out of bed.' The Akor woman spoke again, her tone thoughtful this time. She shot me a sly look when my face reddened. *'You may not have access to men in X'shmir, but that certainly hasn't kept you from*

thinking *about it. A lot.'*

'It's a good thing her thoughts are so well-shielded.' The tanned Oracle nodded her agreement with the Akor and then tapped her fingers to her temples. *'Otherwise all of the Adinvyr in the city would be chasing after her tail.'*

'Speaking of chasing her tail,' the Imviir remarked, *'you shouldn't worry so much about hiding your skin and Brands,* Your Highness. *Let us fix that for you.'*

Before I could protest, the women made a motion and a warm, floral-scented breeze engulfed me. Startled, I looked down when I felt my clothes ripping away. Before anyone could glimpse my nude body, the Oracles summoned new attire around me. Although it vaguely conformed to a style befitting an Umbral Mage, I found my face growing hotter as I looked down at the outfit. It looked more like clothes for a dancer in the Scarlet District. I had to admit that I liked it, but the harem-style pants were startling in their gradated translucence.

A circlet held my veil in place, and my mask had been left beneath it. Thankfully, they had left my curls pinned up and adorned me with a hooded half-jacket. *'At least they have the decency to abide by the rules I'm bound to…'*

'Ah yes, this style suits you much better!' The Rylthra cackled in delight, her fluffy tail wagging behind her. *'Come now, you shouldn't be so shy! In Vorpmasia your Brands are less a problem than your mask and veil are.'*

'There isn't much I can do about the mask and veil.' I shifted in discomfort, glancing down at the clothes again. *'As far as these... If I can fight in it, it's acceptable. I might have strangled all of you if these pants were translucent all the way up. Were we in X'shmir, showing my Brands or skin would be...problematic.'*

'Do give that man a good ass-kicking for us, won't you?' The tanned one pouted and crossed her arms with a huff, causing me to look at her in surprise. *'I've been trying to get into* that one's *pants for* decades! *But he's so gods-damned picky! Sometimes I wonder if he's taken* anyone *to bed in his two hundred twenty-six years!'*

The rest of the Oracles muttered their agreement and reflected the tanned one's miffed attitude. Somewhere amidst all their muttering they dismissed me, so I made my way back toward Darius. I tugged at my clothes and chewed on my lower lip as the other mages openly gawked at me. I couldn't help but wonder if it was because of my Brands or my figure.

'What pushy women...' I grimaced. *'I can't say I disagree with his choice not to bring any of them to his bed—if that's even true. They'd probably be a nightmare to get rid of!'*

"That seemed intense," Darius remarked dryly. He grabbed both of my hands and lifted them, examining the Brands on my skin with a look of confusion. "What's this, a chaos star on each hand...and a white crescent on the right, black star on the left?"

"Born to be an Umbral Mage, perhaps?" I shrugged. "You have another physical examination after this, right?"

"Yep!" Darius grinned. "Maybe there'll be a *really* hot healer, and—?"

"And you'll get an awkward boner and get all embarrassed?" I offered quite seriously. Darius didn't seem to appreciate my joke. Instead, he turned brilliant scarlet, turned on his heel, and stormed off in search of the examination hall. *'Oh. Well, it was easier to get rid of him than I thought it'd be. I'll have to remember that one.'*

After brief consideration, I made my way out of the palace and towards the Sapphire Quarter. Nalithor's power radiated from a single large section of the district and I could tell he was *terribly* bored, almost painfully so. I smirked. Perhaps my presence would be a welcome distraction.

'Not that I'm certain that I know how to deal with him,' I mused, lifting one of my hands to examine my bangles for a moment, before letting my arm drop back to my side. *'Well, there's no point in getting hung up on my dream, or on the way Nalithor provoked Darius. He's so damn playful at times… I suppose I should expect him to get a rise out of my brother intentionally.'*

It wasn't long before I caught sight of a long line of people who were waiting for a chance to prove themselves to Nalithor. There were even a handful of women in the line as well, some of which seemed more interested in the Adinvyr than in fighting, and a few who looked more interested in a fight. Every individual present was a Devillian or a Vorpmasian Elf, and few were dressed in a way that seemed conducive to training or sparring. One thing they all shared was their nervousness and visible inexperience.

"Arianna-jiss?" A familiar soldier inquired, frowning when he spotted me approaching. His eyes wandered down my form for a moment before jerking back up. "This line is for those who wish to prove themselves worthy of joining the Vorpmasian military, General. So you shouldn't be—"

"Oh? I was going to be polite and let them all go before I make a slightly selfish request." I crossed my arms under my bust and brought a finger to my lips in thought. "*He* doesn't seem like the sort to appreciate interruptions, after all."

"I-I think...he'd make an exception." The soldier coughed and glanced away from my cleavage, his face flushing. "This way, Arianna-jiss."

I bit back an amused smirk and followed the soldier. That was too easy. The waiting men and women began protesting the moment they saw me passing them. Nalithor soon came into view and I arched an eyebrow. He was nestled on a sturdy chair with his legs crossed as he leaned against the armrest on one elbow. He had his chin propped atop his fingers as he watched the recruits. Something about his poise was regal, and there was something fiercely predatory about his gaze while he observed one of the hopefuls' sparring match.

As we drew closer, he must have caught my scent in the air. His gaze shifted to focus on me as I followed the soldier toward him. The way Nalithor examined my figure made shivers run down my spine. A small smirk crept across his features the longer his frosty gaze trailed over my skin.

'And here I thought he couldn't look any more predatory.' I bit back a laugh and examined the smirking Adinvyr.

"I knew I smelled trouble," Nalithor remarked, causing several people to turn and look at me. "Rather the drastic change in attire, *Your Highness.*"

"The Oracles took offense to my choice in clothing," I replied, shrugging. I glanced to the side at the recruit who was still attempting to prove himself, and then looked back to Nalithor. "I had a request for you—one that might ease your boredom. I was going to be polite and wait until the trials end, but…it looks like your hopefuls could stand to learn a thing or two."

"Oh? A request?" Nalithor's eyes ran over me again as I approached him. "Dressed like that, one has to wonder what sort of request you have in mind."

"I would like you to spar with me," I answered plainly, ignoring the choked laughter from the waiting recruits. Nalithor's smirk shifted into a boyish grin.

"Ahhh… I was *hoping* you would say that," Nalithor purred before rising to his feet and shrugging off his overrobe. He turned to drape it across the back of his chair and then turned to look at me once more. "You've 'recovered' then, have you?"

"I've *been* recovered," I retorted, motioning loosely at him. "I figured you would come ask me to spar when you were done studying the texts I lent you. However, patience isn't my strong suit. I decided to come challenge you again instead."

"*Challenge* me?" Nalithor inquired with mock-surprise as the rookies laughed at my proclamation. "Maric, you heard General Black. Clear the pit. It's high time we gave the rookies a thoroughly *educational* experience."

"Rules?" I asked, following the delighted Adinvyr into the pit and watching him brush his braid over his shoulder.

"I think another purely physical match is in order," Nalithor replied, turning to face me with a grin. "It would seem they don't believe you can handle me, Arianna."

"Don't worry, *ladies*, I'll be gentle with him," I called to the crowd of rookies. Nalithor's devious chuckle pulled my attention back to him as I settled a hand on my hip. "Weapons, Nalithor?"

"*Kick her ass!*" Several rookies hollered, making me break into a crooked grin.

"That wasn't quite the type of manhandling I had in mind," I retorted sweetly, shooting a smirk at the rookies once more. Turning my attention back to the slightly flushed Adinvyr, I had to hold back a laugh. "Tsk, tsk, tsk. Am I going to have to come up with the rules, *General?*"

"Choose your comfort weapon," Nalithor replied in a playful tone as he summoned his spear. "Ahhh… I suppose we should dull our blades, lest you land another strike against me. We can't have my blood sending our audience into a frenzy, hmmm?"

Once Nalithor was satisfied that we'd both dulled our weapon's edges he leapt for me unannounced, a delighted grin stretched across his face. I parried his strike and then chased him when he leapt backwards from me. Nalithor snapped out with his tail in an attempt to grab me when I swung my scythe at him, but I used my momentum and the weight of my scythe to sling myself out of reach. He was delightfully difficult, but I had a hard time believing this was all the strength a god would have.

"Starting off close to full strength, are we?" I inquired with a small smile, adjusting my grip. *He doesn't seem like the type who would disrespect me by going easy on me. If I'm this close in strength to him…then something else is off.'*

"I decided I should take this opportunity to *fully* enjoy your company." Nalithor chuckled and spun his spear, leveling it with my throat. "It is so *rare* to find you outside of your secluded habitat, after all."

"Maybe you just haven't found the proper bait to lure me with." I smirked at him. "Come now, it's like you've never hunted a vixen before!"

Instead of waiting for a response, I sprung toward him with my scythe trailing behind me. I thought he would dodge to the side as he had many times before, but this time he chose to block my scythe and push back against me. He chuckled again as I bored the blade of my scythe against the shaft of his spear.

The crowd's laughter had shifted to an uneasy murmuring, but

I just grinned and leapt away from Nalithor. The tip of his spear almost grazed my throat when he followed through with his strike.

'Good. He is taking me seriously.' I landed in a crouch and examined the new stance Nalithor had adopted. *'Dealing with his tail is a problem. Perhaps if it wasn't longer than his legs...'*

My thoughts trailed off as I caught sight of an opening and propelled myself forward, aiming to strike Nalithor's shoulder. However, something must have given me away because he met my strike with ease and sent my weapon flying out of my hands. He attempted to grasp me with his tail in the same motion, but I managed to dance out of reach again.

"This time it is *you* who is disarmed first," Nalithor teased, stalking me. "How do you plan to fight me without a weapon or magic, *hmmm*? If you surrender now, I promise to make it as *pleasurable* as possible."

"A weapon is just an extension," I replied with a laugh, bringing my fists up in an offensive stance. "You forget that *I* am a weapon without a worthy master. I'd argue *that* is more dangerous than my scythe!"

The Adinvyr grinned broadly as I flew at him. I slung kicks and punches at different sections of Nalithor's body, but he blocked them all, several of which with his spear. Dealing with his extended range was a challenge, but fun. Beasts in X'shmir had become so boring to deal with over the past few years. Fighting someone who was arguably more dangerous than the Chaos Beasts thrilled me.

I danced between Nalithor's strikes and observed his movements with interest. I deflected his spear to the side at the last moment and bit back a curse when the blade grazed the edge of my hood. Nalithor followed through with the strike, and I took the opportunity to grab his forward hand. I jammed my thumb into a pressure point and twisted, pulling his arm past me as I slammed the ridge of my foot into his ribs. Nalithor's grip on the weapon slipped and I kicked his spear clear out of the sparring pit. Though the contact was brief, I discovered the weapon was hot to the touch. I would have to check my foot for burns later.

Instead of making another playful comment, Nalithor shifted to unarmed techniques and pursued me around the sparring pit. His strikes were quick, and he didn't telegraph, making it difficult for me to dodge them. I had to react to the strikes while they were already in transit, and it was becoming more and more difficult to keep up. My mostly-Human body strained to move with the speed and strength I needed from it.

'Ugh, I can't decide if I'm more Human than I thought, or more Devillian.' I sprung out of Nalithor's reach for the umpteenth time. *'Either he's getting faster or I'm getting slower.'*

When Nalithor shifted to techniques that would force me to the ground I realized I was in trouble. Grappling was *not* my strong suit.

"Ah, ah, ah. You aren't escaping me this time." Nalithor chuckled, sweeping my legs out from beneath me with his tail. He pinned me face-first into the ground, taking care not to bend my arm too harshly behind my back, but firm enough to keep me from struggling. "I think I've won this round...don't you?"

"This time," I answered dryly as Nalithor's tail snuck around one of my thighs and squeezed. "Clearly I require a great deal more practice when it comes to grappling techniques."

"Now that I've caught my *prize*," Nalithor began with a chuckle as he slung me over his shoulder. "I think I'll have you remain with me for the remainder of the afternoon."

"Prize?" I laughed, watching his tail swish back and forth as he carried me toward his chair.

'Yes, prize.' Nalithor chuckled. He shifted his grip on me and pulled me onto the large chair with him, nestling me tight against the side of his torso. *'I'd have to be a fool to let you wander off when you look so...delicious.'*

'I guess I was having too much fun again if you're able to speak with me like this. Again,' I commended dryly, earning another chuckle and a squeeze around my waist. *'That aside... These rookies are* horrible! *I understand why you seemed so bored.'*

"Maric, Oliver," Nalithor called out as he looped his tail around my thighs a few times. "Let's have the greenlings fight each other. It would seem we're all too much for them...and it would be a little cruel to have 'The White Fox' here break them in for us."

'The White Fox?' I laughed.

'That's what many of my men have begun to call you.' Nalithor

grinned before shifting his gaze over my head slightly. *'Speaking of white foxes...'*

"Alala! What are you doing out of the house, hmmm?" I exclaimed as the white fuzz ball barreled between the legs of soldiers and rookies alike. Once she drew nearer, she took a flying leap into my lap. "Did Darius let you wander off? If so, I'll skin him later."

Alala warbled at me and then scampered off my lap and onto Nalithor's shoulder, earning a surprised look from me. That was twice now that she'd gone to Nalithor over me. The Adinvyr in question looked very amused, but I was perplexed. In Sihix, Alala had always been rather attached to me. It had been difficult to keep her from following me out of the forest when I left. But now...

'She apparently decided that our company is more favorable than Djialkan's or Darius',' Nalithor offered with an amused smile as he reached up to stroke Alala's fur. *'Something about his tests going poorly?'*

'Ah...yes. He's probably having a temper tantrum over all his tests.' I frowned. *'As I expected, he didn't weather the fortitude tests very well. Whatever the Oracles had to say to him flustered him beyond belief as well.'*

'And what did the Oracles say to you?' Nalithor asked innocently. I couldn't help but laugh in response. His tone wasn't convincing in the slightest.

'They knew I was going to come challenge you again. So, they spent most of their time complaining that I needed to kick your ass as

"punishment" for not taking any of them to your bed,' I replied dryly, earning a displeased huff from the Adinvyr who seemed so intent on keeping me at his side.

'Well. If your intention was to "kick my ass" I suppose that didn't turn out very well for you,' Nalithor remarked sarcastically. I laughed again when I felt his grip twitch.

'They can kick your ass themselves if they're so miffed!' I replied with a smirk. *'I, for one, have no intention of playing their games. I'll fight you because I want to, not because some little girls are upset that their crush won't pay them enough attention.'*

'They're older than you are.' Nalithor pointed out as he glanced down at me. Somehow his expression managed to be both miffed and cautiously optimistic.

'Then they should act like it,' I countered, earning another chuckle. I felt him relax a little, so I continued, *'They do piss me off though. I'm of half a mind to drag you back to the pit for another round.'*

'As fun as that would be...' Nalithor trailed off and carefully took my right hand in his, examining it in silence for a moment. *'The pattern of your Brands is intriguing. May I see your other hand as well?'*

Instead of replying, I shifted against Nalithor's side so that I could show him both of my hands. I watched, intrigued, as he gently took both of my hands in his. Despite how rough our sparring matches were, he was now handling me as if just touching me would cause harm.

'I'm not going to break just from you holding my hands,' I commented finally, amused. Nalithor twitched and a touch of color rose in his face. *'You* should *know that by now.'*

'You are deceptively small,' Nalithor informed me with a small smile, running his thumb over the back of one of my hands. *'You said your jewelry is a relatively new acquisition. What of your Brands?'*

'I've had Brands for as long as I can remember,' I answered. *'As for my jewelry, Djialkan and the High Priestess of Sihix, Corentine, have been trying for years to get me to accept Aurelian's gifts. However, the hum of magic that accompanied them made me reluctant. Corentine told me not to hide my Brands or jewelry while here, but...'*

'"High Priestess" Corentine, hmmm?' Nalithor sounded curious but his attention had shifted from my Brands to my rings.

'She's like an Oracle...which I suppose makes sense, since her sister is one.' I shook my head with a slight grimace. *'She communicates with Sihix instead of whatever normal Oracles speak with. She's still also a Seer, and once lived in Vorpmasia somewhere.'*

'She's right that you shouldn't hide your Brands or your jewelry,' Nalithor stated after a brief pause. *'The only time we ever hide such things is when we're trying to be stealthy. Hiding such things not only drains a great deal of power but will also make you seem untrustworthy.*

'Considering you're required to hide your face...' he paused to cup my face and lift it toward his, *'I'm sure there are many people*

who are uneasy about your motives.'

'What about you?' I asked, a small smile creeping across my lips when I saw his surprised expression.

'We've fought enough for me to determine that you don't intend to harm me or Vorpmasia,' Nalithor replied with a smirk. *'Any lingering unease I have is because I can't accept that you're* Human. *The notion is utterly ridiculous. You wouldn't be this physically strong or fast, and I think you are aware of that.'*

"Nalithor-zir!" A female rookie shrieked, causing me to cut my eyes to the side at her. "You shouldn't let that bitch sit so close to you! She might—"

"You will refrain from referring to my quarry in such a derogatory way." Nalithor's voice was like ice. He pulled me into his lap fully and wrapped his arms tight around my waist. Whatever look he shot at the rookies over my head made them shrink back in a panic. "Arianna-jiss could harvest your skin and organs without lifting a finger. I'm inclined to let her if you disrespect her again.

"That *would* be an appropriate punishment don't you think, Arianna?"

I couldn't help but laugh in response to his question. Nalithor nuzzled into the side of my throat and squeezed my waist tighter. A small purr escaped him as he rubbed his cheek against my neck.

"I can't imagine there's much demand for pieces of people too weak and unwilling to challenge me,' I answered, arching an eyebrow when Nalithor purred again and his tail twitched. After a pause I turned my attention to the indignant rookie that had agitated Nalithor. "Don't you think you're insulting your *precious* prince's abilities by suggesting he's unprepared for anything I could attempt? I'm just a *little Human princess* after all."

"One that fights like an angry bear," Maric pointed out, grinning.

"I like to think that I'm at least a *little* more graceful than a bear," I countered as Nalithor chuckled into my throat. *'You seem to enjoy making your rookies jealous, Nalithor.'*

'Maybe you just smell that good,' Nalithor suggested, nuzzling me again for emphasis.

"*Human?!*" The woman from before shrieked. "I'll rip you limb from limb you little cu—"

"Ahhh... I really can't stand people like you." I sighed, summoning tendrils of darkness around the woman. With a subtle motion of my hand, my darkness lifted her upside down into the air and tugged her tail, horns, arms, legs, and head in different directions. "You had a good idea, at least. Ripping you limb from limb *does* sound appropriate at this point."

"I'm of half a mind to let you..." Nalithor grumbled. "Still... I don't think either of us would enjoy dealing with the political hassle. Do you?"

"Nalithor-zir, would you really let this monster—?!" The girl shrieked when I started laughing at her.

"Ahhhnnn… But it's so wonderful to be like a monster, isn't it?" I purred, watching the color drain from her face. "You—"

"It's monsters like us that have the *pleasure* of slaughtering Avrirsa's filth," Nalithor interjected, his voice little more than a husky purr. His hand rose to grip my jaw and part of my throat as he tilted my head to the side. "Am I…going to have to force the *'monster'* back in her cage, Arianna?"

'Ah… I've said that to him before, haven't I?' I realized with a start as Nalithor examined my face, his gaze lingering on my lips. *'He didn't have an answer to that question back then.'*

"I shouldn't kill her?" I asked with a small pout, hoping to distract Nalithor from the familiarity of my remark. His claws bit into my skin as he chuckled, but his expression was unreadable.

"What do *you* think?" Nalithor countered, releasing my jaw and then sitting up straight once more.

"She doesn't *need* to die. But she was going to call me a—"

"Stupid cunt! Get off Nalithor-zir!" The Devillian rookie shrieked at me.

I let out a heavy sigh and raised my fingers to my temples for a moment.

"Are you going to challenge me, or are you going to just bark like a small dog?!" I demanded in a feral snarl, using my darkness to toss the woman aside. The rookies around her scrambled out of her path, letting her land in the dirt.

A pair of soldiers hoisted the woman to her feet as she wailed something about her arm. I didn't particularly care, but the soldiers seemed concerned for her, at least.

"If you don't intend to challenge Arianna-jiss for the right to my lap," Nalithor began with a devious chuckle and made a show of squeezing my thighs with his tail for emphasis, "then you can *leave*. I have no use for disrespectful warriors, nor weak ones.

"Jyors, Falzyn, see the woman to the infirmary. I do believe the White Fox may have thrown her a little too hard."

'She's lucky that throwing her is all I did,' I pointed out with a small huff.

"Is my sister troubling you, Rely'ric?" Darius' terse question came from somewhere to our right, causing Nalithor's grip to twitch tense again. "Ari, we should leave before—"

'Can't he think of any better question?' I shot a glare across Nalithor and at my brother. *"'Oh no, is my sister troubling you, Rely'ric? What a travesty!'"*

"No." Nalithor shifted to shoot Darius an icy look. "It should be rather obvious that *I* pulled her into this situation. Or do you think your sister is *forcing* me to let her sit on my lap, boy?"

"Ari. Aren't you supposed to be *avoiding* Nali?" Darius sighed in exasperation when Alala began making angry noises at him.

"He beat me in our sparring match. Apparently, I'm his 'prize' and his '*quarry*,'" I informed my brother with a slight shrug, listening for a moment to Nalithor's devious laughter. "Besides, he's *surprisingly* comfy."

'I'm comfy, am I?' Nalithor laughed as both the rookies and my brother grew more indignant.

'Surprisingly,' I answered, dismissive. *'I would like to know how exactly I'm your* "quarry" *considering you already won our match earlier.'*

'I still have to prove I'm worthy of your interest and your indulgence.' Nalithor's teasing purr sent a shiver down my spine. He trailed his claws along the Brands on my arm and then added, *'I must say, I wasn't expecting quite this much fury from our audience or your brother.'*

"Fine. I'll challenge you, Ari." Darius crossed his arms at me. It took almost all my self-control not to laugh at him. "That *is* how it works here, isn't it?"

'Really? He was trembling in fear after the aptitude tests, yet he wants to challenge *me?'* I stared at Darius in disbelief. *'After his abysmal display... What is he thinking?'*

"Even if you somehow beat your sister, what am I supposed to do with a *male* in my possession?" Nalithor inquired even as he let me pull myself off his lap and onto my feet. "I'm rather certain your sister both tastes and smells better than you can ever hope to."

'Thanks, I think.' I glanced down at Nalithor's self-satisfied expression and then turned to my brother. "Well, what are you going to fight me with then, Darius?"

"You're...actually going to accept?" Darius blinked at me. "Even though I'm an *Astral Mage?*"

'He doesn't even have the control required to call himself a mage yet,' Nalithor scoffed. His intense displeasure brought an amused smile to my lips for a moment, but my amusement evaporated as I examined Darius. My twin seemed serious.

"Yes, I'm going to accept." I huffed, placing a hand on my hip. "What shall I dissect you with?"

Darius scowled and *attempted* to strike me with a bolt of lightning. I just sighed, watching the small bolt fizzle out before even reaching me. The temptation to terrify him pulled at me, and I bit my lip as I contemplated it.

It didn't take me long to decide. Even though he'd pissed me off, I knew better than to scare him after his reaction to our tests today.

I motioned with one hand and enveloped Darius in cobalt flames. With another simple motion, I tossed him clear across the training pit and onto the other side. I watched, bored, as he scrambled to his feet and grabbed a bow and arrows from a rack nearby. He loosed several arrows at me in rapid succession. Dim magic extended from my brother and coiled around the arrows, causing me to narrow my eyes at him.

"Are you done yet?" I yawned, snatching the arrows from the air and then fanning them out between my fingers. "You could have waited until after your schooling was over to challenge me, you know."

The sensation of Nalithor's tail wrapping around my waist

startled me into looking up at the Adinvyr when he appeared beside me. Nalithor plucked the arrows from my grip. He examined them with a displeased grimace and then settled a fierce look on Darius, releasing a savage growl. Nalithor's dark power sent a shiver through me, making my skin prickle. He was *incredibly* angry with my brother, to a point that his power felt almost solid to the touch.

"Darius-zir, I am aware you've been forbidden from using magic outside of your classes and training," Nalithor snarled. Frost crept from his fingers and down the arrow shafts. The air around us grew so cold I could see my breath. "I won't have you endangering my men, my prospects, *or* your sister with such careless displays!

"Leave, before I find more classes to assign you."

'I insist you stay with me a while longer,' Nalithor added as my brother turned crimson and stormed off. *'It would be best if you waited for him to calm down before you return home. Such unpleasant matters aside, I do hope I can convince you to keep your mind open to me. Being able to speak with you through telepathy is convenient...and pleasant.*

'Or...are you still concerned that X'shmiran law will force you to slay me?'

'You say that as if I even can,*'* I scoffed, watching Nalithor walk away from me and back to his oversized chair. He perched on it and settled his intense, predatory gaze on me once more. I still felt anger coming from him in waves, but his expression softened the

longer he looked at me. *'Very well. I'll keep this pathway open so that you can speak with me. That should be a suitable reward for besting me in our match.'*

'I should probably be rewarding you for not destroying that girl.' Nalithor grinned, tracking me as I moved to lean against the side of his chair. *'I still owe you another drink as well. You should join me once these trials are over, my dear.'*

'As pleasant as that sounds, I should decline,' I replied, noting the disappointed expression that crossed Nalithor's face. *'I won't go into detail but... Darius' mental state is shaky, at best, after his tests.'*

'Is that why you didn't simply turn your darkness against him?' Nalithor had a slight frown on his face when he glanced up at me. *'It's a little strange, you know. Most of us expected that you would be the unstable one. The Old Ways have a way of destroying the humanity of Umbral Mages.'*

'Humans were never meant to wield darkness.'

'I was a monster long before I became an Umbral Mage,' I muttered, distracted as I watched one of the rookies. *'That man smells strange. I don't like it.'*

'A "monster" huh...' Nalithor chuckled, shooting me a warm look before turning to look at the rookie that had grabbed my attention. *'Ah... A recruit weak enough that he resorted to drugs to boost his performance. Pitiful. Alas, there's always one...'*

I fell silent and watched as Nalithor instructed several of his men to escort the rookie, by force, to the nearest hospital. My attention soon shifted back to the deity himself. He seemed relaxed but had an undeniable aura of power about him. Every movement was graceful and predatory.

A closer look at the recruits gave me the feeling that I wasn't the only one that sensed it. The recruits seemed mesmerized by Nalithor, but also fearful. Although I didn't find him frightening, I could understand their fear. If they were as green as they seemed, I doubted they knew how to read his hunter-like demeanor.

The feeling of him nuzzling my throat still lingered, distracting me yet again. More distracting yet, I didn't understand why my threats to that woman, and to my brother, seemed to draw and excite Nalithor in such a way. Even his purring had been attractive. It was beyond me how Nalithor managed to be so...sensual all the time. At first, I thought it was because he was an Adinvyr, but I had yet to come across another Adinvyr that had quite the same air as Nalithor.

Perhaps that, and his demeanor, indicated that he was indeed hunting. Hunting me. I shook my head a little at the idea. I doubted it.

"Alala, you seem rather comfortable," I remarked dryly, turning my gaze to the fox in an attempt to distract myself from the Adinvyr deity she'd perched on. "You know, Nalithor, she usually hates *everyone*. This is a little strange."

"She apparently approves of my scent." Nalithor laughed and shifted in his seat, turning his intense gaze to me. "You're certain that I can't convince you to join me for a drink, Arianna?"

"Ah… Do you have siblings, Nalithor?" I questioned, earning an inquisitive look.

"Quite a few, yes." Nalithor nodded, tilting his head as his eyes drifted from my face and down to trace my figure.

"Then the best way I can explain it… Hmmm. My duty as a *sibling* takes precedence tonight." A small frown formed on my face as I thought, hoping he wouldn't require further elaboration. "This has everything to do with me being a concerned sister, and nothing to do with our status as mages or royalty."

"I understand." Nalithor smiled at me and caught hold of my hand, kissing the back of it. His eyes flicked upward, revealing a playful twinkle in his eyes. "Another time, then?"

"Sure…" I answered, hesitant as I examined that smile of his. "You know, with such a predatory look about you, one has to wonder what your intentions are."

"Nothing unpleasant, I assure you." Nalithor's mischievous purr made me shoot him a suspicious look. "Very well, I'll hold you to it. After these trials are over, I will release you."

"Release—?" I started to question him. Nalithor laughed and pulled me over the arm of his chair and back onto his lap.

'You're still my captive for a little while longer.' Nalithor smiled down at me as I reached up to adjust my hood—not only to make sure it was still in place, but to hide my reddened face. The playful deity shifted me so that I was sitting beside him once more but

kept an arm around me.

'*So difficult to deal with.*' I thought behind my deeper layers of shields, catching the faint tilt of his head as his eyes flicked down at me again. '*Tch, he can sense me thinking behind even* these *shields?! I'm going to have to be even more careful than I thought when it comes to this man.*'

CHAPTER TEN
Protective Services

'Human, or Devillian?' I wandered through the house with a small frown set on my face. *'It really is getting difficult to tell what I am. Before, I would have been inclined to say that I'm physically Human…but I shouldn't be able to keep up with Nalithor if that's the case.'*

I made my way into the kitchen and proceeded to brew a pot of coffee for Darius and a cup of tea for me. My twin hadn't spoken a word since challenging me the previous day. His stifling jealousy had subsided sometime in the morning, but I couldn't sense if he was still angry with me. Hells, I still couldn't believe he had actually challenged me.

As much as I enjoyed sparring with Nalithor, our latest match had left me with more questions that I wanted answers to—and Darius' challenge had only exacerbated that.

Throughout our childhood, I was never certain which of us was the more powerful twin. Darius' unwillingness to learn and to train had caused a great divide in our abilities of course, but I now wondered if there was more to it than that. Darius seemed terrified by the sheer amount of power the Vorpmasian and Beshulthien Archmagi exuded—including Nalithor—and regardless of elemental affinity.

Darius' reaction was like what I would have expected from the Humans back in X'shmir. My twin looked upon the Archmagi with an awe-filled reverence that was muddied by fear. A reverence that I couldn't understand because I found the Archmagi's power underwhelming at best. Was I arrogant? Had I simply become stronger than I first believed? I hoped to the gods that I hadn't grown conceited, but it was a genuine, and growing, concern.

'Djialkan, why doesn't Darius have Brands of Divinity?' I questioned while searching the kitchen for a tray and plates. *'I remember he was terribly jealous of mine when we were children.'*

'The bastards who took us from Vorpmasia had greater success in dealing with Darius' powers. Yours were problematic for them at best.' Djialkan hissed, bristling on my shoulder. *'He had already begun to fear magic far before those fools interfered. They were able to prey on such weakness and use it to make him more "Human" than you are.'*

'Still, I don't think I should be able to fight toe-to-toe with a

deity—let alone one that is also a male Devillian.' I grimaced, arranging snacks and pastries on the first platter I found. *'Darius and I seem as though we're close in raw power. I know he fears his magic, but—'*

'You are physically less Human than the boy is,' Djialkan interrupted me, his voice firm. *'However, you are correct on the matter of Nalithor. He should be capable of destroying you with little effort, and yet he appears to spar you seriously. That he is impervious to a* Godslayer *indicates that he* should *be quite powerful. Perhaps the situation with the Elder Gods is worse than Fraelfnir and I feared.'*

'You're still investigating?' I offered Djialkan a strip of raw meat.

'Aye. Onyre and Aleri are just as concerned as my brother and I.' Djialkan snapped up the bloody meat before continuing, *'They both wish to meet with you as soon as you can find the time. In the interim, I will continue to learn what I can from them and from the Vorpmasians.'*

I finished my task of piling the platter with a variety of edibles and nodded to myself. I'd left a little room for Darius' coffee and my tea and placed those atop it before lifting it.

As much as Darius had annoyed me since we came Below, I couldn't help but worry about my brother and his fragile state of mind. It pained me that Nalithor's apparent interest in me managed to make Darius even more erratic than normal. I wasn't quite sure how to deal with either of them at this point.

I made my way toward the first-floor study in search of my

twin and hoped that a peace offering of hot coffee and his favorite snacks would help him open up—or at least relax. Although I wanted to get on his case about needing to study, that could wait until I'd determined if Darius was going to lose control of his temper or abilities.

"Darius?" I nudged the door to the study open, taking care not to drop the platter. "I brought you some coffee and—"

"Ari," Darius interjected with a heavy sigh, "I really fucked myself by ignoring Fraelfnir and Djialkan's teachings, didn't I?"

I arched an eyebrow and examined my brother as I approached him. His emerald eyes were downcast, his dull gaze fixated on the floor. Even under all the heavy robes I could tell his shoulders were slumped. It had been a long time since I'd last seen my brother look this glum. Little light shone in his usually bright eyes, his expression was demoralized and pensive. Gone was the familiar childish facade.

"I won't pretend that it doesn't set you back," I began, offering my twin his cup of coffee. "Since you didn't take their lessons to heart, you're now lacking both your foundation in magic and as a healer. You have a great deal of raw power at your fingertips and no knowledge on how to control it. *That* is why the Archmagi forbade you from using magic outside of class and training. They're concerned that you will lose control and hurt yourself or others."

"That's why Nalithor was so angry with me? He thinks I'll seriously hurt someone?" Darius asked with a pout after a deep gulp of coffee. When I nodded, he slumped back against the couch, nearly sloshing his coffee onto his white robes.

"Given Nalithor's status, the safety of the people is likely important to him—'the people' includes you and I in this case. You could have electrocuted yourself. Worse, you could have electrocuted everyone present had you called forth far too much," I pointed out, divvying our food onto plates. "Judging by what I've learned of Draemiran culture thus far, I think he may have also taken offense to your comments when you arrived."

"Because he saw you as his 'prize' or whatever?" Darius' expression scrunched into one of immense confusion and he leaned forward, continuing, "What does that mean, exactly? After a claim like that I didn't expect you to come home last night at—"

"I lost our duel," I interjected dryly, holding a plate of food in front of Darius' face and waiting for him to take it. "Nalithor decided he wanted my company for the remainder of the day as his 'prize' for winning. In all honesty, I think he was just looking for a distraction from the recruits—they were mostly awful."

"Speaking of awful..." Darius frowned at his plate for a moment. "Just how bad was my magical aptitude test, Ari? Honestly?"

"I can't say for certain since I don't know the specifics of their testing." I shook my head and motioned with my free hand as I spoke. "Your control is almost non-existent. We're probably lucky that you haven't blown half the X'shmiran castle into oblivion."

"What would you suggest then, Ari?" Darius pleaded. "You know that I want to become a healer. I don't want to hurt or conquer anyone!"

"You need to strike a balance of learning about our new surroundings and about magic…" I murmured, sitting back against the sofa. "Normally I would say learning to control your abilities comes first but…

"Fraelfnir, can you continue moderating Darius' power for a little while longer?"

"You believe his lack of knowledge regarding the Vorpmasians is more pressing?" Fraelfnir cocked his head and stared at me from his perch.

"I think it's safe to say that Darius will be assigned classes at the academy and not field work." I nodded at the golden-eyed fae-dragon. "Darius needs to learn as much as he can about the various Vorpmasian cultures before he begins classes. Furthermore, there's the problem of helping the Vorpmasian Families convince the X'shmirans to allow temples and schools to be built on X'shmiran soil.

"It would be very bad if he was rude to the wrong people, don't you think?"

"He has already been atrociously rude to the wrong people," Djialkan spoke dryly and then stole a piece of meat from my plate. *"Darius, do you not realize how poor of an impression you have given the Vorpmasians—particularly Nalithor—thanks to your childish*

behavior?"

Darius froze mid-bite and stared at Djialkan in disbelief. I could practically hear the gears turning in my twin's head as his eyes widened and his jaw tensed, undoubtedly clamping down hard on his fork. A flick of his emerald eyes to the side at Fraelfnir appeared to make him realize that the fae-dragon brothers were in agreement, for once.

"I'm worried about the rules Ari has to follow!" Darius sighed, lowering his fork. "I... I know I can be a pain sometimes, but I'm scared of losing you to these stupid fucking X'shmiran laws!"

"Nalithor is far too powerful for the X'shmirans to enforce such foolish laws against him." Fraelfnir snorted, shaking his mane. *"You and Arianna have both surpassed the level of 'acquaintance' already with that one, as far as X'shmiran law is concerned.*

"That Arianna has not been directed to slay him, or executed by her curse, is proof enough that their laws mean nothing when a god of his level is concerned."

"Arianna is correct, however. Darius, you will be interacting with Vorpmasians and Beshulthiens of all social standings while you attend the academy," Djialkan began in a firm, lecturing tone. *"It would be best for you to learn what you can about foreign ways before then. You would like to avoid potential war, would you not?"*

"War...?" Darius grew pale.

"That's what I meant by being rude to—in other words, pissing off—the wrong people." I nodded. "As much as I enjoy bloodshed,

I can't do anything against an invading force if we somehow nullify our standing in the Rilzaan Alliance. We also have the problem of deities to consider—all the Family representatives we met were demigods, meaning the kings and queens are all Lesser Gods. The deities are more personally-involved with mortal matters than I think either of us were prepared for."

"And you have angered a very important one, Darius," Fraelfnir added, nudging Darius' elbow with his snout. *"We have been unable to determine Nalithor's exact role thus far. However, we do know that he has power over at least some of the Upper Gods."*

"Darius, you don't have an escort for today, right?" I murmured, examining my twin and his gaudy robes. "I have an idea. How about you and I go into the city and learn what we can? There are plenty of historical landmarks and the like for us to learn from, and then there's the citizens and tourists themselves of course."

"You'll come with me?" Darius perked up, his eyes lighting up when he grinned. "Are you sure? I've been such a—!"

"Well, we do both have a lot to learn." I tilted my head and glanced over his robes again. "I'm your bodyguard *and* your sister, remember? Both mean I'm going to look after you.

"So, finish your food and then go get dressed in something more…casual. We're going to go get ourselves acquainted with our new surroundings."

"Alala will watch the house," Djialkan spoke, beating his wings

a few times and leaving my shoulder. *"I will speak with Nalithor or other academy staff and bring back tomes that are appropriate for each of you."*

"Ari, how do you feel about Nalithor?" Darius asked after several minutes of eating in silence. I shot him a questioning look as I chewed my food, so he continued, "I don't mean this in a bad way but…it's really strange to see you interacting with someone after all these years. If anything, I would've expected you to avoid people at all costs—especially considering the way you're treated back home."

"Back home" huh? I refrained from rolling my eyes, swallowing my food instead before answering, "I'd say Nalithor has gone out of his way to make sure I feel welcome in Dauthrmir. He's fun to spar but, beyond that, I don't know how to deal with him. Hells, I don't even know what to think of him still.

"I'm fairly certain that he just wants whatever information he can get out of me. I can't really think of many other reasons for a deity to interact with a mortal so much."

I stuffed another large heaping of food into my mouth as I felt a stab of pain through my chest. I bit down on my fork as if that would help me bury my frustration. Even though being used was "normal" for me at this point, something about the notion of Nalithor using me was upsetting. For some reason, I felt as if he wouldn't do such a thing. Nevertheless, I didn't know him well enough yet to make that kind of assessment.

Perhaps I just wanted genuine interaction from someone for once.

"I'll go fetch an overrobe and my mask, then meet you in the foyer," I informed Darius while I gathered up our plates and stacked them on the tray. "You do have *something* casual, right? Dressing like you're heading to court is likely to estrange the citizens and tourists, not endear them."

Darius nodded excitedly and then darted off toward his rooms. Fraelfnir took flight and chased after my twin, snorting his displeasure. I simply remained on the sofa for a moment with the platter balanced on my lap, watching as both Darius and his scaly companion disappeared down the hallway.

The idea that Nalithor was using me had left a lump in my throat, and I needed a moment to regain my composure.

Sighing, I pulled myself off the sofa and carried the platter back into the kitchen, locking away my emotions as I walked. I couldn't let myself get distracted by such trivial things while escorting my brother through Dauthrmir. I needed to be focused.

'Trivial...' I shook my head and ascended the stairs to search for a lightweight robe. *'No matter what his intentions are, I can't really claim anything about that one is "trivial." What little memory of the past I have is enough to prove that he cared deeply about whoever I used to be.'*

After pinning my hair up, I donned one of the robes Shir and Gari had provided me with. If nothing else, I had decided to take

Corentine and Nalithor's advice. I wouldn't hide my Brands of Divinity any longer.

The translucent attire the Oracles had conjured for me had disappeared upon removal, so my choices were either full-X'shmiran robes or the ones the Guardians had created for me. Alas, the warmer temperatures in Dauthrmir went a long way toward making up my mind. Admittedly, the previous day's events affected my decision as well. Peoples' demeanor towards me was considerably warmer once my Brands were visible.

I only hoped that Darius and I would find a way to circumvent the laws regarding hoods and masks as well. Both items made me stand out far more than I wanted to, and for all the wrong reasons.

"Ready?" I strode downstairs once more and into the foyer, examining my brother's layers of white, gold, and jade robes. "Is that *really* the most casual set you have, Darius?"

"I wasn't kidding when I said I need new stuff," Darius answered sheepishly. "What about you? I don't recognize those robes...but I know you couldn't possibly have gone shopping."

"Sihix's Guardians and High Priestess knew I'd need new attire for this climate," I answered with a small shake of my head as I passed him. I tugged on one of his thick sleeves and continued, "Let's go. We can poke around the Merchant's Plaza while we try to learn about the city and its people. Since the temples to the gods are there, perhaps we can learn about those as well."

"Oh yes, please!" Darius nodded with startling vigor. "After you left our meeting the other day, the Families suggested that I learn what I can at the temples themselves. They said it might help us figure out ways to convince Mother and Father to allow such additions to X'shmir."

"It's still going to go over terribly with our parents." I grimaced, shaking my head once more. "You hope to learn enough about the gods and their temples in order to convince them, then?"

"Uh-huh!" Darius fell into step with me. "They don't understand the importance gods hold to outsiders—and I have to admit I don't understand it either. At least, not to the full extent. I want to learn about the gods so that I can make a valid argument with our parents and convince them to sign the bill that will allow the construction of temples."

"Well, I suppose we did see *some* hint of the strain disallowing foreign religions could cause," I murmured, watching as Darius nodded. He looked delighted that I understood, even though it was such a simple concept. "Darius, I need you to do me one favor."

"Hmm? A favor?" Darius blinked in surprise. "What favor?"

"You recall that yesterday, before our tests, I was speaking to Nalithor about the books I lent him?" I watched a brief scowl cross Darius' face. He huffed and nodded, so I continued, "Our texts are outright offensive to those of Vorpmasian origin. Nalithor was concerned about how many of the texts I lent him are in circulation or otherwise taught publicly."

"Offensive? Oh dear…" Darius frowned, crossing his arms

over his narrow chest as he thought. "Is that why he seemed so tetchy? His behavior struck me as strange… Actually, his behavior is always strange—what am I saying?"

"Another example of why you need to learn about Devillians in particular," I commented as I glanced around the surprisingly empty Sapphire Quarter, taking in the blooming trees for a moment before motioning for my brother to follow me down a road. "Most of what I know is outdated as well, mind you.

"Back to my favor… I want you to do your best to put the X'shmiran teachings about deities and Devillians from your mind while we're here. We already know that even *if* I'm assigned classes, I won't be partnered with you. You and your partner will be responsible for each other's wellbeing, and they *won't be Human*."

"You have a point…" Darius murmured, still frowning. "It's so strange to think that you won't be acting as my bodyguard soon. Then there's the fact we must work while here! I wonder why nobles and royals are required to work?"

"It's probably so that they don't become entitled brats that look down on commoners." I shrugged, surveying our surroundings and examining the elaborate yet eclectic assortment of estates that had been built in the Nobles' district. "Besides, can you really claim that a city—or country—like this could be maintained with only the commoners working? I'd imagine the barrier itself requires a great number of mages to maintain it. *You* for example 'work' as an ambassador. Well, ambassador-in-training."

"Wanna keep an eye out for potential jobs while we explore the city?" Something about Darius' huge grin made my stomach sink. "Maybe we can find work at one of the temples—that'd be killing stones with one bird or whatever, right?"

"Two birds with one stone, Darius." I couldn't help but laugh despite my unease. "Let's focus on learning first. Job-searching should be secondary, for now."

Darius pouted and then seemed to ponder the notion for a moment. Finally, he voiced his agreement. I hoped that I could keep my brother out of trouble while we wandered through the city at least, but I knew that would be difficult. I could already sense trouble brewing and we weren't even halfway through the Nobles' District yet!

The pair of scents following us were distinctly familiar. I growled, glancing around again in search of any close-by threats. Darius shot me a questioning frown, but he was familiar enough with my stance to understand what was going on. A brief expression of panic crossed his face before he pursed his lips tight and focused his gaze forward, eyes wide.

'We're being followed,' I stated, glancing to the side at my brother. *'What do you know about servants from X'shmir being sent here?'*

'Servants? From the castle?' Darius sounded befuddled. *'There shouldn't be anyone from X'shmir here aside from you and me. One of the teams of Vorpmasian scholars recently returned from an extended*

stay, but I doubt they would've brought anyone back with them.'

'They're not here to be friendly.' I glanced at our surroundings, confirming the district was empty except for us, the X'shmirans, and the spies that Vorpmasians had tailing us at all times. *'You're prepared for the usual?'*

'Your ice is cold *you know,'* Darius whined. *'But yes...'*

I stopped on the crystalline road and took a deep inhale of the cool morning air, shutting my eyes. I concentrated on the myriad of shadows that littered the district and found myself thankful for the endless night that this part of Vorpmasia experienced. It provided me with so much to work with. Satisfied with my "grip" on the shadows, my eyes snapped open and wove the shadows across the sky above the Nobles' District. In an instant the light from the stars, neighboring planets, and waning crescent moons were blotted out.

"Wh-what was that?!" A familiar male voice whimpered some yards behind us.

"Shh, you fool! They can't see this in this darkness either! This is our chance!" A husky-voiced woman snapped. "Let's take out the prince and be done with it. The contract will kill his bitch sister for failing to protect him!"

'Humph, fools.' The corner of my eye twitched when I sensed their bloodlust rising. I felt them slinking through the shadows again, but this time it was the ones I had gripped.

With a small motion, I erected a hollow sphere of ice around my brother just as the Humans leapt toward us. I caught the acrid scent of crude poison on their blades as I turned to face them. I pulled darkness around my hands and forearms like gauntlets while examining the Humans' startled faces. Their expressions twisted into fear when I leered at them, revealing my fangs. I sunk into a crouch for a split second before launching myself at them.

Darkness formed into an elongated blade in my right hand, which I tore through the man's shoulder. His knife arm went tumbling to the ground in a spray of crimson, his screams echoing through the district, but I felt no sympathy for him. Instead, I leapt for the woman next.

"Who sent you?" I demanded, shifting my darkness into a blunt object once more. I caught the woman's blade arm with one hand and then twisted it until it cracked, making her wail in agony. "Ahhh… While that *is* better, it isn't very informative."

"L-l-let me go, you monster!" the Human woman spat furiously. I tilted my head and watched her squirm, tightening my grip on her broken wrist and ground the fragments of her shattered bones together. "Fucking bitch!"

Sensing movement from the side, I released the woman and stepped back as her companion attempted to slice me open with a second blade. Irritated by the interruption, I gripped the man with several tendrils of darkness and tossed him dismissively against a stone wall. I rounded on the woman once more; she looked as if she couldn't decide between terror and fury.

"The first one to tell me who sent you gets to live," I stated, bored, as I examined the nails of my left hand. "Whichever one doesn't speak up will have the honor of being the test subject for this new torture technique I've been considering…"

"We're not telling you anything!" The male groaned from where he lay crumpled on the ground, unable to move any longer due to the blood pouring from his amputated arm.

"Fine. Then I'll just—" I began with a growl, preparing to shred them with my darkness.

"Arianna-jiss, if you'll allow me," a voice offered from behind me. I pursed my lips, irritated, when I caught Eyrian's fresh ocean scent approaching me. "I believe my men in the Dauthrmiran prisons are more than capable of pulling information out of them. By your fury, I take it this isn't your average 'disagreement.'"

"These two are servants of the X'shmiran royal family," I began with distaste, allowing the shadows to return to their proper places. "It would appear they were sent by *someone* to assassinate Darius."

"Thus, the ice chamber?" Eyrian questioned dryly as he passed me. He ruffled my hair through my hood with one of his large tan hands and added, "Don't have much patience for torture, do you?"

"Humans don't have much in the way of pain tolerance," I retorted with a huff, turning to stalk towards the icy orb I'd conjured around Darius. "You'd think they'd be more forthcoming than this but *nooo*, they couldn't possibly spill their secrets to the 'family monster.'"

Rolling my eyes, I made a dismissive motion and burst the orb of ice into frost. Darius sneezed a few times as the particles tickled his nose, and then turned his attention to Eyrian and the Humans. When Darius spotted the severed arm on the ground nearby, he turned a shade of pale green and turned his back to the scene with trembling shoulders.

If he thought *that* was bad, he was in for a rude awakening if he truly wished to become a healer.

"I'd offer you escorts…but I guess you weren't kidding when you said you don't need one." Eyrian frowned at me. "I smell poison. They didn't nick you, did they?"

"I'm fine, thanks." I shook my head and then glanced to the side as several more men from the Imperial Guard trotted down the street toward us. "This isn't an uncommon occurrence, Eyrian. I want to know who sent them and how they received permission to come to Dauthrmir."

"Not your blood then?" Eyrian motioned at his own cheek and then pointed at mine.

"Hmmm?" I brought my fingers to my cheek and then examined them, my mouth turning into a wry smile upon spotting the scarlet blood. "No. Not mine.

"Shall we get going, Darius? I know you can't stomach the smell of blood for long."

Darius promptly latched onto my arm and dragged me down the road, so I half-turned to wave a farewell at the uneasy Draekin.

Clearly if I wanted to speak with Eyrian, this wasn't the opportunity to do so. My twin's wellbeing would have to take precedence.

CHAPTER ELEVEN
Realization

"Ari, are you sure it's still okay for us to go out?" Darius whispered, his grip on my arm trembling. "What if they're not actually here to assassinate me? What if they're here to take me back to X'shmir? I'd rather—"

"They were talking about assassinating you in order to make the contract kill me," I informed Darius, casting a brief frown down at his trembling hands. *'Fraelfnir, are you close? It would seem we have a problem already.'*

'I am on my way; I caught the scent of Human blood whilst hunting,' Fraelfnir answered with a growl. *'Is my ward alright?'*

'He's been extremely shaky since yesterday's exams, and now he's even worse.' I led Darius toward the residential district, noticing

that my twin didn't even cast a glance at Nalithor's café when we passed it. *'I was hoping to educate him while distracting him from whatever is bothering him, but...'*

'Perhaps a visit to the temples first is in order,' Fraelfnir commented as he swooped down from the sky and landed on Darius' shoulder, earning a flinch from my twin. *'There are several deities visiting Dauthrmir today that Darius may take a liking to. One or two of which would have the power to calm his nerves, I believe. I cannot promise that they will react favorably to your presence however, Arianna.'*

'My main concern right now is Darius,' I informed Fraelfnir as I sent tendrils of my power slinking through the city in search of other threats. *'We'll take a brief break in the plaza itself before heading for the temples. If worst comes to worst, I get the feeling that the Vorpmasian spies will lend us a hand.'*

'Aye, I do not think they are monitoring you out of concern that you may harm the citizens.' Fraelfnir lifted his muzzle into the air and sniffed a few times. *'The Vorpmasians seem intent on keeping the two of you safe. More shadewalkers have joined the first.'*

'Eyrian's doing, I'd bet.' I grimaced.

The farther away we got from the bloodthirsty Human assassins, the more I relaxed. Although I still wanted to rip them into unrecognizable pieces, I knew it would be better to have the Vorpmasians question the bastards—perhaps the X'shmiran's fear of Devillians would come in useful.

Even so, I was disappointed that my fun had been interrupted.

"Darius, are you alright?" I glanced at my shaky sibling.

"That…was so much blood!" Darius exclaimed, his grip on my arm tightening. "All from just having his arm cut off! Why—?"

"You haven't learned much about anatomy, I take it?" I frowned as Darius turned to me with a questioning look on his face. "Well, I guess I'll be sharing some books with you then. You can't heal without intimate knowledge of anatomy, Darius. If Djialkan doesn't return with tomes on such subjects, I'll fetch some from the library myself."

"I will inform my brother of our needs," Fraelfnir offered with a small tilt of his head.

The three of us fell back into silence as we meandered through Dauthrmir's streets. I found myself constantly searching for potential threats as we walked. I had to force myself to calm down so that I wouldn't make Darius any more nervous than he already was, but it was difficult. Even the "shadewalkers," as Fraelfnir had called them, seemed to have sensed my mood and had put more distance between them and us.

Despite our frequent disagreements and differing views, I was impressed that my brother was able to hold himself together—to an extent—despite the assassination attempts.

'Just who wants to kill him, though?' I pondered, examining the throngs of Devillians, Elves, and Humans that wandered through the Merchant's Plaza. *'Without him, the king and queen no longer*

have an heir—it wouldn't make sense for them to seek his death. However, the commoners wouldn't have the coin to hire assassins from the castle. Hmmm… The nobles, then?'

I took a deep, calming breath and refocused my attention on our immediate surroundings. The people here seemed so genuinely cheerful, especially if compared to the citizens of X'shmir. It still stuck me as strange to see smiling commoners moving about their duties with joyous expressions on their faces. Unlike the people of X'shmir, the Dauthrmiran commoners weren't dragging their feet, their expressions weren't dark and cast at the ground. Their gaits were peppy. Sure, there was the occasional moping soul here and there. However, in X'shmir, all of them would have been moping.

My twin and I headed for the central section of the plaza and perched on an ebony bench that faced the plaza's centerpiece; a massive statue. The monument depicted Devillian children amongst a myriad of adults and Elves of all ages. The pale blue-white stone shone brilliantly in the mixed rays of Magelight, glowing plants, and dim moonslight. A quick look at our surroundings told me this statue was important for some reason or another, because Devillians and a sprinkling of Elves were present and leaving offerings at the monument's base or otherwise had their eyes shut as if praying.

"Oi, Darius!" A vaguely familiar voice with a light Draemiran accent called.

I glanced to my right and past Darius to find a familiar face approaching us. The caramel-skinned man was one of the two "Not-Elf's" that I often saw in Nalithor and Eyrian's company. His short, spiky black hair and unnaturally pale blue eyes were unmistakable. This time, however, I spotted his upper fangs when he grinned at us—as well as the absence of the lower fangs I'd have expected from a Devillian.

'A Vampire, then?' I narrowed my eyes and watched Darius' expression light up when he grinned at the taller man. *'He's not quite as muscular or tall as Eyrian and Nalithor... Though, he is nice to look at. It's strange he doesn't smell like those other Vampires did. Something really* was *wrong with them, then?'*

"Ahhh, the feisty princess is here too!" The man grinned and bowed flamboyantly, offering me his hand. "I apologize for my lack of manners during our previous meetings, Reiz'tar. I'm Xander Leukos, Nalithor's adopted younger brother."

"Pleasure, I'm sure," I replied simply, arching an eyebrow when the Vampire's grin broadened prior to kissing my hand. "Adopted brother you say? That's interesting..."

"It's thanks to these kids," Xander motioned at the monument after straightening, then cast a glance over his shoulder at the pale stone. "Though, I suppose that's a history lesson for another time. Suffice to say that Nalithor and his partner—your namesake— rescued many Elves and Devillians from a terrible fate. Afterwards, the Vraelimir Family took me in.

"Now then, what's with the glum face, Darius? You look like

someone stole your favorite drink!"

'Part...ner?' I stared blankly at the statue in front of me, completely forgetting about my surroundings as a torrent of mixed emotions rushed through me. *'I was his...partner? We rescued people from something? We were* children*! What in the infernal hells could we possibly have accomplished at that age?!'*

My eyes ticked back and forth in thought, and I crossed my arms tightly. I brought a knuckle up to my lips and bit it as I tried to make sense of it. Fifty years of age for a Devillian was the equivalent of a Human's five years of age. I couldn't fathom children that young doing *any* of the things Xander had so casually mentioned. Yet, I didn't sense that he was lying.

I found myself examining the statue again, at a loss of what to think. Partner. That one word managed to send feelings of intense confusion, loss, and frustration through me. Suddenly the fact that I once lived in Dauthrmir had become more "real" to me, and I didn't know how to cope with it.

Careful reexamination of the monument allowed me to spot the carving that was clearly in the likeness of Nalithor as a child. Adjacent to him was a carving that could only be me, engulfed in rage. Nalithor was reaching for me while stylized darkness and flames tore through faceless Elven bodies that were dressed in Susthulite clothing.

The Devillians and Elves of the monument that I'd noticed before were all running away from the slain figures and toward our much smaller forms with relieved expressions on their faces. Several of the Devillians had Brands of Divinity etched into their skin, adding to my unease. Shackles and chains littered the ground around the faceless people that "my" fire and darkness devoured.

Everything seemed to stop when I finally read the inscription on the memorial.

In memory of Her Highness, Arianna Jade Shujare, heiress to the Dauthrmiran throne.

It was with this act that she laid the foundation for the formation of the Vorpmasian Empire by striking down the corrupted elite of V'frul, alongside His Highness Nalithor Vraelimir, heir to the Draemiran throne. Together they liberated Elven and Devillian slaves alike, without care for affiliation, and going against their mission in favor of the greater good.

We shall all remember Her Highness's unrelenting desire to adhere to the greater good and seek justice for wrongdoings. Even in the face of the Elder Gods, she did not back down.

We are forever in her debt.

"—her body was never relinquished to us by the Elders." Xander's lecturing tone snapped me back to reality, and I continued to stare at the statue in silence. "The bastards wouldn't even let us bury her properly. The citizens were outraged, as you can imagine, so we built a monument to her deeds instead. They saved several Devillian gods and demigods amongst the slaves, I'm sure you can imagine that they felt indebted to Her Highness.

"Nalithor, though… He couldn't even look at the memorial for nearly a century."

"That's awful!" Darius exclaimed as I maintained my silence and attempted to calm my racing heartbeat. "Why would the Elders do such a thing?"

The false innocence and curiosity in my twin's voice grabbed my attention. I slid my eyes to the side and peered at Darius from behind my mask. His shocked facade wasn't convincing. Was he simply trying to humor Xander, or…was there something else I was missing?

'Djialkan, why didn't you tell me Nalithor was my partner?' I demanded, unable to keep the snarl out of my voice when I turned back to the monument.

'What would it have changed?' Djialkan countered with a snort.

'I don't like surprises, Djialkan,' I spat.

"Always the quiet one, eh?" Xander moved in front of me, blocking my field of view. I swallowed the lump in my throat, irritated, and tilted my head back to look up at the Vampire. I couldn't read his expression at all.

"A habit from X'shmir," I replied. "It's still unusual being allowed to speak freely."

"Darius says you both came into the city to learn about all of us, right?" Xander broke into a grin and jabbed his chest with his thumb. "Why not let me be your tour guide? I don't have any duties to attend to today, so I was *awfully* bored before I spotted the two of you over here."

'Ah…right. He was one of the Archmagi at our exams yesterday.'
I frowned, considering the offer. "On your day off? Aren't we a
little too boring to be playing host to an Archmagus?"

"So, you did spot me!" Xander's grin broadened. He leaned
down slightly and offered both of us a hand, though his gaze was
on me for the moment. "*Arianna-jiss,* Nalithor told me about your
encounter with the Vampires several nights ago. He said you
noticed they seemed strange?"

*'Did he really need to say my name like that? Fuck. Is he suspicious?
I don't need this right now!'* I grit my teeth for a moment as Xander
pulled Darius and I to our feet. "Yes, we ran into Vampires on the
way back from dinner. They were strange. They were different
from you in scent and in appearance."

"Dealing with 'strange' Vampires like them is one of my
duties," Xander began as I reclaimed my hand and stuffed them
into my pockets. I strongly considered withdrawing one in order
to punch the Vampire when he began examining my cleavage,
though. "If you discover any other Vampires that are unusual, I
would appreciate it if you bring the matter to my attention."

"Sure, if I don't kill them first." I spoke dismissively, ignoring
the frown they both shot me. "The inscription says that she stood
her ground against even Elders. What is that referencing?"

"A few days after returning from V'frul with all of us in tow,"
Xander began, shifting to look at the monument as well, "the

Elders appeared in the original throne room of the Dauthrmiran palace—I'm sure you saw the door to it, it's the one Lucifer keeps sealed off.

"The Elders were enraged that the princess had slaughtered the majority of Vfrul's nobility in the process of rescuing us from the slave auction, even though there were *gods* in the mix of slaves. She insisted that rescuing us was the right thing to do, that it was for the 'greater good,' and that leaving us to the slavers would have caused some terrible tragedy. The Elders took offense. They believed that she was claiming to know better than the beings that created our world. So…they had her slain."

"What?!" Darius yelped, for once voicing my own thoughts; and finally sounding genuine. "The *Elders* took offense to… That's absurd! By that logic, they of all people should have known she was in the right! How could Nalithor go and serve the people that murdered—"

"The Elders stand divided, from what I understand." Xander shook his head, his expression strained. "I don't know the details, but *dozens* of children like Her Highness were slain by one faction of the Elder Gods. The Elders that Nalithor serves are the faction that is trying to *stop* the murderous ones."

"Politics." I rolled my eyes behind my mask, biting back a slew of sarcastic remarks. "Gods and demigods amongst the slaves, though? I would have thought they'd have the power to escape…"

"I'm afraid I can't explain that one to you, *Arianna-jiss.*"

Xander shot me an odd look when he enunciated my name again. "The reason for *that* is still classified after all this time, as it could become a very real threat again if the wrong people find out. I'm sure you understand."

"Of course." I nodded to him. "Thank you for the answers you *could* give us, at any rate.

"I believe you mentioned something about playing 'tour guide,' hmmm?"

"I did!" Xander grinned mischievously. "I'll teach the both of you *anything* you like. Darius mentioned something about wanting to learn more about the gods and their temples. What about you?"

"This is about Darius." I shrugged. "Darius needs to learn about the cultures he will be exposed to at the academy, and for political reasons he needs to learn about the gods—I'm sure you heard some of what transpired at our meeting with the Families."

"Are you saying that you don't need to learn about them yourself?" Xander's grin shifted into a subtle frown as he examined me. "I'm sure Djialkan has taught you some, but—"

"I just don't care right now," I interjected flatly, crossing my arms beneath my bust as I attempted to battle down my displeasure. "My grasp is basic while Darius' is nonexistent. I will garner what information I can while he *begins* to learn. I believe it would be best to focus on getting him up to speed."

I closed my eyes briefly, shutting the shining memorial out of my vision as I tried, again, to calm myself. My pulse still raced at an alarming pace, worrying me that Xander or others near us might hear it. To make matters worse, I felt as if I'd been hit in the gut. Crossing my arms seemed to be the only way to keep myself from trembling or fidgeting. I wanted nothing more than to run back to the house and sulk in the dark under my fluffy blankets.

This new-found knowledge was slowly ripping me apart and I found myself growing numb and distant in response. I didn't know how else to deal with it, and I sure as hells didn't know how I would face Nalithor again after hearing even a *hint* of how poorly he had taken my "death."

'I should have known from his reaction to seeing me in Limbo,' I contemplated, gritting my teeth as I followed Darius and Xander. *'Personal feelings aside…this is strange. Warring factions within the Elders? Enslaved deities? The Elders Nalithor serves are in opposition of the ones that "killed" me? I don't like this, not at all.'*

"What of my namesake, Xander?" Darius inquired, drawing my attention to their backs.

"He was raised by his mother." Xander shook his head. "His Highness was rarely seen in Dauthrmir or in Draemir from what I understand. Mentioning the twins' mother is a taboo—I strongly recommend against it."

I only half-listened as their conversation veered away from the past and back to the present. Instead, I focused on every minute detail I could spot in the Merchant's Plaza. *Anything* to distract me from the sensation of my heart being ripped from my chest. How close had Nalithor and I been as children? Were we partners for a single mission, or had we worked together for longer than that? Why were we traveling and accomplishing missions at such a young age? Just how hard had my "death" been on him?

'This is giving me a headache and then some...' I complained to myself, clenching my hands into fists within my pockets and turning my gaze to the crystal road beneath me. *'After rescuing me from Limbo, how did he...how did he cope with losing me all over again? That false hope must have been devastating. Or...had he recovered sufficiently by then?*

'No, no. I doubt that was it. He seemed truly distraught when he realized who I was.'

The emotions were beyond my comprehension. No matter how I thought on it, I simply couldn't understand or fathom the possibilities. It was a kind of pain that I couldn't relate to, and I wasn't sure if I wanted to.

"What do you mean 'I need to learn about Draemiran bathing customs?!'" Darius yelped, just barely catching my attention. "I-I can't possibly bathe with other people! That's—"

"It's not like you have anything they haven't seen before," I stated flatly.

"She has a point." Xander laughed, motioning at me. "Any preference on what temple we visit first, Arianna-jiss?"

"None." I watched as Xander's cheerful expression faltered, his mouth turning down into a frown as he examined me. *'So, he is suspicious of me, then? Does he think that perhaps his "savior" has returned? Ugh, that's such a strange thought after all of the things and people I've killed in X'shmir.'*

"I still don't quite understand the purpose of temples." Darius shook his head, sighing in frustration.

"They serve multiple functions," Xander began, casting me one more look before motioning to the nearest temple; a massive structure built from pink and red marble, adorned with gilt accents. "When a deity comes to visit a capital city for one reason or another, they stay in their temple. The faithful often come to the main floor of the temples in order to pray, leave offerings, or acquire services related to that deity's role.

"For example, the gaudy pink one there is the Temple of Love, owned by the God Arom'il and his Goddess, Erist'il. You can have all manner of fortunes read there regarding relationships—sexual or otherwise. People can also have the priestesses or priests cast a spell on them to keep them from becoming pregnant."

"Like what the healers who examined Ari and I did?" Darius questioned, perking up. "I told them we didn't need it—"

"Yes, the same kind of spell." Xander laughed, nodding. "Luckily, these two aren't in the city right now. They're a big pain in the ass. Let's see…"

"Something regarding healing, justice, or mercy would probably be a good start," I offered.

Xander looked surprised that I'd spoken up but nodded his

understanding and then motioned for us to follow him. I still just wanted to flee back to the house and sulk, but I knew I couldn't. After the assassination attempt on Darius, I needed to be there to protect him. Even so…that event already seemed like a distant dream. I was trying so hard to wrap my head around this new knowledge and I just couldn't.

"Nalithor-y'ric!" I caught the sound of female voices screeching and I felt my heart sink as I bit back an irritated snarl. "Why won't you let us into your temple? Surely you're hungry, we'd be happy to—!"

"For the last time, I do not require *any of you*!" Nalithor snapped in Draemiran, his voice harsher than I'd heard it, which only served to pique my curiosity—and make Xander laugh, apparently. "The temples are for the *faithful* not for *food* or would-be *prey*. Go home."

I caught a glimpse of Nalithor's pale white braid as he turned and stalked toward the doors of a nearby temple, a scowl set on his face as he walked away from the group of shrieking men and women. Many of the people present were trying their best to look sexy or alluring, some going as far as to pull down the collar of their blouses and dresses to reveal long stretches of their throats. They seemed oblivious to Nalithor's lack of interest, and to our approach.

Despite my growing depression, I found it difficult to keep myself from commenting.

"Ah-ah. Aren't you girls at the wrong temple if you're looking for some *physical love?*" I called sarcastically, settling one hand on my hip and motioning over my shoulder with the other. "You can't *all* be colorblind, can you? The colors of their temples are quite different, you know."

"Arianna-jiss, you've wandered away from your natural habitat, have you?" Nalithor stopped at the door of his temple, pivoting to look past Xander and Darius, and straight at me instead. "Did the Vampire actually find a way to lure you out?"

"My brother's education and some unfortunate 'business' did." I shook my head in response and then glanced at my uncomfortable twin. "That said, it's time to return to my 'natural habitat' soon. Darius, you shouldn't dawdle."

"Oh? I can't convince you to stay for a bottle of mri'lec, Arianna?" Nalithor questioned. I stopped for a moment with my back to him and considered it for a moment. Some part of me wanted to take him up on the offer...but no.

"No... Not this time." I finally replied with a small shake of my head, my eyes drifting down to the road as pain stabbed through my chest again. "I should really see if Eyrian has learned anything from my captives."

I began waking again and gritted my teeth when I heard Nalithor's dejected sigh. For some reason, rejecting his offer hurt. A lot. But why? Hadn't I decided he only wanted to use me for information? After all, since he didn't seem to realize who I was, I was just another source of information and occasional entertainment. '...*right?*'

"What captives?" Nalithor questioned, startling me as he seemingly appeared in front of me. A breeze passing my cheek was the only indication that the Adinvyr hadn't teleported. "I thought I smelled Human blood, but I don't see any— Ah. You missed some on your mask it would seem, my dear."

"Assassins," I stated simply, batting Nalithor's hand away when he reached toward my mask. "They were after Darius, as usual. Eyrian is *'questioning'* them since I don't have the patience for it. I wasn't going to leave them alive long enough to—"

"*Ari*, let's go!" Darius cut me off with a whine. "Sorry, Rely'ric, but she's mine today!"

'Ugh, I could punch him sometimes. I swear!' I sighed, tugging at my hood. Nalithor growled at my brother and shot him a murderous glare. *'Seems like Nalithor is in a foul mood as well. Lovely.'*

"Why does *she* get your attention, but we don't?!" One of the men in the crowd behind me demanded with a snarl. "We, at least, have been loyal for *years*! Unlike Human *scum*, we—"

"Ugh, you filth are giving me a headache!" I snapped, turning on my heel. Flames spat outward from around my feet as I shoved the encroaching crowd with a wall of darkness. They toppled over each other, but the mouthy one pulled a sword from his hip. My darkness gripped his arm and snapped it at the elbow, sending him to the ground in pain. "Honestly! If you don't shut your mouths I might say 'fuck the alliance' and liberate your heads from your chattering corpses!"

I took a step forward and growled at them, watching as they shrank back in fear. Even the one with a now-broken arm scrambled backwards best he could. Ripping them all to tatters was an alluring idea at this point, I could even make a game out of seeing how many I could kill before the deity behind me managed to stop me.

My frustration with the maelstrom of emotions I was experiencing made my temper short, and I didn't understand why the tale of the memorial distressed me to this extent. Something I *could* understand, however, was shredding these obsessed idiots into scraps of meat.

'Are you alright?' Nalithor questioned, placing a hand on my shoulder, though I immediately shrugged it off. I'd almost forgotten that I had left a connection open to him. *'I can't imagine that the assassins would have made you this—'*

'No, I'm not alright. Just leave me alone,' I stated icily, dodging him as he went to grip me again. Without another word to him, I sank into the shadows and rushed through them, heading for the nearest pathway back up to the Sapphire Quarter. Instead of addressing Nalithor again, I reached out to Darius, *'Have Xander bring you home when you're done, or something. I'm going to bed.'*

'Bed? It's not even noon yet!' Darius protested, but I didn't care

anymore.

I was too upset to care about my role as a bodyguard. All I cared about was getting away from everyone and everything before my tears could make it past the rim of my mask. My eyes stung, making me rush through the shadows at a dangerous speed. I needed to get away from everyone, get somewhere where I could cry and work out my frustration in peace, without fear of further embarrassment.

Why did it hurt to turn him down? To brush him off?' I didn't understand it. Nalithor was, effectively, a new acquaintance. I shouldn't have been attached enough to be affected like that, and yet it hurt so much. I hoped that crying alone in my room would make me feel better.

Alone.

I spilled out of the shadows and onto the porch of our house, catching myself against the door frame. Wide-eyed, I just stared at the door for a moment as fear ripped through me and I began to tremble. Alone. I didn't want to be alone. The last time I was alone, those Angel bastards—

A small whimper escaped me as I shook my head hard and struggled with the lock on the door. I managed to unlock it, stumble inside, and then slump back against the door. I tried to shove the thoughts from my mind as my heart raced in my throat.

'Alone. Alone. Alone. I don't want that. I don't want that ever again! I don't... b-but...' I bit down on my lower lip hard and shut my eyes, shivering. *'Stupid, stupid, stupid! I should've stayed in the Merchant's Plaza with them. Now I'm alone. I don't want this. This sucks. I hate this. What the fuck was I thinking? This is bad. I should—'*

Alala's loud warble from the stairs made me jump and yelp. She warbled again, and this time I just stared at her.

"Alala…" I pursed my lips when I heard my voice crack, and felt tears trickling down behind my mask. "Let's…go upstairs."

I didn't want to think anymore. My pain, Nalithor's pain, Darius' pain. Especially Nalithor's pain…why did that seem to upset me more than anything else? I should have been more concerned about my sibling, and yet it was the Adinvyr's pain that upset me most. I knew that wasn't right, or at least it shouldn't have been right. Perhaps I was a terrible person.

'Hate this…' I thought blearily as I staggered into my room. I stripped off my mask and robes haphazardly before throwing myself face-first onto the bed. "'lala, don't leave me alone…"

Alala chirped in response and hopped on to the bed, curling up against my ribs. I yanked the blankets over my head and buried my face into the pillow. My heart ached so much that I wanted to rip it out of my chest so I wouldn't have to feel it anymore. I didn't want to be alone, but I didn't have anyone to go to with my problems either; comfortably or otherwise. Going to Nalithor would just bring us both more pain, and Darius didn't know what had happened to us. He wouldn't understand.

"I...don't wanna be alone..." I whimpered into the pillow, clutching it tight as I shivered. "Why'd I have to be so stupid? Running from Nali isn't going to fix anything..."

'What if Nalithor hates me because of how I just acted?' The thought came unbidden, and everything shattered.

That simple, unfounded notion was enough to break me into a million sobbing pieces. I wailed into the pillow with such force I grew dizzy and my nails pierced the fabric. I couldn't remember the last time I had cried, let alone if I had ever cried so hard. Alas, it didn't matter. Soon, Alala nudged my forehead with her cold nose and I collapsed into my tear-soaked pillow, limp, as everything went black.

CHAPTER TWELVE
Uncertainty

I made my way through Dauthrmir's streets at a slow pace and reluctantly headed towards my temple. Although the X'shmiran princess spoke of going to meet with Eyrian to question "her captives" I hadn't found her there. Eyrian claimed to have not seen her since the morning, either.

'No, I'm not alright. Just leave me alone.'

Arianna's words echoed through my mind for what seemed like the hundredth time that evening. I sighed and shook my head, unable to comprehend her behavior. She'd seemed so distraught, yet intent to push away any offer of help, company, or conversation. *'Why did she say that to me?'*

She had finally begun to let her guard down around me, or so

I had thought, but now it felt as if everything had been undone. For the life of me, I couldn't determine what had upset Arianna to such an extent. It seemed to conflict with what I'd heard of her unnervingly calm reactions to the mental fortitude testing.

Nearing the Merchant's District, I paused. The smell of death was faint but unmistakable. Something foul lingered nearby.

I wrapped myself in shadow and followed the scent to an alleyway near the temples. Several vile figures lurked behind boxes and barrels. Their presence and their stench both made my lips curl in disgust. The creatures' visages were twisted, grey, and lipless. I had thought perhaps they killed something, but no. *They* smelled like death, though they were clearly alive.

My presence didn't stir them. Instead, their cloudy eyes remained on the face of my temple as they whispered amongst themselves.

"We should just kill the crowd and snatch the mage," one hissed to his comrades, drool trickling over his broken, jagged teeth and down his chin. "If we wait too long—"

"Fool! I hear she's able to fight *him* evenly!" The sole female of the group snapped, spittle flying from her mouth. Her bony, skin-covered tail snapped behind her. "We can't deal with the whelps *and* her at the same time."

'*Mage? Her?*' I glanced in the direction of my temple and remained in the shadows to observe both the twisted creatures and their focus.

To my surprise, Arianna was sitting with her back against the door to my temple. She had her knees pulled up to her chest with her chin resting on top of them. The corners of her full lips were turned down in a small frown as she sat there, seeming oblivious to the crowd of men and women in front of her. Even from here I could tell the crowd was chastising her, likely for her presence or for the dim shield of magic Arianna had erected between them and her. I could sense her attention was focused elsewhere.

'What is she doing here?' I frowned, my gaze flicking back to the whispering creatures. *'Perhaps I should warn her.'*

I went to reach out to Arianna and then stopped short. She had told me to leave her alone, despite whatever had upset her earlier in the day. Her behavior was startlingly cold, yet for some reason she hadn't shut me out of her mind again. Despite her clear distress, she kept her emotions locked behind the deeper barriers that I couldn't breach.

On some level, I wondered if she was so upset that she simply forgot to shut me out again.

My thoughts were interrupted by the shadows around me shifting and taking on the form of snarling foxes. The shadowy conjurations bristled and stared at the grey creatures. Traces of Arianna's presence mingled with the darkness she'd used to conjure the foxes, hinting at the emotional turmoil still wracking her mind.

Although I sensed it was beginning to subside, I still didn't understand what had caused her to act in such a way. Discomfort seemed to be overtaking her distress now, at any rate.

"You are right about one thing." I stepped out from the shadows and glared at the startled creatures. "Twisted filth like you can't hope to handle a woman like her.

"*Let alone someone like me.*"

I silenced the shrieking creatures with a dismissive motion when they attempted to flee and watched with satisfaction as their bodies erupted into pillars of blue-white flames. Their necks broke with an audible snap and they each crumpled in place, lifeless. My first instinct was to move forward and rip the filth apart to make sure they were fully and truly dead.

Instead, I froze when Arianna's dark foxes flowed past me to sniff and paw at the flaming corpses. My pulse raced, uninvited, as a feeling of dread washed over me. I looked down at the foxes, expecting to sense fear or disgust from the watchful princess.

Ripping apart the creatures was a suitable punishment as far as I was concerned, but Arianna's foxes and her watchful senses gave me pause. I had already slaughtered the bastards without much thought. Wouldn't such an action disgust a mortal? Let alone a princess? A "*Human*" princess.

I took a step back from the foxes and the disintegrating corpses, my thoughts spinning into a maelstrom. Arianna had already proved she was in a terrible mood this morning—perhaps even a fragile one. Thoughtlessly, I had slaughtered living creatures for the "sin" of trailing the princess and speaking of kidnapping her. At the very least, I should have waited until Arianna's foxes had ceased watching.

'Now I can't question them either...' I bared my fangs in an irritated growl. My gaze shifted to the side at another corpse when one of the foxes pawed at a pile of ashes and released a displeased huff. *'Still no fear...?'*

'You could have at least left me one.' Arianna's voice pierced through my thoughts. Her foxes rushed to me and wrapped around my torso, their displeased huffing shifting to a happier-sounding warble.

'Left...you one?' I questioned, wary of both the shadowy foxes shifting around my torso and their attempts to nudge me in the direction of my temple. *'Ah... I'd forgotten you said something similar regarding the Vampires the other night.'*

'What, exactly, were those?' Arianna's tone was conversational even as she nudged me, hard, with her darkness again. *'And are you going to hide back there all night? I'm not sitting here, staring down your adoring fans, for my own entertainment you know.'*

'Eyrian was right—she's a piece of work.' I grimaced, twitching as Arianna's shadows slid over my chest and abdomen. She seemed intent on pulling me away from the reeking bodies and flickering flames. *'Just what sort of "duties" did she have in X'shmir? She shouldn't be this accustomed to death.'*

Sighing, I nudged stray hair from my eyes and resigned myself to approach Arianna and the waiting crowd outside the temple.

Arianna's warm darkness slid across my skin in a questionable manner, making me twitch even as I braced myself for the onslaught of comments from the waiting crowd. Despite her poor mood, Arianna's presence was intensely sensual. It was a strange contrast to the expression on the lower half of her face, which was more like that of a predator.

I was unsure who she intended to make her prey: Me, or the crowd of people between us.

"Nalithor-y'ric!" One of the women turned to me, excited, and then shrunk back in fear. "S-shadows? What—"

"Aren't you a little old to be scared of the dark?" Arianna teased, a sly smile resting on her face when she lifted her head from her knees.

"Rely'ric, why is her crest so similar to yours?" One of the men demanded. He opened his mouth to continue but all that came out was a strangled yelp as one of Arianna's dark foxes lunged for him.

"If you want to know more of our crests, you should ask Aurelian. *He* is the one responsible for Her Highness," I replied icily, sweeping past the crowd and toward Arianna instead. Her conjurations were quite capable of parting the crowd for me, at the very least. "Arianna, have you been waiting long?"

"Ah...no," Arianna muttered quietly, her smile vanishing as she averted her gaze. "Haven't been awake for very long."

Although I was still cross with the princess for her behavior and dismissals, I found it difficult to see her sitting there like that. Were she twenty years younger, she would have been the mirror image of Lucifer's daughter; she too sulked in discomfort after throwing even the slightest of tantrums.

That likeness pained me more than her behavior earlier today ever could.

Seeing her as a "fake" created by the Exiled Gods grew more difficult by the day. I had thought that any similarities would make it easier to realize she was a fake…but I had been sorely mistaken. Lucifer, Eyrian, and now Xander, seemed so ready to accept that this Arianna was the same one we had lost.

I couldn't. Not yet, and not so easily.

"Let's get you inside." I strode up the stairs to my temple and passed through her shield with ease. She glanced up at me when I stopped before her to offer her my hand. "You look like you could use a cup of tea."

"What?! Why are you allowing that *Human* bitch—" The woman's voice cut off in a terrified shriek when I pivoted to glare at the collective crowd. I allowed my darkness to burst outward from me and rage through our immediate surroundings.

"That's enough." I growled at them, pulling Arianna to her feet. "Addressing Arianna-jiss in such a manner is unacceptable. You would all do well to remember that *Her Highness* is quite capable of putting each of you in your place…if I do not do so first."

"Aren't you projecting Princess Shujare onto Princess Black?!"

The question made my blood run cold.

However, this time, it was Arianna's temper that snapped. She yanked her hand from mine and stalked several paces past me so that she could glower at the people by the base of the stairs. A cyclone of darkness and cobalt flames raged around her feet. Arianna released a feral growl, aiming blades of ice at the startled mix of Devillians and Elves. Despite her outward anger, I sensed calculated calmness from the princess. Was she bluffing? I honestly wasn't sure, and it made me wary.

If she truly intended to slay them, I would have to intervene.

"How poorly do you view your *precious* prince? Do you really think he's that weak?" Arianna demanded, bristling as she drew her vulpine creations away from me and back to her. "My name is Arianna Jade Black—and whether you like it or not, this is *Nalithor's* property. *A deity's* property. If he wants me to join him, then that's none of your damned business!

"And really, *projecting*? Do you say that because of my name? Or are you just so stupid that you can't think of any other reason for—"

"Don't waste your words on them," I interjected coolly before slipping an arm around Arianna's waist and pulling her back from the top of the stairs. "Let's go."

Arianna glanced up at me, her lips parted as if she were going to say something, but instead she flushed and looked away again. I drew her toward the door of the temple and the shot a warning glare over my shoulder at the crowd, having sensed them drawing upon their magic. The fools shrunk back and lost control of their magic, allowing it to disperse harmlessly before too much had gathered.

I placed my free hand on the carved stone door in front of us and infused the intricate design with my darkness. The subtle tilt of Arianna's head and the expression on her mouth gave away her curiosity, and I found myself biting back an amused smile. Perhaps the situation could still be salvaged before she retreated into her shell in full.

Moments later, the sections of the stone door retracted into the granite walls long enough for us to pass through. I willed the pieces back into place behind us, silencing the still-shrieking gathering outside.

"You may be trapped here for a while now," I informed Arianna, moving away from her so that I could touch my fingers to a nearby sconce. Pale flames burst to life in the device and then spread to the rest of the temple. "It will be several hours before my 'adoring fans' give up and leave, despite the time."

"I get the feeling that they have no idea what your role as a deity is," Arianna grumbled, fidgeting with her robes while she glanced around.

"Do you?" I strode past her, beckoning for her to follow.

"No," Arianna replied simply as I pulled off my overrobe and tossed it over a chair. "'Who' you are matters more than 'what' you are or what your role is.

"That said, I thought the Elders would have some law that dictates you must disclose that kind of information. They seem like the sort who would enjoy stuffy rules."

"They are, but no such rule exists." I chuckled, leading the princess into a plush room filled with ebony woodwork and sapphire velvet upholstery. "Would you like tea or mri'lec?"

"Tea…" Arianna trailed off and then fidgeted with her hood again as she took a seat on the sofa I'd motioned her toward. "I probably shouldn't stay. Dealing with your 'fans' on my way back to the Sapphire Quarter will be quite easy."

'She doesn't want to stay?' I frowned as I moved to the back of the room to start a pot of tea anyway. "I take it you wandered from your 'den' for a reason then?"

"I…just came to apologize for my behavior this morning," Arianna grumbled, causing me to turn and examine her uncomfortable demeanor once more. "I don't have any excuses. I just wanted to say sorry."

I stared at Arianna in disbelief as she rose to her feet and made her way back the way we'd come. Even from across the room I could hear the nervous racing of her heartbeat. Arianna's entire body was tensed as if she was expecting me to lash out with a harsh response. She likely thought she was hiding it well, but I heard her voice crack when she said "sorry." However, most startling of all, was her aura. Arianna had drawn it so tight behind her barriers that

I almost couldn't feel it.

It was like she was trying to make herself invisible.

Fear tinged the few wisps of aura that escaped her grasp. It was similar to what I'd witnessed when Djialkan had me carry the princess back to her rooms in the Sapphire Quarter. Even the erratic sound of her heartbeat was the same. *'Yet it isn't* me *she's frightened by. Just what...?'*

"I can't let you wander off by yourself." I caught up to Arianna in several long strides. "The obnoxious ones aside, more of those creatures are likely hunting for you still. You heard their whispering, didn't you?"

"You don't need to babysit me..." Arianna protested half-heartedly. I gripped her gently by the shoulders and steered her back to the sofa as she added, "What were those creatures? You didn't tell me."

"They were likely once Human or Elven," I answered with distaste, satisfied that Arianna wouldn't flee the sofa again; she wasn't putting up much resistance. "I'm more concerned with your mental state at the given moment, Arianna. From what I understand, you aced the mental fortitude examination. I received a slew of concerned—and bewildered—notes from the staff stating as much."

"Torture and death don't bother me," Arianna muttered dryly, sinking back against the cushions.

"You've made that quite clear." I shook my head, returning to the task of making us tea. "After all, I just returned from putting that assassin's arm back together. You know, he nearly bled to death."

"Pity." Arianna huffed.

"If the exams aren't what set you off, what did?" I frowned, settling into a chair across from the princess. Her face flushed and she began shifting in discomfort once more while I studied her. *'Xander and Darius believed it was due to the story behind the monument. But that shouldn't be the case unless she's—'*

"I... Perhaps I tried a little too hard to empathize with the events surrounding the monument in the center of the plaza." Arianna looked away from me and gripped her knees hard enough to turn her knuckles white. "Maybe I don't deal with tragic or emotional information as well as I thought I did. Even so, that's still no excuse for my behav—"

"Arianna, those events aren't the kind that can be understood." I sighed, shaking my head at her even as she pouted. "Those of us involved will likely be unable to ever *fully* comprehend what happened in V'frul or in the aftermath. We all bear scars related to those events and I doubt that will ever change."

"Some wounds *don't* heal with time?" Arianna offered hesitantly, a small frown tugging at her lips. I nodded my confirmation, unsure what to think of the woman before me. "I see...*that* I can understand at least. You...were close to the princess, then?"

I remained silent, considering how to respond. If Arianna—Lucifer's daughter—was truly alive, she wouldn't have any recollection of her life before Limbo. A fake might. Although it was painful to think about the past, let alone speak of it, discussing such things with the woman before me had the possibility of revealing who, or what, she was.

"You don't understand?" I questioned, keeping my tone neutral.

"I don't understand a lot of things." Arianna tilted her head a little, pausing as if in thought. "You're aware of my situation in X'shmir. I don't quite grasp the concept of being 'close' to anyone, or what it's like to lose someone you're close to. And I *definitely* don't understand how or why such young children would have been sent on missions by—"

"You should." I arched an eyebrow at her. "You've been protecting X'shmir, and your brother, from the beasts for *how long?*"

"But that's not—"

"Whether or not it's an assigned 'mission' is irrelevant." I chuckled, crossing my arms as I leaned back in my seat. "You of all people should be aware that children can be quite capable. My…partner and I were young, yes, but it's because we were young that we were able to do so much.

"Those were harsher times. More chaotic times. Our age and small size let us go places where adults couldn't. Our missions often involved posing as orphans so that we could gather information. The fact that we were the children of deities helped matters. Alas, such programs died with the founding of the Vorpmasian Empire. Though the concept of 'partners' remained, obviously."

"Then, you and your partner worked together for quite some time?" Arianna murmured, confusion still tinging her voice.

"You asked me if she and I were close," I began, spotting the princess flinch in response. "Think of your blade, how it feels like an extension of yourself when you wield it. Having a partner is similar. We acted as extensions of each other, but also as anchors when one spiraled out of control."

"An extension…?" Arianna trailed off and tapped her fingertips against her arm. It did nothing to hide the sound of her startled, nervous pulse. "So, like a weapon? But squishier and more talkative?"

I couldn't help but laugh at her comment, causing her face to flush crimson. She muttered a small "humph" and crossed her arms, looking away from me.

"It was our responsibility to keep each other safe, alive, and focused on whatever our mission at the time was," I answered, still chuckling. "The idea of being 'close' to someone is truly so foreign to you? What of your brother or Djialkan?"

"It doesn't sound like you were *that* kind of close with her, it sounds like a different type of 'close,'" Arianna pointed out. I couldn't claim she was wrong. "I'm a *X'shmiran* Umbral Mage,

Nalithor. They think that so much as bumping into me will curse their entire bloodline.

"Darius and I are somewhat close, I guess, but I'm more his bodyguard than his sister. We're not supposed to even hug each other. I must stay several paces behind him at all times. The only times I'm allowed physical contact with him is if I have to yank him out of harm's way."

"You're not allowed...?" I frowned at her, my amusement giving way to something like pity. "What of Djialkan or the people of Sihix then?"

"The scaly one prefers his fae-dragon form," Arianna pointed out with a half-shrug. "Djialkan is more like a bossy, talkative pet because of that. As for the people of Sihix... I was already conditioned to avoid contact by the time I met them. They respected my attempts at avoidance, for the most part."

'Not allowed even the simplest forms of contact with others?' I bit back my frustration, instead studying the princess before me once more. *'If...if she's truly our Arianna, I don't know if there exists a punishment appropriate for the X'shmiran bastards—let alone the Elders responsible for sending her there.'*

"If the two of you wiped out V'frul's elite, then why aren't they under the Empire's thumb now?" Arianna's question startled me from my thoughts.

"I thought you would ask about the deities present among the slavers." I arched an eyebrow at her.

"Xander said that's information the Empire can't let leak," Arianna replied, shaking her head. "I won't deny I'm curious, but I also know I'm not on the 'need to know' list."

"The Elves' own deities were among the captives," I began thoughtfully, watching as the princess grew still and stared at me, "as were several Devillian deities and their children. The nobles in V'frul intended to sell the deities and their children into an eternity of servitude. Children like Xander were to be sold to brothels or to nobles who wanted to begin training their concubines…young."

"Tch, bastards." Arianna glanced away from me as her mouth curled into a disgusted snarl. Just thinking about it made waves of bloodlust radiate from her. After a moment she sighed and turned her attention back to me. "Thank you for answering my questions. I apologize again for my behavior, and now for prying as well."

"Not at all. I appreciate that you're willing to take such history seriously," I responded, discovering that she seemed surprised when I didn't chastise her. "The younger generations treat what happened in V'frul as a trivial matter. As for the events that follow it…they have no understanding, certainly. Worse, they have no respect."

"I gathered as much from the ridiculous proclamation of that one whore—" Arianna cut herself off, her face turning scarlet. She raised one of her knuckles to her mouth and bit it, fidgeting in her seat when I laughed at her.

"I'll admit that I'm relieved you don't share *that one's*

sentiments." I chuckled, rising to my feet so that I could check if the water had come to a boil yet. "You prefer your tea sweet, yes? How much—"

"There you are, Nalithor!" a male voice spoke with excitement, causing me to scowl. I shot a glare over my shoulder at Sebastian as he stepped out of the shadows and settled his gaze on Arianna. "*Oh, what's this?* You finally decided to let someone other than a deity in, Nalithor?"

"You have ten seconds to explain to me why I shouldn't kick your ass," Arianna stated flatly, earning delighted laughter from the God of Chaos. "Afterward you can thank me for being generous enough to give you ten seconds—if your answer is sufficient enough for me to let you live."

'If she keeps talking like that...' I shook my head to myself and closed my eyes briefly. When I reopened my eyes, I turned to keep an eye on them.

"Well, aren't you cute?" Sebastian grinned down at the princess with an unmistakable hunger in his gaze. "I'm the *God of Chaos,* dear girl. Do you *really* think you could—"

"Oh, so *you're* the one I have to thank for this?" Arianna shot to her feet and leveled the Godslayer with Sebastian's throat in a fluid motion. The bastard seemed unconcerned, but Arianna's jaw was set firm. I got the feeling she would use the weapon against him if he gave her reason to.

"As you can see, Sebastian," I began as I strode over to Arianna and picked her off the ground by her waist, "we are busy, and you are interrupting. You can file your report later."

"Am I going to have to fight you and Aurelian both for her, Nali?" Sebastian questioned with wide eyes, making a mock-hurt gesture with his hands over his heart. "I'm kidding! Don't give me that look. Are you sure your 'business' with Arianna-jiss can't wait?"

'...I didn't tell him who she is.' I narrowed my eyes at the God of Chaos. 'So, he really is responsible for giving her that blasted sword? Is she...'

"I really *should* be going." Arianna shook her head when I opened my mouth to tell Sebastian off. "Someone has to deal with Darius' inevitable post-assassination attempt breakdown."

"This happens often?" I frowned at Arianna as she dismissed the Godslayer and then tightened my grip on her waist. *'I don't want her to go... Or, at the very least, I can't let her wander through the city knowing creatures like that are interested in her.'*

"Yes, quite often," Arianna replied, glancing up at me. "I assumed that the Royal Family stated as much when they agreed to let Darius study here. Am I wrong?"

"They mentioned nothing of it, neither did he." I shook my head. "I will speak with Eyrian. We should be able to form a more permanent protective detail for him so that you aren't required to spend all your time on him. You're likely to be quite busy once you're assigned a partner.

"Sebastian, you can make your report after I've taken Her Highness back to the Sapphire Quarter. It won't be long."

Arianna attempted to protest as I guided her out of the room and down the hall toward the temple's exit. Sebastian just laughed and perched on a nearby chair, conjuring a book to entertain himself with while I was gone.

'I can't in good conscience let you return by yourself this late at night,' I told Arianna as I reclaimed my overrobe and shrugged it on. *'Those creatures that were tailing you aren't to be trifled with, and there's likely more of them. You need to be careful.'*

'It's fine, I can protect myself!' Arianna protested, attempting to slip away. *'You don't need to—'*

'I want to.' I cut her off, my tone firm. I slipped an arm around her shoulders and escorted her to the door. *'If something happened to you because I chose to indulge your protest…I wouldn't forgive myself. You understand, don't you?'*

'I understand…' Arianna sighed. *'I just don't want to be a bother.'*

'Haven't I made it clear by now that I enjoy your company?' I countered, watching her face flush as she struggled to think of a retort. *'Now then, let's get you home in one piece.'*

When we exited the temple, I was surprised to find the crowd from before had dispersed already. The only signs of life in the streets, aside from nocturnal animals and birds, were members of the Imperial Guard…and the spies we had assigned to keep an eye on the princess.

'G-General?' One of the spies questioned when my gaze snapped to his hiding place. He appeared out of the shadows beside us and knelt, bowing his head. The man, R'fahl, was a Sundreht and one of our best spies. However, even he trembled when the princess' attention turned to him.

'Double the number of people keeping watch of Arianna-jiss,' I ordered, leading the princess herself past R'fahl. 'Next time you and yours find strange creatures stalking her…contact me immediately. I won't warn you again.'

'As you command,' R'fahl flinched when I glanced at him over my shoulder. 'Even if Her Highness can contend with the threat, General?'

'Even if. Contact me.' I glanced down at the princess, sensing her attention shifting somewhere away from both me and R'fahl. 'She's made a habit of drawing strange things out of hiding. If I am unavailable, you are to contact General Il'thar instead.'

R'fahl vanished into his hiding place once more and then sped away towards his people's lair, leaving his other spies to follow the princess. Arianna seemed unfazed but returned her attention to me once the spy had left.

'You were aware of their presence?' I asked, glancing at her.

'Of course. I still don't think I need an escort of any kind…but as long as they don't get in my way, I'll tolerate them.' Arianna shrugged, her attention flitting off to our flanks again. 'Tch, those creatures you *killed still reek. Here I was, thinking they smelled bad before burning. Ugh.'*

'You still refuse an escort?' I questioned, earning a brief nod in reply. *'You've made it quite clear you can protect yourself, and others, Arianna. There's more to the matter than keeping you and your brother safe, you know. There's also—'*

'If they're not at least as strong as you are, they will get in my way.' Arianna slowed to a stop and turned to look up at me, crossing her arms. *'I appreciate your concern, Nalithor, I really do—even if I don't understand it.'*

'She…doesn't understand it?' I wondered, studying the firm set of Arianna's jaw. A small smile crept across my lips as I shook my head. *'You know as well as I do that none of our soldiers would come close to either of us in strength. However, as I said, keeping you safe isn't the only concern.'*

'What else is there?' Arianna seemed as if she was trying to make herself seem firm and imposing, but her small stature and pouty lips dampened the effect. *'I'm well aware that the spies aren't watching me out of suspicion. Nor are they watching me because you lot are concerned I might hurt people. There's something else going on.'*

'It has to do with the Vampires—and by extension, the Beshulthiens.' I decided to answer her with honesty. Not only would this woman sense if I lied…I didn't *want* to lie to her. Earning her trust, and her interest, was important to me. *'Most Vampires are under Beshulthien rule, as their Emperor is the first*

Vampire—their god. Vorpmasia and Beshulthien do not get along well. We are allied because otherwise the beasts and Exiled Gods would wipe us out.

'We need to determine if the Vampires who took interest in you were sent by the Beshulthien Empire, or if they are rogues. If they were sent by the Beshulthiens…it would mean war.'

'War? Over me?' Arianna sighed and shook her head, her tone one of disbelief. *'Seeing as X'shmir isn't even officially part of the Rilzaan Alliance yet, I'm assuming this has something to do with whatever treaty was drafted between the two Empires.'*

'You're correct.' I smiled and tugged at the front of her hood once before glancing up the street. *'We can talk while we walk. I don't want to stay in one place for too long.'* Arianna nodded her agreement and then accepted my arm when I offered it to her. *'Until a permanent solution to the beasts and Exiles is found, the Alliance is vital to our mutual survival.*

'More important yet are mages. *Without mages, we wouldn't have barriers around our territories capable of keeping the beasts out. Before we found a way to erect and sustain barriers, we had to keep large numbers of soldiers on-hand in every city to protect the people in case of attacks from beasts.'*

'I was half expecting you to say it has something to do with me being a "princess."' Arianna snorted, shaking her head.

'That…is part of it as well,' I informed her, sighing. *'Before the Alliance was forged, the Beshulthien Empire practiced many things*

that are frowned upon in Vorpmasia. They still try to get away with such things on occasion, regardless of the treaty signed between our Empires.

'Stealing princes and princesses away from their kingdoms and forcing them to join the Beshulthien Emperor's harem is one of those things.'

'So there's a concern that the Beshulthiens have taken a strong interest in me or my brother,' Arianna murmured, her tone contemplative until she looked up in response to my laughter. *'What? What's so funny?'*

'They have no interest in your brother, my dear,' I informed her, squeezing her waist briefly. *'Darius has yet to prove his usefulness. You, however, have already gained a reputation. You need to be careful, and it's our responsibility as your hosts to make sure nothing happens.'*

'Fine, I will tolerate their presence. For now.' Arianna paused and glanced down at my arm around her waist. She seemed a little lost for words, or perhaps lost in thought. I couldn't quite tell this time, as her expression remained neutral. *'Is... it really fine for you to escort me like this?'*

'Do you mind?' I countered, watching as she glanced away.

'No... But you're a deity, with business to attend to, and I'm just—' Arianna attempted to protest, but went silent when I squeezed her again. Relief washed over me when she said that she didn't mind. Her worries, however, were another matter.

'*Being a deity just means that I have extra responsibilities, Arianna,*' I informed her. '*I took out the creatures who were stalking you, and I decided that I'm going to take responsibility for seeing you home in one piece tonight.*

'*Unless you'll let* me *take a piece out of you.*'

Arianna bristled and shot me what was probably a glare as her face flushed. I chuckled, doubting she realized just how adorable I found her reactions to be. She would probably have tried to react differently if she understood.

'*You're impossible!*' Arianna huffed, her shoulders slumping.

I smiled. "Impossible". No, "impossible" was a word better suited to her. Whether she turned out to be a fake, or if she was somehow *real*...that word would describe her perfectly either way.

CHAPTER THIRTEEN
Coming to Terms

I rolled over in bed and grumbled into my pillow, attempting to flee Alala's cold nose. She seemed intent on waking me up even though *I* just wanted to sleep. *'Mmm...something* does *smell good though.'*

Alala released a head-splitting warble and then clamped her jaws down on my hand, making me flinch. I shook her off and then sat up in bed, letting the sheets fall to my hips. With a grimace, I examined my hand for puncture wounds and then shifted my gaze back to Alala when she resumed making loud noises.

"Wha is it, 'lala?" I mumbled while trying to stifle a yawn. "Sleepy..."

Alala ran in circles beside the bed for a few seconds and then summoned one of the larger trunks from my shrizar, yipping the entire time. She skidded to a halt by the trunk and pulled herself onto it, sniffing at the familiar scents that accompanied it. Compared to the excitable fox, Djialkan looked and sounded bored.

"You did *decide to abide by Corentine and Nalithor's warnings, did you not?"* Djialkan shot me a look when I went to argue. *"Stop fretting uselessly. If Nalithor is truly impervious to a* Godslayer, *then—"*

"I know, I know," I muttered, pulling myself out of bed. "Too early for lectures. It's just that I have a hard time reading these people, especially Nalithor. I can't tell if he just delights in getting a jealous rise out of people, or…if he's actually interested in me for some reason."

"I will not pretend to understand Draemiran ways," Djialkan began with a snort. *"However, his signs of affection should be genuine. That he continues to go out of his way to make others jealous is simply another sign of affection in his culture."*

"I won't pretend to understand that either," I remarked with a crooked grin. "That he frustrated Darius into *challenging me* was quite entertaining though."

Djialkan snorted with laughter, leaving me to rummage through the exquisite contents of the trunk in search of something less…X'shmiran. After a few minutes, I finished dressing myself, adjusted a few things in the mirror, then left the room. I jingled much more without my jewelry hidden beneath layers upon layers of robes. However, I didn't mind the sound at all. It was oddly enjoyable.

"Oh. I didn't wake you with my clanking around in the kitchen did I, Ari?" Darius asked when I entered the kitchen.

"No, it's just weird being in a different bed. Still can't sleep well, and Alala is bitey," I grumbled, flopping into a chair. Darius walked over and set a cup of tea in front of me. "Did you have breakfast already, Darius?"

"Actually, I was gonna see if you wanted to come have breakfast with me at Nali's café!" Darius replied with a bright grin. "I can't cook, and we don't have any groceries left. What happened to the clothes the Oracle gave you? I thought you'd wear those more often after the way people reacted."

"I guess they were temporary. They dispersed into aether when I took them off," I answered with a small pout. "So I'm—"

"Oh? We should go fix that!" Darius grabbed one of my hands excitedly and bounced on the balls of his feet. "I was going to go get some better robes myself. After all, Nali already told us the best place in the city to go! Let's go together after breakfast, okay?"

"But I don't need—" I cut myself off when Darius leaned forward with a determined expression on his features. I sighed. I couldn't say no to that face. "Fine, we can go together. I just thought you'd rather go without an escort. Besides, you're not really 'allowed' to buy me anything."

'I really don't know if I want to run into Nalithor so soon. He seemed to accept my apology but… I just don't know.' I gnawed the inside of my cheek as I thought. *'Partners? An extension of each other, like a blade? I don't…how can two people be that close?*

'Who is Nalithor's partner now? Is he or she even worthy? I can't imagine they are, given how interested he's been in sparring me.'

I frowned to myself, unsure of why I cared. There was no reason for me to care if Nalithor had a partner, let alone care who they were or if they were worthy of him. Although I was still a little upset to discover that we'd once been partners, it was more because it meant Djialkan had indeed been keeping information from me. Important information. Nalithor's answers had helped me understand, a little bit, but I knew better than to pry further.

Nalithor didn't need to suspect me, and I didn't want to cause him further pain by bringing up such memories.

"We're going as siblings!" Darius interrupted my thoughts and pointed his finger against my nose. "I…did want to ask you something though." My brother paused, fidgeting as his expression grew timid. "Afterwards…will you help me with my training? Our tests made me realize just how lacking my abilities are."

"You're serious? I certainly don't mind but…what do you want to work on?" I examined Darius' expression, finding that he looked unusually determined. *'More like his ridiculous challenge made it obvious, honestly. Though I guess he doesn't want to admit that. I guess I should just be happy that he wants to do something productive after shopping. Though…he doesn't even understand that I don't* need *new clothes, does he?'*

"You…don't mind? Really?" Darius inquired, placing his hands flat on the table and leaning toward me with an eager expression. "I-I thought, with the way you were blushing when you came home last night, that you and Nali probably had plans, so…"

"Hardly," I mused, shaking my head. "He *does* owe me a drink still, and we have more to discuss about both the Beasts and our differing cultures.

"However, that isn't what I was 'blushing' about. The other Adinvyr in Dauthrmir have been pelting me with *very* specific thoughts…"

"You too, huh?" Darius frowned and then glanced at the clock. "Well…we should get going I guess, we have food to eat and shopping to do. We can brainstorm about this later tonight."

I shook my head slightly and then let Darius drag me by the arm through Dauthrmir and to Nalithor's cafe, *The Little Orchid.* Much to my twin's displeasure, Nalithor wasn't there. I, however, was fine with that. Nalithor's behavior still had me flustered and on edge.

'Seeing me home? Insisting on "protecting" me from those creatures?' I settled back in my seat at the cafe and suppressed a sigh. *'If I didn't know any better, I would think he's courting me.'*

"What do you think, Ari?" Darius spoke up while I browsed my menu. "Should I go with Dauthrmiran, Draemiran,

Beshulthien, or Susthulite attire?"

"Can I just pretend to know what *any* of those are and pick a random one?" I countered dryly, causing my twin to pout. "Just wait until we get there and see what you like. It's not that difficult of a concept. I can't believe you've been researching clothing styles and *still* can't pick something."

"But I wanna figure out what Nali likes...so maybe..." Darius averted his gaze as his face flushed crimson. All I could do was stare at him in disbelief. "He talked to you a lot at dinner earlier this week. So, I thought maybe you might have an idea about what he likes..."

Perhaps I hadn't noticed it before, not fully, but it seemed as though my twin had a *genuine* crush on Nalithor. Somehow this was different than his usual interest in men. I'd never seen him act like this before. I'd known for a long time that Darius had no interest in women, and the X'shmiran bastards had used that as fuel for their abuse.

However, I'd never seen Darius act so shy about someone he liked. Until now, whenever he was interested in someone, he was *too blunt*—to a point of making his confessions far more awkward than they needed to be.

"Why are you being shy?" I set my menu down and then pointed at Darius. "This is highly unusual."

'I-I don't know if Nali even likes men or not,' Darius grumbled, his face flushing darker as I rushed to extend my shields around his

thoughts. *'And what if he likes you? What if he likes both men and women? I don't wanna fight my own sister over a guy. I know that's kinda contradictory to what happened the other day, but—'*

'Darius, keep in mind that I barely know him. You have *interacted with him more than I have since coming to Dauthrmir.'* I shook my head and returned my attention to the menu. *'It's very unlikely that there's anything there aside from* maybe *physical attraction. Even that's a stretch though, considering I have to hide my face.'*

'You really think so?' Darius rested his cheek against his fist as he looked at me. *'What do you think then, Ari? What do you think his sexuality is?'*

'It's not something I've been paying attention to; I don't particularly care about who people want in their bed.' I shrugged and ignored the displeased look Darius shot me. *'That said, I get the feeling he doesn't like people who put on airs. So, if you're planning on winning him over, it's probably best to be yourself.'*

Darius frowned at me, but I was saved from further questioning when a waitress in a frilly uniform approached us to take our orders.

The Little Orchid was a themed cafe that boasted waiters and waitresses in varying styles of butler and maid attire. Apparently, the commoners loved it because it gave them the illusion of having their own personal staff.

Several of the staff had attempted to learn of both Darius'

preferences and mine, but we'd politely refused each time. We went to *The Little Orchid* for the good food and drink, not for roleplay. Darius had plenty of servants back in X'shmir, and I'd never been fond of the formality that revolved around them. One of the few things we seemed to agree on was that we wanted to be more "normal" while living in Dauthrmir.

Eventually they had gotten the hint, but a few of the waiters and waitresses still attempted now and then to determine our sexual preferences. Their interest in my brother I could understand but, for the life of me, I didn't understand why they were interested in me—let alone why so many Adinvyr in the city were still prodding me with their power. Was I really that strange?

'Darius, you said the people here are prodding you with their power too?' I inquired.

'Some, yeah,' Darius replied, his expression scrunching in thought for a moment before he motioned at his wrists. *'It's actually been worse since your Brands and jewelry were revealed. I think they've been trying to figure out if I'm "different" too.'*

'My crest has also been drawing a lot of attention.' I motioned down my back with my thumb. *'Apparently Nalithor's men have already nicknamed me "The White Fox" because of it.'*

'It fits!' Darius laughed. *'Especially with that new pet of yours. She doesn't seem to like me much though.'*

'The only people Alala likes outside of the Sihix Forest seem to be Djialkan, Nalithor, and myself.' I shook my head, a small smile

settling on my face. *'Both Djialkan and Nalithor can speak with her it seems, while I can't. Apparently, she told Nalithor that she likes him because he smells pleasant.'*

'He does smell good,' Darius agreed, his expression observant. *'Really though, Ari... The fact I'm interested in Nali aside, aren't you walking a really fine line? I thought you wanted to avoid him so that you wouldn't be forced to kill each other?'*

'Didn't we already go over this? Both Djialkan and Fraelfnir believe that Nalithor is high enough in rank to be exempt from those laws,' I pointed out with another shake of my head. *'You need to learn to listen to the scaly ones better. If you pull this with your professors you're never going to get anywhere.'*

'So, since the magics that bind you haven't forced you to kill him...' Darius murmured, frowning as he considered it. *'Even the Upper Gods aren't exempt from that law if I recall. Does that make him an Elder?'*

'I think he's somewhere between, something new,' I answered, swirling my tea in its cup as I thought. *'At the very least, he is more powerful than Lucifer—the emperor is another "anomaly" as far as power among the gods is concerned. Lucifer is somewhere between a Lesser and a Middle God since he rules over all the Devillian Lesser Gods. He's like a patriarch of patriarchs.*

'Nalithor seems to be in some sort of in-between situation himself—the God of Chaos showed up to give Nalithor his "report" last night. That doesn't seem like a normal—'

'Do you think we should be scared of him, Ari?' Darius interrupted, surprising me with his odd question. 'He terrifies me to some degree. I don't think it's because he's a god though, it's something else. Like how you frighten me sometimes.'

'Like me, he's rather close to his darkness,' I answered with a lopsided grin, while Darius just grimaced. 'I find him confusing, not frightening. I think once you've had more training, you'll understand why our darkness shouldn't scare you so much.'

'Training huh...' Darius sighed heavily. 'It's hard to accept that I'm not the amazing Astral Mage our people think I am. Especially when you're already so strong.'

'I had to be strong though,' I pointed out with a small smile. 'You remember how much time I spent outside of the city walls, Darius. My options were to learn fast or die.'

"Arianna-jiss, Darius-zir, were you looking for Nalithor?" Marius inquired, his tone and expression both curious as he approached us. However, it didn't take long for his eyes to drift down my exposed neck and to my cleavage. His face grew redder the farther down his eyes went. "I can...uh... I can call him here if you like."

"Oh, no." Darius shook his head at the flushed Adinvyr. "We're out of groceries and Arianna likes sweets, so I figured this would be a good stop on our way to run our errands."

"My brother thinks he and I both require new attire," I added, shifting in my seat to look at Marius, who quickly snapped his eyes back up to my face and reddened further. "I have more than enough to wear but I'm accompanying my brother anyway. Since I do *all* of the cooking, it's best I choose our groceries."

"She buys too much meat," Darius stated, pointing at me.

"And he buys too many vegetables." I motioned loosely at Darius as Marius began laughing.

"I guess the deer on your brother's robes are fitting, then!" Marius grinned, motioning to the hems of Darius' sleeves. "And meat for *'The White Fox,'* of course."

"Ugh, just how widespread is that nickname becoming?" I sighed, raising my fingers to my temples. "I'm beginning to think that *The Black Dragon* has something to do with this. Am I going to have to kick his ass again?"

"Didn't you lose your match?" Darius inquired, arching an eyebrow at me.

"I've lost two and won one!" I retorted, crossing my arms.

"I'll let Nalithor know you stopped by," Marius grinned and then motioned at me, seeming to leave my brother out of the statement. "His pouting when he realized he missed out on such entertaining conversation will be *well* worth it."

'The White Fox? The Black Dragon?' Darius shot me a suspicious look once Marius was away from our table.

'Apparently Nalithor's nickname is "The Black Dragon," thus he chose a dragon for his crest,' I offered with a small shrug.

'Ah right, and you handled training his men for him that one day,'

Darius remarked, frowning. *'Similar crests…and you're probably just as strict as he is if not more so. I guess I can see why they'd start calling you that. His nickname came* before *his crest though? I wonder why?'*

'Let's hurry and finish our breakfast,' I suggested. *'At this rate we won't have much time to work on your training before it's time for sleep!'*

Darius nodded his agreement, so we turned our focus to our drinks and then devoured our meals once they came. If I hadn't been so nervous about encountering Nalithor, I likely would have ventured to *The Little Orchid* more often. Their food was excellent, as was their vast assortment of teas. It would likely have taken me months of daily visits to sample their entire offering of blends. Alas, I wasn't quite ready to risk bumping into Nalithor more often.

I breathed a sigh of relief when we left the cafe, then took a deep inhale of the morning air. The interior of *The Little Orchid* smelled too strongly of its owner. Exposing myself to his scent for too long made me start questioning things I didn't want to think about. At least, until my mind started trying to wander off to ponder his alluring physique.

'Ugh, I just make things worse for myself.' I sighed, shoving my hands into my pockets as I followed my brother.

Soon enough, Darius tugged out a map he had scribbled on and then led me through the streets of Dauthrmir, taking us through a series of shops in the Merchant's District and neighboring areas. I found myself grateful that most of the shops delivered. I probably would have strangled my twin if I'd had to carry everything he'd bought.

Clothing was next-to-last on the list, and the boutique Nalithor had suggested looked to be quite upscale.

"Ari, I insist," Darius informed me as I tried, for the umpteenth time, to decline purchasing clothes. "You're a *girl*! You can never have too many clothes!"

'Woman. Not girl… And won't he get punished for this?' I sighed, holding my fingers to my temples. "I already have so much… Ugh, fine. *Fine*! Stop giving me that look!"

Thankfully, the seamstresses that worked at the boutique didn't bother me about my veiled mask. Instead, they helped me choose appropriate styles of Umbral Mages' robes and some other items to have made. On the downside, they informed me that they had nothing ready-made that would fit both my measurements and my unique requirements. I would have to wait a week and a half at minimum for everything to be finished. However, they agreed to make a few things that I could wear while waiting, and they would have the items delivered within the next few days.

For whatever reason, they refused to attach hoods to any of their designs. So, I ended up ordering several traveling cloaks for varying climates instead.

'The disgusted looks from the citizens seem to have stopped…' I glanced around our surroundings distractedly as we made our way through the Merchant's District along the road that would take us

back to the Sapphire Quarter. *'Is this Nalithor and Eyrian's doing? Nalithor said something about giving the military and academy staff a firm talking-to... Did it trickle down to the commoners as well? Or was hiding my skin, jewelry, and Brands really* that *big of an issue?'*

"What now, Ari?" Darius latched onto my arm, a bounce in his step. "Do you wanna do more shopping, or—?"

"Let's go get groceries so I can cook for us," I started with a small sigh, shaking my head. "After, we can go find somewhere to work on your training. Though you never told me what you want to work on."

"Control first?" Darius offered in a contemplative tone. "I don't wanna be fizzling out! Once I call on *any* element, I can't seem to control how much comes."

"Very well. When we get back, I'll see if I can find somewhere on academy grounds where we can practice without disturbing anyone." I nodded to my brother, allowing him to lead me off in the direction of nearby grocers.

About an hour later, I left Darius to stock the kitchen pantry while I strode off in search of one of the district's many guards. If anyone would know somewhere safe for me to take Darius, it would be them. Judging by the nervousness of any guard I spoke to, I could only assume that word of my sparring matches with Nalithor had spread through the ranks like wildfire. If I was *truly* Human, they would have had no reason to be uneasy around me.

'Well, I guess I can't pretend to be Human anymore after all that's

happened,' I reminded myself, striding back towards our house to fetch Darius. *'Still... Are Devillian women not weaker than their men, unlike with Humans? Is there some other reason that Nalithor has no women under his command?'*

Finding an empty, secluded training area proved easier than I thought it would be. I had Darius sit on the ground inside of one of the areas and began with the basics. He'd always had quite the affinity for earth, so I figured having him try to work with the existing ground and pebbles of the training yard would suffice to start.

Darius was much less nervous than he had been at the test, so he was capable of manipulating and even levitating some of the pebbles on a small scale. However, his control was still awful. He ended up shattering the pebbles into dust by exerting too much power over them. It appeared as though he couldn't maintain anything for more than a minute and a half.

'Just how much of Fraelfnir's training did Darius disregard?' I frowned deeply. *'This is the most basic level of training. It's what any mage would start with, and it's the first thing they would master!'*

Humankind's lack of magic was certainly a detriment to our upbringing, but Djialkan and Fraelfnir had done their best to make up for the X'shmiran's ignorance. As a child, I had spent hours a day on this same exercise and Djialkan's other strict lessons. I thought Darius would have retained at least *some* of the knowledge the fae-dragons gave him. *'Is he really going to have to start from the very beginning? Will he be a laughing stock in the academy?'*

"You're trying too hard, Darius," I offered after the eighth broken pebble. Pausing, I picked up another one and tossed it up and down a few times as I considered what to say. "This is a rare case of you focusing *too* hard. You have a strong affinity for earth. Because of this, you don't need to exert as much power to keep it floating.

"Just…relax and tune everything but the sound of nature out. You need to *feel* how much power you're letting through, and you need to *feel* how that flow of power effects the things you're trying to interact with."

"You're sure?" Darius pouted as I handed him the pebble.

"Take my ice, for example." I summoned a ball of ice, allowing it to float above my open palm. "Like rocks, it isn't meant to float in the air. However, using our control of the element, we can bend the rules. If I exert too little pressure, it falls. If I exert too much…" I paused, sending a spike of power through the ice and causing it to shatter into frost. "It loses its integrity and breaks.

"Whether you're creating or using already existing elements, you need to be able to feel the movement of both your energy *and* the innate energy of the element you're working with."

"So, when using multiple elements at once, you have to 'feel' all of them?" Darius frowned.

"It's more complicated in our case." I grinned, motioning between us. "Fire and ice oppose each other. Water and lightning oppose each other. So, we have to use our own power as a buffer when we try to use opposing elements at the same time.

"That's why you fizzled so fast during the exams. Instinctively, you attempted to correct for your opposing elements. You overdid it *and* exerted too much for light."

Darius looked as though he pondered what I said for a moment, before nodding his understanding and letting the pebble rest in his right palm. He took a deep breath and closed his eyes to concentrate, so I pivoted in place to look at the academy clock tower.

However, Nalithor's scent caught my attention instead. I found the Adinvyr in question approaching us from the nearby walkway, his posture relaxed but confident. *'Why…am I excited to see him?'*

I raised a finger to my lips and shushed him before he could attempt to speak. With my free hand, I motioned at Darius. Nalithor nodded and broke into a crooked grin. His gait shifted into that silent, predatory movement that I admired. Once he was standing beside me, he shot me a small smile and then looked down at Darius.

Examining the Adinvyr beside me, I realized that I didn't mind the fact he seemed intent on exposing his muscular chest and abdomen with his choices in attire. He looked damned delicious, and I would've needed a lot more screws loose in order to deny it. I found myself tempted to engulf him in shadows again just for the chance to feel his honed body. I gritted my teeth and looked away from Nalithor, mentally chastising myself.

'I take it that the boy is displeased with his performance?' Nalithor inquired, his voice full of curiosity and his expression thoughtful.

'Displeased is an understatement,' I replied, watching as Nalithor crossed his arms. *'He hates studying anything aside from culture and politics. He hates practicing. So, for him to ask for help with training is...unusual.'*

'Speaking of unusual,' Nalithor remarked, reaching over to pull my hood completely over my face. *'What happened to your more revealing attire, hmmm? This is quite nice as well...but much more teasing.'*

'It was temporary,' I replied, readjusting my hood with a disgruntled huff before turning my attention to Darius as my arms prickled into goosebumps. *'Ah...there he goes again.'*

Watching my twin, I spotted his nose twitching. He must have smelled Nalithor, and it had distracted him. I couldn't blame him for that, not at all, so I simply watched with amusement as the pebble burst into fine dust once Darius realize just whose scent he'd noticed. Darius' eyes snapped open and his face turned dark pink when he looked up at Nalithor. Shrugging, I glanced up at the clock.

"Well, you held it longer this time," I informed Darius. "How about you try—"

"Perhaps watching us would give him a better understanding?"

Nalithor offered, causing me to look towards him in surprise. Alas, his attention was still settled on my brother. "If Arianna and I fight each other, can you watch us with your other senses and not just your eyes, Darius? Feeling the flow of our magic should give you a better understanding of the interaction between both elements and an individual's own power."

"Uh...y-yeah, I can," Darius responded, his face reddening further as he glanced down Nalithor's chest and to the low-rise trousers the Adinvyr wore. After a moment, my brother scrambled out of the training arena and settled down on a bench. "Ari, try not to break him, okay?"

'He thinks you *will break* me?' Nalithor arched an eyebrow at me as I growled at my brother.

'Darius is convinced that I'm overly destructive,' I replied with a small huff before turning my attention to a device by the edge of the training yard. I made a small motion with my finger, directing my darkness to flip the switch. A barrier whirred into life around the training yard. Satisfied, I looked back at Nalithor. *'Since I've fought Chaos Beasts more than I've fought* people, *Darius thinks that means I'll use too much strength when fighting an actual person.'*

Nalithor chuckled, shaking his head, and then summoned several orbs of pale flame around himself. *'Well then, my dear, how shall we teach your brother? A mages' sparring match to complement our more physical matches? Or should we simply display how we exert our power in response to other elements?'*

'You really have to ask?' I smiled, summoning shadows around me and using them to levitate myself just off the ground. Breaking into a grin, I added, *'I think he'll learn much more from a true sparring match, don't you?'*

'I like the way you think,' Nalithor smirked, his tail swishing behind him. *'Loathe as I am to admit it, fighting each other at full strength isn't advisable. I doubt the barrier will hold.*

'Besides, if this *is the extent of your brother's knowledge... He probably can't grasp or follow a fiercer fight.'*

'You're probably right.' I nodded. *'Suggestions?'*

'Mmm... I'm sure you can match the strength I choose to exert.' Nalithor grinned, summoned several more fireballs, then lobbed the entire volley of them at me.

Deciding to make this as *educational* as possible, I reached out with one hand and caught several of the orbs. My power spread through the flames, converting them from Nalithor's pale blue-white to my cobalt blue fire. The Adinvyr had a wild look of excitement on his face when I threw his own flames back at him. He crouched and sprouted six pairs of black feathered wings before bursting upwards into the air to avoid the orbs.

"Isn't that cheating?!" Darius yelped.

Nalithor made a graceful motion with both hands, pulling massive boulders out of the ground and poising them in the air above me. I grinned, examining the boulders with tendrils of my power to determine just how much Nalithor had reinforced the boulder's strength. When he flung the first boulder at me, I summoned an array of thin ice blades. The blades tore through each of the boulders in turn as he lobbed them at me.

This time it was Nalithor who grinned. He summoned more boulders, this time setting them alight with flames.

'Fighting earth with ice instead of that wind of yours?' Nalithor inquired, his tone giving away his curiosity.

'I can't be too predictable, now can I?' I countered, leaping upwards.

Nalithor looked startled for a moment as I used his flaming boulders as stepping stones. Before he could question my methods, I crouched on the boulder that was level with the Adinvyr and launched myself at him. Nalithor flew upwards to dodge as I slung a wind-infused kick towards his chest.

I smirked as I began to fall back towards the ground and called on my darkness, letting my shadows rush the flying deity. My shadows wrapped tight around his arms, torso, and throat. Nalithor sent the boulders hurtling toward me, but I just kicked one out of my way and crashing into the barrier. The rest missed.

I dragged Nalithor back down to the ground with my shadows and watched him struggle for a moment. Grinning, I summoned several more blades of ice above my shoulder and aimed them at the Adinvyr. Darius shrieked with panic, but Nalithor had a look of approval and eagerness on his face. I launched the blades at him, engulfing them in both wind and shadows as they traveled.

A charge of static in the air was the only warning I had, giving me just enough time to leap back. Black lightning struck the spot I'd been standing, and I let out a laugh—that would have *hurt* if it had hit! I darted toward where my darkness had Nalithor bound, weaving my way through the series of lightning bolts he trained on me. Once close, I aimed a shadowy kick towards his head. One of his arms broke free and he caught my ankle. In almost the same motion he tossed me towards the barrier.

Although the motion seemed casual, almost lazy, my back slammed into the barrier with almost enough force to knock the wind from my lungs. However, I'd taken *much* harder tumbles when fighting beasts. This was nothing in comparison.

Nalithor chased after me with both shadows and flames surrounding his clawed hands and forearms. I ducked under his swipe and then encased his legs in solid ice, rooting him in place.

'Your brother and the rest of our audience appear rather concerned that we're going to kill each other.' Nalithor laughed, his tail snapping back and forth playfully. *'Do you think we should stop?'*

'I don't know about you, but I am having fun!' I retorted, watching as my ice began to crack.

Nalithor summoned pure shadows around himself and disappeared from view the moment my ice shattered. I could tell from the brief glance that his darkness appeared to be his comfort element. It was obvious in the fluidity with which he worked. Alas, I didn't have much time to admire it.

Large pillars of shadow erupted from the ground around me, forcing me to dodge. He was attempting to lure me somewhere— that much was obvious.

Pursing my lips, I summoned a shield of ice beneath my feet when I sensed a pillar forming beneath me—one I couldn't dodge. The pillar launched me into the air when it struck my ice. However, Nalithor's shadows were more liquid-like than I anticipated. They poured over the sides of my shield and ran toward my feet. With a displeased click of my tongue, I opted for the riskier move and dismissed my shield entirely.

Nalithor's shadows engulfed me as I fell into them. They ran over my skin as if my clothing wasn't even there, leaving trails of hot tingles over my entire body. I did my best to ignore the rather intimate sensations, and summoned flames around my entire form as I shifted to dive-bomb through the pillar of shadows to where I sensed Nalithor.

He leapt back from me, his shadows dispersing as my flames flared out around me. Nalithor arched an eyebrow at me and then shook his head, making an upwards motion with his index finger. The ground beneath me rolled, throwing off my balance, but I didn't fall. Instead, I summoned a burst of wind beneath my feet and launched myself into the air.

Once satisfied with my altitude, I conjured a scythe of ice and sat on the staff portion like it was a swing. I tilted my head and looked down at Nalithor, curious as to what he might do about the situation.

'That was a risky move,' Nalithor pointed out. *'Are you really so accepting of darkness that you don't fear mine?'*

'You're calmer when working with shadows,' I replied, swinging my feet back and forth. *'It would appear we're both most at ease with our inner darkness.'*

'You're more observant than I gave you credit for,' Nalithor remarked, thoughtful, before leaping into the air and hovering in front of me. He reached for my face, his expression deceptively soft. *'What's it going to take to end this match of ours, hmmm?'*

I laughed, having sensed the sleep spell that he'd intertwined with the shadows surrounding his hand. He cupped my face, but his expression faltered when I shot him a smirk and adjusted the grip on my scythe. With no other warning, I pulled the weapon out from beneath me and slashed at him with it. Of course, he was quick to leap out of harm's way. As I fell back toward the ground, Nalithor shifted to pursue me.

"Are you two quite done?!" Eyrian roared at the both of us as we summoned shadowy gauntlets and squared off. "Not sure the prince here can take many more heart attacks from you two!"

'Mmm... Your brother is rather concerned.' Nalithor purred, biting his lower lip briefly as we circled each other. Our shadows stretched and warped in the air around us, testing each other as we both waited for the other to make the first move. *'You're quite calm by comparison, despite your excitement. That's interesting.'*

'He probably can't figure out who is going to break who,' I commented sarcastically, earning a sultry laugh in response. *'I give it maybe thirty seconds before* General Il'thar *loses his patience and manually shuts off the barrier to stop us.'*

'Yes, he does tend to make a habit of interfering...' Nalithor muttered, casting a cold, sideways glance in the direction of his Draekin friend. *'I'm of half a mind to give him a start as punishment.'*

'Hmmm...agreed,' I murmured, adjusting my grip on my shadows. *'What do you have in mind?'*

'Perhaps I should kidnap you and fly somewhere he can't interfere,' Nalithor suggested in a rather serious tone, shooting me a suggestive look before breaking into a grin. *'However, suspending him in the air with our darkness should be sufficient. He dislikes the air and the shadows both.'*

Before I could respond one way or the other, Eyrian had smashed his fist into the barrier's control box. Nalithor and I both gripped the large Draekin general with our combined power and hoisted him several yards into the air. Nalithor simply trained an icy glare on Eyrian, while I crossed my arms and smirked. More shadows rippled around my feet as I contemplated attempting to punish Eyrian further.

"Really?!" Eyrian yelped. "*Both* of you? So you *were* communicating still!"

"You couldn't tell?" I asked, tilting my head. "Maybe you need to join Darius in some of his classes at the academy."

Nalithor burst into laughter as the Draekin turned a special shade of crimson. I just smiled sweetly at the angry Draekin as he spluttered, unable to think of a quick retort. After a moment, I withdrew my shadows and glanced around at the rather large crowd that had gathered to watch Nalithor and I fight. I could only assume that the pressure of our combined power had drawn them. The training area I had chosen was surrounded by too many buildings and trees for people to have spotted us from the main road.

Shaking my head to myself, I turned and looked at Darius. He was visibly distressed, and it was most likely because of how aggressive my fight with Nalithor had been. I doubted it was *me* he was concerned about, though.

"I do believe your brother could use a cold drink and some lunch, Arianna," Nalithor stated as he dropped Eyrian unceremoniously to the ground. He closed the distance between us and slid an arm around my shoulders, continuing, "And as fun as our sparring matches are, I did actually come to discuss something with you."

"How can you call that 'sparring?!'" Darius demanded finally, stalking towards us with an exasperated look. He shoved Nalithor's arm off my shoulder as soon as he was in range to do so. "Look at you two! You're not even sweating!"

"I think you sweated enough for both of us," I pointed out, nudging Darius' damp collarbone with one finger. Nalithor remained silent and just arched an eyebrow at my brother. "Really, Darius. That was just a light sparring match. You needn't be so nervous."

"*Light* sparring match?!" Darius yelped, grabbing both of my shoulders. "Are you out of your mind?! You two were trying to kill each—"

"She's right. That was a light sparring match," Nalithor interrupted, resting a forearm on top of my head and leaning lightly on me to peer down at my brother. "However, *as I was saying*, I need to borrow Arianna for a bit."

"But—" Darius started to protest but cut himself off with an exasperated sigh. The corner of his eye kept twitching as he looked at me and then over my head at Nalithor. "Fine. But I demand compensation."

Before Nalithor could respond, Darius stalked off in the general direction of our house. I reached up and nudged the Adinvyr's arm and, after a moment, he relented and removed his forearm from my head. Nalithor motioned for me to join him and then started walking in the direction of the main road. Eyrian was quick to fall into step with us, so I glanced to either side at them and waited for someone to explain what they wanted.

"What was that little outburst about?" Nalithor inquired, motioning back over his shoulder with a jab of his thumb.

"He's probably going to ask you out on a date," I answered thoughtfully, causing *both* of them to look at me with disbelief.

"What? Men he likes is the *only* area of his life where he gets *that* pushy."

"Hear that, Nali? You're going to break another boy's heart." Eyrian snorted sarcastically, earning a glare from the Adinvyr. "Tch, don't even like men and you draw em' to you like the plague."

"To be fair… If it moves and it's hot, Darius wants in its pants." I shrugged as both the Adinvyr and the Draekin glowered at each other over the top of my head.

"Hear that, *Nali?* You're *hot.*" Eyrian snorted, causing me to glance between the two curiously again.

"Keep that up and I'm not going to be able to tell if you two are best friends, worst enemies, or passionate lovers," I remarked, shaking my head and bringing my fingers to my temples.

"We're *straight.*" They both retorted, causing themselves to glare at each other again.

"He is right, however," Nalithor began, looking down at me with a more teasing expression. "You did imply you share your brother's view."

"I won't deny that my brother has decent taste in men—in the looks department," I replied dismissively, shrugging. "He would have a much better time in life if he was just as exacting when it comes to personality, seeing as the majority of men who catch his fancy are little better than clockwork dolls."

"Yee-ouch." Eyrian grinned and placed a hand on my shoulder.

"That's some tough love there. Darius doesn't have good taste outside of looks, you say?"

"A shoestring has more personality than most of the men he's interested in," I retorted bluntly. After brief consideration, I motioned at Nalithor and looked over at him, noticing he'd smoothed his face into a more neutral expression. "Not to inflate your ego, Nalithor, but you're probably the most complex man I've ever seen my brother set his sights on, and probably the first that's out of his league *without* taking sexuality into account.

"My brother and his choices aside, however, what is it you wanted to speak with me about, Nalithor?"

Nalithor's gaze flicked to the side at me, but I caught the small smile that was growing on his mouth. I had realized that I must have made him think that I thought he fell into the "pretty but unintelligent" category that most of my brother's interests did. I hoped that my latter comment had rectified the situation. Both the expression on his mouth and the returned swishing of his tail made me think perhaps I succeeded.

"Before that!" Eyrian interjected, moving so that he was in front of us and walking backwards. "The assassins you apprehended are surprisingly resistant, Arianna. At least...the woman is. The man still hasn't woken up yet. We need more time to pull information from them—or permission from the emperor to use more *convincing* methods."

"They're Human, aren't they?" Nalithor frowned at Eyrian.

"Shouldn't they be fragile creatures?"

"I'm not sure what kind of training they're subjected to," I began, drawing both men's attention, "but none of the ones I've caught in the past were willing to speak. Some went as far as to bite off their own tongues. That's why my patience with those two was so short. Well… That, and the fact that they were Darius' personal servants."

"Personal servants…?" Nalithor's eyes widened briefly, before he turned to exchange a serious look with Eyrian. "Speak with Lucifer. Let him know that I'm advising we lift our usual restrictions. We need information, and that woman is going to give it to us."

"It'll mean more if you tell him that yourself," Eyrian pointed out, his tone flat.

"It would, but I have other plans," Nalithor spoke dismissively.

Eyrian shot Nalithor a disgruntled glare as the Adinvyr shooed him away, but Nalithor didn't seem to care. Instead, he gripped me lightly by my shoulders and steered me down a different hallway in the palace. I wanted to kick myself for becoming so absorbed in our conversation. I should have noticed where we were, and yet I didn't even recall entering the palace itself.

'I would like your opinion on something, seeing as you're at least somewhat familiar with Sihix,' Nalithor answered my prior question telepathically as he guided me in the direction of his private wing of the palace.

"Oh, there you are, *Nali*!" The Rylthra Oracle called happily when she spotted us. I felt my eye twitch in response to her tone. "How's the boy doing, Arianna? He was such a mess after his exams!"

'I really don't like this bitch,' I thought, bristling as I toyed with the possibility of not answering her at all. More petty irritations aside, something about the Oracles unsettled me in a way that Corentine simply...didn't.

"Darius is a little better," I replied, deciding to at least be cordial since she was Corentine's sister...and she *had* helped me. "At least, he's finally decided that studying is something he *needs* to do. Well, *after* he was done dragging me all over the Merchant's Plaza..."

"He's quite angry with the princess and me for our duel," Nalithor offered, glancing toward me briefly with a questioning look. Had he sensed my displeasure with the Rylthra woman?

"You two did draw quite the crowd." The Oracle sniffed haughtily before laughing at Nalithor's expression. "Of course I was watching! The two of you are quite impressive, you know. It's such a shame you insist on working alone, Nalithor."

"Oh? Does the big, scary Black Dragon eat all of his assigned partners?" I teased, nudging Nalithor with my elbow. The Oracle burst into giggles as Nalithor turned toward me.

"More like all of my past partners get eaten by *Beasts* if I don't babysit them," Nalithor spoke pointedly, tugging my hood over my face, then chuckling when I batted his hand away.

"You know, *this one* is quite cute!" The Oracle exclaimed with a huge grin, pulling me away from the Adinvyr. She wrapped her arms around my shoulders and giggled again when Nalithor shot her a dangerous, irritated glare.

"You didn't make her remove her mask during her test—" Nalithor started with a snarl, but the Oracle's laughter interrupted him.

"Come now, Nalithor! I can See through her mask plain as day. *Besides*, I got to see her without it while in Sihix." The Oracle laughed again, squeezing me tightly. "Oh, Ari, I made sure the seamstresses and armor smiths in the city have your crest in their records already. The new attire you ordered today *should* be emblazoned properly when you get it.

"Now then! I have to go inform your brother of his test results and introduce him to his new partner. Nali, you're going to fill in Arianna before you start picking her brain about the *Aledacian Forests*, right?"

The Oracle didn't even give him a chance to respond, instead walking off with a grin on her face. Nalithor released a low growl and then pulled at my shoulders gently, guiding me the rest of the way to his wing of the palace. The room he brought me to was several stories high and filled to the brim with complicated-looking devices, tools, tomes, scrolls, and many containers of what looked like samples of uncountable things.

It was much different from the library that I'd seen before. This looked more like a laboratory and was much messier.

'Once again I find myself alone with the inquisitive Adinvyr deity.' I rolled my eyes behind my mask, examining the room and the various fragile-looking items scattered through it. *'Much better than being stuck with the Oracle or my brother, at any rate.*

'I wonder what he wants from me today?'

CHAPTER FOURTEEN
A Gesture of Trust

"I get the feeling that you dislike Oracles," I remarked dryly, watching as Nalithor hung his overrobe nearby and then strode shirtless to a nearby desk. *'Really? Is he just that comfortable around me, or is he* inviting *me to stare? Humph.'*

"They are weak and interfere incessantly," Nalithor replied, shaking his head. "Didn't she say you went to acquire new clothing? Why are you still wearing something so *warm* indoors, if that's the case?"

"Ah…" I muttered awkwardly, causing Nalithor to turn and shoot me a questioning look. "They didn't have anything ready-made that fits me."

"So that's why you weren't wearing pants or a skirt underneath your robes," Nalithor remarked thoughtfully. My face burned hot and I looked away with a huff when I realized that he must have seen up my robes while we were sparring. He seemed unfazed and instead turned to his desk to rifle through stacks of papers, continuing, "I suppose I can't, in good conscience, offer for you to hang up your overrobe in that case.

"If you had plans, I can try to keep this short. Though, I was hoping you might have time to indulge a selfish request as well."

"Plans?" I arched and eyebrow, tracking Nalithor's movements. "No plans. Darius and I already finished all our errands. If my brother is being a good boy, he'll be reading for the next few hours."

"Good, I have you all to myself for a little while then," Nalithor mused, turning from his desk and offering me a small stack of papers. "The Oracles requested for Lucifer to order a rush on your brother's test results. They claimed it was due to something they sensed in relation to one of his prior tests—and your 'hinting.' Darius has been assigned classes, which will start immediately, and he has been paired with a Vampire from Beshulthien.

"Would you like some tea? We may be here for a while, and it is still too early for mri'lec."

"Tea sounds great." I nodded, accepting the stack of papers as Nalithor shot me a warm smile. *What? Did he think I was going to decline and run off already?*

"I will return with tea for us shortly, then," Nalithor stated, before motioning broadly at the room around us. "Sit wherever you like."

Nalithor left through the door we'd entered from, and I released a small sigh. I made my way over to a chaise and perched on it, unsure what to do with myself. A mixture of relief and disappointment went through me as Nalithor's presence disappeared down the hallway, but I wasn't sure why I felt either emotion.

Furthermore, I had no idea where to look when he was wearing nothing but pants. His physique was near impossible for me to ignore, but he was too perceptive for me to get away with freely staring. Although I got the impression he wouldn't mind if I stared, I doubted he would let me get away with it without teasing me for it. I let out an irritated huff at the thought. *'That man is impossible.'*

My shyness and confusion aside, Nalithor's presence made me feel...safe. That was pretty much the *opposite* of what people usually made me feel.

'Not the time to be thinking about this,' I reminded myself, shaking my head hard.

Once I was comfortable and had made sure my overrobe was covering my bare legs, I placed the stack of papers on my lap and proceeded to skim through them. The sheer number of circles and comments in red ink on the first page alone made me snicker. It appeared as though the first several pages were dedicated to the tests of power. Their equipment measured much more than I'd initially guessed and, on some level, I was impressed.

However, my concern over Darius' poor results were quick to outweigh any amusement I found. Darius' raw power was rated insanely high. I pursed my lips in unease and reread the pages at a slower pace. Nalithor had been mindful enough to provide me with a separate page to explain the numbers and ratings, but it only made my unease and confusion grow.

'His raw power is on par with the ratings of the Upper Gods?' I frowned to myself, double- and triple-checking the results. *'I'm not surprised that his power is little better than a child's. But...how is this possible? If he has this* much *power, just where do I fall on the scale?'*

I found myself shaking my head and sighing again as I read on. Darius' scores in both the physical and mental fortitude tests were atrocious. As a X'shmiran prince, my brother had always had everything done *for* him. To exacerbate matters, the fact he was an Astral Mage meant that combat training was something that wasn't required of him—the X'shmirans believed he was above needing such things.

Darius' physical results were so atrocious that the Vorpmasians were assigning my brother an incredible amount of physical training. It was *almost* laughable. My brother wasn't going to take this laying down though, that much I knew. Darius would likely be enraged.

By the scribbled comments, it looked as though the *real* concern was my brother's mental fortitude. It didn't come to a surprise to me; I knew my brother was fragile, and for good reason. I had thought the examiners had brought up painful memories of Darius' past. That certainly would have explained the sorry state he'd been in.

Alas, no. It wasn't that at all.

'He was that *upset over the notion of losing patients?'* I furrowed my brow, reading the explanation of the test. *'I understand him vomiting in response to the fighting portion of the test—he can't stand to look at or smell blood. However, I didn't think his mental state had deteriorated this much. Surely he realized that, if he became a healer, he would see some terrible things?'*

"Darius is being assigned a great deal of both physical and psychological therapy?" I inquired aloud, having caught Nalithor's presence returning. "Since his magical control is horribly lacking... I'm assuming that the Archmagi are concerned about what will happen if Darius' mental state breaks down completely?"

"With that much raw power," Nalithor started as he set a tea tray down on the table in front of me, "we want to take as many precautions as possible. If he can get his powers under control, he will be an exceptional healer and an invaluable asset. If he can't, we're obligated to seek out the Elders and have his powers sealed permanently."

"How can I help?" I offered. However, when I flipped to the next page, I couldn't help but burst into disbelieving laughter. "Ah...so *that's* why he was so embarrassed when he spoke with the

Oracles!"

"He wasn't expecting to be a submissive in work, yet a dominant in bed?" Nalithor inquired dryly as he perched on a chair across from me. "By your laughter, I'm assuming something occurred to you."

"Darius insists that he and I are *always* polar opposites," I replied with a grin, sinking back against the chaise. "As such, he's been insisting that I'm a dominant, and only for one reason; Darius was hoping he'd be read as a submissive. He believes it would mean you're *all his*."

"So, when he 'accused' you of being an alpha female, he thought that meant by default that you're a dominant?" Nalithor shook his head, laughing, then shot me a sultry smirk. "Your brother seems rather concerned about having to fight you for my attention, my dear. Yet *you* seem entirely unconcerned.

"Are you that confident in your ability to win?"

"You already made it clear that you're uninterested in males," I pointed out, settling the stack of papers on my lap and then shooting Nalithor a look. "And if I *did* decide I wanted to fight my brother for something or someone... Do you really think he'd stand a chance in his current state? You saw how poorly his challenge went."

"You do seem like the doting type," Nalithor countered, grinning. "Are you saying you wouldn't at least go easy on him? Assuming he was challenging you seriously."

"If it was for something I *really* wanted, I would have no qualms about destroying my brother for it!" I retorted, causing Nalithor to start laughing. "What? He could do with a swift kick in the ass every now and then!"

"You're adorable." Nalithor purred as he examined me. I growled at him, feeling my face flushing. "Aside from your clear amusement with his DSO results, do you agree with the rest of his scores?"

"I find it difficult to believe that his power is *this* close to an Upper God's," I answered flatly, watching an amused smile twitch across Nalithor's features. "While I can't claim to be familiar with just how powerful an Upper God is… I rather dislike the idea that they're so weak."

"Weak?" Nalithor laughed, shaking his head, and grinned at me. "Ahhh…you really are something else. You think your brother is weak? Even with results like that?"

"He's weak in mind, body, and magic as far as I'm concerned," I replied with a shrug, watching as the Adinvyr smirked. "That aside, he has no inclination toward combat or destruction in the slightest. Certainly, he'll be an excellent healer if he can get his abilities under control…but that isn't exactly something I consider threatening or challenging. What's he going to do, heal me to death?"

"Darius truly intends to take up the mantle of a healer then?" Nalithor inquired curiously. I nodded slightly and then offered the stack of papers back to him as he continued, "You sound as if you don't approve of healers."

"It isn't that," I replied dryly, tracking him as he moved to accept the papers. "My brother doesn't understand the need for people who are capable of fighting. He can be rather passive-aggressive though, so I wouldn't say he's a truly passive individual.

"He believes that manipulating circumstances or facts is safer and more beneficial than my more bloody and direct approach to problems."

"I can see why he believes you're opposites," Nalithor commented in amused tone, his intense gaze studying me. "Still, saying that level of power is 'weak' is a rather bold statement. For a moment I wondered if you were displaying arrogance…but that isn't it… If you truly believe Darius' power is 'weak', then what of mine?"

"You're the most powerful person in Dauthrmir." I shrugged, ignoring the smirk that returned to Nalithor's face. "Considering that Eyrian saw fit to interfere with our duel, I'm uncertain of how I compare. I'll have to challenge you again later."

"You could always challenge me again *now*," Nalithor stated as I reached for a cup of tea. He released a roll of power and I let out an amused laugh response, shaking my head at him. "Now, now. *Laughing?* If you didn't look so amused, I might be inclined to feel insulted."

"I could challenge you now, that is true." I grinned crookedly and sat back with my tea. "But that wouldn't be very conducive to whatever your purpose in bringing me here was, now would it? Please. I do have at least *some* sense of manners."

"It would be a welcome distraction either way," Nalithor smiled and stood up, beckoning me with one clawed hand. "Very well, business before pleasure. Bring your tea if you like, it won't damage anything.

"In my spare time I've been studying the known Aledacian Forests. Both empires consider them as important sources of elemental energy. Despite their reputation of being 'cursed,' we've discovered their existence is integral to our world and its longevity. Due to your relationship with the Sihix Forest, I assume you're aware of this to some extent."

I tilted my head slightly and examined the glowing Brands on Nalithor's back as he spoke. As I followed him up a few flights of stairs, I found myself feeling out the power that seemed to flow freely around the Adinvyr. After reading Darius' test results I was beginning to understand why I believed so strongly that Nalithor's power was beyond that of an Upper God. My brother was like a mouse, and Nalithor was most certainly a dragon by comparison.

'If I can fight him so evenly, then...' I contemplated, my gaze flicking down Nalithor's back until his Brands disappeared into his waistband. *'Actually... I suppose it's stranger that Darius' power is rated so high. I wonder if they're going to rush my results as well? They must be confused.'*

"Ah, so that's the faint hum of magic I heard," I remarked, following Nalithor toward a series of several clear containers with bright crystals inside of them. "How did you manage to prize samples from not one but *five* of the forests?"

"I can be quite charming when given the chance, you know," Nalithor replied, shooting me a sly smile over his shoulder. He motioned to the nearest of the crystals, which shone pale blue. "I've been attempting to compare the power of the five forests I have access to. Studying the similarities in their power, attempting to determine *exactly* what 'corrupts' those who stay too long…and what draws the Chaos Beasts to the forests in such a way.

"Since you said you were on good terms with Sihix, and I am not permitted near it, I was hoping perhaps *you* would give me information about the Sihix Forest."

"That's a little more complicated than you make it sound," I pointed out, passing him so that I could examine the five samples. "So, the forests of ice, wind, light, water, and fire have been found thus far?"

"And now darkness, of course," Nalithor answered. I sensed him moving around somewhere behind me as he continued, "The first five attract beasts like the plague. Many of the Middle and Upper Gods have been attempting to protect the forests from the beasts. In the process, they discovered that the Exiled Gods are *also* trying to protect the Aledacian Forests."

"The Chaos Beasts aren't technically there to harm the forests?"

I asked, turning to look at Nalithor for confirmation, which was given in the form of a nod. "These alone put off more power than Sihix Forest as a whole. I'm sure you've noticed that, seeing as darkness is your comfort element as well."

"X'shmir's relationship with the Sihix Forest struck me as strange," Nalithor commented in a contemplative tone as I turned to examine the crystals once more. "Typically, mortal races seek to destroy the Aledacian Forests out of fear of the 'curse,' or because they fear of the sheer amount of power each of the forests radiates.

"Yet in X'shmir they leave the forest alone completely. Humans aren't exactly known for being a 'holy' race by any means, regardless of what those tomes you loaned me claim."

"It's *because* they're not 'holy.'" I shook my head without turning towards him. "Humans are terrified of the darkness inside themselves and inside their 'fellow man' above all else. If they wander too close to the Sihix Forest they're confronted with that darkness. They don't even have to *go in* the forest. It's easier for them to stay away from it entirely."

"Even though you saved two of Sihix's Guardians, the X'shmirans still fear it?" Nalithor asked, coming to stand beside me.

"*Especially* because I saved two of its Guardians." I laughed. "I was young, and I was cute. The Guardians were of half a mind to take me into Sihix and raise me themselves."

"You're still cute," Nalithor teased, causing me to turn and glare at him. "Especially if you are going to make *that* face. I hope you didn't think I would find your pouting to be intimidating, my dear.

"I assume your loyalty to your brother is why you declined joining them?"

"I didn't decline." I shook my head, earning a frown. "I told you about their High Priestess, Corentine, right? And how she communicates with Sihix instead of deities?"

"Likely because the deities have been unable to contact *anyone* in X'shmir until recently." Nalithor nodded, his tone one of understanding.

"She Saw something of importance and informed the Guardians that they couldn't keep me," I spoke dryly before motioning down at the hem of my overrobe. "My interactions and the two Guardian foxes have obviously had some level of influence on me, but I haven't ever *lived* in the Sihix Forest for more than a few weeks or months at a time.

"They don't have anyone capable of fighting beasts. However, many of the herbs and materials they require don't grow in the forest itself. I decided I rather liked the foxes and their High Priestess, so I often gathered the things they needed and placed it at the edge of the forest for them."

"Forest Guardians are rather strong." Nalithor frowned at me. "How come they are incapable of dealing with the beasts? They should be able to."

"Shir and Gari are a mated pair," I replied without thinking, then grimaced to myself. Revealing that I knew the foxes by name didn't seem like a smart idea, but Nalithor just shot me a warm, knowing smile when I hesitated. I sighed and crossed my arms, continuing, "From what I understand, they are both incredibly weakened until Shir has her kits. Otherwise they wouldn't need my assistance, even with the forest itself in a weakened state. Alala is from their first litter."

"Ah, that makes sense," Nalithor commented thoughtfully, his eyes trained on the crystal samples before us. "It's similar with the Guardians of other forests. However, they all have more than two Guardians on hand.

"So, it *is* like Djialkan said? You've essentially been acting as a Guardian yourself? Do they realize you're no longer in X'shmir?"

"They're the ones who insisted I come Below," I grumbled, tugging at the front of my hood. "I wasn't originally planning to return to the city until well after negotiations were over. Darius had wounded my pride quite thoroughly in his dismissal of me, you see.

"While I was busy sulking, the High Priestess sent me a message to kick my ass into gear. Djialkan insisted we return at once."

"I take it that Darius 'wounded' you around the same time you fled X'shmir and made me chase you halfway across the country," Nalithor spoke dryly and placed his hand on my shoulder. "With your scent being so strong I'm surprised there weren't more beasts attempting to impede either of us, you know."

"Strong scent?" I inquired, curious despite myself. "As for the beasts, I'm quite proficient with using darkness to hide my presence. The beasts are attracted to both Darius' power and mine. Like moths to a flame, as it were. I learned early on that the beasts were terrified of darkness, and that I could use their fear to my advantage."

"Yes, strong scent." Nalithor nodded and then leaned down to nuzzle into the side of my throat, purring as his arms snuck around my waist. "Musky jasmine and vanilla paired with something else that I can't quite place...

"I'll have you know it's quite distracting. I find it hard to believe that cloaking yourself in shadows was enough to hide it."

'Distracting? He's one to talk!' I thought, feeling my pulse quicken against Nalithor's cheek as he nuzzled me again.

"Well in that case, at least I smell better than beasts," I commented, biting back a shiver when he chuckled into my throat. "What else did you want to know? You still haven't told me what this 'selfish request' of yours is."

"I want to know if you've kept anything from the Sihix Forest," Nalithor purred, reaching up to grip my chin. He turned my face toward him slightly and I bit back an amused smirk; he was pouring a great deal of power into both his words and his hands. Did he think he needed to pry information from me? "If you have... I want access to them, for my research."

"That depends on what your intentions with Sihix are," I stated plainly. Nalithor paused, a look of surprise washing over his face, so I smirked and continued, "You don't need to *seduce* me for information, Nalithor. If you can prove to me that you aren't seeking to harm Sihix, then I have no reason to withhold information from you.

"Consider this your only warning. Being straightforward and *honest* with me is a much better method to utilize."

"Maybe I *want* to seduce you, hmmm?" Nalithor teased, tracing my lower lip with his thumb. After a moment he chuckled and released me. "I don't intend to harm *any* of the forests, Arianna. As I mentioned; they are integral to Avrirsa. They are meant to be protected.

"We've received information that a radical group is seeking to annihilate the forests. The Elders decided that I'm best equipped to analyze and research the forests, and their properties, due to my ties to the Vorpmasian Empire and the Academy. If you decide to cooperate with me, I fully intend to return whatever I borrow from you."

'So, I was right. He's a very high-ranking deity.' I examined Nalithor's expression and the firm set of his jaw. Despite his teasing, he appeared quite serious. *'Ah...is this what Corentine meant when she said I'd find an opportunity to help Sihix if I went Below? I hope I'm not wrong.'*

"I want copies of your research on the Aledacian Forests," I demanded, crossing my arms at the startled Adinvyr. "Recommendations on what tomes to read would also be helpful. Attempting to find *anything* in the academy's library is a chore."

"Remember when I said that I had my own goals to pursue in Vorpmasia, and that I had exhausted the tomes in X'shmir?"

"You wish to look into the forests as well?" Nalithor inquired, looking intrigued. "I take it that you noticed something strange about Sihix? Of course, your demands are reasonable, and I agree to them."

"Didn't you see anything odd about Sihix when you flew over X'shmir?" I countered, motioning loosely with one hand.

"The light—or the darkness, I should say—from some of the trees was missing." Nalithor nodded after a moment of thought, then a look of recognition passed over his face. "You believe something is *draining* power from the forest?"

"That's the problem—I don't know for certain." I sighed, deciding to withhold some of my thoughts from him for now. "The Guardians and the High Priestess don't know what could be hurting Sihix in such a way…but the damage is widespread."

"Just how much of the forest are we talking here, Arianna?" Nalithor shot me a frown and then turned to a nearby bookshelf, pulling down a series of tomes.

"Almost forty percent," I replied, causing Nalithor to stop what he was doing and shoot me a look of disbelief. "It's been going on for a long time, they tell me. The forest's inhabitants believe that the sky is 'eating' the forest's aether. When a tree loses its power, they see the glow shoot upwards into the sky and out of view. The fact that X'shmir's sky is the same violet as the tree's glow doesn't help matters."

"But since they're stuck in the Sihix Forest, there's no way for them to prove it?" Nalithor offered, so I nodded in reply. "I assume you have come up empty as well, then?"

"As frustrating as it is, yes," I confirmed with an irritated huff. "If there's a device in X'shmir responsible for it, like the inhabitants of Sihix believe, it must be something terribly commonplace in appearance."

"So you *have* looked for it." Nalithor chuckled and then motioned toward the large pile of books he had pulled down. "This should be a good start as far as tomes are concerned. Making copies of my research notes is a simple matter, but I can't promise they're written well—or that they'll make coherent sense."

"I'm sure I'll manage," I replied dryly, watching as he moved to a rather messy desk. "I have a feeling this wasn't your 'selfish request.' I hope you aren't hesitating to speak your mind, Nalithor. Hesitation is *so unattractive* you know."

"You're feisty today…" Nalithor commented, glancing at me over his shoulder. His tail swayed back and forth as a smirk formed on his mouth. "Since you're so curious, I was wondering if you might be willing to assist me on occasion with some of the classes

I teach at the academy."

"Assist? With *teaching*?" I arched an eyebrow at his back as he returned to duplicating his notes via magic. *'My results haven't even come in yet, and then I threw that unwarranted tantrum. What is he thinking? I'm hardly qualified to teach.'*

"You've proved to be surprisingly observant," Nalithor began without turning around. "A second pair of eyes and senses would be very helpful in some of the classes I teach. There is a regrettable lack of observant mages in the academy; the few that *do* live up to my expectations already have their own classes to instruct.

"My men had nothing but praise for your training methods…aside from complaints about being sore and bruised afterward, of course."

"Ah, the other mages fall into the 'dreamy-eyed scholar' category?" I inquired, earning a rumbling laugh in response. "I don't really mind, but… Would it be appropriate? I'm neither a teacher nor an Archmagus."

"You should be," Nalithor commented, striding toward me with a large folder stuffed with parchment. "If your test results come out the way I believe they will, the Oracles will likely demand you be given the title. They've already shown that they're more than happy to meddle when you're involved.

"However, to answer your question, you would be acting as my assistant. I have a great deal of leeway to do as I please in Dauthrmir and the academy alike, so your rank and your allegiance are irrelevant as far as any questioning parties are concerned. They might be confused, but they will trust my judgment."

"I don't really mind. I'm just…surprised," I grumbled, my face growing warmer as I accepted the binder from Nalithor. He just smiled at me and then moved to the pile of books next. "Fighting is more my forte, but if I can help in some way—"

"It's *because* fighting is your forte," Nalithor interjected, amused, as I tucked the binder into my shrizar. "My classes contain a mix of both healers and destructive mages. Since I am both, I can relate to either side with ease.

"You're more focused on combat and its aspects, so I am hoping that you'll have an easier time determining if there is a rift growing between my students. It has happened in the past, and I would rather identify such a problem as quickly as possible."

"You trust me to help?" I finally decided to be blunt. He gave me a warm smile and carried his collection of books to me.

"You've proven yourself to be quite skilled, and just as powerful," Nalithor replied as he placed the books gingerly in my shrizar. "That, along with your desire to protect one of the Aledacian Forests, makes me inclined to trust you…to some extent, at least. Your insistence that I be straightforward with you helps considerably, though it also goes to further to cement my belief that you aren't Human. Alas, that's another matter entirely."

"Where do you wish me to place the sample from Sihix, then?" I sighed, closing my shrizar as I watched the Adinvyr smile at me yet again before moving to fetch something from a drawer. *'Where does that warmth come from? He seems so much more cheerful than when I encountered him in Limbo.'*

"In here is fine, assuming this container is large enough," Nalithor offered, holding up a crystalline cylinder the size of his forearm. "You seem reluctant."

"Sentimental reasons…" I pouted, feeling my face flush. His poorly hidden chuckle didn't help. "That will suffice."

'There's only two things I can think of that have sufficient power…' I considered, gnawing my lower lip with unease. *'The weapon decoration Corentine gave me certainly has enough of Sihix's power—but it also has mine. And she did demand that I keep it in my shrizar until I find out what the damned thing is for. Well, "for" besides weapons, I guess.'*

Pursing my lips, I opened a different shrizar—the one I kept all my belongings from Sihix in. Nalithor glanced at it with a curious expression on his face, making me wonder if perhaps he sensed the power of the items stowed there. After another moment of consideration, I pulled a box from the shrizar and then lifted the lid to reveal a decorative-looking dagger with a platinum hilt and sheath. The blade itself was obsidian-like as it had been carved from one of Sihix's branches.

"What—?" Nalithor frowned but his tone belied his curiosity as he looked at the weapon. "That metal is like the weapons and armor Aurelian and Elise make, but I sense something else from it."

"The Guardian foxes are capable of working with the same type of metal," I offered, hesitant, as I placed the box down and then lifted the sheathed dagger. I pulled the blade a few inches from the sheath, revealing the obsidian and its violet glow. "Shir, Gari, and many of the inhabitants have gifted me with things they've made. This, in particular, is a blade made from one of the trees in the forest. I don't think I need to explain why I'm reluctant to part with such an item, even if temporarily, do I?"

"There's nothing with less value that you can show me?" Nalithor questioned, looking down at me with a faint expression of concern.

"This is the only item I believe is sufficient." I shook my head. "Since Sihix is weakened, the traces of aether in their other gifts is negligible."

"They must truly appreciate the help you've given them, if they've seen fit to shower you with gifts," Nalithor remarked as I sheathed the blade and offered it to him. "I will be careful with this and will return it to you as soon as I've finished compiling my findings. That aside...what are your plans now that Darius has a partner?"

"Plans?" I inquired, feeling my lips part in as I blinked in confusion. After a moment I remembered he couldn't see my full expression, so I added, "I'm not exactly one to plan *anything*. What do I need plans for, exactly?"

"Partners are almost always assigned to live together," Nalithor replied as he drew the dagger and studied it. "The house you're currently living in was meant to be temporary lodgings for the both of you, used until you were both assigned partners.

"Under normal circumstances you would have been assigned partners at the same time and then moved to separate lodgings based on your results—the academy dormitories for your brother, and your partner's home for you. However, now you will most likely have to deal with both Darius and his partner in the same house as you until a more permanent solution is decided on. For now, it was decided that Darius isn't suited for the dormitories."

"As long as they stay out of my way it should be fine." I grimaced, tracking Nalithor as he placed the dagger and sheath inside of the cylinder and then placed it beside the other samples. "Why do partners typically live together?"

"In the case of students, it's important for them to have partners available for studies and for practice," Nalithor replied as he returned to my side and then offered me his arm. "For individuals such as you and me, it's to help promote comradery, friendship, and understanding. It's important for both partners to know how the other ticks when it comes to fighting together on the battlefield, conducting stealth missions, and so on. We all have our unique quirks that others aren't likely to learn of without spending a great deal of time together.

"That said... I've already eaten up a great deal of your time.

Can I convince you to speak with me some more over dinner, before I see you home?"

"Sure. I don't think you need to convince me this time though," I answered after a moment of thought, glancing up in time to catch Nalithor's triumphant smirk. "What's the look for, hmmm? It can't be *that* difficult to find company for dinner."

"Finding *enjoyable* company is an entirely different matter, my dear." Nalithor chuckled, leading me through the winding corridors of the palace. "You'll find that I share your sentiments on most of the people in Dauthrmir being 'weak' and 'boring.' As a *proper* Archmagus, and professor at the academy, it isn't appropriate for me to state as much.

"Seeing how insistent you've been about me 'proving' my worthiness to you, I consider it a small victory that you've agreed to join me for dinner."

Later that night I found myself staring at the ceiling in irritation. My headphones were clamped tight over my ears and blasting music, but it did little to help matters. Djialkan and I were *both* in piss-poor moods now, despite the fact my time with Nalithor had been quite enjoyable. I now wished that I'd insisted on a late-night sparring match instead of allowing the Adinvyr to see me home immediately after dinner.

Somehow, Alala seemed capable of sleeping through the noises coming from downstairs.

Speaking with someone intelligent had been quite the welcome change of pace, and Nalithor had introduced me to a rather delicious array of Draemiran food and drinks. Although he was a deity, it certainly didn't interfere with the pride he held for his homeland. His love of Draemir was strangely endearing.

If I'd known beforehand that I'd have to listen to my brother and his new partner fucking all night, I would have ordered a *lot* more drinks.

"Ahhh! Vivus, c-careful with your fangs!"

I scowled and attempted to turn my headphones up further, then let out a curse upon discovering they were already at their maximum. Finally, I decided I'd had enough. I swung my legs over the edge of the bed and then stalked to my vanity to grab a hair stick. After pinning my hair up in a loose bun, I yanked on my mask, tugged an overrobe over my satin nightie, and then made my way to the balcony.

Djialkan promptly perched on my shoulder as I swung the doors open. I leapt from the second floor and landed in a crouch on the grassy turf below. My brother and this "Vivus" person were *damn loud*. It was obvious I wouldn't get any sleep soon.

I grumbled curses under my breath as I stalked off toward the edge of the district and through a break in the wall. Once through, I plopped down on the grass with my back against the granite wall and then pulled one of Nalithor's tomes from my shrizar. With a sigh, I resigned myself to staying awake for a few more hours and reading in seclusion.

I wasn't sure how much time passed before I caught Nalithor's spicy scent nearby. My lips tugged down in a small frown as I pulled my headphones off and scented the air again. His scent was growing closer. It had to have been well past two in the morning, so what was Nalithor doing outside the palace at this time of night?

"I was wondering why I caught your scent leading *away* from your house instead of *to* it," Nalithor commented as he stepped out of the shadows to my left. I glanced up at him and then decided it was too much strain on my neck, so I returned my gaze to my book. "Darius didn't kick you out, did he?"

"That boy and his partner are noisy!" Djialkan hissed, indignant, before I could even say anything. *"Were they not such scrawny, sinewy creatures I would devour them myself! I don't understand how Fraelfnir contends with such a raunchy ward!"*

"Pretty much what Djialkan said." I laughed and then lifted my headphones. "Even with *these* turned all the way up I can still hear those two going at it quite clearly."

"Darius bedded his partner *already*?" Nalithor inquired as he perched on a nearby boulder. I glanced toward him curiously, realizing that he was wearing his armor and had a spear strapped to his back.

"I did mention that he wants into the pants of *everything* he finds 'hot,' didn't I?" I asked, causing Nalithor to grimace and nod. "Being picky isn't his forte, even though it *should be.*

"Isn't it a little late at night for you to be wandering around in your armor?"

"Isn't it a little chilly out here for you to be exposing that much leg?" Nalithor countered, pointing down at my left leg. I felt my face burn scarlet when I looked down and found that my skin was exposed all the way up to my waist on one side. "To answer you, however, I was coming to give you back your dagger. I will have to study it later.

"Chaos Beasts have been spotted abnormally close to the Dauthrmiran Barrier and I'm being sent to investigate. I'll be gone for a few days, so I figured it would be best for me to return your dagger to you. Try not to get yourself into *too* much trouble, alright?"

"Aw.... I want to go kill Chaos Beasts..." I grumbled, pouting as I crossed my arms. Nalithor just grinned at me. "Who exactly am I going to spar now, hmmm?"

"Now, now, I'm sure you will get to flight plenty of beasts soon enough." Nalithor chuckled as he examined me. "As for sparring, you're more than welcome to kick my men's ass, or Eyrian's ass. Especially Eyrian's ass, actually."

"You and Eyrian must be good friends." I observed, amused as Nalithor laughed and nodded his head. "I doubt there's much trouble I can get into, sadly."

"I disagree with you there. I can think of *plenty* of ways you can find trouble," Nalithor countered with a sly grin as he handed me my dagger. "If the looks you were getting all night were any indication, there's quite a few individuals that would like to get into trouble *with you* at the very least."

"Really? I didn't notice," I commented dismissively as I accepted the dagger and dismissed it into my shrizar. "They must not have been strong enough to register."

"Ouch." Nalithor laughed, shaking his head as he rose to his feet. "Don't worry, *Your Highness*, I'll give the beasts a good thrashing on your behalf."

Nalithor smiled at me again and then strode away, waving his hand briefly.

"I suppose it's too late to see about making your blade sing?" I called after him, watching as his tail twitched and snapped to the side. He halted in response.

"Is that…a challenge, Arianna?" Nalithor's head turned, but not enough for me to see his face.

"Of course. I'm rather confident in my ability to force you to draw a weapon," I answered, tracking the swishing of his tail. "I won't be satisfied until I can defeat you consistently. Even then, I won't grow bored of you unless you stop being a challenge."

Djialkan sighed at me. *'Arianna, you should watch your words with an Adinvyr.'*

"Tempting as you are…" Nalithor murmured, trailing off for a moment before pivoting to smirk at me. "It will have to wait."

"Duty first." I nodded my understanding, earning a smile from him before he disappeared into the shadows.

Djialkan gave my cheek a firm nudge as I sighed. A glance at the fae-dragon made it obvious that my companion knew I was considering following Nalithor and taking a piece out of the Chaos Beasts for myself. In some strange way, fighting Nalithor almost seemed more appealing that fighting the beasts. I found myself unsure whether it was because Nalithor was more of a challenge, or if perhaps I was growing too comfortable with the Adinvyr's company.

'It is late, you are tired, and are saying foolish things. We should return,' Djialkan stated with another firm nudge. *'You can pout about the lack of a hunt later. While you're at it, you should consider if you truly intend to distance yourself from the Adinvyr. Your words say otherwise.'*

"If Darius and his partner haven't finished yet, Chaos Beasts aren't the only thing I'll be hunting." I snorted, snapping the tome in my lap shut. "Tomorrow morning he's receiving a lesson in sibling etiquette."

'And you will be studying!'

CHAPTER FIFTEEN
Not So Fragile

I flipped through the pages of what must have been my fiftieth book on non-Human anatomy. Although the sofa in our shared study was quite comfortable, we had been there long enough that I'd grown stiff and creaky. Meanwhile, Darius was walking around the room aimlessly while reading a book on restorative magics.

Darius had given up on understanding my choice of tomes *days* ago. Instead, he opted to leave me alone—aside from the occasional question regarding basic magic principles. He seemed like he was taking his studies seriously finally—or was at least trying to. He was proving easier to distract than I thought he'd be.

As for me, I had other things on my mind.

Learning the differences between the varying species of Avrirsa seemed prudent if I was to fight alongside, and potentially against, non-Human beings. The past four days alone had been devoted to studying the Devillians that lived in the territories of the Vorpmasian Empire. I figured that my partner would likely be Devillian, regardless of whether I was assigned classes or to more battle-oriented tasks. While my brother's partner was Beshulthien, it seemed to me that statistics would favor the possibility of a Devillian partner. Most of the people *in* Dauthrmir were of Devillian descent, and that went doubly so for the men and women working in both the academy and military endeavors.

Several times throughout my studies, Darius had snatched my books from me out of sheer curiosity. There were some things about Devillian anatomy that I simply couldn't wrap my head around. The outward appearance of some of the Devillian races may have been similar to Humans, but that was where the resemblances ended. It was quite clear to me now that Devillians were another species entirely.

Even with the detailed illustrations the tomes provided me, I couldn't quite grasp the differences between them and Humans. There were just so many differences between each of the Devillian races—Imviir being more like serpents, for example. Yet, the texts went above and beyond to provide the more…*intimate* details as well. Those differences made me question if they were part of the reasons that Devillians didn't pair with Humans or Elves often. While there were some mixed couples in the city, it seemed as though each species kept to itself for the most part.

'Honestly, Adinvyr look the closest to Humans at a glance, but...' I grimaced and hurried to flip past a few sketches of *massive* genitalia. *'Gods! Their ability to shapeshift almost makes it worse!'*

Devillian genitalia was something I did *not* want to dwell on. I already had to deal with so many unrelenting Dauthrmirans nudging my barriers or sending pornographic thoughts my way. While I didn't understand their apparent obsession with having their blood drunk by me, their other desires were at least understandable—even if I wasn't interested.

What I *didn't* understand, was their interest in *me*. Granted, I didn't understand Nalithor's apparent interest or curiosity either. I was quite certain that my brother should have been earning more interest than me. After all, he always did. I was so accustomed to being a shadow that I didn't know what to do.

'Ugh, he's been gone forever.' I pouted, reaching for the next tome in the series. *'It's been what, four days? Five? It can't take that long to kill the beasts. If he doesn't come back soon...he'll wish he'd stayed with the beasts.'*

One good thing had come of the past few days, at least. Darius had ceased bringing his partner, Vivus, by the house. It seemed as though I'd made my point clear enough when I ripped into my brother for the racket they had made. Darius was so embarrassed that he promised to "meet" his "new friend" elsewhere.

I hoped that the academy would separate us soon. It was far

too awkward when the Vampire came over to study with Darius. The creep was too handsy with my brother, and that alone made me want to rip his head off.

The Vampire's full name was "Vivus Zhool", and he was the other not-Elf that I'd seen accompanying Nalithor, Eyrian, and Xander on many occasions. The cherry-haired, lavender-eyed Vampire was a Wood Elf prior to being turned by Xander. Unlike his "maker" however, Vivus' loyalties were with the Beshulthien Empire.

Beyond that, I hadn't paid much attention. After our formal introduction, the topic of conversation had shifted to the strenuous relations between the Vorpmasian and Beshulthien Empires. In a word: politics.

They'd lost my interest after about two sentences.

"Not going to spar anyone today, Ari?" Darius questioned without looking up from his book.

"Most of Nalithor's men are pushovers. I'm bored of them already," I replied after brief consideration. "From what I understand, most of them are busy with formal duties today anyway and won't have time for training. So, I'd have to hunt down new sparring partners entirely. That's time I could dedicate to my studies instead."

"What have you learned, then?" Darius asked curiously, motioning at the pile of books near me. "Aside from the...uhm... Their rather impressive tail and dick—"

"The Devillians with a similar appearance to Humans have pressure points in areas similar to Humans, with more strewn through their tails and around or *in* their horns," I cut Darius off and snapped my book shut, making him jump. "Draekin, Sizoul, Sundreht, and Rylthra are the most like Humans. Imviir, Akor, N'tarsorn, Jrachra, and Etuln are the least Humanlike. Adinvyr…vary.

"The internal organs and musculature are similar, but not identical, between the races of Devillians. For example, the Imviir are the least like Humans—they are more like serpents inside and out.

"Taking other species into account, Elves are the closest to Humans and the sea species are furthest from us. Vampires, however, vary based on what they were prior to becoming a Vampire. So, it's important that I familiarize myself with *all* the species and races in Avrirsa. Otherwise, I won't be able to fight with or against them efficiently. One thing I haven't found the answer to is why Devillians can't become Vampires—I'll have to look through more of these tomes for answers."

Darius stared at me with a blank expression on his face, blinking a few times as he attempted to process the onslaught of information. I knew it wasn't the kind of knowledge he was fishing for. He wanted more information about the sexual quirks of each species, no doubt. Overloading him seemed like a good way to make him drop the subject before he could get started.

The doorbell ringing from the front of the house startled Darius from his reverie and sent him darting out of the study to see who'd arrived. It seemed to me that he was hoping for a visit from Vivus today. They seemed to be growing too close, too fast. It made me uneasy, and I'd made sure to let Fraelfnir know it. I'd have the fae-dragon's hide along with both Darius' and Vivus' if Fraelfnir didn't keep my brother safe around that fanged creature.

Aside from Vivus, Darius was making many friends already. Over the past week I'd continued to help Darius train. Re-teaching him the basics of magic, how to control elements, how the elements interacted with each other, and how they could each be utilized. Our sessions, for some reason, garnered a lot of attention from the academy's other young mages. They seemed enamored with my brother's determination to improve himself. Conversely, they cowered whenever I made an appearance.

Word that I fought evenly with Vorpmasia's *precious* "Black Dragon" had spread like fire through the city.

I sighed and summoned a mask from my shrizar, pinned up my curls, and then flipped up my robe's hood. In the event that Vivus or one of Darius' other friends stood at the door, it was likely that Darius would drag whoever it was to the study without warning me first. Even though it was "our house" it was still unacceptable for me to show my face to guests.

'What a fucking pain,' I thought, tetchy, as I looked for a book I hadn't read yet. *'Honestly though…just how well does Darius know*

Vivus? As well as I know Nalithor, probably less? Either way, isn't it too soon for them to have a sexual relationship? Are partners even allowed to have sexual relationships?'

I frowned and settled back on the couch. It was actually an interesting thought. Adinvyr fed off sexual energy, right? So, what were the Empire's regulations for partners? I doubted "food" was easy to find when traveling. Did Adinvyr seduce other travelers? Did they feed from their partner? No matter how I looked at it, it seemed like a pain in the ass.

'Huh. I wonder what Nalithor does, then?' The thought came unbidden, making me grimace at the pang of unwanted jealousy. *'He doesn't have a partner, or at least he doesn't keep them for long. That must be quite a burden when it comes to his "needs."'*

I shook my head hard and pushed the Adinvyr from my mind. Nalithor's presence was driving me crazy and I didn't understand why. It wasn't *just* because I desired an interesting sparring partner, but I couldn't identify precisely what was troubling me either. Was it because I wanted to hunt beasts? Did I...miss him? *'No, that can't be right.'*

Several minutes passed before I heard Darius call me from down the hall. I frowned, set my book aside, then made my way to the front door. When I arrived, I spotted a pair of women from the boutique that Darius and I had visited together. Behind them stood a large group of students from the academy. Vivus stood among the students, and fidgeted upon spotting me, averting his gaze.

"Arianna-jiss, we have finished making some of your clothing," the first Sizoul woman spoke up when she spotted me, a bright smile stretching across her tanned face. "If you would show us to your room, we will happily unload your attire and make sure it is to your liking."

I nodded to the women and then turned, motioning for them to follow me upstairs. The first woman had pale blue crystalline horns and deeply tanned skin. The second woman's skin was lighter and closer to the color of caramel, and her horns were dark emerald.

Sizoul had shorter tails than Adinvyr, reaching only a few inches longer than their legs instead of the several feet that Adinvyr boasted. Sizoul tails and claws often bore the same color crystal as their horns. Occasionally, their horns and the scales of their tails held flecks or veins of other minerals.

It seemed as though every Sizoul I'd seen thus far held a job related to creating things—tailors, smiths, jewelers, and leatherworkers to name a few. I didn't want to stereotype, but I was beginning to see a pattern when it came to this specific race of Devillians.

Alala and Djialkan scampered off the bed and perched on a chair across the room when the Sizoul women entered behind me. I kept silent, watching as the two seamstresses summoned an impressive pile of boxes from their shrizars. A small frown formed on my face as I looked from box to box. I didn't recall ordering so much clothing. Especially if it was just a *portion* of it.

'Just how is Darius going to get away with buying things for a Lyur'zi?' I bit back a sigh, my attention flicking to the contents of the boxes when the seamstresses removed the lids. *'Ah. Isn't that...?'*

"Aurelian deigned it necessary to provide us with armor for several of your orders, Your Highness," the paler Sizoul spoke, tilting the box so that I could see it better. "He said something about the Oracles requesting his assistance."

"Is it normal for a deity to just 'drop by' like that?" I arched an eyebrow behind my mask as the two women giggled.

"The gods do and go as they please," the blue-horned woman replied, waving her hand dismissively. "Here, how about this one for today, Arianna-jiss?"

She smiled and opened another box, revealing Umbral Mage robes of Draemiran style. At least, it seemed inspired by Draemiran kimonos, to me. Admittedly, I wasn't sure if it was strictly of Draemir origin or not. The shirt itself was constructed in similar fashion to a kimono but only came down to my hips. Instead of an obi or some other form of sash, a leather underbust corset with plates of platinum armor wrapped around my waist.

Black breeches and thigh high leather boots completed the ensemble. Scale-like plates of armor ran up the shin of my boots to the knee, with larger plates encasing my foot and heel. The plates of armor came to sharp points along the center of my foot and up my shin, creating a wicked ridge.

'*Well, that will be good for kicking something. Or someone.*' I examined the boots and the sharpened metal with an amused smile. '*Seems like Aurelian is insistent on engraving my armor with the elements and foxes, though. Or is that Elise's choice? I do wonder if they're able to communicate with Corentine in some way...*'

The other woman pulled a long coat out of the box she'd originally opened and shook the garment out, letting the folds of leather drape down freely. More platinum-colored armor plated the shoulders, top quarter of the back, and the outer arms of the sleeves. What pulled my attention most was the crest on the back. Embroidery encircled the crest itself and was bordered by the gleaming armor. I'd been concerned that my black lotus would disappear against the black leather, but any such concerns were now gone. The iridescence of the lotus, the embroidery, and the bright armor made it stand out.

I offered brief thanks to the strangely cheerful women and then closed the door behind them once they'd excused themselves. Once my new attire was on, I paused to admire the fit and then tugged on my boots. My armored corset followed, and I adjusted everything again. I'd learned a long time ago that putting on boots after a corset was near impossible.

The coat was quickly becoming one of my favorite possessions and I hadn't even put it on yet. The carved leather paired with armor was exquisite. Stylized darkness, fire, wind, and ice played alongside foxes with varying numbers of tails—all of which danced among stars and crescent moons.

'Was it really necessary to brush the carvings with platinum paint?' I shrugged the coat on and then raised my arms above my head, checking my range of movement. *'I don't mind... but how much did Darius pay for this?*

'...Actually, I'm not sure if I want to know. Scratch that.'

The coat's collar came to just below my jawline and then rounded down in front of my throat where the hems came together at the center. Platinum filigree clasps dotted the garment from my throat and a little past my waist so that I could close it tight, but I decided to leave the coat open for now.

Before I worried about clasps, there was a more pressing matter for me to deal with.

'Darius, this coat has no hood. Neither do any of the new shirts,' I muttered, checking myself out again in the mirror. *'You know the princess-y laws better than I do. What should I do?'*

'If you keep your hair pinned up you should be fine, as long as I give you explicit permission to do so,' Darius remarked thoughtfully after a few seconds of silence. *'You have my permission, of course! So, pull your hair up in a bun or something and you'll be okay. Leaving a few curls down should be fine—and cute!'*

'...since when has he cared if I look "cute?"' I shook my head, sitting down at the vanity to do my hair. *'He's being oddly reasonable. Buying me clothes? Agreeing to let me go without a hood?*

'I'm not sure whether to be grateful or cautious.'

Once I finished pinning my hair up with a multitude of underused platinum hair sticks and clasps that matched my usual jewelry, I painted my lips a deep glossy scarlet and then pulled on a new mask. The mask I'd summoned previously wasn't quite elaborate enough to go with my new attire. A final glimpse in the mirror confirmed that I had a copious amount of pale cleavage on display, but I didn't mind.

I shrugged to myself and returned to the main floor of the house, watching a broad grin stretch across Darius' face when he spotted me. His friends, however, openly ogled me with dumbfounded expressions.

'Can you explain to me why they're gawking that much? I still have my mask on!' I nudged Darius as I passed him and strode out into the sweet-smelling morning air.

'You look kind of deadly and imposing,' Darius offered, motioning at my coat when I glanced over my shoulder at him. *'The clothes underneath fit you really well of course and show your uh…*figure. *That coat screams you're a total badass though. I'd imagine they're surprised by your full jewelry too. You* have *been hiding most of it under X'shmiran clothing after all.'*

'I suppose you're right about that,' I replied, amused by Darius' answer. *'What does your little posse there want with you today, hmmm?'*

'Oh… Apparently there's some important thing that I need to go

to at the academy. It's for new students but I forget what they called it,' Darius grumbled. *'They said I'd get in trouble if I skipped it. So, they came to get me.'*

'You'd better get going then,' I stated dryly, making my way toward the closest military training grounds. *'I'll be over there somewhere looking for a sparring partner. Holler if you need me.'*

I wove my way through the maze of military buildings and moonslight-dappled training areas, nodding acknowledgment to the few soldiers that recognized me. My only assumption was that they identified me by the scent Nalithor claimed I had. On some level I wanted to ask Nalithor just how strong my scent was. Him finding it "distracting" struck me as strange. Furthermore, if he could identify it in such a way, why hadn't he realized my identity?

'Then again, it's not like I'm willing to tell him outright either,' I considered, approaching a series of sparring pits near the Sapphire Quarter's exterior wall. *'Oh? Eyrian is sparring some of Nalithor's men? Did he get bored of the Imperial Guard?'*

Curious, I leaned against a magelamp near their sparring pit and watched the fight that was taking place. Even though Nalithor's men outnumbered the wildly grinning Draekin, it was clear that Eyrian was winning with ease. His movements held bestial grace, and his viciousness often startled his attackers into poorly-timed evasive maneuvers. Both the grace and strength behind his techniques meant that his follow-through was not only accurate, but solid. Human bones would've shattered under the onslaught.

'So, the bone strength of Devillians is much higher as well? Or is the construction entirely different from a Human's?' I wondered, watching as Maric went flying through the air and landed hard fifteen feet away from the Draekin. *'Hmmm, after that kick... I'll assume a different composition. That would've probably broken the bones of a Dux.'*

It took several more minutes before any of them noticed my presence. Once they did, they turned to me with startled expressions on their faces. I arched an eyebrow as several turned slightly red in the face—even Eyrian. He seemed the most surprised out of all of them and was certainly the reddest.

"Don't stop on my account." I grinned at them.

"Arianna? Your hair, your robes?" Eyrian blinked at me, his face flushing darker. His thick tail twitched behind him as he tried to think of something to say. "I-I hope you're not breaking any rules by—"

"Not breaking any." I pivoted to show them the crest on my back. "I guess I can't avoid showing this off anymore. This coat is *so* much nicer than my crestless ones after all.

"It seems there are still some people that didn't get the memo about my crest though. Several soldiers I passed on my way here expressed concern that their *favorite* Adinvyr might be offended by the similarities."

"Nalithor isn't the sort that's easy to offend." Eyrian laugh, looking a little more relaxed now when I turned to face him again. "His nickname for you is appropriate after all."

"Nickname?" I questioned with a heavy sigh, dreading Eyrian's answer. "What do you mean by 'nickname'?"

"*Vixen,*" Eyrian replied with a throaty laugh. "Since you're here, how about sparring with me? I heard you've been giving Nalithor's men a good walloping the past week."

"She hits harder than *you* do!" One of the soldiers sighed, exasperated.

"Sure, I'll spar with you." I tugged my coat off and then hung it over a nearby bench. "Unarmed? You seem like a man who likes to use his fists."

"Aye, unarmed." Eyrian nodded, tracking my movements. "You really *are* a tiny little thing under all those layers of robes you've been wearing."

"Didn't stop her from fighting toe-to-toe with General Vraelimir though..." One of the soldiers muttered. "You better watch your scaly ass, General Il'thar."

'Hmmm, Eyrian is a demigod, isn't he?' I hopped down into the sparring pit and shifted into an offensive stance. *'Maybe I'll use him as a measuring stick to determine where Nalithor, Darius, and I fall on the scale of power.'*

Eyrian wasn't quite as tall as Nalithor, perhaps a few inches shorter, so I knew it'd be easier to kick him in the jaw or the side of his head if I wanted to. A quick glance over his expression and body language made it clear that he was uneasy about sparring someone as "dainty" as I was.

Since he seemed so hesitant, I decided to make the first move. Eyrian didn't seem to expect it at all, and almost didn't bring his arms up in time to block my kick. The plated toe of my boot grazed his cheek but didn't draw blood. *'Pity.'*

Eyrian allowed me to reclaim my foot all too easily, so I sprung into a new series of attacks. Eyrian's expression was more serious now at least, giving me hope that perhaps he'd shifted to the proper mindset.

A punch to his liver, a roundhouse kick across the collarbone, a side-kick to his core—he blocked or otherwise deflected all of them with ease, but his counterattacks barely even registered on my radar. Was he even taking me seriously? The short answer seemed to be no, he wasn't. Eyrian's reaction times were sluggish, as if he wanted to make it easier on me. His strikes were barely noticeable. Even the weakest of Nalithor's soldiers hit me harder than Eyrian was.

The Draekin chose the wrong woman to go easy on. My anger sent a rush of adrenaline into my system, making me shake with both fury and frustration.

"Just how hard am I going to have to hit you before you take this seriously?!" I ducked lazily under one of his punches and then snapped out with a full-force kick.

"If I hit you *seriously*, you would—" Eyrian let out a startled yelp as my kick caught him across the shoulders, knocking him clean off his feet. The plate armor on the front of my boots tore his skin open, staining my shin and the ground with black blood.

"If you aren't going to spar me properly this is a waste of time!" I snapped, planting my foot on Eyrian's chest when he tried to get up. The soldiers nearby snickered and muttered something to each other, but I didn't catch what they said. "Neither of us will learn *anything* if you go easy on me. I suggest you relocate your balls and— Eek!"

I yelped, startled, as a pair of muscular arms wrapped around me from behind and lifted me clear off both Eyrian's chest and the ground. The strong scent of sweet spices slammed into my senses so abruptly that it left me stunned for a moment. When I regained myself, I shot an obscured glare upwards at Nalithor. Grinning, the Adinvyr shifted me in his arms so that one was beneath my knees and the other was bracing my back.

'Why didn't I notice him sooner? Did he learn a new trick?' I wondered, begrudging, as I attempted to worm my way out of Nalithor's grip.

"You don't mind if I borrow Arianna for a bit do you, Eyrian?" Nalithor inquired, chuckling as I crossed my arms with an indignant huff. My racing heartbeat and inability to squirm out of his grip only served to make me tetchier about the situation.

"Actually, I *do* mind." Eyrian growled, pulling himself to his feet. He crossed his arms over his bloodied torso and settled a glare on Nalithor. "We were sparring, and you're interrupting."

"By sparring, I assume you were serving as the princess's training dummy?" Nalithor spoke with false innocence as he examined the Draekin. "Don't you think you're insulting her skills as a warrior by going so easy on her? I'm quite certain she was about to skin you."

"But... She's so *dainty*!" Eyrian protested, motioning at me. "Have you *looked* at how tiny she looks in your arms? When compared to any of us? She's—"

"Hey! I may be small, but I doubt you can hit me as hard as the beasts have!" I retorted, my face flushing in anger. "Nalithor, put me down so I can kick his ass!"

"Can I borrow you *after* you kick his ass then?" Nalithor's strange tone prompted me to look up at him. "Lucifer wants to speak with all three of us, and I need your assistance at the academy afterward."

"You could have just *said* 'Lucifer is waiting for us,'" Eyrian pointed out as Nalithor set me down. "Our match will have to wait, Arianna."

"Good. That gives you time to grow a pair so you can hit me properly!" I snapped, stalking out of the pit to fetch my coat and yank it on. Nalithor and his men chuckled in response, but I didn't get what was so funny. I was half a mind to state as such.

"Oh, so you did get new attire," Nalithor remarked, his hand tracing down my spine. "What do you think, Eyrian? *I* think we may have to start calling her *'The White Fox'* as my men do."

"Aren't you supposed to be scouting the Chaos Beast problem in Abrantia?" Eyrian muttered, but Nalithor ignored him and examined me with a strange expression instead.

"What is it?" I looked up at Nalithor, my curiosity getting the better of me. *'Why is he looking at me like that? What's so damn fascinating?'*

"You found a loophole that permits you to show your hair?" Nalithor asked, flicking the end of one of my hair sticks. He shot the ornament a rather displeased look before gazing down at me again.

"Darius can give me 'permission' to show my hair apparently, as long as I keep it up." I huffed, crossing my arms again. "Why he didn't state as much after your confrontation, I have no idea.

"What's this about Lucifer wanting to see the three of us?"

"Hmmm, if you had horns and a tail you would look like a proper Vorpmasian general in that coat." Nalithor commented, his tone sly. After a moment, he turned and beckoned for us to follow him. "Always straight to business with you isn't it, Arianna?

"You'll just have to wait and see."

'Wait and see? What's with the sing-song tone?' I stared at Nalithor's back, watching the playful dancing of his obsidian-scaled tail. *'Ugh. Does he* have *to smell like* food *all the time?'*

I stuck my tongue out at Nalithor's back and then moved to follow him.

"How is your brother doing, Arianna?" Eyrian adopted a conversational tone and fell into step with me. "They're having orientation and then some classes today at the academy, right?"

"He's already trying to skip things!" I tossed my hands into the air as Nalithor slowed his pace to walk with us, a questioning expression settling onto his face. "A group of his friends and his redheaded fuck buddy—*excuse me*, 'partner'—came to the house and dragged him off right before I came to the training grounds.

"I've had to refocus his attention *constantly* the past few days because he keeps gravitating toward advanced books instead of the ones in his range."

"Even after his horrendous test results he thinks he can just skip the basics?" Nalithor inquired. He frowned with concern and propped one arm in the other, rubbing his chin in thought. "Perhaps I should borrow you for one of his classes today, and not just the physical ones I was going to ask you to assist me with."

"Isn't she a little feisty to be helping with classes?" Eyrian asked dryly, earning him an irritated look from me.

"Her feistiness is a welcome change from most of the women here!" Nalithor laughed, then shot Eyrian a sly look over the top of my head. "You never struck me as the sort to prefer passive women, Eyrian. Is Arianna too much for you?"

"Passive...?" Eyrian stared at Nalithor, flabbergasted, as color rose to his face. "Hardly! But aren't you concerned that—"

"I'll behave myself," I interjected, earning a strange look from both of them. "It's not like I'm going to *eat* any of the students, you know. That's more Djialkan's area of expertise."

'Or Darius', depending on the type of eating, I guess.' I added to myself.

They laughed before falling silent as we approached the palace gates. As we made our way across the palace grounds, I realized that my crest still came as a shock to many of the soldiers and palace staff. I was quite certain that I'd worn emblazoned robes to the palace several times since coming to Dauthrmir, so I didn't understand why so many of them seemed startled.

Seeing me without a hood seemed to be just as surprising to many of them. They were making me feel a little self-conscious.

'You look uncomfortable,' Nalithor commented, shooting me a concerned glance as he led us down an unfamiliar hallway. *'Did Eyrian and I make you—?'*

'I don't understand why everyone is staring at me so much,' I grumbled, hugging myself. *'I can understand why the crest comes as a surprise, I guess. I have been avoiding my emblazoned robes for the most part. However, they almost seem more fascinated by my hair— and it isn't even down!'*

'Well, your attire is a rather stark contrast to your X'shmiran robes,' Nalithor pointed out as he stopped before a pair of double doors and knocked a few times. *'One would think they'd be staring at your ample cleavage or numerous pieces of jewelry...*

'Aurelian really equipped you fully, didn't he?'

"Come in, Nalithor, Eyrian, Arianna," Lucifer called from somewhere beyond the door. The two large Devillians both motioned for me to go first after opening the doors, so I obliged. "Have a seat. We'll try to keep this brief."

I nodded, watching as Lucifer motioned to an empty seat on his right. The expectant look was the only hint I needed. I swept around the large elliptical table and examined the three individuals seated on the opposite side. Xander I recognized easily by his lustful gaze and minty scent. The other two people, however, were unfamiliar to me. One was a nervous female Wood Elf, whom Eyrian took a seat beside. The other was a male Akor.

Akor were quite fascinating to me. They were a fiery race of Devillians, their diet consisting of primarily magma. Their skin ranged wildly from snow white to pitch black, with all the shades between being ashy greys and browns. Their claws, horns, and tails often resembled polished obsidian or other volcanic rock.

In rare cases, such as one of their patron deities, their horns and tails were diamond.

The molten cracks in their skin, horns, and tails often caught fire when the Akor was under emotional or physical stress. In some twisted way I wanted to know how many things they set fire to during puberty. I could only imagine how chaotic that could be, considering Devillians aged so slowly.

'Maybe it's a good thing I grew up as a Human!' I snickered internally.

Judging from the looks the pairs exchanged between each other, the large crest on my coat must have caught the attention of both the Elf and the Ifrit. Telepathic reverberations in the air indicated that they must have been discussing something, and the glances toward me gave me the impression that I was the topic.

Nalithor took the seat to my right and leaned on the left armrest, his expression one of curiosity as he examined me and the loose curls that hung around my face and neck. I decided to pretend I hadn't noticed and shifted my attention to the Vorpmasian Emperor instead. Listening to Lucifer, at least, would be easier than trying to figure out the captivated Adinvyr.

"Arianna, you're aware that General Vraelimir was sent to investigate reports of Chaos Beasts near the Dauthrmiran Barrier, correct?" Lucifer asked, so I nodded my confirmation. "The sighted group consists of several X'shmiran Dux-class Chaos Beasts, and most of my generals are days away from Dauthrmir on other missions.

"Both Generals Vraelimir and Il'thar have stated that you're more than capable of handling yourself against the beasts, and the Oracles have echoed their praise. Would you be willing to lend us your skill in hunting these beasts?"

"Oh? A chance to thrash some beasts?" I grinned, delighted, and punched one hand into the other. "How could I deny such a request? I'd be *happy* to tear the fucking filth apart."

"She looks even easier to break than I do!" The Elf protested.

She pointed at me, a condescending sneer on her face. "How can you expect someone *like her* to work with any of us? *Especially* with *Prince* Vraelimir? She'll just get in the way."

"I can always shred you first, if you prefer." I purred in response, my mouth curving into a wicked grin. The startled Elf's face drained of color when I channeled my bloodlust at her. "Then you won't have to worry about anything ever again, right?"

Nalithor paused, growing still, when I directed my bloodlust toward the woman. His expression was unreadable, but he had stopped mid-reach for one of my curls. I thought that I'd properly shielded my bloodlust so that only the Elf would sense it. *'Does our telepathic connection let him sense it regardless? It shouldn't… Did I fail to shield my bloodlust? I thought I'd grown quite good at it.'*

"You should save that energy for the beasts," Lucifer remarked dryly as my attention shifted back to him. "I'll take that as a 'yes.' You and Nalithor are the only ones here without a partner, so I expect the two of you to function as a pair for this mission. All six of you are to work together; track down and eliminate the group of beasts. See to your preparations. You depart tomorrow morning.

"Generals Vraelimir and Il'thar are in charge. You're dismissed."

Nalithor offered me a hand up from my seat, an amused expression on his face. He seemed unusually insistent that I walk beside him instead of following him or the group, so for the moment I relented and ignored the murmuring from the four people behind us. The Adinvyr seemed oblivious to our comrades despite the seriousness of our mission. He was much more interested in tugging at my curls and examining my attire.

'I'm not a doll you know.' I glanced to the side at Nalithor after several minutes of silence, watching a grin split his face.

'I'm bothering you?' Nalithor asked, amused as he flicked the tip of one of my pointed ears. *'The more I see, the more I want to see, and the more I'm inclined to believe you aren't Human.*

'At the very least, I can already tell you are much *more pleasing to the eye than your twin is.'*

"Nali, just how serious is the situation?" Eyrian inquired from behind us. I watched with faint interest as Nalithor cast a scowl over his shoulder at the Draekin. "Don't give me that look. Normally you would have dealt with the beasts yourself."

"I'll explain in the morning once we're on the airship," Nalithor replied, dismissive, and much to the displeasure of the female Elf. "All you need to know is that they're in the Abrantia Valley and moving north. The ship can only take us to the edge of the barrier, so we need to travel on foot after that.

"Arianna, you should make sure you inform your brother that you'll be gone for a few days. We should run into him at the academy."

'Darius, I may be gone for a few days as of tomorrow morning,' I began simply, then glanced to the side when Nalithor nudged my barriers. He looked displeased. *'I'm going to make sure that I bring*

enough supplies in my shrizar, just in case there's an emergency. Do you need me to pick up anything to restock the house with?'

'They partner you with someone already or something?' Darius inquired in return. *'I shouldn't need anything, no. Vivus and our friends are planning to try out different restaurants all week.'*

'Apparently the Vorpmasians are understaffed and there's a large group of beasts that need to die.' I looked to the side amusedly as Nalithor appeared to grow frustrated and began tugging at my curls again. *'Generals Vraelimir, Il'thar, Xander, and two people who have yet to introduce themselves have been assigned to take care of the problem. The emperor wants to keep things even and requested that I work with Nalithor temporarily since he has no partner.'*

'No fair!' Darius whined, then sighed. *'Fine, fine. Try not to kill any of them alright? I want to fuck at least one of them first.'*

'No promises. This Elf is pissing me off!' I retorted before shoving my brother out of my mind. Turning, I reached up and snatched Nalithor's wrist when he reached for a curl by my cheek. "Am I going to have to string you up to get you to stop that?"

Eyrian, Xander, and the Akor burst into laughter but the Elf was anything but amused. She released an indignant shriek and spluttered something in a language I didn't understand. I glanced to the side at her, my lips parting as I thought. She seemed rather taken with Nalithor, considering how flushed and angry she was growing. Nalithor, however, hardly even acknowledged her presence. He seemed more determined to ignore her than he did my brother.

"Unhand him!" The Elf demanded. "How *dare* you touch Nalithor-tec!"

'Is she just going to yap instead of challenge me?' I shot the haughty Elf a wary look. "Don't you think you're being overly presumptuous, Elf?"

"Forgive her, Arianna." Eyrian grimaced and grasped the back of the Elf's tunic. "Illyana only recently returned to Dauthrmir. She hasn't yet heard of your combat prowess."

"Surely you jest! This *Human* couldn't possibly impress Nalithor-tec with skills in combat!" Illyana snorted, making a graceful yet dismissive gesture with one hand. "What sort of farm did this one grow up on? The creatures must have been impressive it trained her to accept an Adinvyr's girth."

'I don't know whether to laugh or feel insulted. Mmm... Maybe I will kill her later.' I shifted slightly to look up at the now-irritated Adinvyr in question. "-tec?"

"It's an honorific to indicate endearment or affection for *boys,*" Nalithor offered, shaking his head. He grasped my hand and brought it to his lips, shooting a glare at Illyana. "You forget yourself, Illyana. Arianna-z'tar is royalty, as am I. *You,* on the other hand, are Eyrian's partner.

"It would serve you well to focus on him, lest your lack of knowledge and training bite you in your Elven ass."

'-z'tar?' I asked as he smiled and allowed me to reclaim my

hand, looking satisfied by Illyana's amplified fury.

'*The female equivalent of -y'ric, and short form of Reiz'tar,*' Nalithor responded, leading me toward the academy's grounds and away from our would-be comrades. '*Effectively -jiss and -zir are the equivalents of "princess" and "prince," while -y'ric and -z'tar are somewhere above that.*

'*They are terms meant to show an even higher form of respect than -jiss and -zir, but it isn't uncommon for Draemiran men and women to refer to people they wish to pursue as -y'ric or -z'tar. Unlike the titles and honorifics in the common tongue, ours are interchangeable based on the level of familiarity or respect between individuals.*'

'*I assume by your distaste with the Elf that outbursts such as that aren't uncommon,*' I mused as Nalithor held a door open for me. His frosty eyes studied me intently as I passed him. '*I like that though. The idea of honorifics based on familiarity and respect instead of being expected or given That said, I know primarily of their formal usage.*'

'*The joys of being an Adinvyr,*' Nalithor stated bitterly, before glancing down and tugging gently on one of my dangling earrings. '*Unfortunately, Adinvyr draw men and women to us regardless of whether or not we actually desire to. You could call it our "natural charm" I suppose. Therefore, your resistance is quite intriguing.*

'*But yes, it is a terribly common occurrence and a major factor in why I do not keep partners overlong. They simply can't focus when I utilize my full power in battle.*'

'*And lack of focus is deadly,*' I nodded, then batted at his hand again. '*If you keep looking at me like that, I'm going to grow worried you want to put me under a microscope.*'

'*I assure you that what I have in mind is much more pleasant,*' Nalithor replied a little too seriously. After a moment he frowned, his gaze sliding to the ornaments keeping my hair up. '*It's a shame you have to keep your hair up. Your hair must be quite long...*'

'Maybe, *if you behave yourself,* I'll accidentally *misplace some of them.*' I rolled my eyes and crossed my arms, noting the grin that replaced Nalithor's frown. '*That said, shouldn't you be telling me what class you're pulling me off to help with? Or explaining why such a small group of us will be handling the beasts?*'

Nalithor just chuckled in response and led me to a door at the end of the hall on the eighth floor. When he opened it, he revealed a room of around fifty students. Darius looked delighted at first when he spotted Nalithor, but a scowl soon overtook it when he spotted me following the Adinvyr into the classroom.

"I apologize for the delay," Nalithor began, taking on a formal tone as he approached his desk. He beckoned me to join him and then looked at his students. "Arianna-jiss and I had a meeting with His Excellency to attend to. I'm sure I don't have to explain why that takes precedence."

"Arianna-jiss?" A male Elf with sandy-color hair perked up, his eyes sliding down to my cleavage. "I wasn't aware we would have *two* teachers for this class."

"I've requested that Arianna sit in and observe," Nalithor replied, pulling up a chair beside his desk and then motioning for me to sit. His amused expression made me suspicious, but I obliged. "As I'm sure you are all painfully aware, you are in my class because you failed the control portion of your exams. Miserably. We are starting from the absolute basics."

'And having eye candy for a professor will help them focus on learning control how *exactly?'* I wondered, taking my time to admire Nalithor's back and ass. *'Well, at least he'll entertain me even if the students don't.'*

'Ari, didn't I claim dibs on Nalithor?' Darius demanded. I smirked slightly, decided not to shield his tantrum this time. *'Since I'm* interested him, *obviously that means he only likes men! You should give up now before—'*

'I'm sure your sibling rivalry can wait until after *classes are finished for the day, Darius.'* Nalithor chuckled, shooting my twin a chilling look that did *not* match the sound of his laughter. He then smacked my rear with his tail as he passed my perch. *'You forget that I have seen your test results, Darius. Even if I did happen to have an interest in men—which I don't—dominants are of no interest to me, let alone ones so much weaker than I.*

'Now, be a good boy and focus on class.'

I bit back my laughter as Darius' face grew a bright, angry red. Nalithor shot me a knowing smirk over his shoulder, his tail swishing a few times before he turned to face the class once more.

Crossing one leg over the other, I leaned back in my chair and examined the students as they *attempted* to follow Nalithor's instructions. The exercises were basic, but the students were already struggling. Most of them appeared to be Elves, with only a few Devillians peppered throughout the room.

Even with how much I'd helped my brother over the past few days, he was still one of the first to lose control over his element, no matter which one he attempted to work with. Somehow, the other students weren't doing much better.

'So, you are *the one who's been shielding Darius' thoughts.'* Nalithor came to stand behind me and rested his hands on my shoulders. *'You decided he needed a wakeup call, did you?'*

'At the very least he needs to be knocked off his high horse,' I replied, biting back a purr as Nalithor massaged my shoulders. *'I can't decide if you're intentionally riling him up at this point...'*

'He does seem quite flustered, doesn't he?' Nalithor remarked innocently before releasing a devious chuckle. *'Your presence here is distracting his classmates a little more than I anticipated. It would appear to be a mixture of their disbelief that you're not taking classes alongside Darius...and your succulent cleavage?'*

'Succulent?' I grinned crookedly, resisting the urge to look down at my chest.

"Professor Vraelimir, forgive me for asking, but..." A blushing Devillian of the Imviir variety looked from Nalithor and then to me a few times. "Arianna-jiss is the twin sister of Darius-zir, is she not? Should she not be a student here as well?"

"Arianna aced her first test, and the results are not back on the rest." Nalithor smirked, motioning at me. "She can fight evenly with me, so I wouldn't claim that she needs to study here. Alas...this room is too small and fragile for a sparring demonstration.

"My dear, if you would be so kind?"

Nalithor nudged me, the mischievous twinkle in his eyes matching the growing smirk that played on his lips. Clearly, he wanted me to give them a different sort of demonstration. I focused my attention forward once more and examined the mixture of expectant and smug expressions on the student's faces. The smug ones sealed the fate for them all.

"A demonstration then, is it?" I inquired sweetly, earning a chuckle from Nalithor. "Very well. I will indulge you *this time*, Nalithor."

I didn't wait for his reaction to my chosen wording. Instead, I summoned all four of my elements into the room and startled shrieks from the entire class. The whirlwind of elements tore around the room, displacing papers and other lightweight items. After a few seconds most of them calmed down, realizing that I was using my own power to buffer the elements and keep them from doing actual harm.

However, a surprising number of students were incapable of sensing that fact. Feeling their growing panic, I called my elements to my side and separated them, shaping each one into a different fox. Nalithor gave my shoulders another squeeze, laughing, and then released me. He approached the large shadowy fox I'd created, a rather boyish smile on his face.

"As you can see... Arianna is quite controlled," Nalithor commented dryly. "Perhaps a bit playful, but her power and control are both exceptional.

"You really do like foxes don't you, Arianna?"

"They're cute..." I grumbled, heat rising to my face. "Is that sufficient proof, *class*, or will it take a brawl?"

"You are tiny. He would break you." An Akor narrowed his eyes at me as I grinned and Nalithor laughed.

"Ari, are we really that tiny?" Darius whined as I rose to my feet. "We're about average height in X'shmir, aren't we? So—"

"You are both small," Nalithor confirmed, closing the distance between us in a few strides. He lifted me by my waist without warning, startling a yelp from me as he smirked up at me, hoisting me upward until his face was level with my stomach. "That said, she kicks harder than General Il'thar does—and she's considerably cuter too. Gave me a nice gash with that scythe of hers as well...

"Ahhh...enough of that. Perhaps if enough of you beg us *properly*, Arianna-jiss and I will see fit to give you a true demonstration of our power through sparring when we return in a few days. For now, back to your exercises!"

Nalithor placed me down again and shot me a warm smile

before shifting his attention to his students. I pouted slightly, attempting to straighten my attire. He was so difficult to deal with, and yet it seemed as though I couldn't avoid interaction with him at all. Hells, I often found myself rethinking my desire to distance myself from him—especially after his near week-long absence.

'I'm…glad he's back.'

CHAPTER SIXTEEN
Revealing the Past

As I strode through the Sapphire Quarter, I glanced up at Avrirsa's moons, feeling contemplative. My prolonged exposure to Arianna today had left me with more questions than I'd anticipated. *'She was quite cooperative today. Playful as well... Is her resistance waning?'*

Arianna's behavior for most of the day struck me as strange after having witnessed her rage this morning. I expected her to remain in a foul mood after Eyrian's poor excuse for going easy on her. Eyrian was a fool for treating her in such a way—he should have known from my mistakes, and from watching the princess rip into a beast, that she shouldn't be treated as a Human. Alas, I could understand his concern. If he truly believed she was Lucifer's daughter, I doubted he could bring himself to use his full strength against her.

Instead of remaining bitter, Arianna's demeanor had improved—for a time. Something other than her playfulness pulled me even now, hours later. She had looked troubled during classes. The constant tremble of her thoughts behind her deeper barriers confirmed my suspicions, even if I wasn't privy to the contents. With every new glare or curt comment from her brother, Arianna's visible concern and confusion grew.

By the end of the day Arianna had slipped into a brooding mood. That she had shown even a hint of emotion before leaving my side seemed like a minor miracle.

'Why am I jealous of that brat?' I covered my face, coming to a stop as I took a deep breath. I needed to calm myself. *'Why does she dote on him so much? How can she still care for someone that has done nothing but help the X'shmirans continue their abusive behavior?'*

I truly couldn't understand it. The entirety of the X'shmiran Royal Family, including Darius, seemed intent on breaking Arianna down until she was just a tool. What reason could she *possibly* have for tolerating such treatment? Had she grown accustomed to it? The only thing that made even a modicum of sense was that, perhaps, it was related to her mentions of the ties between them. If the death of one meant the death for the other, I could only assume that there were other issues alongside.

'Perhaps I just want her to dote upon me instead.' The

unwelcome thought made me scowl. I shook my head hard, cursing myself. *'My first concern should be determining if she was created by the Exiles. Troublesome as they are, it's hard to believe they would have left one of their creations in a place like that…'*

My train of thought trailed off as I caught Darius' weak scent in the air. I grimaced to myself before adopting a more pleasant expression, pivoting to look over my shoulder. Sure enough, the brat himself was approaching me. He wrung his trembling hands together as he walked, his green gaze flitting around as if searching for something other than me. The brat *almost* looked concerned or panicked.

"What is it, Darius?" I sighed, frowning as Darius' demeanor remained nervy. *'Strange, the brat normally perks up when he sees me or if I address him. What could possibly have concerned him so?'*

"Have you seen Arianna?" Darius asked with a worried frown, pointing towards the academy's main clock tower. "I was going to ask her to come to dinner with me, but I can't find her anywhere!"

'Now he actually wants *Arianna's presence at dinner?'* My brow furrowed as I examined Darius. *'That is rather strange… I doubt this is because he is going to miss her whilst she's gone.'*

"I have an idea of where she went. Would you like me to check?" I offered after brief consideration, watching as anger, jealousy, and reluctance flashed across Darius' face.

"Oh, I can check for myself. It's alright." Darius shook his head hard. "I wouldn't want to bother—"

"Where she went is off-limits to mages with minimal control of their abilities," I informed Darius with a dismissive wave. "If she is still there, I will have her meet you for dinner. Where should I tell her to go?"

"The house!" Darius laughed, quickly shifting gears from pouting to a cheerful grin. "She absolutely *hates* the stares she's been getting, so I ordered all her favorites. They'll be delivered soon. I'll be at the house. Let me know if she's not there, okay?"

'Her favorites?' I suppressed my suspicious frown, considering the boy's words. *'Is he planning to bribe her? And what is this about hating the stares? Arianna seems quite comfortable as long as the looks are not malicious... Is she hiding more from me than I thought?'*

Darius grinned, revealing the fangs that didn't suit him, then waved and ran off. I shook my head and shot a disgusted look at his back before turning to make my way towards a nearby lift. If my instincts were correct, Arianna was on one of the more unusual islands below the city. I couldn't imagine what business she would have there, or who would have given her access to it, but her power radiated from that point quite clearly.

Upon first meeting the boy months ago in X'shmir I had noticed how unusual he looked for a Human. Slit pupils, fangs, and his almost metallic pale gold skin were traits not associated with being Human. Nor were his magical abilities. Regardless of the number of elemental affinities and lack of control, he shouldn't have had *any* access to magic if he was truly Human. The Elder

Gods had stripped their species of magic long ago.

'I suppose the difference in their ability to wield magic is also of concern,' I thought as the lift descended. *'The fae-dragons clearly schooled Arianna well. How could Darius erase* that *much from his mind willingly?'*

Despite my curiosity I found it difficult to ask Arianna about such things outright. Not only did I fear that conversing about such things could threaten her mental state...I found myself in a position where I no longer wanted to confirm or deny her identity.

Confirmation of either possibility would result in different kinds of pain, and both were terrible.

Even so, Arianna's Brands of Divinity fascinated me—though I would never have admitted it aloud. After all that had happened, the distinctive Brands running along her smooth pale skin shocked me most of all. The pattern was reminiscent of the Shujare family, though there were too many differences for me to be certain without seeing the rest of her. I kept telling myself that this wasn't *my* Arianna...but it was becoming more difficult with every day.

'As a child her *Brands were white, weren't they? Where would these new patterns, and color, have come from? Am I misremembering?'*

Aside from myself there were few deities or demigods with bi-colored Brands. The chaos star-like flowers on the back of her hands were unusual enough themselves, let alone the black star on her right hand and the white crescent on her left. Coloring and pattern aside, the radiance of her Brands was closer to that of a deity of *my* ranking. It shouldn't have been possible. Then there were her strength, speed, and power…she seemed so delicate, yet she kicked just as hard as Eyrian could—if not harder.

I caught Arianna's maddening scent in the air and glanced down at the island below, curious. The air was thick with the mingled jasmine and vanilla aroma, indicating the princess had been down here for quite some time. Alas, Dauthrmir's Guardian Dragons quickly drew my attention away from the princess.

Both Onyre *and* Aleri rested with their chins on the island's shore, their telepathic reverberations indicating that they were conversing with the young woman sitting between them. Arianna's form was lit only by the moons above us. Her Brands glowed along her legs and down to her toes as she swung them back and forth in the water. Unfortunately, she had pulled one of her damnable hooded robes on, obscuring her hair from view once more. The rest of her skin seemed almost luminescent beneath the glow of the moons.

Most noteworthy was the smile on her face as she conversed with the dragons. Her cheerful laughter gave me pause. Unlike the majority of expressions I'd witnessed on her delicate features since her arrival, this one was not tinged with sadness or hollowness. It was a genuine cheer and happiness.

Something about her smile made me desperately want to pull away her mask and hood. I battled the urge down and then turned my attention to her third, familiar, companion.

'Djialkan?' I hesitated, leaning against the base of a nearby magnolia tree. It didn't seem wise to interrupt the princess's conversation with Dauthrmir's Guardians.

'You understand, do you not?' Djialkan snorted, shadows spilling from his maw as he glanced toward me. *'If she can speak to Onyre and Aleri, then she's—'*

'Royalty of the Vorpmasian Empire,' I murmured, my gaze resting on Arianna as my blood began to boil. *'You mean to tell me that a Devillian prince and princess have been in the possession of twisted Human scum?!*

'She should still be an infant if she's Devillian, yet she looks slightly younger than I!'

'The creatures responsible for sealing most of the twins' power also obscured their true species,' Djialkan snapped. *'Those seals began slipping decades ago, if not more. The seals on Arianna's abilities have almost completely vanished, whilst Darius' are sturdier.*

'The Oracles have strengthened Darius' seals on both his power and species due to his fragile state. Arianna's, however, continue to weaken.'

I remained silent, examining Arianna once more. Aside from her Brands and *exceptional* figure, I didn't see anything visual to indicate that her species was something other than Human. The occasional flash of fangs when she spoke or laughed, and the pointed ears I'd discovered today, were my only visual hints at her being something "else."

Her power and intoxicating scent were what truly made me suspicious of her origins. Alone they brought up many questions, but together they painted her as anything other than Human. Her apparent resistance to the natural charms of an Adinvyr was both worrying and appealing, and *not* something other Devillians shared.

Even so, I seemed to fluster her with ease despite that resistance.

'I should have asked Sebastian about the Godslayer.*'* I frowned, examining the Brands on the backs of Arianna's hands as she motioned to the dragons. *'Its power should have consumed her when she drew it, especially with the fear that shot through her when she realized what weapon she had drawn. Those weapons aren't meant to be wielded by full mortals, let alone Humans.*

'Her Brands are quite unique but...they still have traces of Lucifer's bloodline in their patterns. That shouldn't be possible for a mere reincarnation. Either she's a near-perfect fake...or she is the real Arianna and has some recollection of that damned weapon. There are no alternatives left.'

My pulse quickened and a pang of pain pierced my heart as I examined the smiling princess. I didn't know whether to feel delighted or saddened. We had spent so long looking for her, yet I still struggled to accept that the woman before me might truly be Arianna. Sometimes I wondered if perhaps it would be easier for everyone, including her, if she was just a reincarnation. That she might remember even a fragment of her time in Limbo tore at me.

All I knew for certain was that Lucifer would be *livid* if he had already decided, fully, that the twins were indeed his children. If he had confirmed it in some way, he would focus every ounce of his power as a god and as an emperor to destroy every last X'shmiran he could find.

My instincts as the God of Balance told me that such actions would be a mistake.

'She must have her memories of Limbo,' I observed, my eyes flicking to her scarlet smile as she laughed up at the dragons. It was a pleasant sound, and it hadn't changed much since she was young. *'The way she said that phrase to was unmistakable. I should have known then.*

"'But it's so wonderful to be like a monster, isn't it?"

'She really has grown into an exceptional woman. It's…impossible for me to see her as the same child I once knew. Still, it's a relief that she hasn't been destroyed by the Old Ways at least. Not for lack of effort. Did her time in Limbo prepare her?'

I fell still, considering the possibilities. Clearly my heart wanted to accept that this Arianna was *my* Arianna from the past. My mind, however, still screamed that it wasn't possible. Why would the Elders lie to me, after all? The Exiles were still gods in their own right; they could infuse a "fake" with memories from the deceased if they wanted, couldn't they?

Taking a deep breath, I shook my head. *'The Elders are*

responsible for her "death." I can't trust them.'

'Are you going to hide there all night, Nalithor?' Onyre's voice jolted me from my whirlwind of thoughts, his gaze flicking toward me. 'If you think you are being sneaky, you are sorely mistaken. We noticed you as soon as you boarded the lift, as did Her Highness.'

After shooting the white dragon a grimace, I pushed away from the tree trunk and strode silently across the grass to join them. Arianna scented the air subtly and then tilted her head a little towards me, her lips parting in surprise for a moment. Before I could say anything, her attention snapped back to Onyre and Aleri as she giggled at something.

"Your brother is looking for you, *Your Highness*,' I stated, crossing my arms and smiling as she twitched in response. She really did hate being called that. "He appears quite frantic."

"He is?" Arianna frowned after a moment and then tilted her head back to look up at me again. "It hasn't been that long since I came down here has it?"

"Several hours, I'd wager,' I offered, watching as she pursed her lips and shifted her gaze to the lake's surface.

"Really? Several hours already? Hmmm…" Arianna frowned further. After a moment, she motioned up at the sky. "I was hoping to look at *those* a little longer, seeing as we don't have them in X'shmir. However, after his classes today, Darius *is* in a sorry state…

"He wouldn't tell me what his therapist said to him."

After a small sigh, she pulled her legs out of the lake and then rose to her feet in a fluid motion. That faintly sad expression had returned to her features now. Instead of moving for the lift she crossed her arms beneath her bust and nibbled on the knuckle of her index finger. I could practically hear the gears turning in her head, though whatever she was contemplating was well beyond the portions of her mind I had access to.

'What is it going to take to rid her of that sadness?' I wondered, feeling guilty that *I* had caused the shift in her mood. *'Although...she looks more worried than sad. Darius again? Tch...'*

"He did seem particularly nervous," I remarked, frowning as I watched Arianna. Something was agitating her. I could feel her frustration and turmoil bubbling just out of reach now, but I couldn't determine the source. I only hoped I wasn't the cause.

"Too bad you lot didn't just conquer X'shmir..." Arianna muttered under her breath, striding past me as the dragons disappeared beneath the surface of the lake.

"You don't seem like the type who would be disloyal to her people," I began, watching as she turned to face me with a surprised expression on those lips of hers. "For you to make such a bold statement—"

"Has everyone really been so transfixed by *this*," Arianna snapped, motioning at her mask and hood with a growl, "that you've all forgotten how Astral Mages are *'worshiped'* in the Old Ways? Or is that another thing that's 'unique' to X'shmir?!" I looked down at her as she stalked toward me, unsure of how to respond when she jabbed her finger into my chest. "I *told* that airheaded brother of mine that he should withdraw from the mental fortitude tests—and potentially from therapy—in case he wasn't ready for it... But he insisted on going through *both* anyway!

"Am I going to have to spell it out for you, Nalithor?"

The treatment of Umbral Mages according to the Old Ways was enough to make most people's stomach turn. The torture with molten chains, the insane restrictions to every facet of life, and other problems made them little better than slaves. Historically speaking, such treatment was well-known in Vorpmasia even though we had never taken part. We had saved many mages bound by the Old Ways and learned of the true horrors through them.

However, the twisted so-called "worship" of Astral Mages in the Old Ways was lesser known and was what truly made my blood boil. Arianna seemed satisfied when a scowl split my face. I tracked her as she moved several feet away from me to perch on a nearby bench. The small sigh that escaped her almost sounded *relieved,* of all things.

"You're telling me that the X'shmirans practice the Old Ways to their *full* extent?" I questioned, grimacing at my own dangerous tone. *'At this rate I will frighten her instead of— Who am I kidding? I should have frightened her many times over by now, yet I haven't.'*

"They use it as an excuse to get away with the things they do to my brother." Arianna nodded after a moment, crossed her legs, leaned back on her palms, and then sighed again. "We were quite young when we came into our abilities, but…*they* had already been abusing Darius for years before that. They apparently… Ugh. They claimed that such things were *'suitable punishment'* for a boy who was unable to beat his sister in the 'race from the womb.'

"I…I read that Adinvyr have a special sort of hatred for people that bring harm to children. Especially, you know, *that* type of harm. Judging from the rage pouring off you…I'm assuming that isn't information you actively seek or otherwise 'sense?'"

"You're hardly picture of calm yourself," I retorted, bristling as I ran a hand through my hair. Sighing, I looked down at Arianna again. "There must be a reason you haven't torn them to shreds yet."

'A blunt question like that, the slight tremble in her lips as she spoke… She was fishing to determine if she should be angry with me.' I considered, examining her face. *'For once I'm thankful for the mask and hood. Although she's not crying, at least not yet, the quavering gives her away. She's distraught.'*

To my surprise, Arianna's answer to my comment was a twisted grin and a short laugh. She looked genuinely amused despite the bitter edge to the sound. I sensed her bloodlust spiraling out of control as she pondered what to say, attempting to break free of her inner defenses. Somehow, she managed to beat it back into submission as she looked up at me once more.

"As much as I may or may not have fantasized about *ripping that fucking filth to shreds*," Arianna began in a startlingly icy tone, her murderous intent making me tense. "I've mentioned my 'curse' before—how if Darius dies, I die. The reverse is also true. Beyond that, it will kill me if I so much as *scratch* any of the X'shmiran nobles or royals! Simple as that. It's similar magic to what you've sensed silencing me before.

"I can't act. Not without throwing both my life and Darius' away…and I'm not that desperate. Yet."

"Would you like me to conquer them for you?" I purred, kneeling before her. She looked startled as I cupped her face, but she didn't pull away. *'Mother and Erist will have my hide for this…but I don't care.'*

"Conquer…? Wouldn't that be a poor move for a deity—" I pressed my thumb over Arianna's plush lips, silencing her as I shook my head.

It was difficult for me to focus my gaze on anything other than those lips of hers since so much of her face was obscured behind that damned mask…but I did my best. The quivering of her mouth beneath my thumb exposed her poorly hidden anguish, igniting my rage further. How she was holding back the tears, I had no idea.

"The agreement Vorpmasia signed with X'shmir is void if they're found to have violated *any* section of the contract—past or present," I informed her, moving my thumb from her lips and watching as her pale face flushed pink. "The physical and emotional damage they have inflicted on your brother is a heinous crime, punishable by death.

"Even if it happened only once, many years ago, their fate is death. By your simmering anger...I assume the problem is ongoing?"

"How else would they continue with the excuse of 'worship?'" Arianna spat, turning her head away with a scowl. "Wouldn't it be more accurate to say you're offering to conquer X'shmir for my *brother*, not for me?"

"No, I am offering to act in your stead," I answered with the firmest tone I could muster, stroking her cheek with my thumb until she turned to look at me with a startled expression. *'Shouldn't I be more concerned about her brother? They've both been subjected to things no one should have to face, certainly, yet...I am more concerned about Arianna.*

"So, I will ask you again," I paused, smiling as I examined her flustered expression and attempted to reign in my own bloodlust. "Would you like me to conquer that *filth* for you?"

It was impossible to keep the growl from my voice, but the princess didn't seem to mind—quite the contrary, it seemed to make her blushing grow darker. Even though her thoughts were hidden from me, it was clear that Arianna truly thought like one of my kind. She was startled, of course, that someone would offer to kill for her, but she couldn't hide from me that the notion appealed to her.

Although I couldn't see her eyes, I could tell that she had averted her gaze again by the slight tilt of her head away from my hand. I heard her heart beating wildly, and her lips were parted in thought. I imagined that she was weighing the gravity of my offer against the details of her "curse," against her desire to kill the X'shmirans herself…and perhaps other criteria as well.

Arianna didn't strike me as naive enough to think only two people would die during my conquest of X'shmir.

Perhaps a Human would have found her bloodthirsty reaction and inclinations frightening…but I found them rather endearing. Arianna was adorable, no doubt. It drove my desire to destroy the X'shmirans for her to new heights. Her self-control was admirable, but it was waning. Someone had to do something about those bastards before she was driven to kill them—and herself in the process.

I would not allow her to die.

"Don't you need sound evidence?" Arianna finally asked, her hesitation clear in her voice.

"I do…but I have the feeling you have plenty of proof for me," I replied.

Poking around in Darius' head for proof seemed unwise given his already fragile state. Arianna, however, held strong hatred for their so-called parents. It seemed likely that her emotions on the matter weren't from someone *telling* her about what had happened to her brother. Furthermore, she seemed more stable than Darius in every way despite her distress.

"Let me be your sword and, in your place, I'll see to it that they receive every *ounce* of pain and suffering they deserve for the atrocities they've committed," I spoke in a firm, commanding tone, breaking the prolonged silence.

"How am I supposed to say 'no' to that?" Arianna mused, a bashful smile spreading across her face as she shifted to face me. "I won't deny that I'm surprised by your offer, but I—"

"Think of it as…a gift." I smiled, running my thumb along her lower lip, taking care not to graze her with my claws.

My smile broadened when Arianna's breath caught in her throat and she looked away from me again, her cheeks growing rosier. Earning such reactions from her amused me to no end. She was such a proud warrior, and yet she was capable of such softness.

"Then… I accept," Arianna replied quietly before pausing as if in thought. "You may want to sit instead of kneel if I'm going to show you what I've seen."

I nodded and released her face, then raised up just enough to pull myself onto the bench beside her. She offered me her left hand in silence and, for a moment, I simply looked down and examined the black chaos star pattern on the back of her hand. The white crescent at the very center gave off a soft glow. *'She's still uneasy but seems resolved. Any hint of trembling is gone.'*

After accepting her hand I marveled at how small and delicate it seemed in comparison to mine. Despite her training and inclination to fight, her skin was soft and smooth to the touch. I could have stayed like that forever, but Arianna appeared to be all business for the moment. She advised me to steel myself and waited mere seconds before pushing a series of memories directly into my mind.

At first, I was startled that she had not only the power to single out specific memories to transfer, but that she could do so through *my* barriers. She hadn't even given me the chance to lower them first. Alas, my surprise soon gave way to disgust, nausea, and rage. The scenes Arianna had inadvertently walked in on as a child were something no one, regardless of age, should ever have to see.

Her presence had initially gone unnoticed by the X'shmiran king and queen, but not for long.

Arianna and Darius had both been so young when she first discovered what was happening to her brother, yet her rage was beyond what I'd felt from people many times her age. Her anger and hatred surpassed even what I felt for the Elders and Angels, threatening to sweep me away. What *I* thought was all-consuming rage paled in comparison to what the woman beside me felt towards the X'shmiran Court.

It made sense to me now why Dilonu was missing an arm— Arianna had flown into a blind rage upon entering the room and torn it from him with her bare hands despite her small size. The spray of blood through the air should have fazed her but instead it had fueled her anger and made her lunge for more. I grit my teeth with distaste when I witnessed one of the guards inside the room strike her in the back of the head to incapacitate her. Such a blow would have killed a Human adult, let alone a child.

I opened my eyes and looked down at the silent princess, finding her presence calm despite my own boiling blood. It seemed likely that she had sensed the full extent of my bloodlust and hatred toward such acts, yet she hadn't even flinched. She appeared to have accepted her inability to help Darius long ago, even if it clearly displeased or upset her at times. Her pulse was steady now and I no longer sensed a maelstrom of emotions trying to break free of her deepest barriers. *'That pain in her back was...'*

"Just how young...?" I grimaced at the shaking rage in my voice and continued, "That was before you two officially became mages, wasn't it? I still sensed chains in your back, aside from what they..."

"From what I've learned from the more *humane* servants in the palace..." Arianna pursed her lips, shaking her head. "You *really* don't want to know how young they started with Darius, Nalithor.

"As far as my chains, I can show you that as well if you wish. I'd mostly forgotten about them since Corentine and her sister removed them for me."

"*Forgotten?* You're certain?" I frowned at her, but she just smiled and nodded in reply. "Very well. I can't deny that information would assist me in earning Lucifer's approval.

Though, after seeing that, I'm of half a mind to destroy them with or without it…ugh."

Arianna's laughter surprised me, but she seemed truly amused. Unlike her previous laughter, it wasn't a bitter or sarcastic sound. Perhaps with that filth gone she would be able to laugh and smile like that more often. *I'm getting carried away again. Despite her challenge and eagerness to spar, she's exhibited little interest in me. Though…it seems strange that she would so willingly lend me her precious collection of texts and that dagger. Hmmm…*

'Ah. Is she hiding herself due to a reluctance to taste temporary *freedom?'*

The memories Arianna passed to me this time stunned me, but not for the reasons I anticipated. Somehow, she had learned to cope with the pain of molten metal laid across her back, creating a latticework of scarred skin and pliable metal. Some of the damned chains were so hot that they had dripped globules of metal onto her skin before being laid into place.

Djialkan and Fraelfnir had done their best to heal the young princess after such sessions, using up almost all their stored power each time. Arianna's self-healing capabilities and natural regeneration made it clear that even at such a young age she had already been far from Human. I felt like a fool for ever considering her to be a mere mortal.

For the first few years the Royal Family had drugged Arianna so that she couldn't escape, let alone struggle or cry when they arranged the chains across her pale skin. They would leave her bound and alone while the chains cooled and fused with her flesh, not releasing her until hours later—or longer.

Her hatred astonished me yet again.

It was becoming quite clear that the only reason she hadn't torn X'shmir from the sky herself was because she didn't want her brother to die due to *her* actions. The curse was the only thing holding her back, and it wasn't doing a very good job of it.

After experiencing her full hatred and fury, it was obvious to me that Arianna would have easily ripped X'shmir apart if it was only her life at risk. She would have happily sacrificed it if she could guarantee the destruction of the king, queen, and involved nobility.

Arianna was in-tune with her darkness to an extent that most Umbral Mages could never hope to achieve. The shadows and darkness around us, even those wafting from me in my rage, calmed her instead of enraging her further. Mages who weren't so accepting would have been driven to slaughter the source of their anger long ago. It took my respect, and admiration, of Arianna to new heights.

I had noticed her familiarity with darkness upon her arrival in Dauthrmir, but I hadn't realized it was to such an extent. I had thought her comment about beasts being frightened of *her* darkness was strange, but it now made sense. Most living creatures couldn't fathom this degree of darkness.

It was strangely comforting to know someone other than

myself who was so close with the element.

"Will that suffice?" Arianna inquired, looking up at me when I released her hand. "You took that well, all things considered."

"Draemir, my homeland, was deeply involved with seeking out and punishing those who followed the Old Ways," I began as I rose to my feet, pivoting to offer her a hand. "I may not have been exposed to such atrocities at such a young age…but I was at least somewhat prepared thanks to what I've seen in the past.

"Unlike what the X'shmiran tomes teach, one of the primary duties of an Adinvyr is to find, lure, and eradicate those who would make a mockery of sexual relationships by using them to harm others. Especially if a child, like your brother was, is involved."

'Is she a stronger healer than I thought? The Oracle isn't strong enough to heal such wounds completely, and I would imagine this "Corentine" woman is the same,' I wondered, pulling Arianna to her feet and letting tendrils of power examine her. *'The chains are gone; her back is free of scars…*

'By the Elders, the pain *she experienced. She's stated before that she was "used to" pain. Did her time in Limbo—if she is* my *Arianna— affect her more greatly than she's let on?'*

"A mockery?" Arianna interrupted my whirlwind of thoughts and reclaimed her hand. "That's an interesting choice of words."

'It's a shame she wouldn't let me hold it for at least a bit longer…' The thought sent an unwelcome lance of pain through my chest, causing me to clench my teeth and glance away from her briefly. *'I*

need to calm down. I can't...I can't let myself jump to conclusions about her identity.'

"Perhaps it isn't obvious due to how *some* of us conduct ourselves," I murmured, attempting to find the words to express my thoughts. "Our race sees sex and sexuality as sacred things. Using either one to harm others is one of the biggest 'sins' in our culture—if you want to call it that."

"Then Adinvyr must have strong ties with Erist'il, correct?" Arianna asked as we approached the lift. She grinned when she saw me grimace. "She's the Goddess of 'Love,' right? Physical love, anyway. I would think she'd be rather involved with your race if you all tend to punish the very things she stands against."

'Ugh, I hope I can keep "Auntie" and Mother away from Arianna for at least a little while,' I groaned inwardly, considering the situation. *'They're never going to let me hear the end of it...'*

"You're correct...I just have a particular dislike for both Erist and her husband," I replied dryly, crossing my arms over my chest as the lift ascended toward the city above us. "They mean well, but they both have one-track minds. Erist'il is always focused on the physical aspects of sex...and whether the person she's conversing with has found a suitable 'toy' to bed.

"Arom'il, by contrast, is the God of 'Emotional' Love. I'm sure I don't need to explain what *he* relentlessly pesters everyone about."

"That sounds annoying..." Arianna muttered as she leaned back against the railing and tilted her head back to look up at the starry sky. "Hmmm…are there any other academy tests I should know about?"

"Unless the Archmagi or Oracles determine they want to put you through more tests, you should be done," I offered after a moment, surprised by the abrupt change in subject. "All that's left is to wait on whatever they choose to assign you; classes or a partner. They're likely to request you undergo another medical examination in order to make sure you're healthy and fit for battle…but you shouldn't need to worry about that. Our healers are bound by oath not to disclose personal matters, and that would extend to what's behind that mask of yours."

Arianna just nodded in silence, her gaze still aimed to the stars. It was almost as if the sight of the stars, moons, and planets hanging above us entranced her. I glanced upwards as well and then looked back to the princess in thought. I had almost forgotten about X'shmir's strange violet sky and its lack of celestial bodies.

To us, the Vorpmasians, it had been an unsettling sight. Just thinking of the sickly X'shmiran sky made my skin crawl. While we had determined it wasn't *supposed* to look that way, we hadn't been able to discover what had caused it to take on such an appearance. We were too restricted in our movements in that country. If Arianna's memories were as limited as they had been in Limbo, I realized that coming to what the X'shmirans referred to as "Below" was the first time she and her twin had seen the *real* sky.

"Have you finished making your preparations for dealing with the beasts?" I questioned after a moment, hoping to distract that sad expression from her face. I was rewarded with a brilliant, excited grin when she looked toward me.

"I have! Djialkan is quite eager to leave as well." Arianna motioned at the fae-dragon who had remained silent and motionless on her shoulder. "He's frustrated about hiding in the house and slinking through the shadows of Dauthrmir all the time. Alala is uninterested though and will stay behind to help Fraelfnir make sure Darius doesn't destroy *everything*."

"You are worried about unwanted attention, Djialkan?" I looked to the fae-dragon, who just released an irritable snort in reply. "I suppose I can understand that.

"I will meet both of you at your house in the morning."

The last few minutes of our ascent to the academy grounds were spent in a comfortable blanket of silence. Simply each other's presence seemed sufficient for now. Upon arrival, Arianna quietly dismissed herself. I watched as she swept across the dark grass and traced her graceful movements until she was out of sight. After utilizing my darkness to confirm there were no Vampires or other strange creatures preying upon her, I turned for the palace, satisfied that she was safe.

Lucifer and I were going to have a long discussion and I didn't care how late it was. I was going to make my case, and I would make it clear why *I* needed to be the one to rip those disgusting people apart for their crimes.

Until then, I would do my best to keep the twins' potential identities to myself. Lucifer, Eyrian, and Xander were already far too suspicious. Until I could confirm Arianna and Darius' authenticity for myself, one-hundred-percent, I had to err on the side of caution. I couldn't let Lucifer rip all of X'shmir from the sky, even though I was considering doing the very same. That the bastards would do such terrible things to the twins made me sick. That Arianna—potentially *my* Arianna—had seen such things as a child, been cursed, tortured…

'Why do I keep making this about Arianna instead of Darius? He's suffered just as much, perhaps more, but…' I shut my eyes and attempted to gather my thoughts. *'I* must *calm down before tomorrow's mission. These things can't be distracting me while we hunt, else I will put all of us in danger. Including* her.

'Arianna… I will *keep you safe.'*

CHAPTER SEVENTEEN
The Hunt Begins

"Come on, Ari! If you don't get up soon, you're not gonna get any breakfast before you leave!" Darius yelled from downstairs, eliciting a few choice curses from me as I nuzzled into my pillow.

I paused when the events of the previous night flooded back to me, causing my face to burn so hot that I hid my face in my pillow fully.

Nalithor had shocked me with his offer. Despite his overflowing rage for my situation, and for my brother's, Nalithor's expression had remained *tender*, of all things, when he asked if I wanted him to act in my stead. *'How can someone look so gentle when making an offer like that?'*

"I will move everything into your shrizar while you get dressed,"

Djialkan informed me as I pulled myself from bed. *"You had best hurry."*

"I know, I know…" I sighed.

I yanked on the first set of Dauthrmiran robes I could find, pinned up my hair, and rushed out the door.

Getting Nalithor off my mind was difficult but I was doing my best. I really didn't want to ponder him or his "gift" yet. Any time I did, I couldn't help but think of the expression on his face when he made his initial offer.

"Here you go, Ari!" Darius called cheerfully. "Tea and a hearty breakfast should wake you up. You look uneasy still… What's wrong?"

"Eh… I was speaking with Onyre and Aleri—the Guardian dragons—last night when you sent Nalithor to come find me," I grumbled, sitting down at the table before pulling on my mask. "His presence and our brief conversation raised some important questions."

'Not to mention it proved I don't know how to deal with Nalithor at all,' I added to myself, settling into my seat. *'How am I supposed to keep my thoughts tame around him? Especially if he's going to look at me like that…'*

"Why do I get the feeling that I won't like where this is going?" Darius frowned, drawing my attention back to the matter at hand.

"Considering the way everyone here speaks of the Old Ways, did you really think *that* was going to remain a secret?" I asked quietly, watching as my brother's frown deepened.

"I knew it would come up at some point. That said, you're not *allowed* to do anything—!" Darius slammed his hands down on the table and grit his teeth. "They weren't angry with you for not killing the bastards, were they?!"

"No… Well, Nalithor might have been at first. I'm not sure; sometimes he's hard to read." I muttered, my face growing warm as I stared down at my tea. "Darius… Just how involved were you with the details of the treaty between X'shmir and Vorpmasia?"

"I wasn't involved, I just signed it," Darius shrugged and then leaned forward, peering at me. "You're *really* blushing, you know. Want to *show me* instead? I know you wouldn't divulge something like…like our past…without good reason."

'Right… "Our" past. Still, isn't he a little too carefree? Shouldn't he be angry with me?' I bit back a grimace. *'And…really? He only signed it? What sort of dolt signs a treaty without reading it first?!'*

I sighed and then nodded to Darius as he giggled at me. My twin turned a brilliant shade of burgundy moments after I transferred my memories of last night's conversation to him. I was a little relieved to see that I wasn't the only one startled by Nalithor's offer, but I was more relieved to see that Darius didn't appear angered. He was certainly stunned, but so was I. Perhaps after seeing an offer like *that*, Darius was able to shelve his jealousy—for the moment.

'He isn't going to throw a fit?' I watched Darius grab a napkin

and fan himself, his face still flushed. *'With the way he's been acting about Nalithor I was* certain *he'd fly into some sort of rage.'*

"Okay… I can *definitely* see why you've been so flustered since last night." Darius gulped and slumped back in his chair. "I'm pretty sure if he looked at *me* like that, I wouldn't be able to handle it.

"Really though, a gift? Isn't that a strange way to put it?"

"It is a meaningful way to word it," Djialkan interjected, swooping into the kitchen to perch on my shoulder. Alala came scampering in after him and ran around the legs of my chair before bolting out of the room. *"Even for a culture so steeped in the ways of war and hunting, it is a rare offer for an Adinvyr to make."*

"I've been studying Draemiran culture." Darius nodded, turning to look at me. "What Nalithor offered you is… It's the highest show of respect that I can think of in their culture. As Djialkan said, it's a rare occurrence."

"Offering to act as your sword carries the same gravity and responsibility as if he had asked for your hand in marriage," Djialkan stated bluntly, causing me to choke on my tea.

"You couldn't think of *any* other analogy? *Any*?!" I demanded, rounding on the cackling fae-dragon.

"I can't either!" Darius laughed, shaking his head. "It's a very personal thing and indicates that he cares strongly on some level or another. Of course, he has many reasons to care; our parents have violated something that his race sees as sacred, something they see themselves as guardians of. They also broke some section of the treaty between X'shmir and the Rilzaan Alliance."

"*'Some section.'*" I snorted to myself.

"*As a Vorpmasian General, Nalithor could have simply gone to the emperor without consulting you,*" Djialkan said in a condescending tone. "*As a deity, he could have gone directly to X'shmir without consulting you or Lucifer.*"

"Instead he chose to do *that?*" I sighed when the both nodded at me. "So, Darius, you're wondering how deeply he cares and how I earned his respect to such a degree?" I pursed my lips when Darius nodded again. "I really don't know, Darius. I've sparred with him a few times, aside from helping them with that one beast.

"I doubt any of that is enough. Maybe you two are just underestimating how much his kind hates—"

"I'm not!" Darius interrupted, pouting. He looked like he was going to say something else but glanced over his shoulder at the clock instead. "Don't you have to go soon, Ari?"

"*Nalithor said that he would come by to fetch us.*" Djialkan snorted and then hopped into my lap, shooting me an expectant look. "*Are you going to hog the pancakes to yourself, Arianna?*"

"Darius, you sure you don't want to keep some of last night's leftovers?" I motioned toward the pantry. "I know you said you're going to be trying restaurants with your friends, but don't you want to have some food on hand?"

"Don't worry so much!" Darius pointed his fork at me. "I'll be fine. You need to make sure you have enough supplies in case your mission gets extended, right? After all, who knows how far the beasts have moved since yesterday!"

'How am I supposed to stay sane after Djialkan used an analogy like that?' I pouted, returning my attention to the plate of food in front of me. *'Forget staying sane... How am I supposed to look at or speak with Nalithor without getting flustered now?!'*

As if on cue, the doorbell rang, and Darius bolted from his chair. I shook my head, then offered Djialkan a pancake and used my other hand to devour my own food. Moments later, I caught the sound of Darius speaking in cheerful tones, soon followed by Nalithor's scent wafting through the house. Tendrils of the Adinvyr's power flowed through the house like water. I bit back a grimace when his power paused to examine me before continuing its exploration of the first floor. *'What is he looking for?'*

"Oh? The vixen shares her food with the fae-dragon?" Nalithor teased, coming to perch on a chair beside me. He shot me a smile as he set a stack of papers, and several tomes, on the table.

"His bites are unpleasant, sharing is less unpleasant," I answered dryly, passing the now-cheerful Djialkan another pancake.

"Your brother here seemed quite concerned when he greeted me." Nalithor motioned at Darius as he reentered the kitchen. "Something about being worried that I'd be angry with you for not taking care of the X'shmiran *pests* yourself?"

"She *can't*—" Darius started to protest, but Nalithor raised a hand to silence him.

"This saves me some explaining. I wasn't quite sure how to explain last night to you, honestly, and it's something we need to discuss." Nalithor lifted a sheet of parchment and placed it in front of Darius. "During my discussion with Lucifer, we ran into a problem."

'He already went to speak with Lucifer? But it was so late when we returned!' I glanced between Nalithor and Darius a few times while nibbling my food. "Of course you did. Nothing is safe from politics."

"This matter is rather important," Nalithor stated, his firm tone making me glance toward him again. "Since the two of you are X'shmiran royalty, we would have to take both of you into custody if we were to declare war on X'shmir. We can get around this if…you both become official citizens of the empire."

"And citizenship, especially done secretly, takes time." Darius frowned, sinking into thought.

"I'm assuming you wouldn't be telling us this if you and Lucifer hadn't devised a plan to deal with Darius' scheduled 'visits' to X'shmir." I sighed, turning to look at Nalithor. "What if Darius and I turn out to be something other than Human? Would we still have to wait on citizenship?"

"Keeping Darius away from X'shmir is a simple matter." Nalithor nodded and motioned at the sheet of paper in front of

Darius. "Since your test scores were horrendous, the amount of work you need to invest into your studies at the academy gives us grounds to have you remain in Dauthrmir. I've already had word sent to the X'shmiran filth, informing them that it is unsafe for *them* to see you without an escort of mages.

"And yes, Arianna—the rules still apply regardless of your species."

"*Please*, we're *Human!*" Darius whined. He skimmed the paper and then scoffed. "These are *my* results? I think your equipment needs to be checked and replace. After, I should be tested again."

'*He really believes that you're both Human?*' Nalithor questioned me as he stole the last slice of bacon from my plate. '*Darius' ignorance is astonishing at times...*'

"Darius, try not to destroy the house while I'm gone, alright?" I pushed my chair back and picked up my empty plate. "Also, do us both a favor and keep your fuck toy away from the second floor. If it's tainted with his presence, I'll burn the house down when we return.

"If he taints Alala, I'll skin you both and feed you to the fish. I'm sure Onyre and Aleri wouldn't mind if I plumped up their prey."

"My *what?*" Darius yelped, shooting a panicked look toward Nalithor as if he expected jealousy from the Adinvyr. "Ari, such language is highly inappropriate for a *princess*. You—"

"Shall we go, Nalithor?" I placed my plate on the counter and then turned to look at the smirking deity. "The beasts *are* traveling, after all."

"Darius, if you truly believe your test results are incorrect," Nalithor began as he rose to his feet, "you can challenge your other professors to reexamine you. *I*, for one, will not indulge you. It is quite clear that your results are accurate."

Nalithor offered me his arm, which I accepted, much to Darius' displeasure. The Adinvyr chuckled at my brother's spluttering, led me out of the house, and in the direction of the far side of the Sapphire Quarter. I examined Nalithor subtly from behind my mask, tracking his surprisingly cheerful gait. The expression on his face was just as pleasant.

"Eager to hunt?" I asked, my curiosity getting the better of me.

"Yes, I much prefer hunting to teaching," Nalithor replied, shooting me a broad, almost child-like, grin. "While I would rather the others didn't have to join us, I suppose it can't be helped.

'He'd rather it just be the two of us?' I wondered, watching the cheerful man beside me. A mix of familiar scents caught my attention, drawing my attention away from Nalithor; the "others" were waiting for us in front of a small airship, and I could tell already that the Elf was going to be a thorn in my side.

'Are you always so harsh with your brother?' Nalithor's question startled me into looking at him, but his expression was still a pleasant smile. *'You don't strike me as the uncaring type. Not after what you showed me last night.'*

'Darius asked me not to treat him differently just because of his abuse,' I replied, releasing a small sigh. *'I may be overprotective of him at times but I'm one of the few people in X'shmir that treats Darius as a* person. *Everyone else treats him like an object, a victim, or like their prophesized savior.'*

'I see. So, despite his behavior, he doesn't want you walking on glass around him?' Nalithor frowned, but he was too excited for the expression to stay on his face for long. *'You and Djialkan have everything you need?'*

"We are prepared sufficiently." Djialkan huffed and dissolved into dark mist, disappearing from sight. *"I will remain hidden until needed. Your comrades are too noisy for my tastes."*

"It's unusual for you to be late, Nalithor," Eyrian remarked, crossing his arms at us as we approached. "Darius didn't give you trouble again, did he?"

"The boy is insisting that his test results are incorrect." Nalithor shrugged and pulled me past our temporary comrades, guiding me to the sleek obsidian ship. "See to it that you all have your things. We're leaving as soon as you've confirmed that you have everything necessary for a several-day trip."

I ignored Illyana's foul, condescending glare and instead focused my attention on Nalithor. Something about his smooth, predatory movements never failed to captivate me. It baffled me how such a dangerous man could be so regal. Judging by the mischievous glint in his eyes when he offered me a seat by the window, I got the feeling that he'd caught me staring at him. The curve of his mouth and the swishing of his scaly tail told me he was a little *too* pleased by the attention.

'*Are we going to have to contend with that woman's behavior this whole trip?*' I settled back in my seat and tracked Nalithor as he sat to my right. '*She's going to be dead weight if glaring at me and ogling you is all she's capable of.*'

'*You can see why I don't keep partners for long,*' Nalithor replied with a chuckle, shifting to face me and tug at my curls. '*At least you are much more pleasant and resistant.*'

'*Resistant, yes. Pleasant? Perhaps…*' I batted his hand away from one of my hair sticks. '*You can be very catlike at times, you know. Are you sure a* dragon *is fitting? Perhaps you should have chosen a nice little kitten instead.*'

"Arianna-*jiss*', are you even capable of lifting a weapon?" Illyana's asked in a haughty tone, hefting a longbow made of silver-colored wood. She seemed oblivious to Eyrian's bark of laughter. "You're so—"

I made a small motion with the index finger of my left hand and summoned every weapon, except the *Godslayer*, from my jewelry. After pointing my collection at the Elf, I turned my gaze out the window and spoke dismissively, "Seeing as you're barely worth my time, you should refer to me as *Reiz'tar*.

"Which one of these would you like me to skin you with, Elf?"

"Just how many weapons do you *need*?" The Akor asked in a

surprisingly smooth voice. I had expected the volcanic-looking man to sound gravelly. His attention, however, was on my array of blades. "Nalithor and Eyrian both told us you prefer using your fists and legs more than weapons. So why the arsenal?"

"As much as I enjoy getting my hands dirty," I began, dismissing the weapons, "sometimes beasts are too resistant to martial techniques. In order to kill them I need to have slashing, stabbing, and crushing weapons available to me."

'You should be careful with that bloodlust of yours.' Nalithor purred, leaning down to nuzzle my ear, and earning a snarl from Illyana in the process. *'At this rate you will have me pursuing you long before you give into my natural charms, Reiz'tar.'*

'At this rate,' I countered, twitching away from him as I flushed. *'I'm going to have to peek in your head and give the briefing myself.'*

"I counted at least a dozen X'shmiran Duxes making their way along the Abrantia Valley's eastern edge," Nalithor began, finally, focusing his attention on the rest of the group. "They were moving in the direction of the Ceilail Forest, but their pace was slow. It should take them several days to reach Ceilail with the roundabout way they're following.

"By now the beasts should have reached the northwestern forests. Once there, we will need to be cautious. Amakiir has told the creatures and people of the valley that we are coming. Still, we must be wary in case the young ones have managed to slip away from their parents.

"Amakiir is adamant that we do not use fire magics in his lands. As such, Arianna-jiss and I are both down one element."

'Amakiir is the patriarchal deity of the Varjior,' Nalithor offered when I turned to him to inquire. *'Unlike Rylthra and Sundreht, the Varjior are not Devillian. They are, however, capable of shapeshifting into the forms of animals in a similar fashion. Amakiir himself can take on the form of a tiger.*

'He fancies himself as a guardian of nature and of the hunt. The Abrantia Valley is his *territory. Amakiir will be incredibly angry with us if we so much as singe anything, so I hope you are comfortable without your flames.'*

'I'll be fine. I don't rely on magic much to begin with.' I shrugged. *'I'm more concerned about the number of beasts. Is it common Below for so many to group together?'*

'It's extremely unusual.' Nalithor nestled back in his seat with a sigh, a thoughtful expression on his face. *'I've been meaning to ask... Did I hurt you during our last sparring match? You collided with the barrier rather hard.'*

'Hmmm? I've been tossed rougher by Chaos Beasts,' I replied dismissively, earning a chuckle from the Adinvyr. *'Will the Akor, the Elf, and Xander be alright against Dux-class beasts?'*

'Xander and Illyana both utilize long-range weaponry and magic. They should both be fine.' Nalithor shot me an amused look. *'The Akor, despite his kind's natural affinity for fire, is an Earth Mage. Eyrian is what we like to call a Maelstrom Mage; he wields water,*

lightning, and wind in unison.

'However, unlike Xander and Illyana, most of us prefer to fight at close range. As such, it will be the four of us on the frontline while those two cover us from their vantage points in the trees.'

"My name is Azhar, by the way, Arianna-jiss." The Akor adopted a formal tone, causing me to glance at him. "Eyrian and Nalithor have told me of their sparring matches with you. It is rare for them to praise someone so highly. I look forward to fighting with you."

"He's my partner in the interim." Xander grinned, slinging an arm around the buff Akor's shoulders.

"A pleasure, I'm sure," I responded after a moment, choosing to be polite even though their power and scents didn't interest me.

I spent the remainder of our short trip in silence, half-listening to the others talk and half-examining the scenery of the Dauthrmiran Crater. Soon we shot through the obsidian spires bordering the crater and into the luscious, blooming Abrantia Valley. Our pilot landed the airship where the glassy stone faded into dirt and eventually grass. Nalithor ordered the crew to keep the airship there while we worked, then called for the rest of us to disembark.

My nose wrinkled when I stepped out of the ship and the stench of Chaos Beasts filled my nose. I fastened the clasps of my coat to protect myself from the cool breeze and then sniffed at the air again. It was strong enough that it almost overpowered both

Nalithor's scent, and the woodsy scent of the massive tiger awaiting us.

"Amakiir, have the beasts maintained their pace?" Nalithor asked, but the monstrous tiger ignored him to stare at me instead.

"Djialkan, cease your hiding," Amakiir rumbled, eliciting an irritated huff from the fae-dragon. Djialkan appeared on my shoulder from a ripple of shadow and nodded to the massive tiger. "That's better. Girl, you already caught their scent, didn't you?"

"They're a lot of them." I nodded. "And they're picking up their pace."

"You can smell them from here?" Nalithor studied me for a moment before turning to look at Amakiir. "In that case I suppose that, with your permission, we should hurry."

"Girl, try not to devour *this one* or the Elf." Amakiir snorted, seeming to ignore the Adinvyr altogether *again*. "Enjoy your hunt."

Amakiir bounded off without another word, causing Nalithor to glance down at me with a befuddled expression on his face. Eyrian and the rest of our group had already begun to wander aimlessly through the tall grass and in the approximate direction of the beasts. It irked me. They clearly had no idea where they were going.

"Not that way," I called, my voice firm as I used a small burst of shadow to leap over their heads and draw their attention. "They're veered off closer to the barrier. It seems as though they're trying to follow the very edge of the valley."

Before anyone could question me, I turned and stalked through the tall blue grass, tracking the disgusting scent of the beasts. Nalithor hadn't been kidding when he said there were at least a dozen of them—there was no other way the stench would be so strong or the grass so matted. It had been a long time since I'd sensed or otherwise encountered such a large group of beasts, but something smelled "off" about this pack.

However, too much time had passed and displaced their scent. I couldn't quite detect what was so wrong about it.

I glanced up to my right when Nalithor fell into step with me, and then looked up a little more to examine the blade of the spear he'd summoned and strapped to his back. At least I couldn't claim he was unprepared, unlike most of our comrades. It looked as though he and Eyrian were the only ones with weapons drawn from their jewelry or shrizars already.

That aside, Nalithor was examining me with that strange look in his eye again.

'What is it?' I refocused my gaze forward since he seemed so intent on staring.

'It's unusual for Amakiir to recognize someone as a hunter without *having seen them in action for himself,'* Nalithor murmured, drawing a few fingers down my spine. *'Eyrian implied that your sense of smell was stronger than that of an average Human's, but... I honestly thought he was joking, despite your occasional comments.*

'If your sense of smell is this strong, then I'm even more curious

about why I affect you so little.'

I grimaced at him before narrowing my eyes behind my mask and searching the tree line ahead of us. The trees were enormous, and I could spot where branches had been broken, trunks clawed, and plants trampled by the beast's passing. Score marks dug at least a foot deep into some of the larger trees, revealing their dark blue wood and black sap.

'The sap hasn't dried yet. We must be close.' I pursed my lips and hurried to shackle my bloodlust into place. However, judging by Nalithor's smirk, he had noticed. *'Damn it. Did the others—'*

"You're a frightening woman, you know that?" Eyrian snorted from behind us. "Try to leave us *some* of the beasts, alright?"

"Wait here." I frowned, coming to a stop by the forest's edge as a familiar musty scent filled my nose. Nalithor shot me a questioning glance, so I reached out to him again, *'Something is off.'*

'Will you be alright?' Nalithor asked, his concerned expression shifting into a smile when I vanished into the tree's shadows. "Arianna-jiss is going to scout ahead. She says something 'smells off.'"

I ignored the hint of sarcasm in his voice and instead propelled myself through the shadows of the towering trees, aware of Djialkan still on my shoulder. That disgusting, familiar scent grew ever stronger as we neared the beasts. I grit my teeth, slipping from one shadow to the next at an increasing pace. Dispersing into shadows was a strain, but it was much quicker than making our way through to forest blind and on foot.

I sunk into the shadow of a particularly large tree and frowned, examining the group of Chaos Beasts. They were deep within the forest but had stopped in a clearing. However, it was the people with them that concerned me, not the monsters themselves. I would have recognized those feathered wings—sometimes white, sometimes gold—anywhere. *'What are* Angels *doing alongside beasts...?'*

"Have the lesser beasts prepare a line of defense here," one of the Angels snapped, revealing rows of jagged teeth. "They need to buy us more time for our work."

One of the Duxes nodded his eyeless head in understanding and then turned to relay the information to the other beasts via grunts from the maw in its abdomen. Thick yellow slobber spewed everywhere as it "spoke." I watched for a few minutes as the lesser beasts spread throughout the trees, listening for any more pertinent information. The Angels seemed capable of flight still, but none of the other monsters appeared to have wings.

Scowling, I raced back the way I had come with enough speed to alarm Djialkan, causing him to dig his talons into my shoulder. Mere minutes passed before I burst out of the forest from above my comrades, startling everyone *except* for the intrigued Adinvyr. *'Tch, he must've been monitoring me through the shadows.'*

"You look *pissed.*" Eyrian pointed at my face. "What did—"

"There's at least five Angels with the beasts, and they're giving orders directly to the Duxes. The Duxes appear to be relaying orders to dozens of weaker beasts," I snapped, rising from the crouch I'd landed in. "At least, I think they're Angels. They have multiple rows of *really* nasty teeth."

"Angels corrupted by the blood of beasts?" Azhar frowned, glancing to Nalithor as he growled. "They won't be able to fly well within the trees, but this still poses a problem for us all."

"They've instructed the weaker ones to impede us so that they can 'work,'" I continued pointedly, causing Nalithor to face me with a deep frown. "I couldn't determine what their 'work' is, but I doubt it's anything good considering how close they are to the Dauthrmiran Barrier."

"Show us where they are." Nalithor motioned to his temples. "I don't like this either. We'll move in immediately."

I obliged, much to the dismay of our comrades. However, none of them questioned me. Instead we all turned and raced into the forest in search of our prey. I caught sight of Nalithor leaping through the branches above me as I slipped into the shadows. He kept casting me curious glances as we ran, looking as if he was judging the way I moved through the darkness.

Hearing a grunt, I turned my attention forward and leapt out of the darkness, swinging my scythe through a deer-sized beast. My blade cleaved it two and less than a second later I had entered a new shadow. I increased my speed and turned in the direction of the closest Dux I could sense. My bloodlust was beginning to slip but my concern about hiding it was deteriorating faster. Finally, I had things to kill!

'You take the one on the left, I'll take the one on the right,' Nalithor offered, veering away from our comrades to follow me. *'You must have spent a lot of time hunting beasts in the forests around X'shmir. You move incredibly well through the trees.'*

'There wasn't much else to entertain me,' I replied as Djialkan snorted and flew off my shoulder. *'Djialkan will stay in the trees and alert us if he spies any aerial beasts or Angels while we're dealing with the Duxes.'*

Nalithor nodded and dropped to the ground beside me as I sprung out of the shadows to run on foot. I admired the Adinvyr's graceful, predatory movements for a few seconds before refocusing on our task; we had beasts to kill, and with any luck I could take out some of the Angels as revenge for the torture they had put me through.

CHAPTER EIGHTEEN
Unmasked

I took in Arianna's graceful movements as she ran through the underbrush beside me. She had a determined, yet delighted, expression on her face. The more I watched her run, and occasionally leap over a branch or boulder, I realized that the fox on her crest was incredibly fitting. Her movements were distinctly vulpine down to the very way she scented the air. However, something about the set of her jaw and slight furrowing of her brow made me uneasy. It seemed as though something was still bothering her.

Without warning, Arianna suddenly crouched and pulled shadows from all around us, gathering each of them beneath her feet. In less than a second, she used the condensed darkness to launch herself through the air, leaving an arc of residual shadow in the air behind her. The glint of icy blades running along her forearms was the only hint I caught of a weapon before she was out of sight. I shook my head, laughing, as her bloodlust rippled through the forest untamed. As foxlike as she was, bloodlust like *that* rivaled even my own.

Within moments Arianna's victim was wailing in pain. I decided to make my way to the beast I'd promised to deal with. As tempting as it was to watch the princess rip the beast apart, it was obvious that she could handle herself. Arianna didn't require my help, let alone an audience.

I chased after my prey and swung my spear through the few beasts that attempted to slow my pace. From what Arianna had seen, I had expected more of the little ones. Yet, by the time I had caught up to the Dux, I could count the lesser beasts on a single hand. I stalked the Dux for a moment, a frown settling on my face. Its movements seemed strange.

'Have you ever heard of someone drugging beasts?' Arianna's inquisitive tone was a distinct mismatch to the overwhelming bloodlust laced with her presence. My breath caught in my throat and I grew still, rushing to strengthen my barriers against the troublesome woman. She seemed oblivious to her effect on me and continued, *'The one I just killed was wobbling around like a drunkard.'*

'As is mine,' I replied once comfortable with my strengthened

shields. *'Only three lesser creatures attempted to get in my way. However, they weren't acting the same as this Dux.'*

I had experienced small tastes of Arianna's bloodlust before, but this degree of it made the previous instances look like nothing by comparison. It astonished me. It was comparable to the near-blinding rage and desire to kill that I felt whenever I detected something that needed to die for disrupting the Balance. Even most Adinvyr, let alone other races of Devillians, couldn't relate to what such things made me feel. Yet this woman matched or even surpassed it. *'What could possibly elicit this type of reaction from a "Human" princess?'*

'Their blood smells different,' Arianna offered. *'Gods, kill yours already! Otherwise I'm going to get there first, and you'll be all out of fun!'*

Arianna's presence faded from my mind, but I felt her closing the distance between us fast. It was as if the shadows themselves were molding to reflect her ferocity. I chuckled and shook my head before drawing my spear once more. A set of white and platinum armor shimmered into existence around me before I launched myself at the wobbling beast.

If Arianna wanted a contest, I was more than happy to provide her with one.

A Dux should have taken me at *least* several minutes to slay, however the creature was far too disoriented. I was able to dispatch it in a matter of seconds—and through pure physical strength.

Leaning against my spear, I grimaced at the corpse and studied it. Arianna was right; their blood smelled different. There was a sickeningly sweet undertone that I couldn't recognize.

"You still insist on calling *that* armor?" Arianna dropped down from a branch above me and the pointed at my exposed torso, her face flushing when I smirked. "What do you think? Do you recognize the scent?"

"No. I haven't smelled anything like it before." I shook my head and then glanced over my shoulder, listening to the sound of distant beasts roaring in pain. "We should see if we can find where the Angels ran—or flew—off to. I don't like the idea that corrupted Angels have 'work' to attend to so close to the barrier."

Arianna nodded and motioned for me to follow her. It made me wonder if perhaps she could smell the Angels as well, but I didn't quite understand why her sense of smell was so strong to begin with. As far as I could tell she was still mostly Human, for now, and much to my displeasure. Despite that, she followed her nose and instincts better than most of the Devillians I had grown up with. *'Is this the product of hunting beasts so often in the wilds around X'shmir? Or is something else the reason for her strong senses?'*

'The princess said there were five Angels, right?' Eyrian's grim voice burst into my thoughts, causing me to frown deeper.

'She did, but why are you asking me?' I countered.

'None of us can break through those damn barriers of hers!' Eyrian snorted. *'Looks like the beasts turned on the Angels. They've been*

mauled and are very *dead. We're hunting down the rest of the Duxes now.'*

'You blocked the others from your thoughts?' I asked Arianna, watching as she leapt into a tree and crouched on a branch. She looked as if she was searching for something.

'They talk too much.' Arianna's reply was simple and to the point, yet it clashed with the wild grin growing on her face. The sound of her heartbeat grew faster with excitement as she leaned forward on her branch. *'So, what do you call a beast that's larger than a Dux?'*

'Larger than...?' I leapt into the tree beside Arianna and stared at her quarry in disbelief. The creature certainly resembled a Chaos Beast, but it was many times the size of a Dux. I couldn't comprehend how something of its size and shape could possibly move on its own. Like X'shmiran beasts, it smelled of death. *'We've...never found a beast this large before.'*

'It's weaker than a Dux,' Arianna stated conversationally, shivering as she drew shadows to herself once more. *'Let's kill it!'*

Before I could caution her, Arianna leapt through the branches and then into open air. She summoned her scythe in one hand and conjured darkness along its blade to extend its reach. In one smooth motion she had removed one of the creature's house-sized arms. Platforms of darkness popped into existence around the creature's body, giving the princess something to land on before she sprung forward again. I couldn't help but laugh as I watched her ping-pong herself around the beast's body. Her fighting style was chaotic, as always, but her movements were fluid.

Watching her hurtle around the unknown beast made it quite clear that this petite woman had many times the strength of a Human.

'Or is it really that weak of a beast? Is she truly so strong?' I trained my eye on the princess's blade, watching as it cut through the beast's hide and bone like a hot knife through butter. *'She is strong… But she shouldn't be capable of slicing through bone like that. Something is wrong with this monstrosity.'*

I detected Aurelian's familiar ripple of magic as Arianna's Dauthrmiran-style clothing disappeared, overtaken by one of her sets of light armor. The dancer-like armor gave her better range of movement and allowed her to increase her speed. The mixture of leather and cloth didn't seem like it would do much to protect her from a physical blow, but I had a feeling that mobility was all she was concerned with. I certainly wasn't going to complain about the shift. She was quite nice to look at.

I shook my head at myself and then dashed forward to join her in the assault. Arianna said nothing but seemed aware of my presence. She shifted her patterns slightly as if to adjust for my incoming strike. I frowned when my spear bit into the beast's flesh—it ripped through muscle and bone as if air was my opponent. Once again, the princess had proved correct; this beast was weaker than a Dux despite its size. Nor did it appear to have any poisonous features.

We gradually dismembered the gigantic monstrosity. Despite Arianna having dismembered the creature long ago, the damned thing was still alive. The bloodthirsty princess's chest was rising and falling more quickly now as we rested in the air above the beast. Arianna looked displeased while she studied the creature, but we both soon grew still as something unexpected happened; the beast had begun regenerating its arms. Thankfully, it hadn't begun to regenerate its legs or head at least…yet.

'That's new…' I frowned and then glanced at Arianna, watching another twisted grin cross her face. *'Still not tired, hmmm?'*

'Who has the time to be tired when we're having so much fun?' Arianna turned to shoot me a cheerful smile that made my heart melt. *'If I distract it, can you examine it? It should have a heart somewhere. We need to find that and put it out of its misery. As much as I enjoy fighting to the soundtrack of screams… Well. Its wailing is quite pitiful with its head missing, don't you think?'*

'You really are something else, you know that?' I chuckled. *'Very well. You fight, I'll observe. Our comrades seem to be dealing with the remaining Duxes still.'*

'Let's hurry, then, so we can kill those too!' Arianna exclaimed with a little too much excitement. She slid from her perch and hurtled to the beast with renewed vigor.

'Perhaps her labored breathing was from excitement and not

exhaustion?' I arched an eyebrow, tracking Arianna's movements for a moment before shifting my gaze to the immobile beast itself.

I watched in disbelief when Arianna tore one of the regenerated arms from the creature's body. A single yank from her bare hand was all it took. While it hadn't regrown completely as of yet, it had still reached the size of a Dux's arm by now, if not more. Her strength made me wary.

Eyrian was quite right in his original assessment of the princess; she truly enjoyed herself while fighting. Perhaps too much. I had noticed it in our sparring matches of course, but her arousal had never been *this* high whilst fighting me. The Archmagi would have a difficult time finding someone to partner her with if hunting made her excited to such a degree. Despite being one of the oldest Adinvyr, I found the sweet scent of her arousal mingled with the immense pressure of her bloodlust near-unbearable.

I bared my teeth in a feral growl when the beast slashed upwards at Arianna out of nowhere. It was the first move the damned creature had made since we stumbled across it, and it had moved fast enough to land a strike against her. My rage bubbled over the moment I caught the scent of Arianna's blood in the air.

'How dare that…that thing *touch her?!'* I shifted my grip on my spear, prepared to tear the beast to ribbons for what it had done. *'I'll see to it that—'*

"You son of a bitch!" Arianna roared. Unrelenting power and bloodlust exploded outward from the princess, startling me from my own rage as her unadulterated fury drowned out any hint of her prior arousal.

The pure hatred and anger pouring off the princess was so thick that I could barely breathe. Everything in the forest grew still as the princess's bloodlust threatened to consume it all. It took me longer than it should have to determine what had infuriated her to such an extent. The beast's strike had shredded her mask from her face, leaving a bleeding gash down her left cheek and down to her jawline. It had missed her eye but, judging from the amount of bleeding, the wound was deep.

I watched in fascination as Arianna reached up to her hair sticks and withdrew them with a flourish, sending the sheaths of their miniscule blades skittering across the ground. She fanned the concealed weapons between her fingers and then, with a sharp motion, flung them into the beast's hide. Without pause, Arianna hacked into the creature's body with her scythe. Her long dark brown curls cascaded down her back and to mid-thigh, bouncing and swaying chaotically to the rhythm of her attacks. She didn't stay in one place for long, and instead carved chunks of meat from the creature in one place before darting to one of her other platforms to repeat the process.

Despite my love of long hair, Arianna's eyes were what captured my attention. They were an incredible, and familiar, shade of electric blue. As with Darius, Arianna's pupils were slits. Although she was consumed by rage, I still found her beautiful.

The scent of poison caught my attention when a chunk of meat flew through the air and passed me. Several of Arianna's hair sticks were lodged in it and were the source of the offensive smell. I frowned, wrinkling my nose at the acrid scent. Perhaps she was angrier than I had initially given her credit for. Arianna didn't seem like the sort to use poison against her prey and, judging from the beast's scream, her poison wasn't the kind meant to induce paralysis or death—she wanted the beast to suffer.

I chose to remain on my perch and watched Arianna make quick work of the beast. Shimmering shields generated by the crystals in her jewelry protected her from the seemingly endless spray of beast blood. It would have been catastrophic if the creature's blood came into contact with the wound she'd sustained. If I sensed any sign of the shields faltering, *then* I would intervene. Until then, keeping my distance from the enraged princess seemed safer.

'Her wound…' I shifted my gaze to Arianna's cheek before reaching out to Djialkan. *'Black blood? She is less Human than I believed?'*

'She is,' Djialkan replied. *'Once the beast is dead you should be able to approach and heal her. Arianna usually calms once whatever injured her has died. She gets quite tetchy when someone or something managed to wound her. It is a rare occurrence.'*

I shot a filthy look up at the circling fae-dragon, cursing him for the lack of information. Sighing, I turned my gaze downwards to study Arianna once more. Her movements were still graceful and precise despite the bestial fury with which she tore into the monster. Then again, her fighting style often seemed bestial even when she wasn't enraged. It didn't take long for her to finish off the beast, and I couldn't help but find myself impressed that she had refrained from using fire magic during her rampage.

She certainly hadn't neglected her other elements.

I hopped from my perch and landed lightly on the ground, preparing to approach the princess. However, she turned to face away from me, cradling her wounded cheek in one hand. Blue-black blood poured between her fingers and trickled down her forearm, but she seemed intent on avoiding me.

"Don't look!" Arianna grumbled, bristling.

"You don't want me to heal you?" Frowning, I sent several tendrils of my power towards her in an attempt to ascertain why she was being defensive toward me.

"But..." Arianna trailed off with a heavy sigh and an almost imperceptible shake of her head. "I'm not... Ugh. I'll be fine, okay?"

I smiled and placed a hand on her shoulder when I realized what was bothering her most. Of all things, she was concerned that her rampage had made her seem undesirable. *That*, at least, was something she couldn't hide from an Adinvyr.

Perhaps the Old Ways had affected this half of the twins more than I had come to believe. Arianna didn't strike me as someone who lacked self-confidence. Umbral Mages were forced to hide their faces so that others wouldn't be drawn in by a pretty facade, only to encounter the "ugliness within." Had she taken it a little too literally, or had the X'shmirans warped that as well?

Either way, it surprised me that the little vixen was concerned about what *I* might think of her after such a display. It made it clearer that Arianna still hadn't acclimated to our cultural differences. Had she put on a display in front of younger Adinvyr, they likely would have proposed to her. I bit back a smirk. *'She would either skin them, or she would turn bashful and hide somewhere.'*

"I can't just sit back and let that pretty face of yours bleed." I sighed at her and then gripped her chin. I leaned down to kiss her wounded cheek, tasting her sweet blood on my lips. Her face flushed scarlet and she averted her gaze again. "You really are adorable, you know that? Now, hold still so I can heal you."

I wasn't sure if she cooperated because she was flustered, or if she was feeling obedient. Alas, I knew I needed to focus on healing her before pondering such things. Preferably *before* the scent, and brief taste, of her blood drove me insane. I wasn't even hungry and yet I still considered taking a bite out of her for myself.

Shaking the thoughts from my mind, I held Arianna's face in my right hand and summoned shadows around my left. Arianna grumbled a quiet curse when I pressed my fingertips to her wound and began healing it. That it stung came as no surprise. The gash was much deeper than I first thought; the damned beast had torn almost all the way through her cheek.

"Not going to run off to find your mask?" I inquired, carefully working my darkness through her wound.

'No point,' Arianna replied, her grumpiness tinging her thoughts. *'Bastard tore it into pieces. So, it's not like I can put it back on.'*

"Good. I can enjoy this treat for a little longer then," I mused, chuckling when her face turned a pretty shade of pink. "Do you sense anything else 'wrong' nearby?"

Arianna paused, her plush lips parting as her eyes grew unfocused. She cast her power through the forest and, after a few moments, her gaze refocused. She glanced up at me with such an adorable, pouty expression that I wanted to reach down and squeeze her.

"They're all dead already," Arianna answered with a heavy sigh. She shot me a confused look when I laughed. "What's so funny?"

"I wasn't prepared for such a disappointed and pouty response." I smirked, wiping the blood from her cheek. Her left eye closed and she pouted more as I stroked her cheek a few more times for good measure. "Correct me if I'm wrong, but I get the feeling that's the face you would make if someone stole your tea."

"Hmmm. Tea... I want some," Arianna murmured, averting her gaze shortly in thought. "Did you get all of the blood off?"

I couldn't help but tease her more. After releasing her face, I brought my fingers to my lips and slowly lapped her blood from my fingertips. I was well rewarded. Her face turned crimson again, yet she seemed entranced and unable to look away from me. Her pupils dilated as she tracked me. She was almost like a fox, ready to pounce. Grinning, I leaned down and gripped her chin again, tilting her head up so that she had to look me in the eyes.

"Does that answer your question, *princess?*" I asked with false innocence, watching as she nodded and looked up at me with wide eyes. "Ahhh... You are just too cute. How am I supposed to keep this treat to myself? We need to return to the ship with our comrades soon..."

'Such a shame. This was meant to be a several day trip...' I kept the thought private, burning Arianna's features into my memory. *'I will skin Darius if he attempts to have Arianna wear masks again.'*

"Not a treat!" Arianna protested when I released her. Her expression remained bashful, her cheeks still rosy, as she turned to look away from me. Arianna's armor disappeared into her jewelry as her clothing from before returned, though she fidgeted with the fit for a few moments before addressing me again, "I'm more concerned with 'what' that damn thing was, and what made the beasts seem so...drunk."

"Let's take samples then," I offered, summoning several crystalline vials and fanning them between my fingers. "Amakiir will dispose of the bodies after we've left. If we want to investigate this issue, we will have to take the samples now. There won't be another chance."

Arianna nodded and then turned her attention away from me. She seemed to consider something. Her eyes ticked back and forth almost as if she was reading a book, but they had grown unfocused again. After a moment she braced one arm in the other and began tapping her fist against her cheek as she thought. It was almost like she was oblivious to her surroundings, but the occasional spike of bloodlust gave me the feeling that she was reviewing her battles with the beasts. I decided to leave her to her thoughts and focused my attention on collecting samples of the unknown beast.

"What, exactly, corrupted the Angels?" Arianna broke the silence after several minutes as she followed me back to the Dux I had slain.

"Beast blood." I motioned at her cheek and then continued, "It can happen when Chaos Beast blood enters someone's system through an open wound or ingestion. That's why the crystals in Aurelian's creations create shields around us in battle—they exist only to repel the blood of beasts.

"However, in the past few decades, many Elven, Human, and other 'weak' species have begun using beast blood as a recreational drug. Small doses won't cause corruption. Alas, it has mind-altering properties. Consumers usually can't limit themselves to 'small' doses."

"Since you said 'weak' species, I'm assuming it grants them increased strength?" Arianna questioned. I nodded my reply, so she continued, "Well, I guess that explains why they smelled so similar to beasts…"

I watched Arianna as she fidgeted with both her robes and her curls in discomfort. Her cheeks were still a little rosy, but it looked as though it was because she had settled into being shy, seeing as she had finally calmed down. She kept gnawing on her lower lip as her gaze flicked around the woods surrounding us. Despite the fact her killing frenzy had subsided, her heartbeat was still elevated from nervousness.

"You're this unaccustomed to revealing your face?" I asked, earning her full, albeit surprised, attention once more. "I assure you that you don't have anything to worry about. If, for some reason, someone sees fit to cause you trouble… Well. You are more than capable of handling them yourself, are you not?"

"Actually, I'm worried about something else," Arianna replied, her eyes flitting down my arms and tracking my hands as I resumed gathering samples. "Remember? Darius said that only my partner is allowed to see my face." She paused to motion up at her chin, a small pout forming on her lips. "What if they force you to accept me as your partner?"

"I can't claim that I'm opposed to the idea," I replied, rising to my feet. I dismissed the vials into my shrizar and then turned to face the princess fully. "That said, you should keep in mind that I'm not the only one who will have seen your face by the time we return to Dauthrmir. I don't think they will be able to use that excuse."

Arianna sighed and nodded, then followed me once I beckoned for her to join me. Her sigh almost sounded like one of disappointment, but I pushed it from my mind for the moment. Although I wasn't quite prepared to return to the city so soon, I didn't want to remain in the forest for much longer either. If more beasts, or worse, the Exiles, showed up to see what was taking so long, the results would be disastrous.

The more distance we put between us and the corpses, the more Arianna appeared to relax. Even so, her face remained alert. Finally, being able to see her face made it clear to me just how different she was from Darius. Arianna's gaze was bright and clear, even fierce at times. Darius' was often lost or foggy. At this point it came as no surprise to me that they appeared to be opposites in that regard. Darius was clearly the scatterbrained one.

"Does Darius share your sense of smell?" Curiosity got the better of me after several minutes of walking in silence. Arianna turned her head and blinked up at me for a moment with her head tilted to the side; it was much cuter now that I could see her entire face. *'I get the feeling Alala isn't the reason for the foxes on Arianna's crest and robes.'*

"He isn't as good at separating or identifying scents, but yes," Arianna replied after a moment of thought. She then pointed a finger against my bicep and shot me a heart-melting yet devilish grin, continuing, "Darius has barely been able to concentrate for the past few *days* you know. All because of your scent clinging to the books you assigned him!

"It's kind of funny, honestly. He tends to pace when he's reading, so he keeps walking into things."

"*My* scent?" I frowned at her. "The two of you can detect the scents of *individual people?*"

"That's right." Arianna nodded, then begun counting off her fingers. "Darius smells floral. Lucifer smells like old books and leather chairs. Xander smells kind of minty. Azhar smells like wood smoke. The strumpet smells like honeysuckle—which I *hate*, mind you. Eyrian smells like the ocean, sans fish."

"And me?" I arched an eyebrow when she flushed and averted her gaze.

"A mix of sweet spices, musk, hints of sandalwood…" Arianna trailed off, seeming lost in thought.

"Hmmm? '*Sweet*' spices?" I nudged her, earning a sheepish smile. *'That was rather more detailed than her descriptions of the others. Why?'*

"Yes. 'Sweet' spices. I'm not sure what else to call it." Arianna laughed, tugging her long hair over one shoulder. "Like the type of spices used to bake sweet pastries. I just can't identify which specific ones—it's like a mix, or perhaps a spice I'm unfamiliar with. Likely the latter, all things considered."

"Was it necessary to call her 'the strumpet?'" I teased, ruffling Arianna's hair.

"Absolutely!" Arianna responded with a nod, before reaching up with both hands and attempting to dislodge mine from her head. "Oh… You said we should be gone for several days, didn't you? Do we have more beasts to hunt somewhere?"

There was an eager, bloodthirsty gleam in Arianna's eyes when she looked up at me. I couldn't help but grin at her expression. She was like a kitten begging for milk, except *blood* was what she wanted to spill. I found it terribly endearing. Furthermore, I found myself growing ever more curious about the results of her DSO test.

I wasn't sure if I would accept anyone, aside from myself, as her partner.

"Do you sense any?" I countered, watching her face with amusement.

'I…want another chance to kiss her.' I studied the full lips that Arianna always seemed to have painted scarlet. *'Her lips were soft, and sweet… Perhaps I should have given her a longer kiss.'*

"No. Nothing." Arianna sighed, disappointed. "Amakiir and his people are waiting a little outside the forest. I don't sense anything else interesting."

Intrigued, I spread my own power through the air and, sure enough, Arianna was correct. Dozens of Varjior waited in the fields beyond the forest's edge, accompanied by the tiger bastard himself. They seemed to be in pleasant enough moods, and the little vixen beside me didn't seem concerned in the slightest.

"You two could have waited!" Illyana snapped from somewhere behind us. This time, I saw the corner of Arianna's eye twitch. The princess didn't turn, and instead reached up into the air, snatching the arrow that the Elf had fired between us.

"I don't know about you, but *I* rather dislike the scent of those fucking creatures and their blood!" Arianna retorted, breaking the arrow in half before she rounded on our comrades. She settled one hand on her hip and pointed at the Elf with her other. "*You* still have twenty-eight of your thirty arrows. Did you even *do* anything while the men were fighting? Or did you just sit in a tree and try not to piss yourself, *Elf?*"

Neither Eyrian nor I could contain our laughter. Illyana flushed with rage, her haughty sneer twisting into a more menacing and foul expression. Arianna glared back at the Elven woman, an aura of cold, calm anger surrounding her. It seemed as though the princess was gauging whether to end Illyana where she stood, or if she should give her the chance to redeem herself. I got the feeling that Arianna's cold anger could burst into a fiery rage at any moment...yet I didn't feel concerned. Quite the contrary. I wanted to see it.

The princess had hit the nail on the head. Illyana had fired one other arrow aside from the one that she had shot between Arianna and myself. By the feel of the Elf's aura, she hadn't tapped into much of her magic either—there was almost no perceptible hum around her.

Arianna seemed to hold particular distaste for someone who had tagged along and contributed little to nothing. Instead of confronting Illyana further or attacking her, Arianna simply turned on her heel and resumed walking towards the forest's edge.

I exchanged an amused look with Eyrian before catching up to Arianna and falling into step with her once more. From a distance her silent fuming was unnoticeable, but once beside her I could feel the simmering anger rippling around her.

Alas, it appeared that Illyana was far angrier than Arianna. I sensed several more arrows, this time aimed at the princess's back. Scowling, I raised a shield of stone behind Arianna at nearly the same time as the princess herself summoned a barrier of thick ice. The arrows pierced my stone and bore several inches into Arianna's ice. In an instant, I turned and grabbed Illyana by the throat and lifted her into the air. The Elf's vertebrae strained and popped beneath my grip on her neck. It took a moment for the Elf to register that I had closed the distance between us, let alone that I was threatening to end her.

"Explain to me why I shouldn't execute you for turning on one of your comrades," I demanded, glaring at the Elf.

The sensation of feminine hands against my torso and warmth leaning into my side made me glance down. Arianna had pressed herself against my left side, but her eyes were focused on the dangling Elf. The princess nibbled at one of her fingers as she watched Illyana's struggle. Arianna looked like she was trying to choose between pastries, not like she wished for someone's death.

That bloodthirsty glint had returned to Arianna's eyes and, after a moment of watching Illyana's legs swing, the princess looked up at me with an almost begging look.

"If you decide to execute her, can I do it instead?" Arianna purred, startling me as one of her small, soft hands slid up my torso and her long nails grazed my exposed skin.

I faltered, unable to think of a response as I stared down at the bloodthirsty woman. My grip on Illyana's throat twitched as I considered it, earning a fearful shriek from the Elf. Arianna dug her nails into my abdomen when my attention drifted away from her, almost hard enough to draw blood. I glanced between Illyana and Arianna for a moment, before returning my full attention to the considerably more dangerous of the two. *'It is tempting, but…'*

'You're really *considering it, aren't you?'* Eyrian asked dryly, though I kept my eyes on the demanding, bloodthirsty princess beside me. Arianna bit her lower lip and shot a sideways look at the Elf. *'Are you really going to let the girl lure you into trouble like* that?'

"She's not my comrade!" Illyana hissed, continuing to struggle. "This lowly little Human *bitch* needs to—"

"Eyrian, get your partner under control before I decide to grant Arianna's request," I spoke, my tone frigid.

Eyrian grew pale in response to whatever look Arianna shot him.

'She's cute, but…' Eyrian winced and then grabbed Illyana,

slinging her over his shoulder. *'Come to think of it, what happened to the girl's mask?'*

'A Chaos Beast shredded it off her, nearly tearing through her face in the process,' I replied, shooting a bitter look at the Elf as Eyrian carted her past us.

'That what the overwhelming spike of rage and power was about?' Eyrian sighed, shaking his head. *'I can't blame you for almost giving in to her request. Arianna is damn adorable, and Illyana is a haughty bitch. They need to find me a new partner already!'*

I shot a glare at Eyrian's back before glancing down at Arianna and giving her a gentle nudge. The way she was tracking Illyana almost made her seem hungry. It made me wonder if her bloodthirst was perhaps literal. Arianna glanced up at me and then took several quick steps away from me, a bashful look forming on her face. I wouldn't have minded if she remained close to me...but I got the feeling that saying as much would only serve to make the princess even more skittish.

We followed Eyrian and his struggling partner through the forest, with Azhar and Xander bringing up the rear. They both seemed content to linger behind us, keeping a safe distance away from Arianna.

"The princess is quite the huntress," Amakiir remarked, settling his gaze on me the moment we stepped out of the forest. "It would appear she shaved several days off your hunt, no?"

"It would appear so." I nodded, glancing down at Arianna. She was examining the Varjior with faint curiosity, but I could feel her mind whirring beneath her shields already. "Was there anything else you needed assistance with, Amakiir? Or—"

"Hmmm…" Arianna grumbled, tensing beside me. I looked down at her, watching as she narrowed her eyes and surveyed the Varjior again before shooting me a sideways, questioning, glance. *'What is Amakiir's stance on his own people partaking of beast blood?'*

'His own…?' I frowned at her, earning an inquisitive look from Amakiir as he approached us. *'She wants to know what your stance is on your people drinking the blood of beasts.'*

'Let me speak with her privately.' Amakiir's frown deepened as he turned to Arianna. "Your Highness, let us step away for a moment."

I watched in silence as Arianna and Amakiir walked quite some distance away, speaking in low tones. Shaking my head, I turned my attention to the rest of our group. They all appeared to be in one piece, though Xander had sustained intentional damage as usual. Xander, Azhar, and Eyrian were all watching Arianna with a little too much interest for my tastes—and they seemed oblivious to my displeasure.

'Hmmm… I don't recall telling Amakiir that Arianna is royalty. Did Lucifer tell him?' I glanced at the pair and then back to my comrades, narrowing my eyes at them. *'Even Eyrian looks like he wants a piece of her! Honestly. What am I going to do with that woman?'*

"What do you think, Eyrian?" Xander asked, his eyes wandering down to Arianna's round ass. "Her test isn't back yet, is it? Mistress or slave?"

"Hard to say." Eyrian frowned, studying the princess from head-to-toe. "I'm going to say switch. Before I would've been inclined to say Mistress, but seeing how shy she is behind that mask of hers… I'm not so sure now."

"As if shyness is any indication." Azhar snorted with disdain, his tail snapping behind him. "You didn't catch the look she gave Nalithor when she asked if she could perform the execution in his stead. She is a slave."

"*I* think you're both wrong," Xander argued, shaking his head before licking his lips and grinning. "She'd make a fine Mistress, I think."

"I think that I may have to skin all three of you and hang your tanned hides in my study," I offered in a conversational tone, causing the three of them to turn towards me with startled expressions. "Now then—"

The four of us turned when we sensed Arianna's bloodlust spike high. In a flash, the dangerous princess had leapt into the group of Varjior. There was a strangled scream, followed by curses in multiple languages. I glanced nervously at Amakiir, but he looked pleased as he watched Arianna drag one of the females out of the crowd by the throat. Arianna seemed oblivious to the woman clawing her arm. The princess threw the frightened woman down at Amakiir's feet. The God of Varjior said something to Arianna, who simply nodded and began walking back to join us. She licked some of the blood off her forearm as she walked, much like a cat grooming itself. Yet there was something decidedly…erotic, about her mannerisms.

"What was *that* about?" Xander grinned down at the princess. "I'd be *happy* to clean that up for you, *Your Highness.*"

"If I was going to let *any* of you do what *you* are thinking, it'd be Nalithor!" Arianna retorted, bristling as she shot the Vampire an irritated glare. Xander's rising bloodlust was plain as day. Even if Arianna had truly been Human, I had no doubt that she would have still sensed it. Arianna turned her attention to the rest of us and spoke again, "That woman has been drinking beast blood. Amakiir is going to find out where she's been getting it, or from whom. Since they live a tribal lifestyle here, their contact with traders is limited, and he wants to make sure it didn't come out of Dauthrmir.

"He wants to know if we will stay in their village for the night and invited us to celebrate the success of our hunt with them. Of course, he said we're welcome to cleanse ourselves in the village's springs."

'Me? Oh, I am not letting her get away with that comment for free…' I shot an amused glance at the sulking Vampire before settling my attention on Arianna in full. She didn't seem to know what she had done, but she would soon enough.

"Illyana, will you behave? Or are you going to try to kill the princess again?" Eyrian asked.

"Let go of me!" The Elf snapped, kicking her legs in her renewed struggle.

"Just make her watch the airship." Arianna snorted, letting her bloodied arm fall to her side.

'The Varjior gouged you deeply.' I held out one hand, palm up, and waited for Arianna to give me her arm. *'Let me heal you.'*

'You seem to be doing that a lot today.' Arianna pouted, though she complied. *'I'll have to be more careful. Thank you.'*

'Xander is likely to take a bite out of you at this rate,' I informed her, amused by the disgusted grimace she made. *'Then again, so might I. You taste very sweet.'* I laughed when she twitched in response and her face flushed. *'Is that a bit of bias there, my dear?'*

"Is it really safe to tease her?" Eyrian asked pointedly, earning a filthy look from the princess in question. "I can't hear the two of you but, if you've turned that color, I can only assume he's teasing you or making you *very* angry."

"Neither of you are making a good case for me to remain unmasked, you know!" Arianna placed her free hand on her hip and shot both of us an agitated glare in turn.

"I'm of half a mind to 'accidentally' damage any masks you attempt to wear," I informed her, causing her to arch an eyebrow at me. "After all these cute expressions you've been making? Only a madman would sit idly by and let you resume wearing such things, Old Ways or not."

"He has a point." Eyrian jabbed his thumb at me as he looked down at Arianna. "Enough of that. Nali, are we going to accept Amakiir's offer?"

"We should." I nodded. "There's a chance that whoever the woman obtained beast blood from is still in the valley somewhere, and it'd be our job to deal with them if that's the case."

'If you want to return to Dauthrmir I can have the airship return you there,' I offered, releasing Arianna's arm. She examined her healed skin for a moment before yanking her sleeves down and shaking her head.

'I'm fine, and they have meat,' Arianna replied. *'I'm enjoying the time away from my dolt of a brother too. I swear he's been trying to kill me with the amount of vegetables he's been buying. I'm overdue for a barbeque.'*

'Then I'm going to have to ask that you stay nearby,' I started, earning a questioning look from her. *'I've known Xander for a long time, and he's a little too interested in you. The smell of your blood is driving him crazy despite its resemblance to Devillian blood.*

'While I trust him in battle, I don't trust him to keep his hands or fangs off you.'

'You said something about taking a bite of me yourself.' Arianna shot me a look and then crossed her arms, glancing at the Varjior as they called for us to follow them. *'Not that there's anything wrong with a little bite every once and a while, but... Why would an* Adinvyr

be considering a bite, hmmm?'

'Because we can feed on blood as well,' I replied with amusement, examining her from behind. *I'll have you know it's sexual* energy *that we feed on. Not sex itself. Of course, sex is the easiest way to access such energy. However, we can draw if from our surroundings—such as the shenanigans going on in the Scarlet District—or through blood.'*

'Through blood?' Arianna shook her head, seeming curious despite herself. *'How exactly does* that *work? I know traces of magic are carried through blood but—'*

"Because, my dear," I began in a whisper, pulling her back against my chest. I leaned down to speak into the right side of her throat, smirking when I felt her quickening pulse against my lips. "While we carry an aphrodisiac-like venom in *all* of our bodily fluids… Our venom is purest in our bite." I smiled into her skin when I heard her breath catch, then nipped lightly at her soft throat. "My fangs aren't for show, I assure you.

"Perhaps if you're a *very good girl* I will give you a personal demonstration, hmmm?"

'T-that's enough out of you!' Arianna yelped.

I chuckled and released her, watching as she hurried to catch up with the Varjior ahead of us.

She would truly be a fun chase.

CHAPTER NINETEEN
Damsel in Distress

"Arianna-jiss, are you alright?" A woman with sharp, birdlike features asked. "Andrea wounded you deeply."

"I'm fine." I shook my head and then pulled my sleeve back to show the woman. "Nalithor already saw to my wounds."

The woman frowned at my arm and then nodded before turning her attention to Amakiir and the other Varjior that had chosen to accompany us. Moving through the village in such a large group seemed unnecessary to me, but it looked as though my comrades had much to discuss with the Varjior and their god alike.

'Really though, does Nalithor have to tease me so much?' I kept the thought private and pulled my sleeve back down before shooting a glance in the Adinvyr's direction. *'Maybe I should just conjure a new*

mask and be done with it. Somehow he's managed to grow even cheekier now that I'm without one!'

I remained silent as we followed our Varjior hosts through a maze of tribal tents and roughhewn buildings. Decorations made from felled prey and scavenged treasures hung everywhere, even from sections of massive skeletons. I could only assume the large bones belonged to slain Chaos Beasts. Although I wanted to know more, it felt inappropriate to interrupt my comrade's deep conversation with Amakiir and his warriors.

Somehow, Eyrian managed to ignore Illyana's shouting and kicking as we made our way through the small village. The Elf remained hysterical and unapologetic. Some of the looks Nalithor and Xander both shot Illyana sent chills down my spine. They both looked like they wanted to kill her even more than I did. How Eyrian tuned out her struggling and constant shrieking was beyond me.

We soon came to a stop by a cluster of trees with dark brown bark. The cracks in the bark were filled with a sky-blue glow that flowed upwards through each tree, and led to leaves in varying shades of blue, green, and silver. The glow in the leaves was paler than what ran through the bark and shone brighter. A glance upward at the thick, twisting limbs revealed blankets and cushions nestled into almost every nook and cranny. *'Do some of the Varjior sleep in the trees? Some of those cushions are much too low to be for lookouts...'*

"Arianna, I hope you'll forgive me for underestimating you," Eyrian offered, coming to a stop beside me. "Would you be willing to spar me again? I won't hold back this time."

'A sparring match huh?' I shifted away from the looming trees and examined the serious expression on the Draekin's face. "Now?"

"Yes, now." Eyrian nodded.

"Don't you think sparring can wait?" Nalithor came to stand on my other side and frowned at Eyrian, his tail sway behind him. "I may have healed Arianna, but she lost a great deal of blood from her injuries. It would be ill-advised for you two to fight at full strength while she's recovering."

'He has a point, but...' I glanced between the two men a few times, then settled my gaze on Eyrian. "Do you plan to fight while restraining the bitc— Ahem. The Elf?"

"My warriors will see to it that the traitor is looked after." Amakiir motioned at Illyana before turning his attention to Nalithor. "It is unlike you to worry needlessly about a huntress, Nalithor. Beasts don't allow us breaks when we sustain injuries. I'm sure she has plenty of experience fighting while weakened."

"You can always interfere if you think their match has gone too far," Azhar pointed out when Nalithor opened his mouth to protest. "Assuming you can handle her wrath, anyway."

'If he truly is going to take you seriously... You should be careful.' Nalithor sighed and ran a hand through his hair, shooting me a concerned look. *'At full strength you should easily best him but—'*

'He isn't at full strength either. They handled more of the beasts than we did,' I countered with a small smile, watching as several Varjior women carted Illyana away. It was a shame we hadn't executed her instead.

'She is *Beshulthien royalty.'* Nalithor gave me a knowing look.

Amakiir led us through his maze-like settlement once more to find somewhere for Eyrian and I to fight. I found myself examining my surroundings and the Varjior deity himself. Now that had shifted to a bipedal form, Amakiir looked mostly Human. His bright orange hair hung in shaggy layers to his earlobes, his skin was tanned, and his jade green eyes had slit pupils.

It was beyond me how *anyone* in or around Vorpmasia had tanned skin.

The Varjior's sparring areas were significantly smaller than what I'd grown accustomed to in the Sapphire Quarter, but I had expected as much. This was a small village, and their sparring areas comprised of sandy soil lined in river stones. Eyrian and I took positions on opposite sides of the ring, whilst our comrades and Varjior hosts stood what they probably thought was a safe distance away.

Nalithor shot me another concerned look. His tail swayed slowly as he prodded me with tendrils of magic. I considered teasing him or perhaps making a joke, but I chose against it. I appreciated his concern and found it a little cute, even if unnecessary. *'Don't worry, I'll be fine.'*

"How about 'anything goes?'" Eyrian offered, a boyish grin spreading across his face. "Ah! Afterward we should go bathe in the springs before tonight's festivities right, Nalithor?"

"Bathe...?" I blinked at Eyrian and then looked toward Nalithor as well, finding a slight flush had entered the Adinvyr's face.

"She has only just now been freed from her mask and yet you would already ask her to bathe in the Devillian way?" Djialkan perched on a nearby boulder and snorted at the grinning Draekin. *"I will never understand Devillians."*

"To be fair, you also don't understand why 'fleshy two-legged creatures' like us wear clothes to begin with." I shot Djialkan a crooked grin, earning a small "humph" in return.

"Eyrian, you know full well that Varjior men and women do not bathe together. We expect you to abide by our customs while here." Amakiir grunted, shooting the Draekin a disapproving glare. "Arianna-jiss will bathe with the other unmated women of the village. You four will join the unmated males."

"Awww, what a shame." Xander shot me a sultry look, tilting his head as he examined me from head to toe. "You know, Your Highness, it's quite disappointing that you and your brother won't join us in the baths. Darius sure is quick to decline."

"He doesn't exactly want to see women—especially his *sister*—nude," I pointed out, shaking my head at the Vampire's attempt at an alluring expression. "Eyrian, let's get started, shall we? Be forewarned, I want to spar you again after we've both fully recovered."

"Of course." Eyrian nodded, then turned to shoot a devilish grin in Nalithor's direction. "Your turn to stand on the sidelines, Nalithor."

'That's a strange comment...' I glanced between them, watching as Nalithor crossed his arms and released a low growl. *'Is he... Is he jealous? I don't know how to take that. Not after all his teasing.'*

Eyrian gave me almost no time to react to his fist flying past my face. I danced backwards and adopted an offensive stance as the Draekin darted toward me again. He wasn't quite as fast as Nalithor, but he still moved with greater speed than I expected from a man of his size. *'I'm going to have to throw out my notions of large men being slow. Tch.'*

Eyrian really meant it when he had suggested "anything goes" for our fight. He showed no sign of hesitation when he summoned lightning, wind and water. The Draekin twisted the three elements into gauntlets, encasing his hands and forearms up to the elbow. His maelstrom-like gauntlets crackled and warped with power, charging the air with static.

Blocking his strikes would be difficult if I had to deal with condensed elements, and not just flesh against flesh.

'I'm still limited to ice, darkness, and wind.' I reminded myself, darting to the side of Eyrian's charge. *'His techniques and movements follow a different style from both mine and Nalithor's. I*

guess I'll use this as a learning experience.'

My head swam when I summoned darkness and twisted it around my hands, feet and shins. I clenched my jaw and forced my eyes to focus on Eyrian. *'Did I lose more blood than I thought? Maybe I should just end this quickly.'*

"Ha! You really do kick hard!" Eyrian laughed when my shin and pointed foot slammed across his chest. "It'll take more than that to bring a Draekin down!"

I slipped away as he pivoted to slash at me with his tail, nearly clipping me with it. Unlike Nalithor's more whip-like tail, Eyrian's was more draconic and lined with both ridges and spikes. Being hit by *that* was something I wanted to avoid at all costs.

'Shit!' I grit my teeth as my vision spun, leaving me with a split second to guard against Eyrian's kick. His shin crashed into my darkness-encased forearms and lifted me clean off my feet, sending my flying backwards. I attempted to slow myself with wind and darkness, but my head spun again, causing me to lose my grip on my elements. *'Maybe...I really did over do it.'*

"I knew you weren't alright." Nalithor sighed, catching me against his chest. One of his arms slipped around my waist to help me remain upright as I started to slump to the ground. "Arianna?"

"Dizzy..." I grumbled, lifting a hand up to my head. I attempted to pull away from the Adinvyr, but his grip tightened.

"Ah, ah, ah, careful." Nalithor purred, leaning down to nuzzle my shoulder. "Don't rush it. Let the dizziness subside first."

"Just how much blood did you lose, Arianna?" Eyrian approached us with a concerned expression on his face. "Your reaction times are suffering."

"You should have known it was a lot," Nalithor muttered, shooting Eyrian a look. "I wouldn't have suggested waiting if it wasn't serious."

"Ella, Kaera," Amakiir called to two women. "Escort Arianna-jiss to the springs. Djialkan, you will join the rest of the males and I."

'Will you be alright?' Nalithor questioned, squeezing me again before allowing the two women to pull me to my feet. *'That oaf shouldn't have—'*

'It's my own fault for being careless.' I cut him off with a small shake of my head, before turning to follow the cheerful women away. *'I've sustained worse wounds in the past. I'll be fine.'*

Unfortunately, the two Varjior women seemed incapable of *not* talking while they led me through the village. The springs weren't far from the sparring areas, but I quickly grew agitated.

Trees with glossy blue foliage and pale flowers loomed over the springs, shielding them outside elements. Each of the natural springs was surrounded by colorful blinds made of painted skins and furs, shielding them from unwanted eyes while also identifying which section was which.

Women were separated from men, and then further separated based on whether they were mated, unmated, or elderly. It made even less sense to me than the Draemiran bathing customs did.

I learned that the two women escorting me were sisters. Ella was the woman with knee-length pewter hair and scarlet eyes. Kaera had the same long, straight hair but hers was black, and her eyes were pink. Their animal form was that of something called a "vrandool"—a wolf-like creature native to the forests surrounding the Dauthrmiran Crater. In their non-shifted forms, the sisters looked like Elves.

"Here, let us help you," Ella offered, watching me plunk down on a boulder to strip. "You should really be careful about letting one of our kind hurt you! It wouldn't do for you to become one of us, now would it?"

"Our men sure wouldn't mind. They're always looking for strong mates," Kaera pointed out, rolling her eyes while Ella unfastened my corset.

"Become one of you?" I frowned at them. "What do you mean?"

"Varjior are similar to Vampires in the sense that we can 'turn' others into a Varjior," Ella replied with a small huff, tracking me as I dismissed my clothing into a shrizar. "Like Vampires, we can't turn Devillians, Angels, or divine beings. I can't tell what you are…but you should be careful."

"Damn!" Kaera whistled at me. "How do you keep the Devillians from hunting you? You must drive them wild in the baths. Varjior men would tear each other apart for a chance at you!"

"She's definitely got birthing hips." Ella nodded sagely, pushing me toward the steaming water. "How do you keep your breasts in place while fighting? Mine are smaller but still such a burden!"

Really? Birthing hips? I fucking hate that term!' I sighed inwardly, wading into the warm water. "I bathe by myself. Suffice to say, my people's customs are not conducive to anyone seeing me—nude or otherwise."

The sisters nodded their understanding and then joined me in the spring. I released a small sigh, sinking into the water up to my chin. There was no denying that it felt nice, though I would have preferred to bathe alone. I remained silent and, after a few minutes, decided to hurry about cleaning myself. There were several dozen Varjior women present, and their cheerful conversations with each other didn't take long to gnaw at my patience.

I hated it. I couldn't understand their fascination with their chosen topics—clothing, trinkets, men, flowers, and rearing young, just to name a few. Trinkets, perhaps, I could understand. After all, I had to wear a great deal of jewelry now and I didn't mind the shiny, jingly contraptions. The other topics? No.

How could they be so relaxed when living in the wilds, defending against beasts on a daily basis? Not only did they have their homes and belongings to protect, but they also had their children there. Their settlement didn't seem safe by any stretch, nor was it encased in a barrier like Dauthrmir. *'Are these women stronger than they look? At first glance I would have thought they're homemakers like the women in X'shmir… But, if they survive out here, the women must fight too.'*

"Have you found a potential mate yet, Arianna-jiss?" A woman with sharp features questioned me, a bright look in her eyes. "I hear you handled a Dux by yourself! Surely someone so strong has at least *someone* courting them."

'Courting, huh? Well at least they're choosier than Darius, I guess.' I pulled my soaked hair over one shoulder and then turned to address the woman. "No one is courting me, no. I don't really have the time for such matters anyway. My days are filled with studying and training."

"What about Nalithor-zir? He *is* your partner, isn't he?" Another woman probed.

'Ah, I know that expression. So that's what this is about.' I shook my head, feeling a pang of mingled irritation and jealousy. "We were paired for this mission since Nalithor doesn't have a partner of his own, and they needed someone who has experience with X'shmiran Chaos Beasts. I haven't been assigned an official partner yet."

"Maybe I do have a chance with Nalithor-zir still!" The second woman exclaimed, bolting out of the spring. She dressed in a hurry and then gathered a basket of flowers before disappearing from view.

'Sure you do. Tch, just how brainless does he make women?!' I bit

my cheek hard to keep myself from saying as much. My face flushed as anger and jealousy both threatened to rear their ugly heads. *'What a pain… This would be much simpler if Nalithor didn't seem…interested in me.'*

"What do you think, Kaera?" Ella examined me, a thoughtful expression on her face. "Blue or red mrifon?"

"Mrifon?" I questioned, looking between the scheming women.

"These are mrifon." Ella reached over the edge of the spring and plucked a pale blue flower from a nearby basket. "Most of the blooming trees you see this time of year in Draemir, the Abrantia Valley, and Dauthrmir Crater are mrifon trees. We use the tree's sap in healing salves and their flowers are—"

'Shit, shit, shit!' I slumped back against the stone and stared at the flowers. *'I remember the Adinvyr women in Sihix talking about mrifon. They're used to signal "availability" and related information.*

'I don't want it! This is why I can't stand women!'

"Red is for warriors, and Arianna is clearly a warrior," Kaera pointed out flatly, picking up one of the large rose-like blooms.

"Blue is for people of high birth though, and she's a princess!" Ella argued.

"She can wear both," Kaera countered.

"I'm not wearing *any*," I stated, pulling myself out of the water and then conjuring a plush towel to dry myself with. "I came to Abrantia to kill beasts, not to find a mate."

"B-but..." Ella trailed off and fidgeted with her hair for a moment before holding out the blue flower to me. "The only tribeswomen that don't wear mrifon are either mated or provide 'services.' You know? Like..."

'Great, so they took a Draemiran concept and further complicated it.' My eye twitched as I wrung water from my hair. "You're concerned that your men will misinterpret my intentions and my 'purpose' at the feast?"

"Yes, exactly." Kaera nodded. "Someone of your status should be adorned with many mrifon."

"I don't particularly care for status..." I conjured undergarments and tugged them on, then looked at the troubled sisters. "One mrifon will do. Two at most.

"Ah... Damn, I'm not supposed to use my fire. How am I going to dry my hair?!"

The Varjior sisters started arguing over mrifon colors again, so I released a sigh and attempted to towel my hair dry. Perhaps, if I dressed quickly, I could slip away unnoticed. Smiling to myself, I dressed myself in the first thing that came to mind and inched away from the arguing women.

One of the other Varjior women moved to block me, a knowing smile on her face. Instead of calling Ella and Kaera's attention, the woman offered me a scarlet mrifon and then let me pass once I accepted it.

I examined the flower while making my way through the maze

of tents, keeping my footsteps light so that I wouldn't draw attention. The blooms were like a cross between a rose and a spider lily. Its sweet smell reminded me of the way honey tasted, but there was a subtle citrusy undertone to it. I couldn't claim that the flower wasn't beautiful. The Varjior women attempting to cover me in them, however, was another matter.

Pursing my lips, I glanced up at the clear starry sky and then scented the air. I smelled roasting meats nearby. Dizziness still lingered, but my empty stomach was much more important.

The village gathering was so raucous that I was able to slip through the throngs of Varjior unnoticed. I plucked large slices of meat from a few separate platters, filled a tankard with sweet-smelling liquor, and then slinked away to find myself a perch nearby. No one seemed to notice me, but I still pulled more shadows around me just to be safe.

My perch, I had decided, would be high up in a mrifon tree that bordered the festivities below. From there I had a clear view of the large fire pit, more roasting food, dancers, and many tables lined with Varjior. Children ran around freely, occasionally taking on their animal form to dart between the legs of adults. Many warriors still had weapons strapped to their back or their waist, their eyes alert even as they feasted.

I settled back against the tree and nibbled at a piece of meat, hoping that the height of this branch and the dense foliage would keep me hidden. As far as I was concerned, I had received enough attention for the day. Eyrian, Xander, and Nalithor all seemed a little too intrigued now that my mask was gone. Azhar, though, I couldn't read—which made me more nervous than outright attention did.

'Why are these called mrifon anyway?' I glanced down where I had set the flower. It was almost the size of a tea plate. *'There's nothing "little" about these trees or their flowers. Perhaps they're small in comparison to other flora in Draemir? Hmmm...'*

Surveying the party once more, I spotted Illyana speaking cheerfully with the deer-like women that had escorted her away before. I still wanted to rip the strumpet's head from her shoulders and bristled when I spotted her. Alas, Nalithor had denied my request. Disobeying a deity seemed like a poor course of action, tempting as it was. *'I'll behave myself...for now.'*

Pouting, I searched the crowd for the deity in question. He was easy to spot—all I had to look for was a gaggle of Varjior men and women. They were pestering him, tugging at his robes and attempting to pull him every which way. All of them were speaking at once, occasionally shooting glares at each other as they vied for his attentions. Nalithor himself looked like he was searching for something, likely a way to escape. I wasn't sure if his power as an Adinvyr was to blame for his surroundings, or if it was because we had eliminated a threat to their village. Either way, it looked problematic. The one saving grace was his height and strength, which made it impossible for them to push him around.

'Assuming their animal qualities aren't limited to their shifted form... His scent must drive them crazy.' I took a swig of my drink and crossed my legs at the ankle, attempting to find a comfortable position. *'Though... I suppose they could just be weak enough that his mere appearance is sufficient to send them into a frenzy, Adinvyr or otherwise.'*

In contrast, Eyrian looked like he was enjoying the attention he was receiving from several Varjior women. Azhar and Xander had both sequestered themselves away in a corner together, looking bored as they discussed something. The Varjior seemed uninterested in that pair. If there were similarities between Varjior and Vampires, I could see why they might not find Xander interesting. And Azhar...well, he did *look* intimidating.

I was happy to find that I had managed to give them the slip. They must have been too distracted to notice me when I fetched my food—I doubted Nalithor would have missed my manipulation of the shadows, otherwise.

"Not going to rescue him?" Amakiir's voice from above startled me into looking upwards, finding that he was perched on the branch above me. He tilted his head, shooting me a curious look. "He seems like he's searching for you, after all."

"He can find another scapegoat." I huffed around a slice of food. "I'd say he's looking for a means to escape, not for me."

"Varjior are pushy," Amakiir remarked dryly, landing in a crouch next to me. "Though if he spotted you wearing *that* I doubt he'd leave you alone the entire night. You are avoiding him?"

"What's wrong with this?" I frowned, looking down at my satin kimono and the sliver of leg it revealed. "It's comfortable, I can fight in it, and—"

"It's Draemiran." Amakiir shook his head at me. "*That one* is soft for all things from his homeland, and he has a soft spot for *you*. I've never heard him speak so highly or passionately about someone's skill or their bloodlust. I doubt he will let you out of his grasp if he sees you like this. If he does, he is a fool—and I will put him in his place on Lucifer and Lysander's behalf.

"You should consider saving him, you know."

I arched an eyebrow at the Varjior deity as he leapt down through the branches to rejoin the party and then shifted my gaze to Nalithor again. He wore a set of black Umbral Mage robes in the Dauthrmiran style, so his skin was covered from the throat down. Despite his uncharacteristically modest attire, the Varjior men and women were still intent on garnering his attention. Nalithor's expression made it clear he wanted no part of whatever they were clamoring for, but they didn't care.

Tilting my head, I ate several more slices of meat and watched for a little while longer. Once I was convinced Nalithor was truly displeased, dissatisfied, and uninterested in the gaggle of strumpets clinging to his robes, I decided to intervene. I stretched my arms above my head, rested my plate on my lap, and then nudged the Adinvyr with a few tendrils of power. *You look like you could use some help down there.'*

Nalithor's gaze snapped up, then he imploded into darkness, much to the displeasure of the pouting Varjior. Almost instantly Nalithor reappeared to my left and stole the largest remaining slice of meat from my plate.

"Payment, for not giving away your location...sooner..." Nalithor trailed off, his gaze wandering down my form, his eyes widening. "How did you manage to sneak by in *that* without notice?"

'A reaction so fast? I guess Amakiir meant it.' I shrugged, ignoring Nalithor's slight frown. "You were all too busy talking."

"You could have joined us," Nalithor offered as I dismissed my plate.

"Mmm... Eyrian is a loud drunk." I shook my head and then motioned down at the rosy-faced Draekin.

"Good point," Nalithor muttered, his icy gaze taking me in for a moment more before his gaze fell to the mrifon beside me. "You intend to hide here all night, then?"

"Too noisy. I was considering returning to the ship to sleep." I sighed, tilting my head back to look up at the Adinvyr. "Then I remembered we left the soldiers there, and that I don't know them. As such, I trust them about as much as I trust the bitch down there."

"She's probably going to be sent back to Beshulthien after what happened." Nalithor's voice filled with disgust as he looked down at Illyana. When he returned his attention to me, he adopted an amused expression. "Didn't I ask you to stick close?"

"You said *nearby*. Up here qualifies," I corrected him, earning a laugh.

"It wouldn't be so worrisome if you at least had Djialkan keeping an eye on you, but I don't see him." Nalithor smiled and leaned back against the tree beside me.

"He dislikes the noise as much as I do; he's skulking about by our tents somewhere," I replied before downing the remainder of the liquor in my tankard.

"We can go somewhere quiet if you like," Nalithor offered, so I glanced up at him again. "You might grow a little cold if you leave the fire pit while wearing that, however."

"I'm sure I can manage," I replied, rising to my feet. Nalithor paused as he looked down at me, openly examining both me and the kimono I wore. "Now, now. My attire is rather simple. There can't be *that* much for you to stare at."

"My dear, you have *plenty* for me to stare at." Nalithor shook his head and smirked. "I do hope you don't have some ill-conceived notion in your head that you aren't attractive to look at, Arianna. I would hope that our reactions indicate that we find you rather exceptional.

"That little rampage of you fuels our...interests. Especially mine."

"It's also what made the Elf fly off the handle," I pointed out, earning a crooked grin from the Adinvyr.

"Illyana is an Elven princess—she looks down on Humans and fails to see that you are most certainly *not* a Human." Nalithor laughed before crouching to pick up the mrifon I'd left lying on the branch. He twirled it between his fingers for a moment as he straightened, shooting me an odd look. "The Varjior women are attempting to assimilate you already?"

"They're concerned that I'll be mistaken for a strumpet myself if I don't wear one." I sighed, tugging at my curls as I cast a dirty look at the party going on below. "I was able to slip away with just one mrifon, at least, instead of being covered in them like they were plotting."

"Ahhh, so you are avoiding *everyone*." Nalithor chuckled, tucking the stem of the flower behind my left ear. "Hmmm, it suits you even if you're adverse to it. Though, the color *is* questionable."

"I didn't say I was aver— Eek!" I yelped as he scooped me into his arms and leapt from the tree. Startled, I clung to his chest and tensed, expecting a hard landing due to the height. Instead, he landed smoothly as a cat and then burst into a sprint. "H-hey! I didn't say I was ready!"

"You were ready," Nalithor stated, bounding away from the village and toward a nearby hill. "Perhaps not for the jump, but you were well past ready to leave."

I huffed and crossed my arms. Nalithor was correct but I refused to admit as much aloud. It took maybe a minute or two for us to reach the hill he'd chosen, thanks to his startling speed. Once he'd slowed to a stop he grinned and set me down on my feet. I glanced around at our new surroundings, keeping my expression passive. It was a great vantage point and gave me a clear view of the large river that snaked through the Abrantia Valley. However, Nalithor was correct. It was much cooler there compared to the village, and he looked as if he was waiting to see if I would say something about it.

Instead, I summoned a pile of furs and pillows from my shrizar, kicked off my sandals, and plopped down amidst the fluff.

"Much better," I remarked simply.

Nalithor laughed and shook his head, examining me for a moment. He seemed to approve of the sight of me lying amongst all the fur.

"Is there room for me?" Nalithor settled a hand on one hip and motioned at my furs with the other, an amused smile playing on his lips.

"Of course," I replied after making him wait for a few seconds. "I didn't summon *all* of this just to be greedy, you know."

"Yet you hogged most of the fun with that strange beast you discovered," Nalithor pointed out as he removed his shoes. He took a few paces toward me and then stretched out on the furs at an arm's distance from me, linking his hands behind his head. "Remind me to *never* make you angry."

"I'm not that bad." I smiled, turning my gaze up to the sky as well. "Besides, do you have room to talk? With all the teasing you do?"

"I believe you would at least *attempt* to kick my ass if I've been bothering you," Nalithor countered. "If you want me to stop… I can certainly try. However, you may be too cute for me to resist."

"'Cute' huh?" I rolled my eyes at the stars and bit back a sigh.

I didn't know how to take it whenever he referred to me as "cute" or "adorable." Perhaps "beautiful, "pretty", or even "sexy" would have been better, though I probably still wouldn't have known how to react. Receiving compliments wasn't exactly something I was used to, let alone expecting. "Cute" and "adorable" just made it even harder to tell if he was actually interested in me. *'Aren't those more… I don't know, friendly terms? Or is something lost in translation?'*

"You seem uninterested in our comrades," Nalithor spoke up after prolonged silence. I glanced toward him, only to find his gaze still fixated on the stars. "I thought at least Eyrian would have interested you to some extent."

"He's boring," I stated dismissively, earning a rumbling laugh from the Adinvyr. "He *is*! I'm still cross with him for being too careful when sparring me! It makes him too easy to take down. How am I supposed to find *that* interesting?

"Our brief attempt at a match earlier wasn't enough to tell me if he's really going to take me seriously."

"Too careful?" Nalithor shifted so that he was resting on his side, facing me. He propped his head in the palm of one hand and shot me a soft smile. "Do elaborate. Eyrian probably puts less thought into his actions than your brother does. I only caught the tail end of your duel in Dauthrmir...but I'm admittedly curious. You were incredibly upset with him."

"He's too fixated on how..." I sighed heavily, feeling my face flush with irritation as I motioned at myself, "...on how dainty I am in comparison to all of you. Like he's scared I'm a porcelain doll that will break."

"Ah, perhaps he really is interested in you then..." Nalithor frowned, seeming oblivious to the questioning look I shot him— until he spoke again, "I've seen him spar with Rylthra women before—several of which are members of the Imperial Guard. Rylthra are much smaller than you are and yet he treats them the same as anyone else."

"Well if he doesn't have the respect to fight me properly, then he can find a new sparring partner." I growled, drawing Nalithor's attention back to my face. "Sparring someone who won't take me seriously isn't worth my time, regardless of how he's praised my combat ability."

"You really are a Devillian under there somewhere, aren't you?" Nalithor mused. He reached out with his free hand and gripped my chin, tilting my head as if he was looking for something. "Hmmm, no seam or zipper. Where are you hiding, *hmmm?*"

I couldn't help but laugh, batting his hand away. However, he caught both of my wrists in one hand and shot me a knowing look.

"I will gladly spar you as much as you like, to make up for General Il'thar's incompetence," Nalithor began in a mock-formal tone. He then smirked and pulled me across the furs toward him. "For now, you appear tired and cold. Should I carry you back to the village?"

"Too noisy." I shook my head as Nalithor released my wrists. "You're a scoundrel, you know."

"You think so?" Nalithor inquired as he pulled some blankets over both of us. "I'll have you know that *I* think I'm more of a hero. Clearly I'm coming to rescue the princess before she freezes to death."

Nalithor cupped my face in one hand for a long moment, his pale eyes tracing my features. For a moment I thought he was going to steal a kiss, but instead he plucked the flower from behind my ear and set it aside. Before I could scoot away from him, Nalithor reached out and shifted me so that my back was against his chest and he draped an arm over me. I couldn't deny that both his scent and his warmth were comforting to me but being so close to him was making me blush furiously despite his hands remaining in appropriate places.

"Did I really look *that* cold?" I asked once my pulse calmed enough to let me think. Nalithor just laughed and squeezed my waist briefly, before reaching past me to fetch a pillow, offering it to me. "Thanks... I think."

I accepted the pillow and placed it under my head. Only seconds passed before Nalithor slid his other arm beneath the pillow and my neck, allowing him to pull me even closer to his chest—which seemed to suit him just fine.

"You really should sleep and, if you insist on sleeping out here, I'm staying with you," Nalithor spoke after a moment, tensing as if he expected me to tell him off. "So, if my maintained presence is objectionable, you—"

"The thanks wasn't just for the pillow." I pouted, gnawing on my lower lip for a moment before continuing, "Nor would I have 'rescued' you from the gaggle of Varjior who seemed so intent on stripping you of your robes if I found your presence 'objectionable.' You're…just a little difficult to deal with. That's all."

"Difficult?" Nalithor mused, running a hand down my side and to my hip. "I wouldn't say I'm difficult. I'm appreciative of your resistance to Adinvyr, perhaps overly so.

"As bashful as you are, you haven't revealed even a *hint* of interest, let alone desire…and perhaps it's a little frustrating."

'Not even a hint, huh?' I wondered.

Of course, upon arriving in Vorpmasia and discovering how powerful the Devillians were, I had strengthened my shields. However, mental barriers did nothing against the instincts of Adinvyr. They were capable of detecting physical desire regardless of such things, no matter how many layers were utilized. I found it hard to believe that Nalithor couldn't sense anything from me, yet he seemed sincere. *'Are my occasional thoughts not as bad as I believed?'*

"You must be really tired of easy women if you welcome frustration." I laughed.

Nalithor gave my waist another squeeze and nuzzled the top of my head, a small purr rumbling in his chest.

"Go to sleep, Arianna," Nalithor spoke quietly, wrapping darkness around me. My eyelids fluttered involuntarily as I attempted to resist. "You overdid it against the beasts, and you know it. *So, rest.*"

"But I...wanted to talk with you...more..." I tried to protest but it was useless. His magic was too strong for my weakened state, and I slipped into a deep sleep before I could finish my sentence.

CHAPTER TWENTY
The Ceilail Forest

I looked around within my dream, overcome by confusion. This place was familiar. I knew it from my dreams of being taken from Dauthrmir, but this clearly wasn't that *dream. The granite floor and its obsidian inlays were pristine, as were the pillars and tapestries within the room. Members of the Imperial Guard were spread throughout the room, hands on their weapons. Unlike the nightmare I so often relived,* this *scene was calm and composed—and I was a mere spectator.*

'What's going on? I've never seen this before.' *I examined the dais at the back of the throne room, my gaze falling on where Lucifer sat. He looked less tired here and was dressed more casually than I'd ever seen him. His posture was relaxed, and his expression was cheerful instead of reserved.*

"There you are, Arianna!" Lucifer called with a bright smile when the throne room doors swung open to reveal a young Devillian child. "You didn't give Djialkan and Maric a hard time now, did you?"

'Arianna…?' My confusion grew as I examined the child. Her bright blue eyes, pale skin, and long dark curls were all-too-familiar. 'Is that… Is that me? This has to be a dream.'

The child's face flushed as she clutched the skirt of her frilly black dress. Her scaled tail tucked between her legs as she shifted from foot-to-foot and gnawed at her lip. Small platinum horns protruded from above her temples and curved back around either side of her head. The shape and twist of her horns mirrored Lucifer's horns, yet were more slender and not yet fully grown.

"She wanted to stay with Onyre and Aleri," Maric laughed, ruffling the child's hair.

I looked at Maric, my confusion growing. That laugh was unmistakable. Although the man in the dream bore less scars, this "Maric" was clearly the same one that now served under Nalithor. His armor clearly identified him as a member of the Imperial Guard—so why was he not a member of the Imperial Guard in the present day?

Maric nudged the princess's back, urging her to join Lucifer at his throne. The child looked around nervously and then scurried across the dark blue rugs to join her father. Lucifer picked her up by the waist and sat her on his lap, giving her a broad smile and pinching one of her rosy cheeks. She flushed darker and averted her gaze from the section of the throne room that was troubling her.

'This has to be from long before I was taken from Dauthrmir. "I" am a lot smaller.' *I looked around the room in search of what was flustering "me" so much, and then paused, surprised.* 'Isn't that...'

"The princess really is like a doll!" A smiling woman with pale blue hair exclaimed, approaching the dais with her family in tow. She placed her hands on her knees and bent over until her face was level with the princess's. "Hello there, little one. My name is Ellena Vraelimir—but you can just call me 'Ellena' alright, cutie?"

'Vraelimir...' *I shifted my attention away from the Adinvyr matriarch and to the rest of her family.*

With Ellena was a man that I could only assume was Lysander, her husband. He seemed more reserved than his wife, but his expression was still pleasant. Lysander's hair was the color of pewter and his eyes were a pale blue-grey. Nalithor was easy to identify by his wild white hair and icy blue eyes. The second child was merely an infant but had a full head of bright blue hair. The infant shared his mother's molten orange eyes, while Nalithor resembled their father most.

"Arianna" was trying her damnedest to avoid looking at the young boy in front of her, all the while growing redder in the face. She clutched her father's robes in her small fists, her knuckles turning white. Her overwhelming shyness wafted from her in waves. I was a little impressed that she wasn't trembling.

'This is so confusing!' *I huffed.* 'Why am I seeing this from such a strange perspective? Hells, why am I dreaming about this at all?

It's hard to care about something I don't remember…let alone reminiscence about what might have happened. What am I supposed to think of this? Learn from this?'

"I'm Nalithor!" The boy offered with a bright smile, offering Arianna a hand. He only bowed slightly after Lysander nudged him. "We're going to be playmates—! What's wrong?"

Arianna let out a small squeak and scrambled off her father's lap, darting behind the throne to hide. She felt so shy and embarrassed that she was almost in tears.

Had I really been that skittish as a child? It was difficult for me to believe, even as I watched the scene play out. I glanced at the Vraelimir Family and found that both Ellena and Lysander looked amused. Nalithor, on the other hand, looked concerned.

'Wouldn't most children be hurt by such a reaction?' *I examined Nalithor and then my child-self in turn.* 'I wish I could sense these people's auras. I can't imagine why I would be that flustered by them. Was I just that shy as a girl?

'No, no. Stupid me, this is likely just a dream… Right?'

"Arianna, sweetheart," Lucifer chuckled, shifting in his throne so that he could reach behind it and tug on one of her curls, "you shouldn't hide from your new playmate. Nalithor will be living with us for a few years while the two of you train with Aurelian."

I wanted to look away from the scene, but I couldn't bring myself to do it. Lucifer's words were like a knife through my heart. A loving parent, a luxury neither Darius nor I had. A luxury that had been stolen from us. I shut my "eyes" briefly, hoping that everything would disappear, but it didn't.

"B-but..." The princess bit her lower lip, practically eating her own chin as she clenched and unclenched her hands. "I-I don't know h-how to—"

'Boys just disappear like my brother did...' The thought pierced through my mind, startling me. I whirled around, examining the faces of those present, but only Nalithor seemed to have heard it. Either that, or the adults present had expected this reaction from "Arianna."

The young Nalithor's brow furrowed with concern and determination as he attempted to skirt around the throne to check on the trembling girl. Ellena and Lysander caught him by the shoulders and held him back, reminding him that in Dauthrmir he was just a visiting royal from an allied nation—he couldn't do as he pleased here, regardless of his intentions.

Djialkan appeared in a puff of violet smoke, perching on "Arianna's" shoulder. After a moment, she let out another startled squeak, turned cherry red in the face, and fled the throne room entirely. The corner of my eye twitched. Knowing Djialkan, he'd said something blunt that only made things worse. Likely for his own amusement. Rascal.

The adults looked vaguely concerned, but nowhere near as worried as Nalithor was. He looked torn, and like he wanted to chase after the younger girl to comfort her.

'Right... Nalithor is an empath of some degree.' I glanced

between the faces of the royals present and then settled on Nalithor's once more. 'I guess at this age I wouldn't have had much control over my thoughts or the barriers around them. He must've been able to hear my thoughts and feel my emotions clearly back then.'

"Your Majesty, may I—?" Nalithor began, earning a chuckle and warm smile from Lucifer.

"Of course, Nalithor." Lucifer nodded. "You and Arianna will be spending a great deal of time together. I'm sure you can find a way to make her open up."

The vision swirled into a cacophony of colors, making me dizzy to a point where I would have fallen had I been standing. When I opened my eyes, I found myself floating in a garden scene, still somewhere in the Dauthrmiran palace. "Arianna" was hiding behind a large mrifon tree and had a stack of books beside her. She was wearing a light blue gown now instead of the frilly black one from before.

I caught movement in my peripheral vision and shifted to find Nalithor walking across the blooming garden. It was rather obvious that he was looking for "Arianna." I was surprised to find that he already knew how to walk without making a sound. After a few more paces Nalithor perched on a bench and placed his violin beside him so that he could shift to get comfortable.

'What happened? My hair is longer here.' *I reexamined "myself" and then Nalithor.* 'His too! Just how much time has passed? Why didn't I get to see where I ran off to? Why am I *still* hiding from him?'

Looking at my younger self, I noticed that her hands were trembling now as she flipped through one of her books. Her tail was limp in the grass and her body was coiled as if ready to spring from hiding to flee. I could only assume that she had caught Nalithor's scent.

'Is he going to just wait there?' *I looked back to Nalithor again as he lifted his violin.*

"Arianna" flinched when Nalithor began to play his instrument. Her knuckles grew white as she gripped her book tighter. She was trying, and failing, to hide the curiosity from her face and the twitching of her tail. Nalithor pulled an alluring melody from his instrument, one I didn't recognize. My younger self became entranced and placed her book back with the others. Soon, she rose to her feet so that she could peer around the tree.

A small smile curved across Nalithor's lips as he continued to play. The lower half of his tail swayed in time with the music as he flowed from one song to the next. He must have sensed "Arianna's" attention shift to him. However, it took five full songs before she worked up the courage to leave her hiding place and approach Nalithor.

"You like music?" Nalithor asked, lowering his violin.

"I... I do. I play the piano." Arianna hesitated and shifted her gaze away from Nalithor.

"Would you like to play with me?" Nalithor's tone and expression were both bright, his smile genuine. "I can teach you these songs if you want, or you can teach me the ones you know!"

"You'll...play with me?" Arianna stared at Nalithor in disbelief.

"*Even Darius won't play with me. He's…too scared of the dark…*"

"*Is that what you're worried about?*" Nalithor giggled, placing his violin aside. He slipped off the bench and turned to face Arianna, then summoned an orb of darkness in his left hand. "*See? I'm a Lyur'zi too. I promise you can't scare me.*"

Arianna looked like a transfixed cat as she stared at Nalithor's darkness, even if only for a moment. She took a few hesitant steps toward Nalithor and then snatched the orb from him. Nalithor looked startled and shot Arianna a questioning look when she turned her back to him. Crouching, Arianna rested her elbows on her knees and held the orb of darkness between her hands. She studied it with an intensity that didn't fit a child. It was like she was judging him by his darkness, and Nalithor seemed to have realized that. The silence dragged on for over a minute, causing even him to grow nervous.

"*Hmmm…*" Arianna murmured, standing back up. She stared at the orb for a moment longer and then turned her attention to Nalithor, examining his Brands of Divinity, a strange look on her face. "*'Kay. I'll believe you.*"

Nalithor's darkness dispersed as he released a sigh of relief, a smile returning to his face.

'What was I looking for? Why does he have Brands at this point, and I don't?' *I looked between the slightly less nervous children, unsure what to make of them. 'This…feels like a dream yet it's so vivid. Why would a dream have this much detail?*

'My memories were erased completely, weren't they?

Does...does that mean this is Nalithor's dream? Have I somehow intruded on his dreams?'

Everything spun again but this time I found myself drifting in darkness. Warmth engulfed me as Nalithor's scent filled my nose. This time, the scene didn't shift. That was fine by me. Darkness and warmth were all I needed. There was no point in pondering things I couldn't remember.

It was all too confusing, too frustrating. I didn't want to see more.

When I began to wake up it didn't take long for me to realize that I had sprawled halfway across Nalithor's chest at some point. However, I was much too comfortable to move. My head and shoulders were nestled into his upper abs, while my left arm hung over his torso. My left leg had somehow ended up hooked around his. However, he didn't seem to mind. He was stroking my back absentmindedly with one hand and, by the occasional rustling, it sounded as though he had a book in his other.

'How long have I been asleep?' I wondered, relaxing into Nalithor's warm skin. 'He could've woken me...'

I was tempted to go back to sleep but Nalithor's scent filling my senses was far too distracting. After sleeping so deeply it was difficult to doze back off. That said, I couldn't help but purr the next time he ran his hand firmly down my back.

"You haven't decided you're a kitten instead of a fox now, have you?" Nalithor chuckled, pausing as I nuzzled my cheek into his abs. "I was surprised you didn't wake when our comrades came along. Though, not quite as surprised as they were to see you sprawled across me like this…"

"Don't care. Comfy," I mumbled, groggy, earning an outright laugh from him this time. Which meant he stopped stroking my back. I pouted and grumbled, "Don't stop, felt nice…"

If Nalithor said anything else, I didn't catch it because I had begun to doze off. However, it finally clicked that I was cuddling with a *deity*, and that it was probably *very* inappropriate of me to do so.

"Oh! I-I'm sorry, uh…" I jolted away and hurried to extract myself.

I sat up and turned my back to Nalithor, my face burning hot. My pulse pounded in my throat as both unease and regret filled me. I'd been quite comfortable, but he was a deity. A deity I couldn't read well. There was no way in hell a mortal should have been cuddling with him. It was too late to go back to cuddling now anyway.

Nalithor's chuckling and his tail squeezing my hips didn't help matters.

"Now, now, I wasn't complaining, was I?" Nalithor purred, sitting up and pulling me backwards into his lap. He nuzzled into the crook of my neck and released a playful laugh when I twitched. "Everyone else has left for Dauthrmir already. You can be as lazy as you like."

"We…don't have anything else to hunt?" I tilted my head back to look up at Nalithor, my heart falling in disappointment. The Adinvyr shot me a crooked grin and squeezed me like a stuffed toy.

"The woman you captured was hunting weak beasts, not buying blood from others. As such, we have no crooked traders to punish," Nalithor replied, coiling his tail tighter around me as he spoke. "I do have some...'*business*' to take care of in the Ceilail Forest, if you wish to join me. If not, I can take you back to the airship first. It should have returned by now."

"Does this 'business' include killing things?" I asked, attempting to mask my excitement. Nalithor nuzzled into the side of my throat again, making me shiver as he grinned into my skin.

"Mmm... Killing quite a few things, yes." Nalithor purred, hugging me as he released a roll of power, giving me pause. "Do you think you can handle fighting alongside me with all of my seals broken?"

"With your seals broken?" I questioned, but he just chuckled deviously and released his power all at once.

I bit my lower lip hard as tendrils of his power slid over my skin, wrapping tight around my body. Glancing down, I found Nalithor's Brands of Divinity shining brighter than ever before. However, Nalithor's lips brushing against the side of my neck brought my attention back to the matter at hand.

Someone had to distract him from whatever it was he was thinking.

"I'll be fine," I stated wryly, biting back a shudder as he drew his fangs along my skin. "I think the *real* question is whether or not you can focus enough to tell me about our new hunt."

"Oh? You're…still unaffected by me?" Nalithor shifted me so that I was sitting sideways in his lap. A small frown tugged at his lips as he reached for my face. "Hmmm…you should be at least a *little*—"

"You shouldn't tempt me with a hunt and then change the subject!" I prodded him in the chest, shooting him a firm look. "You can worry about whether or not you 'affect' me later. For now, we should be killing—"

"Does the vixen grow cross when teased?" Nalithor inquired innocently. He shot me a smirk and then released me, rising to his feet. "Very well then. Straight to business already, is it?"

'I get cross when teased…and he gets cross if I focus on "business" instead of him?' I looked up at Nalithor, curious. *'He looks so disappointed…'*

"Well, I get the feeling that we won't get much in the way of breakfast before we go kill them," I pointed out, pulling myself to my feet. Nalithor's downtrodden expression didn't change, so I added, "The sooner we're done, the sooner we can return to Dauthrmir and I can make us pancakes. *If* you would like to join me that is."

"You're inviting me?" Nalithor perked up, faint surprise showing on his face as he tracked my movements. "Weren't you attempting to avoid getting to know anyone, Arianna?"

"Well," I nudged on my sandals and then began dismissing everything into my shrizar, "if you're going to conquer X'shmir for me, I don't really see a reason to continue following X'shmiran laws. Though, I'm sure Darius will try to make me wear my masks again."

"I won't allow it." Nalithor growled and embraced me from behind in a possessive manner, his chest rumbling against my back as he held me. "If *anyone* attempts to make you follow the Old Ways, they will have *me* to contend with. Including that brother of yours."

"You won't 'allow' it, hmmm?" I laughed, amused, as Nalithor lifted me off my feet and nuzzled my shoulder. "If you keep doing that, I'm going to start thinking you want *me* for breakfast."

"That is an excellent idea…but no, that isn't why." Nalithor chuckled, his lips brushing against my skin as he spoke. "You should call for Djialkan. The Ceilail Forest is easily a half a day's walk away."

"Oh? So, this is potentially turning into a several day trip after all?" I asked, attempting to hide my excitement. Once I detected Djialkan's presence, I prodded him with a few tendrils of my power and then turned my attention back to Nalithor. "Is it actually alright for me to join you?"

"Consider it another test." Nalithor grinned, releasing me. "If you can handle fighting alongside me while I'm displaying my full power, instead of the brief exposure you've seen during our duels,

I may just have to claim you as my partner.

"I don't believe anyone else is capable of handling that delicious bloodthirst of yours. Even *I* had to shield myself so that I wouldn't give into your whims while we hunted yesterday."

"Mmm? Am I really that bad?" I tilted my head, then summoned a coat around my shoulders.

"You're that *exquisite*," Nalithor teased. "Few of our comrades can fathom such intense bloodlust."

"Hmmm…seals, huh?" I muttered, fastening the coat's clasps before turning to shoot Nalithor a firm look. "Nalithor, you haven't been restraining yourself during our sparring matches, have you?"

"Give me *some* credit." Nalithor laughed, ruffling my curls. "The seals I maintain on myself hide the 'feel' of my power, my aura. There are times when they weaken and my aura seeps through, such as when we spar. They do not alter my performance, they are purely there to diminish the number of 'problems' I run into in the city."

"I was going to be rather angry with you if that wasn't the case," I grumbled, attempting to dislodge his hand. A playful smirk crept across his face as he watched me.

"How do you feel about killing *people* instead of beasts?" Nalithor questioned.

I considered my response for a moment, glancing to the side briefly when Djialkan swooped down to perch on my shoulder.

The fae-dragon, to my surprise, had no quip for me. Instead, he stretched and then settled himself into a comfortable position.

"I suppose that depends on what kind of 'people' we're talking about," I replied, falling into step with Nalithor. "There's plenty of people who need to die, and plenty who need to live. X'shmir is a good example of that—many of the commoners are innocent of the crimes that the nobles and royals have committed."

"How about a caravan of slavers that is using beasts as an escort?" Nalithor offered, causing me to arch an eyebrow at him. "I was contacted by an acquaintance of mine in Ceilail while you slept. The caravan has somehow acquired Chaos Beasts and are using the beasts' power to hide themselves in the forest and away from Amakiir's scouts."

"I'll try to let you get a few strikes in this time." I grinned at him. "No promises though. I can enter quite the frenzy when beasts are involved."

"Your battle yesterday doesn't count as a frenzy?" Nalithor shot me a curious glance.

"I am not certain if a god of even your caliber could stop her when she enters a true frenzy," Djialkan muttered. *"There is a reason, aside from her status as a Lyur'zi, that makes the X'shmirans frightened of her, you know."*

"Show me," Nalithor demanded. "Or do you intend to make me wait on that as well?"

"Where's the fun in just *telling* you everything?" I countered with a smile, shaking my head. "Speaking of making you wait... You don't even know what my DSO results are, yet you want to 'claim' me as your partner? Tsk, tsk, tsk."

"Regardless of your results, I meant what I said. I don't think there's anyone else in Vorpmasia capable of handling you," Nalithor answered dryly, reaching up to ruffle my curls again. "Since you're so 'understanding' of the situation with our quarry, kindly remember to leave the captives and forest creatures in one piece. We're only to take out the slavers and the beasts."

"That won't be a problem." I huffed, batting at his hand. "You've warned your friends in Ceilail not to corrupt me, I hope?"

"Fear not, I told them to leave the corruption to me," Nalithor replied with a smirk, earning him a laugh. "You truly refuse to show me what a 'real frenzy' consists of?"

"Mmhmm, you seem like you could use some mystery in your life," I teased while opening a shrizar. "You said Ceilail is half a day away, at minimum?"

"Ah, so you were prepared for something like this?" Nalithor asked as I pulled a pair of lacquered boxes out. "You have learned to use your power over ice to chill things even while they're sequestered away in your shrizar?"

"I always cook too much food, and Darius wasn't going to eat any of it." I nodded, offering him one of the boxes. "It would be best if we didn't fight on empty stomachs, right?"

"You still owe me breakfast when we return to Dauthrmir."

Nalithor smiled at me and accepted the box. "I must admit, I'm a little disappointed that you're not affected by my power."

"Really? Why?" I shot him a surprised look before pulling the lid off my box.

"Not being able to tell what someone thinks of me is...strange," Nalithor replied after a moment of thought. "I'd imagine it's similar to the way you feel about suddenly being without your mask."

"Except instead of being accustomed to hiding your face, you're used to fending off hordes of strumpets?" I offered, earning a crooked grin in response. "I suppose it's the 'same' in the sense that you're almost like a normal person when around me, instead of some piece of meat for the usual sorts to chase around."

"You sound as if you dislike them even more than *I* do." Nalithor chuckled, shaking his dead.

"Well, take last night for example." I pointed my fork at him. "The Varjior men and women were all trying to tug you off in different directions and putting their hands all over you, even though your body language made it clear you wanted no part of it. I rather dislike people like that. Darius only gets away with it, *to some extent*, because he's blood. Even then, I'm of half a mind to skin him sometimes."

"At least fry him until he's crispy before you feed him to me," Djialkan commented all-too-seriously.

"And then there's you, the mysterious anomaly that seems

unaffected by my power despite how easily I can fluster you."
Nalithor laughed again when I pouted and glared at him. "You
have barely indulged me and, aside from that brief bias of yours
yesterday, there has been little to indicate one way or the other
what you think of me."

"I, for one, am not inclined to tell you," I informed him,
smiling when I caught his brief pout. "Such topics can wait until
later anyway.

"What sort of beasts are escorting the slavers? Do we know
what species the slavers themselves are?"

"Oh, species?" Nalithor shot me an inquisitive look. "That's an
interesting question."

"I decided that if I'm going to fight alongside, or *against*, non-
Human species that I should learn their physiological differences,"
I replied with a flourish of my fork. "It's easier to kill things when
I know where to stab them. Of course, it helps with the healing
aspect of things too."

"You really are a huntress," Nalithor remarked dryly, shaking
his head. "None of the beasts are X'shmiran as far as I'm aware.
Therefore, you should exercise *some* caution. There are no Dux-
class beasts, only lesser ones. As for the slavers themselves, they are
assorted.

"Slavery is prohibited by all of the countries in the Rilzaan
Alliance. Caravans, such as this one, are usually an assortment of
outlaws from the Empires or are from outlying countries with no

affiliation to the alliance."

"Hmmm…" I grumbled, lifting my box so that Djialkan could eat the rest. "Why couldn't our 'comrades' tell where the beasts were, yesterday?"

"You appear to be more experienced than them when it comes to hunting beasts in the wilds," Nalithor offered, an amused smile settling on his face. "Is that why you were so agitated with them?"

"Partially." I shrugged the shoulder opposite of Djialkan, then cast Nalithor a sideways glance. "I don't usually like to share my prey."

"Yet you adjusted quite expertly for *my* incoming strikes," Nalithor pointed out with a small smirk.

"I did say *'usually'*," I countered. "*You,* at least, I've found to be capable of keeping up with me in a fight."

"Do not let her fool you, she does not like to share anything." Djialkan snorted. *"Arianna, you should travel in your armor. It is likely the beasts will have ambushes prepared, and I doubt you wish to find yourself injured again."*

I released an irritated sigh as Djialkan hopped off my shoulder and onto Nalithor's. Traveling in my armor wasn't something I was against, it just wasn't the most comfortable thing in the world. Alas, I knew Djialkan was correct. That didn't stop it from annoying me. With reluctance, I opted for my full plate armor and chose to leave the helm off until we actually *found* beasts.

We were close enough to the Gron'kial Mountains for it to be too chilly for my lighter sets of armor. Furthermore, I knew Ceilail was the Forest of Ice. I didn't want to freeze to death before killing our prey.

"Oh? You have this kind of armor as well?" Nalithor inquired, flicking a wicked, curved point on one of my pauldrons. "Mmm…it still hugs your curves quite nicely."

"*Focus*," I commented dryly, glancing up at him. "You're looking at me like I'm food. Again."

"Well you *are* food." Nalithor purred, smirking. "You know, I'm surprised no one has taken a bite out of you yet."

"Don't you think they'd have to be rather foolish to try 'taking a bite' out of me without permission?" I shook my head at the frisky Adinvyr. "Ceilail is the Forest of Ice, isn't it? How have you managed to make contacts there? Or do you happen to have power over ice as well?"

"My affinity for ice is…a work in progress," Nalithor informed me. "Dauthrmir has done minor trade with the inhabitants of the Ceilail Forest for many years, as have Amakiir's people. Most inhabitants of Ceilail are peaceful creatures and not capable of fighting off the beasts who occasionally rampage through the forest. They usually contact one of the Vorpmasian Generals when in need of assistance, such as now."

"Can we really afford to take such a leisurely pace when beasts and slavers are involved?" I questioned, causing Nalithor to shoot me a curious glance. "Don't you think it's possible that the slavers want to capture some of Ceilail's people as...'unique merchandise?'"

"Slavery itself should be the last issue on our mind since we're talking about people who've been 'corrupted' by an Aledacian Forest. They won't live long if the slavers take them."

"It's quite likely, but..." Nalithor frowned, his brow furrowing. "Djialkan, can you carry Arianna?"

"Why make me *carry her, when she could just ride you?"* Djialkan hissed, shaking his mane. I shot him a confused look. *"He is 'The Black Dragon' for a reason, Arianna."*

"So instead of walking we could be flying?" I demanded, placing a hand on my hip as I settled a glare on them both. *"Nalithor?"*

"You're that eager?" Nalithor inquired, stopping to turn and look at me. He sighed and glanced away from me after a moment, his shoulders falling. "All business then?"

"The sooner we're done, the sooner we can go back to Dauthrmir and analyze the samples you took from the beasts yesterday," I began, earning a dejected sigh from the Adinvyr. Shaking my head, I continued, "Secondly, you don't need an excuse like walking half a day to Ceilail just to speak with me, Nalithor. If you want to get to know me, all you have to do is ask."

"She is right, you know." Djialkan cackled, shaking his wings. *"Taking care of the filth should come first. You are letting your typical, selfish Adinvyr instincts—"*

"Djialkan, kindly refrain from stereotyping me." Nalithor

grimaced and brushed the fae-dragon from his shoulder. "Unfortunately flying is not an option. That form is…draining. If we flew from here to Ceilail I would not have the strength to fight the beasts or the slavers, let alone take the captives to safety. You would be on your own."

'He should not be that weak as a deity,' Djialkan began, bristling. *'The Elders should have gifted him with power. At the very least, he should be stronger than a demigod—namely, you.'*

'You suspect something?' I asked Djialkan as Nalithor looked between us with a frustrated expression. "Walking is fine then. Can you have your contract instruct the forest and its creatures to impede the slavers in the even they attempt to leave?"

'If my hunch is right, we will have many important things to see to before we can so much as think *of returning to X'shmir or helping Sihix,'* Djialkan replied, clenching my shoulder tight with his talons. *'Onyre and Aleri have noticed strange happenings as well but cannot leave the lake. I will delve deeper into my search when we return to Dauthrmir. Fraelfnir's time is ever-consumed with caring for Darius. Until your brother can manage himself, Fraelfnir will not be able to assist us.'*

"Already done. Give me *some* credit, Arianna." Nalithor chuckled, shaking his head at me. "I suppose that, at the very least, we can pick up our pace."

Nalithor handed his empty box to me and shot me a small but unreadable smile. I dismissed both of our boxes into my shrizar as we resumed our trek across the variegated blue grass.

I wasn't sure what to think about the Adinvyr after my dream the prior night. The details had grown fuzzier by now, but him using his music to lure me out of hiding was still quite clear.

'You must still be connected to your heart. I can think of no other way for you to share dreams with a deity. Strange that you did not wake when he did, but I suppose it is for the best,' Djialkan remarked, rubbing his scaly cheek against my head. *'Such a shy child you were. Much has changed.'*

'Why didn't I have Brands of Divinity?' I scratched Djialkan's scales while examining our surroundings, taking in the lush, glowing scenery. We were almost entirely away from the forested section of the valley now and entering the more plains-like portion.

'You hid them. You were ashamed of being different.' Djialkan snorted at me. *'The fact that having no Brands whatsoever was also "different" escaped your grasp back then. However, does any of this really matter, Arianna?'*

'No...I suppose it doesn't.' I relented, disappointed. *'None of that matters now. I was just curious...'*

"Are you feeling better?" Nalithor interrupted my train of thought, lifting a scarlet mrifon up in front of my face. "You should keep this with you. We are likely to run into more of Amakiir's men while we see to business."

"Won't it wilt?" I accepted the flower from him and stared at it for a moment, before looking up at Nalithor again.

"Besides…where am I supposed to put this?"

"It wouldn't be such an issue if the Varjior had not twisted our tradition…" Nalithor sighed, flipping his braid over his shoulder. He plucked the flower from my hands and then tucked it behind my ear himself. "Mrifon drink aether, they will not wilt so easily. However, the color would be questionable outside of Abrantia."

"So, the Varjior decided to change the meanings of the colors as well?" I rolled my eyes. "I heard of the tradition from some of the Adinvyr women in Sihix, but only enough to get the general idea. Nothing more."

"You didn't notice that all of the workers in the Scarlet District wear red mrifon?" Nalithor laughed as my face burned hot. "In Amakiir's tribe, red is the color of warriors—the color of most things' blood. They chose to take 'liberties' when adopting Draemiran tradition."

"What a pain." I sighed, my shoulders slumping. "What about blue and white?"

"Blue is for mages, white is for nobility." Nalithor smiled at me, the swaying of his tail giving me the feeling he was stalking me like prey. "You're not thinking of going around hunting for a mate now, are you?"

"Hardly!" I huffed, crossing my arms. "These are the kinds of things that are important to know if I'm going to keep myself out of trouble. Right, Djialkan?"

"The day you keep yourself out of trouble is the day the entirety of

the Gal'edean freezes to the ocean floor," Djialkan retorted with disdain.

Silence fell around us for a while as we made our way through the thigh-high grass. Nalithor remained a pace or two ahead of me, occasionally glancing back as if I might simply disappear. A few times he looked as if he wanted to say something, but he'd just shake his head to himself and refocus his gaze forward again. I couldn't figure out what was bothering him, but it didn't seem appropriate for me to pry either. Instead, I chose what seemed like a happy medium—I picked up my pace and fell into step with him. *'Now he won't have to keep checking on me, right?'*

"You…said that I don't need an excuse to get to know you?" Nalithor murmured, his voice surprisingly quiet.

"That's right." I nodded, glancing to the side at him.

"What if it's a personal question?" Nalithor asked, shooting me a troubled glance.

"Ask me whatever you want. If I think you're out of line I'll say as much," I answered.

"Why…are you so loyal to Darius?" Nalithor released a heavy sigh and ran his fingers through his hair. "I feel as though I should understand, since I myself have siblings, but with his behavior…"

"Self-preservation," I responded. "My life belongs to X'shmir. Not because I have love for the country, but because Angelic magics bind my life—and Darius'—to X'shmir. I can't act out against the royals or nobles, let alone put Darius in his place, without risking my life.

"I would argue that a truly 'loyal' sibling would have set Darius straight long ago."

"Angelic magics again?" Nalithor slowed to a stop and pivoted to frown at me. "We've found no traces of Angels or their magics in X'shmir aside from…you. Darius laughed us off when we asked about the presence of Angels in X'shmir, claiming that they were just as 'mythical' as Devillians were."

"They are there, and they are 'corrupted' like the ones I spotted with the beasts yesterday," I murmured, tilting my head for a moment in thought. "You're worried about something?"

"What will happen to you if I execute the X'shmiran Court?" Nalithor narrowed his eyes and crossed his arms. "I intend to act as your blade, but if harm will—"

"You must make certain that X'shmir is far from Arianna," Djialkan interrupted, snorting darkness from his nostrils. *"Arianna's well-being is integral to the survival of the X'shmiran kingdom. As such, the Angels worked in numerous loopholes that keep her from death. If she is not physically there to handle a threat, the curse will not execute her—after all, without her, the X'shmirans would not be able to reclaim their lands."*

"Wouldn't the 'curse' force you to war with us to reclaim X'shmir then?" Nalithor glanced between Djialkan and me, his expression still one of unease. "Perhaps if we find a way to remove—"

"Nalithor, who is this woman?" An unfamiliar voice questioned from behind.

My skin prickled into goosebumps and adrenaline spiked into my system. I whirled around and summoned one of my swords to hand, leveling it with the throat of the robed man behind us. Nalithor quickly moved alongside me and caught my wrist, pressing firmly to indicate I should lower my weapon. When I shot him a questioning look, I found that his gaze was instead on the man that had appeared. Nalithor's expression gave me pause. His outer demeanor was calm and collected, but the fire in his eyes revealed his hatred and distrust of the robed creature.

The only thing I recognized about the intruder was his long white robes. They were like what the Elder Gods were wearing when they had taken me from Dauthrmir. However, this man radiated much less power.

"You didn't inform us that you finally selected a Chosen," a woman spoke, appearing beside the male.

"Arianna-jiss was assigned as my partner for a mission of Dauthrmiran origin," Nalithor spoke with intense distaste and pulled me slightly behind him, his grip firm enough to hurt my arm. "I have told you before that I loathe this practice of "Chosen" amongst the gods. I would not lower myself to such a level then, and I still will not now."

"Ah, hello there, Djialkan," the male of the pair remarked, earning a low hiss from the fae-dragon. *"We can find you a more*

worthy ward if you desire. Guarding a Human is beneath your capabilities."

"I am content with this one." Djialkan's voice dripped with acid, enough to make Nalithor tense and shoot him a warning glance. My companion bristled and looped his scaly tail around my shoulders. *"Arianna, I do not know these gods."*

'They're nowhere near as powerful as an Elder should be,' I agreed, watching as confusion crossed the pair's faces. *'You're going to go investigate?'*

'I will return to Dauthrmir on my own and consult Fraelfnir, Onyre, and Aleri—once this filth departs,' Djialkan confirmed.

"Our mission is a pressing matter," Nalithor spoke up, causing the Elders to exchange a glance. "I will make my report after we've concluded our business."

"Very well." The woman nodded, turning to her partner. *"Let's return. It would seem as though we jumped to conclusions too early."*

After the pair vanished Djialkan released a ferocious snarl and leapt into the air, making directly for the Dauthrmir Crater. Nalithor shot a frown after the fae-dragon and then shifted his attention down to me with a more pleasant expression on his face. However, he wasn't hiding his concern well, and I could only assume my elevated heartbeat was to blame.

The appearance of the "Elders" made me want to run and hide.

"Where is Djialkan going?" Nalithor gave me a brief squeeze before releasing me.

"…Djialkan doesn't recognize either of those 'Elders'. He's going to speak with Onyre, Aleri, and Fraelfnir on the matter." I decided to be honest. After a moment's hesitation I dismissed my sword and began following Nalithor again in the direction of Ceilail.

"I see… He must be concerned that perhaps his memories were tampered with…." Nalithor's mutter was barely audible, his demeanor pensive. "They *are* Elders. More precisely, they are the ones who were not pleased with my 'promotion.'"

'If the other "Elders" are as weak as those two were, I question whether or not Nalithor has actually become a deity.' I frowned to myself at the thought, then reached out to Djialkan once more. *'From your experience, how would you rate those "Elders" on the scale of power?'*

'Middle Gods, not even Upper,' Djialkan replied, then paused when I passed on what Nalithor had told me. *'This is a problem. I will investigate the other deities as well. Neither Nalithor nor the Elders should feel so weak. I knew it was strange that you could fight Nalithor so evenly, but the Elders… They feel weaker than him.'*

"Most people would have fainted with fear. Are you alright?" Nalithor pulled my attention back to him and cupped my face in his hand. I paused, a little surprised by his concern. Unfortunately, speaking my mind didn't seem wise.

"They startled me, more than anything." I sighed, twitching a little as Nalithor's hand slid from my cheek and he trailed his fingers down my throat. A small smile formed on his face as he let his hand drop to his side. "I'm fine, Nalithor. Don't worry about it."

Silence fell around us once again, aside from the soft swishing noise of the grass as we strode through it. The mrifon trees were now far behind us as we waded through a sea of grass and wildflowers. The Ceilail Forest was visible in the distance, its pale blue crystalline trees rising hundreds of feet into the air, if not a thousand. However, it was still far enough away that I couldn't make out any details aside from the color and the soft glow the trees emitted.

We both seemed content to remain silent. I wasn't sure about Nalithor, but the appearance of the Elders had put me on edge. It didn't seem "safe" to speak anymore. Nalithor shot me subtle glances of concern, but soon I sensed his attention pulling away from me and refocusing on something else. Small reverberations in the air around him gave me the feeling that he was communicating with someone, but the ripples were so minuscule that I couldn't be certain.

"We...have a problem." Nalithor's voice was little more than a growl, causing me to glance to the side at him. Waves of heat came off him as his anger simmered.

"What's wrong?" I asked, shifting my gaze up to his dark expression. *Hmmm... Angry Nalithor is kind of sexy.*

'...shut it, Ari.'

"The slavers have captured the chieftain's children. Three sons and two daughters." Nalithor bristled, his tone terse. "How many provisions did you prepare?"

"Enough for at least a week." I kept my reply simple, watching as the angered Adinvyr slowed to a stop.

"We are flying to Ceilail then," Nalithor stated in a tone that left no room for argument. "It will take a few days for me to recover, but we can't just wait idly by while the slavers have children in their grasp."

Nalithor seemed as if he was avoiding looking at me now. Anger shook his limbs and his tail thrashed behind him as he glared off in the direction of the Ceilail Forest. His expression was murderous and the heat wafting off him was growing hotter by the second. I did find his passion oddly attractive, but I also knew we were still in Amakiir's territory and weren't supposed to use our fire. Nalithor was losing his grip on his temper and, if I was his partner, then it was my responsibility to keep him in check. *'I think that's how it works, anyway.'*

"I suppose at this rate, 'breakfast' will become lunch or dinner," I remarked, smirking as I pulled the mrifon from my hair and dismissed it into one of my shrizars. My smirk shifted into a grin when Nalithor turned to me with a startled expression on his flushed face. "Which *reminds* me! Are mages *always* required to wear robes of status? Or are we allowed to wear other clothing as well?"

Somehow, my attempt at distracting Nalithor from his boiling rage appeared successful. At the very least, his muscles relaxed a bit and his tail stopped thrashing wildly. It was an improvement. Though the temperature around him didn't decrease, it did stop increasing.

"Other clothing? Nalithor arched an eyebrow, watching as I sheathed a pair of swords at my hips. "When we aren't officially on duty, we can wear anything we like. What are you plotting, hmmm?"

"Me? *Plot?*" I asked innocently. "I would never do such a thing."

Nalithor laughed and shook his head. He seemed to know I was ready, because in the next moment darkness enveloped him. Once his power dissipated, I was met by his *massive* draconic form stretched in the grass before me. I tilted my head, curious, and examined him. His claws and horns were both platinum in this form. The scales covering his body were like the scales on his tail in his Adinvyr form; obsidian with veins of platinum throughout. His eyes were still the same frosty blue.

'I was half expecting a smartass remark,' Nalithor informed me as I approached him warily. He was the size of a small airship, meaning that just one of his clawed feet was thicker than I was tall. *'Potential jokes aside, we should get going. Are you ready?'*

'Me? A smartass?' I laughed, hopping up Nalithor's scaly hide and into the saddle he had conjured between his front shoulder

blades. *'I was just thinking that this form suits you. You always manage to look regal, don't you?'*

'Regal?' Nalithor took on a teasing tone. *'Didn't you call me a scoundrel last night?'*

'You're both,' I replied. *'You're quite regal most of the time. Even those predatory movements of yours are quite regal.*

'The rest of the time I can't determine your intentions though, so "scoundrel" seems appropriate.'

Nalithor let out an indignant snort, shooting thick plumes of darkness from his maw. Moments later he leapt into the air. I could only giggle at him. The mannerism was so similar to Djialkan that it struck me as hilarious. That he, too, spit darkness made the resemblance even more apparent.

For some reason I had a strong urge to pet Nalithor's glistening scales, but I resigned myself to clutching the front of the saddle instead. *'I doubt he'd appreciate that...'*

The ground beneath us was a blur as Nalithor's wings propelled us toward the Ceilail Forest at an alarming speed. I used my power over wind to create a pocket of calm around myself, lest the wind tear me from his back. It was a trick I had learned after one of my first times riding one of Djialkan's larger forms around X'shmir— I had fallen from his back, *once,* and that was all it took to teach me that safety came before thrills when it came to riding a dragon.

Mere minutes passed before I caught the vile scent and aura of beasts. I released a feral growl and tensed in the saddle. My amusement with Nalithor instantly faded into intense bloodlust. There were so many filthy creatures hiding in Ceilail, and they all needed to *die*. *I'll rip them limb-from-limb and scatter their shredded bones and entrails across the forest floor! I'll stain the entire forest in those bastard's blood! I'll—'*

'*By the Elders, woman, calm down!*' Nalithor growled at me, causing me to glance at him briefly before returning my attentions to the forest instead. '*At the very least you should wait until I've* landed *before trying to leap from the damned saddle!*'

'*They need to* die!' I hissed in protest, gripping the saddle tighter as I rose up in it. '*I want to go kill* all *of them. What's so wrong with that?*'

'*If you get any more "excited", killing our prey will be the* last *thing on my mind,*' Nalithor retorted in a dangerous tone. My face burned scarlet when I realized what he was talking about, but I was too far gone to calm myself. '*Remember not to kill* everything, alright? Just—'

'*Just the beasts and the slavers. I know!*' I leapt down from his back and landed in a crouch, watching as the Adinvyr returned to his normal form. Power and rage rippled off him freely now, giving him the appearance of a proper, enraged, deity.

I combined my wind and darkness, then launched myself into the Ceilail Forest to hunt. My pulse roared in my ears as I wove my way through the massive branches, climbing high as I could go without losing sight of the forest floor. There was no way in the infernal hells that I was going to control myself when there was so much *filth* nearby to kill. The Adinvyr's warning was of no concern to me anymore. If there were repercussions for my rage-induced arousal or my murderous rampage, I would deal with it later.

I ripped into the nearest beast I could find with a delighted cackle, tearing it into several large chunks with my swords before dashing after the next. Another laugh escaped me when I sensed Nalithor rushing through the forest ahead of me and to the slaver's camp. Perhaps I would leave the slavers to him. There were too many beasts to deal with.

Much to my disappointment, all the beasts I encountered were weak. The smallest one was about the size of a rat, while the largest was around the size of a stag. Unlike their X'shmiran brethren, the Rilzaan Chaos Beasts resembled living things instead of lumps of flesh. They were more like vile, angry animals instead of sewn-together corpses. Though, they still smelled terrible.

It took me at *least* half an hour before I was satisfied there were no more beasts alive in the Ceilail Forest. At least, no beasts of the chaos variety. *'Why are the slavers still alive?'*

My curiosity took over as I made my way in the direction I smelled Nalithor in. I stepped uncaringly across the corpses of fallen beasts as I went. Their oily black blood was a stark contrast to the pale, frosty foliage of the forest. Grimacing, I kicked a few bodies of slavers out of my way before continuing onward. I heard voices ahead, and there was an oddly seductive and sing-song lilt to Nalithor's rumbling voice.

After so much bloodshed my mood was significantly improved. I had a spring in my step and a grin, possibly a wild one, on my face. I giggled to myself when a fun idea crossed my mind. *'Maybe I should play with Nalithor since he's so accepting of my bloodlust. That could be fun!'*

"Now then, which of you would like to die first?" Nalithor purred in a dangerous manner. The Adinvyr shifted slightly in place, listening as I approached him from behind. The slavers he'd cornered released shrieks, their eyes growing wide as they stared at my blood-coated armor. Nalithor settled his gaze fully on the slavers again, but addressed me, "Done with the beasts already, my dear?"

"They weren't any fun." I slipped my arms around Nalithor's torso and leaned up against his side, smirking. "I think you can find me better toys to play with next time.

Nalithor glanced down at me with a surprised expression on his face, examining me for a moment. His attention snapped back to his prey when they began to splutter.

"What's this? The God of Balance has found himself a new whore to do his dirty work?" The less fearful of the men sneered, though he shrunk back when I growled at him.

"Well, I suppose that answers my former question," Nalithor snarled, making a dismissive motion with his left hand. The offending slaver's terrified scream was cut off by an invisible force ripping his head and limbs from his torso. My Adinvyr companion seemed unfazed and slid his right arm behind my back while his tail coiled around my hips. He didn't seem to care at all that I was covered in blood. *'Not so much as a flinch from you, my dear? I never told you my role.'*

'I'm more observant than you might think. I at least had an idea,' I replied with a small shrug, studying the slavers. *'Well, several ideas really. But you seemed like you didn't want your status or role broadcast. So, I decided not to bring it up.'*

"Look at how tiny this bitch is even in plate armor! How could *she* have dealt with the beasts?" One of the slavers snapped to his comrades. "No horns, no tail... But an Elf couldn't handle that many either!"

"Mmm.... Can I kill them?" I looked up at Nalithor and bit my lower lip, dragging the points of my clawed gauntlet down his exposed abdomen.

"I'm not done with them yet." Nalithor chuckled and caught my wrist, a mischievous glint in his eyes. "You are positively *dripping* with blood. How about switching back to your clothing, hmmm? We will have to care for your armor later."

I nodded in reply and let my armor dissolve back into my jewelry, returning to my kimono-like ensemble from before. Nalithor released another low growl when the slaver's eyes wandered to inappropriate places. The Adinvyr tightened his grip on me and shot the group of men a chilling glare. It took the bastards longer than it should have to notice my Brands but, when they did, they started muttering to each other in a language I couldn't understand.

"You're sure I can't kill them?" I inquired, turning my attention upwards to Nalithor again. *'Maybe a cute pout will change his mind?'*

"When you look at me like *that*, it's very tempting to let you do as you please," Nalithor replied after a moment of thought, bringing his hand up to my face. He rested his thumb against my lower lip and then smiled at me, shaking his head. "If you're a good girl, I *might* let you help. For now…you should clean off the rest of the blood before it taints that lovely scent of yours."

"*Fine.*" I sighed as Nalithor loosened his grip enough for me to move away. After taking a few paces away from him I planted myself on a nearby boulder and crossed my legs. "Hmmm? What's *that* look for, Nalithor?"

"You intend to watch me…'question' them?" Nalithor's expression filled with curiosity, though the playful swaying of his tail made me wonder what he was *actually* thinking. The way he tracked me while I cleansed the blood from my skin and hair made me feel like he was considering making *me* his prey next.

"I have to make sure you live up to my standards," I replied sweetly, leaning back on my palms. *'If he wants to be difficult, I'll just have to be more difficult.'*

Nalithor shook his head at me, an amused smirk settling on his face. I just smiled at him and watched with interest as he turned his attention to the trembling slavers. It was strange to me that anyone was so frightened by the Adinvyr. His presence struck *me* as comforting and a little alluring.

'Maybe more than a "little" alluring,' I corrected myself, tapping my foot against the air.

"Arianna, dear, this one seems to think that you're one of the typical strumpets that follows me around," Nalithor called in a teasing purr, so I glanced at the terrified slaver he motioned at. "I'm sure you have something to say about *that* don't you?"

Instead of speaking, I glared at the slaver and summoned a pair of icicles up from beneath him, simultaneously skewering and freezing both of his testicles to the ground. The bastard yowled in agony, so I smirked and turned my gaze to the remaining slavers.

"I would be happy to give the rest of you the same treatment if you think spouting off like your friend there is a wise choice," I offered with mock-innocence. "I'm sure at least one of you can scream better than him."

"What a nasty creature!" One shrieked, pointed at me, then looked up at the amused deity. "With Brands like *that*...did you choose to make this bitch your goddess?!"

"While that's certainly an intriguing option," Nalithor began dryly, crossing his arms, "Arianna-jiss is not a goddess...as far as I'm aware." He glanced toward me as if considering something, then looked at the slavers again. "Ahhh... I really can't stand filth such as you overlong… None of you understand how to treat or address a lady *properly*.

"Let's get going, Arianna. We still have much to do."

I barely heard him. I shot to my feet in a split second and darted past him with a sword in hand. One of the slavers had drawn a weapon and was preparing to stab Nalithor in the back. There was no way in the infernal hells I was going to allow that to happen. I would make them pay.

The poor bastard shrieked in terror as I grabbed him by his blade arm and tore it from its socket. In the next moment I silenced him with a sword through his throat. I removed my sword with a flourish, uncaring as blood sprayed across my clothes and face. With a small "humph" I dropped the corpse on the ground and then moved to take care of the others.

"Now you're all bloody again." Nalithor captured me around the waist and leaned down to nuzzle my throat, releasing a husky chuckle. "Ah, ah, ah, I'm not letting you kill the rest of them."

"But—" I began to protest, pouting as Nalithor pulled me a few paces away from the screaming men.

"I let you have all of the beasts to yourself." Nalithor purred, turning me to face him. One of his hands rose to my throat as he used his own magic to brush away my fresh coating of blood. "Don't you think it's *my* turn to tear things apart?"

Nalithor didn't give me a chance to respond. He leaned down and pressed his lips to mine, his hand shifting upwards to my face.

What I expected to be a brief kiss turned into a lengthy one. He pressed his other hand against the small of my back, pulling me as close as possible.

I thought my heart was going to beat out of my chest, or that my face might ignite—and I wasn't sure which would happen first. Part of me feared my curse might strike at me for the intimate action, but my concerns were soon overpowered.

The Adinvyr was a damned tease. Every time I thought the kiss was growing more passionate, that I would get to taste more of him, he pulled back into a softer and more "innocent" kiss.

Nalithor eventually pulled away with a self-satisfied smirk on his face. He licked his lips, chuckled, then hefted me over one of his shoulders with ease. I couldn't think of anything to say, so I remained quiet as he carried me away from the slavers. I glanced up from the ground in time to see the foul men burst into chunks, ripped apart by some unknown force. With them gone, the forest grew silent again.

I sighed, slightly irritated, as Nalithor's clawed hand wrapped around the back of one of my thighs. There was a surprising amount of pep in his step for someone who *should* have been weakened from flying. His tail had resumed its playful swishing, tempting me to freeze it in place.

"I can *walk* you know," I commented after letting him carry me for a while. Nalithor chuckled and began tracing random patterns on my thigh with his thumb, making me twitch. Maybe I needed to try harder to distract him. "You already dealt with the captives, I'm assuming?"

"Your frenzies are *that* blinding?" Nalithor inquired, carrying me deeper into Ceilail and showing no sign of letting me down. "While you were so *expertly* keeping the beasts occupied, the forest's inhabitants and I evacuated the captives.

"Mmm…your bloodlust is rather infectious, Arianna. I haven't enjoyed a hunt so much in a long time."

"You're welcome…I think?" I tilted my head to the side, listening as he laughed again. "In all seriousness, do you wish to hide the fact that you're the God of Balance, or—"

"Well you *have* seen the problems I deal with merely for being an Adinvyr," Nalithor replied dryly, giving my thigh a squeeze. "As a god without a goddess… Well, can you imagine how much worse things would be if my role and rank were known? Mine is a role between the Upper and Elder Gods, my dear. The types of women who are drawn by power and rank are of no interest to me."

"I see your point." I grimaced. Nalithor finally set me down, so I adjusted my kimono to make sure everything was where it should be, and then looked up at the Adinvyr again. "If you're trying to hide your rank then you should probably try harder. With Brands brighter than Lucifer's, it isn't exactly difficult to tell you're more powerful than him."

"Oh? Is that how you found out?" Nalithor slipped an arm around me again and pulled me tight against his side, a small smile on his face. "Still…you should have been at least a *little* affected by my power. At the very least *your* bloodlust shouldn't have affected *me* so strongly.

"Mmm… Perhaps I should kiss you again to be sure."

"You're the strongest person in Dauthrmir," I pointed out, my tone flat as I tried to distract him from the notion. He gave me a crooked grin and squeezed me again.

"You don't plan on giving away my little secret at all, do you?" Nalithor murmured, lifting his free hand to my face. "Hmmm, if we hurry, I might be able to fly us back to the airship."

"We can walk. I'm in no hurry." I shook my head, then attempted to pull my face away from his hand, feeling my face growing hotter. "I get the distinct feeling that you're attempting to avoid something in Dauthrmir anyway. No need for us to rush back if neither of us are keen on doing so."

"Mmm…" Nalithor pulled me tighter against him and studied me, smiling when I flushed darker. "If I'm being honest, I don't want to share the sight of you in this attire. You were quite the sight while sleeping on my chest… You didn't have to move, you know."

"It didn't seem appropriate for me to *stay* either…" I grumbled, averting my gaze completely.

"*I* knew *you would be a fool and consider returning to Dauthrmir too early!*" Djialkan snapped, swooping down from above. He sent several small branches crashing to the ground around us, startling me. *"The sooner you rest, Nalithor, the sooner we can return. We should not leave that* boy *on his own for long, lest he convinces the whole of Vorpmasia that you are his personal toy!*

"Alala may be capable of protecting the house, but she cannot do anything about that brat's mouth!"

"*Toy?*" Nalithor growled. I arched an eyebrow as the Adinvyr released me and rounded on Djialkan, pointing his finger at the fae-dragon's snout. "Just what do you mean by *toy?*"

"Darius is quite likely to claim that he's making—or has already made—you his pet," I remarked, resting my cheek against my fist as I watched the agitated Adinvyr. "Since he's been called out by the Oracles as a dominant in the bedroom, he's going to assume that means *you* are a submissive. He'll do whatever he can to drive off 'potential suitors.' That's just how Darius is."

"I thought I made it quite clear that I'm not interested." Nalithor shook his head and then pivoted to look at me, his expression softening.

"Darius is Darius…" I frowned, thinking. "Despite everything that's happened to him, he truly believes the world revolves around him. If he finds himself attracted to someone, he thinks it's because they're 'suitable' to his tastes. He believes it's impossible to be attracted to someone who won't be mutually interested."

"What of you, then?" Nalithor examined me, his question catching me off-guard. "You don't seem like you share your brother's views on such matters, and you don't appear to be affected by my power as a god or as an Adinvyr."

"She may not be affected by your power," Djialkan began slyly, *"but that does not mean she is unaffected by you. Can you honestly claim that she would be so easy to fluster if she wasn't at least a* little *attracted—"*

"Djialkan, I really am going to turn you into a pair of boots one of these days!" I clamped my hand around the fae-dragon's snout, then glanced toward the smirking Adinvyr. "Oh please. Don't look so smug!"

"You know, if you're *attracted* to me," Nalithor started with a sultry purr, "I should still be able to sense *some* level of desire from you. Yet the only time I've noticed your arousal is when you're fighting beasts. A younger Adinvyr would probably be insulted, you know."

'Fool!' Djialkan snorted. *'He should know better than to rely solely on his power. Has he forsaken his skills of observation completely?!'*

"Someone so easily insulted wouldn't be worth my time anyway!" I retorted, bristling when I felt my face growing warm again. I averted my gaze and pivoted away from him, then sighed, continuing, "Aren't you supposed to rest after using your draconic form for so long? Should you really be—"

"Djialkan, did you find one?" Nalithor pulled me into his chest and looked to my scaly companion.

"I found several and placed them in Arianna's shrizar. You are certain that mrifon are necessary even here?" Djialkan nodded to

Nalithor.

"They are," Nalithor replied, smoothing one of his hands down my back. "Arianna… You should slip several of the mrifon Djialkan gathered into your hair before our hosts find us. It wouldn't do…for…"

With difficulty, I caught Nalithor when his knees gave out. He rested his forehead against my shoulder as I lowered him carefully to the ground, making sure not to step on his tail. The strength in his limbs was almost nonexistent, and his breathing was slowing despite his pulse quickening beneath my hands.

"You pushed yourself too hard?" I asked, resting him back against the trunk of a tree.

"You smell…amazing." Nalithor sighed, capturing me around the waist. He pulled me closer and buried his face into the crook of my neck. He inhaled deeply and then mumbled, "I…should…"

"You…should sleep." I managed to say, even as his lips traveled down the side of my throat. I carefully dislodged his grip on me and gave him a look, attempting to redirect his attention. "Others are coming, you said?"

"If they so much as *look* at you inappropriately, I'll kill them," Nalithor muttered. His grip loosened as he glanced away from me and slumped back against the tree fully. He looked a little disappointed, but mostly he just looked exhausted.

'Arianna, the mrifon,' Djialkan reminded me as Nalithor's eyelids fluttered shut. '*Tch, your bloodlust must have invigorated him just enough for him to finish the mission. He is utterly drained.'*

I shook my head and opened a shrizar in search of the mrifon Djialkan had apparently gathered. The sapphire blue and snow-white blossoms were, admittedly, gorgeous. However, I couldn't understand why I would need so many. I selected two out of the nearly two dozen and then wove them into one of my less-used hair pieces. Pinning some of my hair up was the only way I could think of to keep some of the large flowers in my hair. Sticking two behind my ear didn't seem possible and putting one behind each ear seemed silly.

'Why did you get so many?' I shifted my attention away from Nalithor and over to Djialkan.

'He is fond of you, and so he requested many.' Djialkan shrugged his wings, then chortled at my expression. *'Men from the village deeper within Ceilail will arrive soon. You should prepare yourself to help them with Nalithor. I doubt it would be wise to leave him in the hands of their women.'*

"Stay…" Nalithor grumbled, catching me by the wrist when I went to move away from him.

'You are both clingy sleepers!' Djialkan cackled. *'Well, Arianna? Are you going to leave him?* Hmmm?'

'You're enjoying this too much.' I shot Djialkan a filthy look before turning my attention to the troubled Adinvyr. *'I guess I can stay…'*

Someone was fond of me? It was such a strange notion. I

couldn't quite comprehend it, and I wasn't sure if I even wanted to try. I already had a hard time believing that he had kissed me again, even though I could still taste him on my lips. It was a little disappointing that he'd ended our kiss when he did.

'Has he realized I'm uninterested in his power and status, then?' I leaned back against the tree beside Nalithor and glanced to the side at him as his grip on my wrist loosened. *'I wouldn't think he'd be this familiar with someone he thinks is using him… Though, perhaps he's just hungry.'*

Shaking my head, I decided not to dwell on it. I could hear several pairs of footsteps approaching through the icy underbrush. Perhaps once things had settled down then, and only then, I could ponder Nalithor's actions.

CHAPTER TWENTY-ONE
Understanding

"Nali, what's wrong?" The bloodied child looked down at me with bright blue eyes, genuine confusion plain on her face. "They were bad men, weren't they? They came to hurt us."

Arianna shifted her gaze to look at the torn corpses of Elves at her feet. She lifted her blood-soaked petticoat a few inches and stepped over the assortment of scattered limbs and other body parts, searching for something. I couldn't comprehend what I had just seen. Her darkness had torn through the Elven assassins like a wild animal, ripping them into nearly unrecognizable chunks of meat.

It was our first mission, yet she had killed them without hesitation.

"How are you so calm, Arianna?" I sighed, my shoulders slumping as I wiped vomit from the corners of my mouth. "You tore them apart *like—"*

The smell of death and vacated bowels made me retch again, but I had already emptied the contents of my stomach.

"I knew you wouldn't understand...no one does..." Arianna paused, sniffling, as she clenched her fists and stared down at her bloodied shoes. "I'm going home."

"Wait, Arianna—" Something hit the back of my head, making my world spin.

The last thing I heard was the sound of the tiny Devillian girl shrieking in rage, followed by the sickening crunch of breaking bones.

Darkness embraced me as Arianna's scent enveloped me. But no, it wasn't the scent of her as a child. This was...

I opened my eyes and stared wearily at the roughhewn beams above the bed. The chill in the air told me that we were still somewhere within the Ceilail Forest, yet I was comfortably warm. Frowning, I sat up and then winced when my body creaked in protest. Glancing down, I discovered many layers of blankets and furs draped across my lap. My robes were missing, leaving me in nothing but a pair of loose trousers.

'By the Elders, her scent...' I took a shaky breath, attempting to calm myself even as my pulse raced. *'It wouldn't be this strong just from the blankets. Where is...'*

My thoughts trailed off as I turned to look around the room and found Arianna laid out on a small sofa opposite from me. She was sound asleep, and her head had lolled to the side, revealing a long stretch of her soft throat. The blankets she had summoned for herself had fallen to the floor to reveal the pale swell of her breasts and the short nightgown she wore. Somehow, she seemed peaceful despite the lightweight clothing and the awkward angle the lower half of her torso was twisted in.

I pulled myself out of bed and strode quietly across the room to her, taking in her exquisite figure as I approached. Her full breasts, round hips, and shapely ass… I couldn't deny that she was an amusingly troublesome woman.

'Nnngh, how long have I been asleep?' I perched on the edge of Arianna's sofa, tracing my fingers down her cheek and along her jawline; she didn't budge. *'I want to taste* all *of her.'*

Grimacing, I recoiled my hand and shook my head to clear my thoughts. Feeding on Arianna wasn't an option. Not yet. Her blood by itself wouldn't be enough to sate my desire for her, and I hadn't yet "earned" the right to possess every inch of her—

I sighed, covering my face with one hand as I took careful breaths. *'Did I overdo it and stay in that form for too long? I shouldn't be this hungry.'*

After a moment of hesitation, I lifted the slumbering princess into my arms and carried her across the room to the bed where it was warmer. Arianna grumbled something incoherent in her sleep and turned into my chest, nuzzling her cheek against my bare skin. She released a contented sigh, her heartbeat growing calmer even as mine threatened to race out of control.

It was a minor miracle that my pulse didn't wake her, but I knew better than to tempt fate.

I carefully laid Arianna in bed and pulled the blankets over her, making certain she wouldn't find herself growing cold. Satisfied the blankets wouldn't fall off, I sat on the edge of the bed and cupped her face in my hand. She seemed truly exhausted. Her mind was completely still.

'Was Djialkan telling the truth? I affect her? Not my power but truly...me?' It was such a peculiar notion.

For most of my life, I had struggled with people desiring me for my power, my status, or because my Adinvyr traits drew them in. They cared for nothing else. Power, status, and wealth were all anyone saw when they looked at me. My parents had the foresight to warn me about such things but knowing beforehand only took the edge off the many disappointments.

The Royal Families of Vorpmasia, and their children, made up the majority of people who treated me normally. Even the rare noble or commoner who *didn't* desire men still only saw me for my power and influence, leaving me with only the other Devillian demigods to call as friends. That had begun to change over the years, thankfully, as I grew to know more warriors.

Alas, most of the women in Vorpmasia still only saw me for my power.

'What does she see?' I wondered, studying Arianna's face as I stroked her cheek. *'Tch... The one woman I truly want to devour*

and she's unavailable. Even a small taste…'

Arianna shifted in her sleep when I leaned down toward her. I froze in place and held my breath as she rubbed her face into my hand, a small smile playing on her lips. I'd thought that perhaps I had woken her, but no. She was still fast asleep, and letting her rest was likely in my best interests. My hunger was rising again just looking at her.

Leaning down, I pressed my lips to hers and savored the sensation of her plush lips and her sweet taste. Reluctant, I rose to my feet and summoned loose robes around myself, then glanced back at Arianna before leaving the cottage. I needed to bathe, and I needed to find someone willing to share their blood with me.

Judging by the state the cottage was in, and how exhausted she was, I could only assume that Arianna had been caring for me while I regained my strength. Although I wanted to drink in every part of that exquisite woman, imposing on her further seemed…inappropriate, at best.

'Just what is it going to take for me to "earn" the right to feed from her?' I huffed, stalking through the sleepy village. My tail snapped back and forth in irritation as I made my way for the nearby springs. *'If just a kiss tastes so amazing, I wonder what—'*

I released a frustrated groan and braced myself against the trunk of a tree just outside the village. This wasn't merely an issue of hunger, though I wanted to tell myself that's all it was. I wanted Arianna for more than just her blood or her alluring physique. My desire wasn't driven by hunger, it was driven by my attraction to her. I had misinterpreted my lust as the need to regain my strength, but the intensity of my desire for Arianna did not match the minute level of hunger I felt.

Perhaps it was time to accept that I genuinely wanted her and began acting as such.

"*She will be quite cross if you are not resting when she wakes,*" Djialkan commented. The fae-dragon appeared on my shoulder and dug his talons into my skin, snorting.

"Waking her did not seem appropriate," I replied, shutting my eyes. Sighing, I shook my head and then looked at Djialkan again. "She...has been caring for me? For how long?"

"*Four days.*" Djialkan tilted his head, violet eyes seeming to look through me. "*The villagers offered to care for you in her stead, but she refused to let them near you. How is your strength?*"

"I'm hungry," I muttered, pushing away from the trunk of the tree. "Most of my power has returned. We should be able to return to Dauthrmir whenever we like. Have the captives calmed yet?"

"*Not as much as we would like.*" Djialkan shot me an odd look and then nosed my cheek. "*You are struggling to accept your attraction to my ward still?*" The fae-dragon cackled when I twitched, then shook his head. "*You are still concerned that she is a fake?*"

"She's..." I looked away from Djialkan, my heart beating in my throat. Part of me still wanted to deny that she could truly be the same Arianna. The whirlwind of both pain and relief that I felt otherwise was overwhelming. "I...know, Djialkan. I know. Do you think I haven't noticed her dream-walking? Her confusion over witnessing memories that are no longer hers? That her power reaches for me even in her sleep?

"I struggle to let myself hope, Djialkan. Even if it *is* her... I promised myself that I wouldn't allow her to be swept back into the role of Balance. She has been through so much. To let her bear such a burden, if I could prevent that—"

"You are a fool." Djialkan pivoted and lashed my face with his tail. *"Unlike you, Arianna was created for the role of Balance! Do you think she would forgive you if you abandoned her? Let alone with such flimsy reasoning? I will destroy you myself if you attempt something so foolish—if Lucifer does not beat me to it."*

Djialkan leapt from my shoulder and disappeared through the trees, leaving me staring after him. I didn't know how to respond to the fae-dragon's threat. My chest constricted as I thought on his words. Abandonment. For so long I had been afraid that Arianna believed we abandoned her to the Elders, to Limbo. That she would hold a grudge against me for not saving her sooner.

I cursed, slamming my fist into the nearest tree. Then I paused, hesitant realization overcoming my frustration. *'Djialkan... Is that your way of giving me your approval?'*

'Break her heart and the Elders, Exiles, and beasts will be the least of your worries.' The fae-dragon's snarling reply left me in a state of

momentary shock. *'She is no longer familiar with Devillian ways of any kind, Nalithor. Be patient with her.*

'Do not...bring up the past. Not unless absolutely necessary. She struggles to understand it, to accept it. Allow her to come to you with it, in time, when she is ready.'

Djialkan's presence faded entirely before I could reply, leaving me to rest against a tree in solitary thought. I never would have thought that Arianna's Guardian would give me explicit approval, not after all that had happened. Not after I failed to stop those bastards from taking her away so many years ago.

I shut my eyes and took a deep, steadying breath. There was nothing I could have done back then. We were small children in the presence of beings far more powerful than we were. Neither of us stood a chance against the Elders or the Angels that had come for Arianna. I knew that, but it was still hard for me to accept.

Up until I had first stumbled upon Arianna in X'shmir, I had spent my life trying to make up for a failure I had never made. The inability to keep the Elders from taking Arianna. Of course, I hadn't been able to protect her back then. But now...

I looked down at one of my hands and clenched my fist, my claws drawing blood from my palm. It was different now. I had infinitely more power now. More experience. The Elder's powers were waning, as was their influence over the other gods. The fools didn't even seem to know who Arianna was—that they truly thought her to be Human was laughable. They, of all creatures, should have known that wasn't the case.

'If I abandon her...there will be no one to protect her.' The realization hit me, eliciting a snarl.

Djialkan and Alala were her Guardians, certainly, but they didn't have the power to go against the Elders. That wasn't their purpose nor was it their role. In theory, I shouldn't have had the power to protect her either...but I felt as though I did.

My mind was made up as I strode toward the springs once more. I didn't want Arianna to experience the pain that could come with the role of Balance, but I couldn't abandon her. She would be mine. I would protect her. Even if it took slaying the Elder Gods to keep Arianna safe, I would do it.

I chuckled to myself as I neared the empty springs and stripped my clothes off. When the Elders took Arianna from me, I had vowed to slay them. Those plans had fallen to the wayside once I became the God of Balance—there were just too many things to "fix" in the world. Yet now I had come back to my original goal; slaying the Elders. If they ever realized who Arianna was, I was certain they would attempt to intervene again.

A shiver of excitement ran through me as I thought on it. To slay the Elders and claim Arianna for myself. *That* was a goal worth bleeding for. Worth killing for.

'No one will take her from me. Never again.'

CHAPTER TWENTY-TWO
Encountering a Lari'xan

'Where is he?' I wondered, sweeping along the frozen roads of Ceilail's central village. Frowning, I tugged my hood over my face and shivered. I hadn't planned on leaving the warmth house today but waking up to a certain Adinvyr missing had changed my plans.

Banayr'e was the central hub of activity within the Ceilail Forest and housed several thousand citizens within its sprawling web of buildings. The people of Banayr'e were surprisingly accepting of my refusal to let them near the slumbering Adinvyr, so I had been surprised when I awoke to find him missing—let alone that he had placed me in bed.

'It's only been four days! Has he already recovered enough to be wandering around?' I gnawed on my lower lip and surveyed my

surroundings, unsure of where to look next. *'Tch, where in the hells did he run off to? I've searched half the town already!'*

I quickened my pace and nodded my acknowledgment to the occasional citizen who greeted me. The village was bustling with people this morning, but most of them stayed out of my way to tend to their own tasks. I found it easy to differentiate between the citizens and the captives that Nalithor had liberated, as the people corrupted by Ceilail's power all took upon icy qualities.

The Devillians of the forest, for example, had horns, scales, and claws made of varying shades of ice. Most of the people there had skin, hair, and eye colors that followed the same frosty theme. Pale shades of blues, purples, and even greens combined with white to create a natural camouflage for the people and creatures of Ceilail alike.

They were lucky that they hadn't turned fully into creatures of ice. If they had, I doubted they would have been able to survive for long without breaking.

'Why am I so desperate to find him? I know he can take care of himself.' I bit back a frustrated grimace and hugged myself as I passed a group of Centaur and Dryad women. Though the people here seemed accepting of me, they dropped their voices to hushed tones whenever I drew near.

"Lady Arianna!" An older Elven woman beckoned me, a bright smile on her face. "'ere, ye prolly fergot ta eat 'gain, din't ye?"

The woman, named En'risa, reached out and offered me a bag

of sweet-smelling pastries. Her smile grew as she urged me to accept it. Along with the rest of the elder generation of Banayr'e. En'risa had declared that they would take care of *me* while I cared for Nalithor. They were kind, but they wouldn't take no for an answer.

That, at least, was something they shared with their brethren in Sihix.

"En'risa, have you seen Nalithor by chance?" I hesitated to ask, accepting the basket. The old woman grinned broadly, her eyes twinkling.

"Tha' boy wandered off already?" En'risa barked with laughter. "Ye best find 'im, milady. I dun know much bou'ta gods, but turnin' inta a dragon mus' be damn drainin'!"

With another smile, En'risa shooed me on my way and I resumed my search for the pesky Adinvyr. I pulled a warm sticky bun from the bag and nibbled at it as I walked through the town. Perhaps when we returned to Dauthrmir I would ask the Vorpmasians about establishing a trade agreement with Sihix; we certainly needed a wider variety of spices and herbs for cooking up there, and I really wanted to make better food for the people in Sihix. They would love it, and it was at least *something* I could do to thank them for all they'd done for me.

"He couldn't stand the taste of your blood either?" The worried whispering of a woman drew my attention to a group of female Adinvyr. *"Rely'ric wasn't acting strange at all. So, why did he withdraw after a brief taste?"*

"At this rate it will take weeks for His Highness to recover, won't it?" A second female spoke, looking distraught. *"What's so repulsive about our blood anyway?"*

"You've seen Nalithor recently, then?" I spoke up, watching as the four women flinched and turned to look at me with fearful expressions. "Did you happen to see which way he went? I doubt he should be out of bed yet."

"A-Arianna-jiss, I apologize. I d-don't know," one woman replied, hiding her wrists in the sleeves of her tunic as if it would keep me from noticing the fang marks on her flesh. "When I saw him, he was returning from Ceilail's temple, but that was bells ago."

"Thanks." I turned away from the women and began walking again.

The corner of my eye twitched as I stalked off and chewed on my lower lip. My jealousy threatened to boil over, tempting me to rip those women apart. Just thinking about it made shivers travel down my spine. I bit my lip harder and shut my eyes for a moment, trying to still my thoughts. This was not the time for unwarranted jealousy. I had a missing *deity* to find.

'Calm down,' I told myself, aware of the darkness rippling around my feet. My shadows traveled up my legs and wrapped around my body as images of ways to kill those women flowed through my mind. *'He's an Adinvyr. I knew he would need to feed after draining himself of so much power. It's not like he would lower*

himself to feeding off me in my sleep, and he's too much of a gentleman to wake me up for—

'Wait. Why in the infernal hells am I jealous that he isn't feeding on me?! That doesn't make any sense!'

I rolled my eyes at myself and continued my way through the ice-covered streets, my jealousy subsiding as quickly as it had come. Nalithor had chosen to bite their wrists instead of more intimate regions, and he apparently disliked the taste of their blood. As such, he wouldn't have recovered much of his strength yet. *'That could be a problem. I need to find him, and soon.'*

I muttered to myself and rummaged around in my bag for another sticky bun, then nibbled on it as I continued through Banayr'e. Eventually I came to the northwestern boundaries of the city and stopped. I scented the air for a moment and then sighed; Nalithor hadn't gone there either. As I begun to turn, I caught the sound of familiar wings and glanced up through the glowing trees.

'Arianna, come with me.' Djialkan growled, swooping down to hover in front of my face. *'Whatever you are searching for can wait.'*

'I was trying to find Nalithor. He snuck out of the cottage while I was asleep.' I pouted, feeding Djialkan the last bite of my pastry. *'You found something important while searching the forest?'*

'We will not require the High Priest's blessing to meet with Ceilail,' Djialkan snarled, drifting a few yards away before beckoning me. *'This way, Arianna. Your search for that one must wait.'*

Nodding, I dismissed the bag of baked goods into my shrizar and then hurried through the forest alongside Djialkan. It had been a long time since I'd last seen him so agitated. It was almost enough to distract me from the concern I felt for Nalithor. *Almost.* The more I thought about him, the more I realized it seemed strange for him to reject the taste of those women's blood. My jealousy was long gone, replaced entirely by my concern for his wellbeing.

The people of Banayr'e had been waiting for Nalithor to recover for *days.* They seemed as if they had more business with Nalithor, beyond the slavers and beasts we had dealt with, but they didn't trust me enough to discuss it with me. Djialkan and I were convinced that it had something to do with the village's missing High Priest of Ceilail—that was all the people seemed to talk about.

Djialkan and I had been trying to meet with the High Priest, and the temple guards claimed that he was ill. A little snooping around late at night from Djialkan, as well as eavesdropping, had revealed that the man was missing. Not ill.

'What did you find?' I asked, pushing translucent underbrush out of my way.

'I do not believe it is a coincidence that we ran into the false Elders on our way here.' Djialkan bristled, spitting shadows from his maw. *'Unlike in Sihix, the temple in Banayr'e does not lead to the forest's core. I found it elsewhere…along with our missing High Priest.'*

I scowled and picked up my pace, weaving through the frosty

forest with what some might have found to be an alarming speed.

Thankfully the ground was not solid ice. The aether that flowed through Ceilail had changed everything from the largest of trees and animals to the tiniest of mushrooms and the dirt they grew from. Each granule of dirt was a deep frosted blue or purple, while much of the grass and other flora was translucent and pale, or entirely devoid of color.

Every person, animal, and insect all looked as if they were made from ice, though I'd discovered that wasn't quite the case. They were indeed fragile, but their flesh was still flesh. It was just…different.

The deeper we traveled into the forest, the more my unease grew. Something felt terribly wrong, but I couldn't determine just *what* the problem was. It made my skin crawl, it made me want to tear something to shreds with my bare hands. I wanted to dig my fingers through its bloody flesh as it wailed for mercy.

'J-just what did you find, Djialkan?' I shivered and bit my lower lip in anticipation. My halfhearted attempts at calming myself were doing nothing. *'I don't smell any beasts.'*

'If you are already reacting in this manner, my hunch must have been right,' Djialkan muttered, shaking his mane. *'It will make more sense if I show you. Stay close. We are almost there, and Nalithor is not here to—'*

'Mmm… I want to kill it…' I shivered again, my skin prickling into goosebumps. My gaze darted around in search of whatever it

was that needed to die, desperate to find my target. *'Ugh! Just what…'*

My thoughts trailed into silence when I shifted my vision and examined the threads of magic that lingered in the air, wrapping around the trees beside us. Flickering runes of Angelic origin twisted around everything near us, from the trees to the pebbles. Their usual gold color was marred by a shifting black substance that was unlike oil and was thicker than molasses.

'This isn't from beast blood.' I rushed through the forest, following the runes. *'What would cause something like this? I don't recognize this smell or this power.'*

I wasn't even following Djialkan anymore, nor was I aware of him. The runes seemed to all lead toward the same cave, stretching as if being drawn into a whirlpool. Since the fae-dragon didn't call out to stop me, or bite me, I assumed that the cave was where he wanted to bring me. There wasn't even a hint of the golden light of the runes there, as they had all succumb completely to the strange black substance.

'This…is what Sihix was once like.' I shivered as the air around me grew colder and colder, speeding through the cave in search of the power radiating from deep within it. *'Why are the citizens oblivious to— Oh.'*

I skidded to a stop upon entering a massive cavern and looked up at the twisting roots thick as buildings. Hundreds of frozen corpses had fused to the roots of the tree. The same thick, black substance that soiled the Angelic runes was flowing from the corpses and up the tree's roots.

Blood still stained the ground where the most recent victim had died. I grimaced, shifting my gaze to the side to examine the freshest corpse and its shaman-like attire.

"So, that's the High Priest, Djialkan?" I questioned, my brow furrowing. *'At least the cold keeps the bodies from rotting... Even I probably wouldn't be able to stomach the smell of this much death.'*

I shifted my gaze toward the crumbling altar at the center of the cavern, frowning. By the size of the roots hanging above us, and the altar in the center of the cavern, I knew this had to be Ceilail's core. Yet it was so far from Banayr'e.

"What do you see?" Djialkan perched on my shoulder and rubbed his warm muzzle against my cheek. *"I have never seen your bloodlust subside so quickly."*

"It hasn't subsided," I muttered, reaching up to scratch Djialkan's chin. After passing him several images via telepathy I continued, "It's like what we saw in the Sihix Forest those years ago. Except I don't see—"

"So, this is the kind of trouble you find when I let you out of my sight?" The voice startled me, causing me to pivot and draw my sword. His spicy scent registered in time for me to stop my blade by his throat. "Ah, the cold is messing with your senses as well, my dear?"

Nalithor smiled and nudged my blade away from his throat.

He approached me and then tugged my hood back to reveal my face and hair. He studied me with a pleasant yet intense expression that I couldn't quite read. After a moment, he shifted his gaze to the freshest of corpses and released a heavy sigh before approaching it. Wary, I dismissed my blade and shifted to track Nalithor. *'He's still too weak to be out of bed. What's he doing here?'*

"You're familiar with a scene like this?" Nalithor questioned, crouching beside the former High Priest. My pulse leapt into my throat when Nalithor reached for the corpse.

"Don't touch it!" I rushed forward and wrapped my arms around Nalithor's upper torso, pinning his upper arms in place. With difficulty I pulled him backwards with me and away from the corpse. "You're a god, can't you see magic?! You shouldn't—"

"Magic?" Nalithor placed a hand over one of my wrists, nudging me. "I get the feeling you're not referring to the elements carried by aether.

"Let me up, Arianna. I won't touch it since you're so concerned."

I hesitated but chose to relent, letting my hands drop to my side. Even so, I tracked him as he rose to his feet, prepared to blast him away from the corpse if I had to.

With him there, it would be difficult for me to investigate the problem. If Djialkan and I were right, and the Elders Nalithor knew were fake, getting him involved would be far too risky.

"Mmm...you smell like pastries," Nalithor remarked, smiling

again as I caught him by the sleeve of his robes and pulled him several yards away from the priest's corpse.

"Shouldn't you be resting?" I chastised, looking up at Nalithor. He shot me a smile that gave me pause and made my face ignite. *'W-what kind of expression is* that?'

"How could I ignore that rather *delicious* bloodlust radiating from you?" Nalithor chuckled. He reached behind my head and pulled my mrifon ornament from my hair, letting my curls fall around my shoulders. "There, that's better."

"I will show him," Djialkan commented when I struggled to formulate a response. The fae-dragon hopped from my shoulder and over to Nalithor's, nudging the Adinvyr's cheek. *"Leave her be, Nalithor. She is familiar with situations such as this."*

"Familiar?" Nalithor frowned, looking equal parts concerned and disappointed as I moved away from him. "But, Djialkan, that crystal is the heart of a god! What would such a thing be doing down…"

I tuned them out and turned to look in the direction Nalithor had motioned.

Under the twisting roots of Ceilail, near the altar, was a massive formation of ice. It was shaped into the form of a flower I didn't recognize. Within the center of the frozen flower was an obscured shadow in the form of a person. Angelic runes covered almost every inch of the ice, flickering and straining to hold its captive. Both the runes and the ice seemed to be weakening.

'The heart of a god?' I wondered, tenderly stepping over the vines that had begun to slither toward me. *'It really is like what happened to Sihix before I found him.*

'Nalithor really…doesn't know? I hope Djialkan can distract—'

My body grew still as power ripped through me. Darkness spiraled outward from my feet. The magic in the cave was foul. I needed to destroy it.

'Mmm… Perhaps the bastards who cursed this place will react if I destroy their runes? Oh, I hope they do. Then I can eviscerate them too! I'll tear, rip, shred, pulverize, destroy *them! Filth like them don't deserve to live. Who gave them permission to keep breathing? Their existence is wrong. I'll get rid of them! Their magic, their corpses, everything.'*

I shivered, nibbling my lower lip in excitement. My gaze flicked to the nearest set of runes; I would start there.

"*Arianna…**stop it**.*" Nalithor's voice was little more than a husky growl by my ear. His tone made my heart skip several beats as my mind struggled to refocus. Everything was fuzzy, and there was less strength in my limbs than before.

"Wha—" I shuddered and fell silent when Nalithor's lips brushed against the side of my throat.

"*I told you not to interfere, Nalithor!*" Djialkan barked from somewhere beyond my field of view, then devolved into a slew of what I could only assume were curses in the draconic tongue.

I attempted to shift my vision to check for the Angelic runes but all that came was a piercing pain through my skull, making me wince. Giving up on that endeavor, I looked around with my normal vision. Nalithor had restrained me against the floor of the cavern and had his torso nestled between my legs. He had pinned my wrists above my head as if restraining me from something. A brief glance up at the cavern's roof revealed that the corpses fused to Ceilail's roots were gone. *'How much time has passed...?'*

"Need I subdue you further?" Nalithor questioned quietly once I stopped trying to wriggle from his grasp. He lifted his head to look me in the eye, but I couldn't read his expression.

"The magic is gone, she will be fine now," Djialkan answered dryly. *"You can let her up."*

'Blood...I smell blood.' I shut my eyes, wincing as everything spun. *'Ugh, what happened?'*

"Ceilail, who is responsible for this?" Nalithor's question made me snap my eyes open. I watched as he rolled off me and into a sitting position.

Nalithor had deep gouges running down his chest and upper abdomen. Blue-black blood still trickled down his pale skin. Blood matching it covered much of my hands. Pain lanced through my chest as worry and guilt threatened to over whelm me. I looked up to Nalithor's face, but his attention was focused elsewhere. *'I...did this to him?'*

'He attempted to keep you from destroying the magic that bound this place,' Djialkan informed me as my concern grew and my pulse

quickened. *'The fool should have listened to my warnings.'*

I carefully sat up and glanced at Nalithor again; was he avoiding looking at me? Was he upset with me?

"That is not for you to know yet, Nalithor." An unfamiliar yet pleasant female voice spoke. *"Arianna, I looked into your mind; Sihix was once bound similarly?"*

"Ah...yes," I mumbled, glancing away from Nalithor and toward the wraith-like woman. She had shifting crystals of ice and frost around her wrists and ankles. Every part of her, even her clothing, looked as though it was made of ice and yet she moved like she was made of flesh. My concern for Nalithor overtook my curiosity, causing me to turn back to the Adinvyr. "Nalithor, I'm sorry. Did I—"

'He cannot know of this yet,' Ceilail reiterated to me in private. *'I will contact my brother, Sihix, as soon as I have regained my strength. If the others are bound similarly, we will have need of your services again. Until then, tread with care.'*

'Because...he will be Exiled if he learns what you, Sihix, and the others are?' I questioned, watching as Ceilail nodded and then turned her back to us. *'I don't like it...but I understand.'*

"Here, let me—" I reached out to place my hands on Nalithor's chest, but he caught my wrists and shot me a look of concern instead. It was better than him not looking at me, at least, but not by much.

"Do you remember what you did?" Nalithor asked, holding my

hands just out of reach from his wounds.

"I remember deciding where to start, and then…" I faltered as a cacophony of destructive thoughts rose in my mind, causing me to shake my head firmly. It was all gone now yet I still hadn't satisfied my want for destruction.

"Enough." Nalithor squeezed my wrists, his expression firm. "I thought you had lost all control of your power, until you commanded '*sh'rlic marnas.*'"

"What? 'Break apart?'" I blinked at him for a moment, then shifted my gaze down to his bloodied chest. "When did *that* happen, and when are you going to let me—"

I squeaked, startled, when Nalithor pulled me to him. He pulled my legs apart with his tail and settled me so that I was straddling his lap. My face felt like it was going to catch fire, but I couldn't think of a quip that would make him release me. Nalithor looked smug, triumphant even, as he brought my hands to his chest.

"You heal, I'll ask questions," Nalithor spoke in a conversational tone. A small smile formed on his lips as he examined me. "Mmm…this goes to show how tiny you are, doesn't it?"

I shot Nalithor a begrudging glare before summoning darkness around my hands so that I could heal him. Ignoring his hands slipping around to pet my back was difficult. He chuckled when I twitched in response to his hands wandering dangerously low, and

I gave him another look.

If it wasn't for the intoxicating smell of his blood, I would have focused on making it hurt *more* as revenge for his teasing. Alas, I needed to heal him before I wound up taking a taste. The scent was far too mesmerizing while I was weakened.

"Sihix was bound similarly?" Nalithor questioned, earning him a nod in reply. "You freed 'it' as well?"

"Djialkan knows of that better than I do," I mumbled, letting my darkness flow through his wounds. *'Ugh. Here I've been taking care of him for days and then I go wound him myself. At least he doesn't seem upset with me for it...'*

Djialkan glided over to perch on one of Nalithor's shoulders. *"When she released Sihix it was while she was in the middle of a trance-like state, such as the one you just saw. It was on the second night of our first stay in Sihix. She began sleepwalking and, when I followed her, we arrived beneath Sihix's temple.* Something *had been defiling the forest's roots with the corpses of past High Priests, High Priestesses, and even some of the citizens.*

"As with what you just witnessed, Arianna commanded the tainted Angelic magics to 'break apart' in the Draemiran tongue. However, she was not consumed by bloodlust due to her slumber. Nor did her elements turn into such a savage storm."

"Mmm, you do have quite the temper under there don't you, Arianna?" Nalithor purred, pressing the small of my back. He inched me closer to his chest until I had to brace myself against him to stop from growing too close. The chuckle he released sent chills down my spine. "Had I not been concerned for your wellbeing...I would have gone and torn *every shred of filth that I could—*"

Nalithor rested his forehead on my shoulder and breathed a shaky sigh, his clawed fingers digging into my robes. His pulse raced beneath my hands, reminding me that I still had healing to do. Power hummed through Nalithor's skin, giving away just how much he wanted to go hunt something—*anything*. It made me question why he had pulled me into his lap in such a way. Was he trying to fluster me, or was he trying to keep himself from misusing his power?

"Shouldn't you be in our cottage, resting?" I questioned as Nalithor's hands traveled up my back. He nuzzled into my throat with a sigh, squeezing me closer. "You didn't need to stop...me... H-hey, stop that!"

"I...can't have a taste?" Nalithor nibbled at my throat.

I couldn't suppress my shiver. I placed my hands flat against Nalithor's chest and pushed him back slightly, giving him a firm look.

"No, you can't," I stated, attempting to ignore his disappointed expression. "Didn't you already drink some of the village strumpets? Why are you this—"

"They taste *and* smell terrible," Nalithor muttered, slipping his arms fully around my waist. He squeezed me tight and laid his head on my shoulder, facing away from my throat this time. "You know…if you are partnered with an Adinvyr or a Vampire, it is likely you will have to serve as 'food' on occasion."

"I can't finish healing your wounds when you're holding me like a stuffed toy." I sighed, turning my face away from his bloodstained chest. The desire to taste his blood threatened to overwhelm me, forcing me to close my eyes as I attempted to calm myself. He smelled like he would make an *excellent* breakfast.

"What happened to not giving into the princess's bloodlust, Nalithor?" Djialkan chortled, causing the Adinvyr to bristle. *"You said yourself that the power of a 'mere mortal' should not affect you, yet you seem quite willing to let her desires sweep you away.*

"Should you not be sweeping her away?"

The corner of my eye twitched. Did Djialkan think he was helping somehow? If anything, I had the feeling he was going to make things worse with such comments. I wasn't sure what I would do if Nalithor began teasing me even more.

"Let me finish healing you. After, we should return to the village," I spoke up while Nalithor growled at the fae-dragon. "You need to finish recovering, and I fear these wounds may lengthen the process… The scaly one and I can look into whether or not the villagers were aware of what was happening here."

"I want to know who is responsible for doing something like this to Ceilail." Nalithor growled again, his grip tensing even as he complied, allowing me to place my hands on his chest once more.

"Ah… Despite your complaints my blood seems to suit you."

"I'm going to assume that's some form of Draemiran compliment that I fail to understand." I rolled my eyes at him and then allowed darkness to flow from my hands again. Nalithor just smiled and lifted a hand to my face, using his own magic to wipe the blood from my skin. "How long do you think it will be before you've recovered enough to make the trip back to Dauthrmir?"

"A few more days," Nalithor murmured, brushing my cheek with the backs of his fingers. "If we discover the citizens are involved with Ceilail's imprisonment…then it will be longer before we can leave."

"It's not like executing them for their crimes will take you long," I pointed out, laughing when he twitched. "While it has been refreshing to be away from Dauthrmir, the incessant knocking on my barriers, and my brother, I'm sure that Alala is growing upset with us for our extended trip."

"You are *far* too understanding of my role," Nalithor informed me, resting his hands on my hips. "Or are you *that* eager to spill blood? It can be difficult to tell with you."

"Neither." I shook my head, letting my hands drift down to the wounds on his abdomen. "I would think that imprisoning a…" I tilted my head in thought for a moment. "Hmmm, what is it that you call the embodiments of the Aledacian Forest?"

"Lari'xan," Nalithor replied simply, then chuckled at me when I paused again in thought. "It is just as it sounds, my dear.

'Elemental Gods' would be the closest translation. However, many who speak the common tongue refer to beings like Ceilail as 'Local Gods' or 'Aetherial Gods.'"

'They have the "god" part correct and the actual rank incorrect.' Djialkan snorted, hopping into the air. *'Can you handle the Adinvyr whilst I return to my investigation?'*

'Define "handle?"' It took all my self-control not to roll my eyes. *'I'll be fine. Your investigation is more important. We need to find out if it's the Elders or the Lari'xan who are lying. One of them is not what they claim to be, and I'm not convinced that it's the Lari'xan.'*

I sighed, unsure of what to make of Nalithor's intense expression. "As I was saying, I would think that imprisoning a Lari'xan constitutes as a heinous offense. If the Aledacian Forests are as integral to Avrirsa as you believe, then people who try to interfere with that balance are—"

"It's a shame you won't be able to assist me with the slaughter if the people of Banayr'e *are* responsible," Nalithor interjected, slipping his forearms beneath my rump. He pulled himself to his feet with ease, chuckling when I yelped and gripped his shoulders. "Granted, after seeing you enter a state like *that*… I am unsure of how to restrain you."

"A state like what?" I frowned. "Are you going to put me down?"

"*Eventually*. When it suits me." Nalithor smirked. "As for the state you entered, I have nothing to compare it to. I feel as though you would have challenged an army on your lonesome had there been one available, and regardless of what the outcome might be."

"Where did you stash my hairpiece?" I nudged his shoulder with one hand. "And aren't you *cold* wearing robes like that in Ceilail?"

"Ah, here." Nalithor chuckled, adjusting his grip so that he was holding me up with one arm. He conjured my mrifon hairpiece in his free hand and lifted it between us. "I will shift my grip so that you can fix your hair. However, I am not putting you down."

"You are difficult," I mumbled. He used his arms, tail, and magic to adjust me until I was cradled in his arms. *'Comfy, warm… No way in the infernal hells am I going to tell him that. Then he'll never set me down!'*

Nalithor shot me a smirk and then carried me out of the cave, into the icy forest beyond. *'I can't understand this man at all. Shouldn't he be rushing back to the village to find out how much the citizens know? Why is he being so familiar with me as of late? Hells, why is he stroking my thigh with his thumb like that?!'*

"You aren't tired?" Nalithor questioned, tracking my movements as I pulled up my curls and nestled my hairpiece into place. "Releasing that amount of magic should have strained you greatly. Then healing me…"

"I'm limited to using my shrizar now, I can't do anything else," I replied, then glanced up at him when his grip tensed. "Must you carry me? I can walk."

"I *want* to carry you..." Nalithor mumbled, glancing away from me.

'Wants to?' I shook my head slightly and then opened my shrizar, retrieving the pastries from before. I nibbled on one and took turns between examining both Nalithor and our surroundings. *'Ugh... Feigning alertness isn't going to last long. I want to sleep.'*

"Want a bite?" I offered, earning a surprised look from the Adinvyr. "Still a little warm."

"You or the bun?" Nalithor teased.

"Oh hush!" I stuffed the remaining third of my sticky bun in his mouth.

"Rely'ric, Lady Arianna!" A Nymph guard exclaimed as we neared Banayr'e's gates. "Is everything alright? We felt intense darkness from deep within the forest. I've never felt anything like—"

"Arianna-jiss found a troubling problem and rectified it," Nalithor responded, carrying me past the guard and into the village as I nibbled on a second pastry. "Will you call the village elders to our cottage? It would be best to talk there."

"At once, Rely'ric." The Nymph bowed and then took off at a run, soon disappearing between buildings.

"Can I have another bite?" Nalithor asked, causing me to shoot him a suspicious look over the remaining portion of this pastry.

"Hungry?"

"In more ways than one."

"…here." I pulled another pastry out of the bag and offered it to him. "Still a lot left."

"Don't foxes usually stash their food?" Nalithor chuckled. "You're going to have to feed me, my dear."

"Or you could put me down."

"Not happening."

I sighed, choosing to relent; I still felt guilty for wounding him. At least he ate the bun in normal bites—I'd half-expected him to take tiny bites to make it last longer. He did seem quite hungry but refused my suggestion of stopping somewhere to pick up more food.

Many citizens expressed their concern as we passed them. Nalithor's grip seemed to grow tighter every time a male addressed us. By the time we arrived at the cottage I was convinced that I would have prints of Nalithor's fingers permanently engraved into my shoulder and thigh.

I thought that he would put me down once we arrived, but instead he sat on the bed and pulled me into his lap. He coiled his tail around my thighs when I shifted to move away, tightening his grip on me.

"I'm not letting you out of my sight," Nalithor spoke softly. "You've been taking care of me for several days…now it is my turn to take care of you. Rest. I will wake you if something happens."

"I can sleep on the couch," I protested as he pulled me closer, bringing my head to his chest. "You...you don't have to—"

"You can barely keep your eyes open." Nalithor chuckled, resting a hand on my waist. "I will see to it that you aren't disturbed while I speak with the village elders.

"We should recover as quickly as possible so that we can return to Dauthrmir. Hopefully Djialkan's investigation doesn't turn up anything else that requires my immediate attention..."

Nalithor trailed off when I relaxed against him. I let my cheek rest against his chest and bit back a sigh. I didn't have the energy or the willpower to argue with him more. He was warm, and he smelled good. That was enough for me.

'Perhaps letting him have his way every now and then isn't so bad...'

CHAPTER TWENTY-THREE
Opening Up

'Didn't he say he wouldn't let me out of his sight?' I rolled my eyes and glanced around for any sign of Nalithor. *'How did he manage to slip away without waking me* again? *I should kick his ass later.'*

My heart sunk in disappointment. Perhaps I took Nalithor's statements a little too seriously. After all, his behavior made it obvious that he was quite hungry. It seemed likely that his hunger was coloring both his thoughts and actions. Still...I didn't enjoy waking up alone. His presence would have been welcome.

I shook my head and then pulled my hood further over my head to protect myself from the frigid winds. For all intents and purposes, I had been "alone" for a long time. I'd thought that I'd grown used to it, but now I wasn't so sure. The lack of Nalithor's company upset me far more than it should have.

I hugged myself and rubbed my arms briskly in a failed attempt to warm up. Ceilail's forest had grown much colder since the Lari'xan herself had been freed. The citizens native to Banayr'e were much more cheerful with their "mother" now available to them. However, they were giving me a wide berth despite the role I had played in freeing Ceilail. Some bowed to me with reverent expressions on their faces, but others shot me fearful glances and then scurried away.

'Did I...do something while asleep?' I shrunk back in my cloak and settled my gaze on the ground, trudging onward. *'Tch, where's that Adinvyr when I actually have questions for him?'*

The air grew colder as I approached the massive tree in Banayr'e that served as Ceilail's temple. Waves of frost drifted in the air surrounding the tree, blurring its form and obscuring some sections from view. Everything about the forest and the village both felt more...*alive* now that their Lari'xan matriarch was free. I mumbled a few curses and made my way closer to the tree-temple.

"Ceilail is expecting you. She's on the top floor," a Dryad addressed me with a smile. "The God of Balance is not with you?"

I shook my head in silence and passed the Dryad, earning a concerned frown. Somehow the inside of the icy tree was even colder than the windy exterior. The furnishings inside the temple were sparse, consisting mainly of ornaments and lamps created from flora found within the forest. On occasion I passed items and decorations of foreign origin, many of which I didn't recognize the style of.

Compared to the temple Corentine looked after in Sihix, this place was bare.

'No guards? No Guardians?' I frowned, my gaze flicking around the pale interior.

"Ah, there you are, Arianna." Ceilail smiled at me when I crested the stairs to the top floor. *"Thus far I have been unable to contact Sihix.*

"Djialkan was kind enough to inform me of what... befell you. You remember nothing of your childhood in Dauthrmir?"

"Nothing," I confirmed. I strode into the wide-open room and glanced around at the large book shelves before returning my attention to Ceilail. "You know of me?"

"It was Our intention to have you or your brother fulfill the role of Balance." Ceilail released a heavy sigh and then motioned for me to sit across from her. *"Your Adinvyr is handling the role We gave him in your stead—and quite well, I might add—but it still poses a problem for Us."*

"He's not *my* anything!" I exclaimed. *'The role "They" gave him... Then, the Lari'xan are truly the real Elders?'*

"So you say, so you say." Ceilail waved one slender hand dismissively. *"How does the power of the gods you've met thus far strike you?"*

"Weaker than they should be," I replied instantly. "Djialkan agrees; the so-called Elder Gods that we met on our way here are nowhere near as powerful as a *real* Elder. Yet Nalithor thought that I should have been frightened by them."

"Djialkan informed me that their power was close to what the Middle Gods should have." Ceilail nodded, a frown tugging at her translucent features. *"If Nalithor is weaker than them, then that would mean his power is around what Our Racial Gods should be. Except..."*

"Except?" I prompted her when she trailed off; her uneasy expression was making *me* uncomfortable.

"His power is growing." Ceilail sighed, shaking her head. She slumped back in her seat and motioned with one hand, continuing, *"I don't know if it is because he holds your heart with his, or if it is due to your presence. I could be missing something else, as well... My power has not fully returned yet.*

"My concern is that he will soon surpass the False Ones and they will send him into Exile. We won't be able to keep these matters from Nalithor if his power continues growing in this manner. If things progress at the current rate, it won't take him long to surpass the False Ones and then reach the height his power is meant to be."

"If the Lari'xan are the *real* Elders, as Djialkan and Corentine claim, how did you fall into this mess to begin with?" I crossed my arms and shot Ceilail an annoyed look. "*You* are supposed to be the ones who created the universe, and yet you've been usurped by lesser beings—how is that even possible?"

"We have created and destroyed this universe countless times!" Ceilail snorted at me. *"Every time We find a critical error in Our creation. Someone, or something, never fails to make everything go down an unrecoverable path. We even experimented with taking away free will—everything still went awry. These failures are what made Us realize that We needed a God and Goddess of Balance, so not everything was pointless.*

"The False Ones amount to little more than imprisoned troublemakers from the past. They broke free of confinement and sacrificed thousands of lives. Through the blood of thousands, they launched an assault on Us to bind Us. Their attack was too weak to kill Us, of course—We are immortal. However, their intention was not to kill us. Their intent was to trap Us, and trap Us they did. Our hearts encased Us in crystal—what you freed me from—to protect Us."

"You *imprisoned* troublemaking deities instead of destroying them?" The corner of my eye twitched. *'I wonder how much trouble I'd be in if I pointed out how fucking stupid that is?'*

Ceilail huffed. *"They are desperate to stop what they think is an endless cycle of destruction and recreation. They believed eradicating Us is the only way to do so.*

"At any rate, I didn't call you here for a history lesson. I have sent others off in search of my remaining brothers and sisters. What I need from you...is to stay alive while you investigate 'who' or 'what' was trying to corrupt both Sihix and I. The runes were Angelic, but I did not recognize the magic. If it belonged to one of the False Ones or an

Exile, they are unknown to me."

"What of Nalithor?" I sighed. "I'm not allowed out of the city without a partner, as far as I'm aware, and *that one* is determined to take the role. Wouldn't that be a problem?"

"It would provide you with an easy way to keep an eye on both him and his growth," Ceilail murmured, tapping her fingers against the arm of her chair. *"As he is fulfilling your role, for now, you will need to consult him frequently anyway. Just… Do try not to get him Exiled? You are in a unique position to do things that he cannot.*

"Djialkan and I have determined that the False Ones are already looking for a way to kill you. They haven't realized who you are, yet, but your proximity to Nalithor is threatening to them. However, you can still afford to be less careful than your Adinvyr is."

"He's not my—!" I started, but Ceilail just shot me a charming smile. "Fine. I get it. Be careful, and keep Nalithor out of trouble to the best of my ability…

"How are the 'False Ones' trying to kill me now?"

"They are unable to interact with the fae-dragons properly since they are not Us." Ceilail motioned to herself, then continued, *"Their offer to find Djialkan a new ward was an offer to kill you so that he would be free of you. Your companion shared his memories with me so that I could see what transpired; they truly believed you are Human. It seems that they are losing their touch."*

"Even I don't know what I am," I pointed out flatly, watching as Ceilail's mouth tugged into a frown.

"*Arianna... I could restore your memories of the past, but...*" Ceilail's frown deepened as she contemplated it.

"But?" I probed, uneasy despite my quickening pulse. The prospect excited me, but Ceilail's hesitation made me nervous.

"*You would lose your memory of everything that happened* after *being whisked away from Dauthrmir.*" Ceilail sighed, shaking her head. "*Everything. Your time in Limbo and in X'shmir, the past few weeks you have spent on the Rilzaan Continent. Everything you have learned, including the strides you have taken in both combat and magical arts. All of it.*

"*The 'current you' conflicts too greatly with who you used to be. If you had both, you would likely brea—*"

"Then I don't want it." I crossed my arms. "I won't pretend that I don't feel...guilty, at times, for not remembering the past. However, I don't want to lose who I am now or what has happened over the past months. Nor do I want to just *forget* everything that has happened to my brother.

"If it works as you say, I'd be little more than a child in an adult's body."

"*You've developed a soft spot for Nalithor, haven't you?*" Ceilail giggled at me as I flushed. "*You should go find him.*

"*My children are...frightened of you, Arianna. It would be best if you and Nalithor gather the slaves you rescued and then depart at once. Djialkan has already returned to Dauthrmir ahead of you—he intends to gather more information on the gods. We need to determine what is weakening all of them so greatly."*

"Frightened of me, huh?" I tilted my head, then sighed. "This is your forest; don't *you* know where Nalithor is?"

"It will be more fun to have you find him for yourself." Ceilail beamed at me as I huffed and rose to my feet. *"He accepts you and your darkness doesn't he, Arianna? Don't let my children's fear upset you. You've already won the favor of someone far more important than they are."*

"You?" I stopped at the top of the stairs without turning.

"Nalithor." Ceilail giggled, making me bristle. *"Off you go now. I'm sure you are both beginning to miss the warmer lands beyond my territory."*

I bit back the urge to glare at the Lari'xan and then descended through the tree once more. Ceilail had given me the chance to regain my memories...yet I hadn't hesitated to turn her offer down. I wasn't sure if it was the right choice, but it felt like it was. The amount of knowledge and maturity I would lose by accepting was staggering.

Although there was a distinct discrepancy in years lived as a Devillian girl versus years lived as a Human, I doubted the girl I once was had *as much* knowledge regarding hunting, magic, and combat as I did now. I would know nothing of X'shmiran beasts, the sins of the Royal Family, or the people who cared for me in Sihix. Nothing.

'She could have at least answered me about what *I am.'* I released

a heavy sigh and fidgeted with my robes as I walked out of the temple. *'Even if* They *meant for me to be a goddess...wouldn't my species matter at least a little bit? Lucifer is the patriarch of all Devillians—so what does that make him? Who is my mother? Does Lucifer have new children? Why—'*

I shook my head hard and shoved the thoughts from my mind. Finding the pesky Adinvyr was more important than dwelling on the past. Without him, I wouldn't be able to orchestrate our rescues and leave the forest. I hastened my pace and questioned a few citizens to find out if they had seen Nalithor recently. Many of them simply screeched and ran away from me, but the older generation was kinder and more forthcoming.

Unfortunately, the general consensus was that no one had seen him in several hours.

'Just great.' I pouted, making my way out of Banayr'e and into the forest itself. *'It's so cold I can barely smell anything. How am I supposed to track him down?'*

Resigned, I summoned an extra cloak around myself and then pulled on a thicker pair of gloves. It was far colder than any of the winters I'd experienced in X'shmir and, much to my displeasure, it was making me miss the Adinvyr's warmth. Looking around revealed a few sets of footprints that I could follow beyond Banayr'e's walls. The people living in the village didn't wander away from their homes often, so it seemed likely that at least one set of tracks belonged to Nalithor.

Despite my complaints about the growing cold, the Ceilail Forest was quite beautiful. It didn't feel like "home" to me in the way that Sihix did, but I still found the pale flora and fauna appealing. Every kick of the wind sent waves of sparkling frost drifting through the trees. Frigid places such as Ceilail were blissfully quiet and peaceful, and *that* was something I could appreciate. *'Right...need to find Nalithor, not bask in the silence.'*

I hastened my stride and followed the trail of crushed underbrush, occasionally scenting the air in search of even the slightest hint of Nalithor. It was strangely disconcerting, and borderline upsetting, that I couldn't detect his scent at all. *'Why did he have to wander off on his lonesome anyway? Finding him is going to be such a pain in this place and I...I don't want to be alone here.'*

A short while later, the sound of frustrated women reached me.

"I told you we were stupid to follow him!"

"B-but...doesn't he need to feed?"

"Obviously he can't feed from us for some reason, idiot!"

"Does that mean he's sick? Do gods even get sick?"

"Should you three be outside of Banayr'e without an escort?" I piped up, coming to a stop behind the three women. They whirled around to look at me with startled expressions, so I crossed my arms and continued, "What's this about 'him' being ill?"

"T-there are very few reasons for an Adinvyr to not feed." The Elven woman with pale blue skin whimpered and ducked behind one of her larger friends. "Now that you've freed Mother Ceilail, it's possible that our blood carries too much ice-aspected aether for him. We didn't think that it would be a problem for a deity. The other option would be…"

"Would be what?" I prompted, tapping my foot with impatience. The trio shifted uncomfortably and looked away from me. "Honestly, why are you so scared of me? I helped Ceilail. Shouldn't that serve to make you more comfortable around me? I really don't understand you people."

"W-we're sorry, Arianna-jiss." One of the other women bowed to me, her greenish-white hair falling around her frozen horns and face. "We're grateful that you released Mother from her prison. We truly are. Your darkness…it frightens many of us. Since we can't determine who you are or what your relationship with Rely'ric is, many of us choose to be cautious."

"There are few reasons for an Adinvyr to cease feeding," the third woman, another Elf, added. "Too much aether, particularly of an element they're not aligned with, is one reason. Second, if they are ill, they are unwilling to 'eat' aside from drawing energy from places such as brothels—of which Banayr'e has none."

"The only other reasons would be if they have entered a relationship *and* are monogamous…or…" the Devillian woman paused, her expression disturbed, "…or if they wish to starve themselves to death. R-Rely'ric does not seem depressed, but—"

"So, he's being stubborn about something." I rolled my eyes

and lifted my fingers to my temples. "Which way did he—"

"Noble and royal Adinvyr have been known to cease feeding as a way to show they've found someone to court!" the first Elf blurted out. "W-we thought that maybe you and he—"

"Ugh… Is it really that uncommon for him to show up with a partner?" I rubbed my temples, then let my hand fall to my side. "Which way did Nalithor go? We need to escort our rescues back to Dauthrmir as soon as possible. Ceilail advised me that it is time for us to leave."

The three women stared at me for a moment with appalled expressions, then motioned off in the way they had come from. I mumbled my thanks and then brushed past them as they began to whisper amongst themselves. From the brief snippet I caught, they thought that I was disgusted by the idea of being closer to Nalithor.

'That isn't the case…' I frowned at myself. *'If anything, shouldn't he be disgusted by the idea of working with—let alone growing close to—a mortal?'*

It was impossible to tell how much time passed before the sound of trickling water and high, giggling voices caught my attention. I was unable to spot the source just from glancing around my immediate area. The proximity of the trees in this part of the forest made sounds bounce and bend in unusual ways, and the enormous trees were to close together to give me a clean line of sight anywhere.

After skirting around a few more trees, I found myself blinking in disbelief at a nearby stream. Not only was it unfrozen and freely flowing, but the water was iridescent and smelled of Spring. My curiosity got the better of me, so I began following the stream and listening as the giggling grew louder. Soon, Nalithor's rumbling voice was added into the mix—but I couldn't understand what he was saying. I'd never heard this language before, and it was too far removed from both the common and Draemiran tongues. There was no way for me to even guess.

I stopped, amazed, and stared at the clearing before me. The grass was a vibrant green and flowers were blooming, or otherwise budding, everywhere I looked. At the center of the clearing was a pond of opaque, rainbow-colored liquid. It looked to be the source of the stream I had been following.

Little points of light with barely-discernible wings flitted through the clearing. Many more rested on the leaves or petals of blooming plants, on felled branches, or on the boulders lining the pond. As with the strange liquid, each of the flying lights was a different color. They seemed to be the source of the feminine giggling I'd heard.

"Am I…interrupting something?" I hesitated to speak up, then flicked my gaze to Nalithor's bare, muscular back. "Aren't you *cold*, Nalithor?"

"Arianna? You should still be in bed." Nalithor stood and turned to look at me, his voice and expression both carrying his concern. "You need to rest—"

If he finished the sentence, I didn't hear him. My attention was on several dozen of the floating winged orbs; they had begun to float toward me while murmuring to themselves in worried tones. The small traces of power emanating from their shining white bodies made my pulse freeze for a moment, before sending a jolt of adrenaline and panic through my system. I scrambled back from the creatures and pressed my back against a tree, my pulse racing in my throat. Light. How I hated the light...

I could have run, but that would have meant taking my eyes off the creatures. They rushed toward me, chittering in worried tones. I didn't know what to do—something told me that I shouldn't kill them, yet that was precisely what I wanted to do to creatures so full of light.

"*Eri'na Jutae, eohim caisa uo.*" Nalithor commanded. The lights drifted to a stop a few feet away from me and then scattered to the far side of the clearing. Nalithor approached me with a worried look on his face. "Are you alright, Arianna? You're shaking."

"I...I don't like the light," I muttered, tugging my hood further over my face in a poor attempt to hide my embarrassment. "What did you—"

"I told the light ones to leave you be." Nalithor pulled at the front of my hood. "You're...scared of the light?" I twitched involuntarily in response, earning a small sigh from the Adinvyr. "Most Shadow and Umbral Mages have at least *some* fear of their counterpart. Light is—"

"The darkest things lurk close behind the light," I interjected, continuing to hold my hood over my face. Internally, I cursed my trembling. "On the surface the light seems so…so *nice*. But those with affinity for light have the deepest shadows."

"I'm sure you didn't come here just to tell me such profound observations." Nalithor chuckled, pulling at my hood again.

'Is he…trying to distract me?' I tensed my jaw, feeling hesitant. After a moment, I pulled my hood down and shot a wary glance in the direction of the light-aspect creatures. "I wouldn't claim it's profound…"

"Hmmm… I smell those women on you." Nalithor leaned down and sniffed at me briefly, his tone giving away his immense displeasure. "If they troubled you, I will—"

"The people of Banayr'e are better behaved than the brats in Dauthrmir." I cut him off and shied away from him. "What *is* this place?"

"You haven't found something like this within Sihix?" Nalithor's surprise sounded genuine. He straightened and then glanced over his shoulder at the iridescent pond. "They're most often referred to as 'fairy springs'…though the term isn't entirely accurate.

"It's a place where dense amounts of aether gather. The pixies, like most Fae, are elemental creatures by nature and often choose to guard locations such as this. For lack of a better term, it is an aetheric fount."

"I haven't explored as much of Sihix as you may think," I mumbled, peering around him briefly. "Alas, that's not what I—"

"You should be *resting*," Nalithor informed me. He lifted both hands to my face, intense worry shaping his features. "If you had run into beasts in the forest, would you have been able to defend yourself in this state?"

"I'm not that weak!" I huffed, batting his hands away from my face before moving several paces away from him. *'Ugh...calm down, Ari. Don't let those little shits rile you up and make you act like a bitch to Nalithor. Calm down.'*

"I apologize. I was just...concerned," Nalithor muttered. The disappointment in his voice tore at me.

"Ceilail wants us to gather the slaves we liberated, and leave the forest immediately," I stated abruptly, turning to look at the sulking Adinvyr. "Between Ceilail's dismissal and the presence of light-aspect...*anything*...I'm moody. So, I'm sorry for snapping. I just...I just really don't like—"

"Will you feel better if we move further away from them?" Nalithor questioned me, his tone and expression both unreadable.

"I'll...be fine. You weren't done with them yet, right?" I averted my gaze. "I'll wait off in the forest somewhere."

I quickly slipped away from Nalithor and the clearing before he could say anything. Once I was several dozen yards away from the blasted light pixies, I took a seat on an ice-coated boulder.

Getting away from the pixies helped a little, but there was still a slight tremble in my hands as I yanked my hood back up. By the time I managed to calm both my pulse and my breathing, a fine layer of frost had formed on my outermost cloak and across the top of my boots.

"You didn't have to flee so far," Nalithor commented as he approached some time later, his torso now wrapped in several thick layers of dark robes. "What's this you were saying about Ceilail wanting us to leave?"

"…I'm scaring her 'children' apparently," I mumbled, clasping my hands between my knees while shivering. "She wants us to return to Dauthrmir immediately and take the former slaves with us."

"Scaring…?" Nalithor sighed heavily and came to a stop beside me, nudging my shoulder before speaking again. "Come, let's fetch our wards and begin the journey back."

Without a word, I rose to my feet and followed Nalithor through the forest. My nerves were still shot thanks to the little twinkling pains in my ass. I didn't like the awkward silence that hung between Nalithor and me, but I couldn't think of anything to alleviate it. He had seemed upset when I brushed him away in the clearing, and that only served to make me feel worse about it.

"You said…they're frightened of you? Your darkness?" Nalithor questioned after several minutes of silence. He slowed to a stop and pivoted to look at me.

"I'm used to it," I grumbled.

"I don't think we *ever* grow truly accustomed to the jolt we feel when someone looks at us with terror in their eyes." Nalithor prodded me over the heart with one finger, a small smile on his face. "You aren't used to it. That much I can tell. I doubt you would be pouting this much otherwise."

"Not pouting!" I pulled my hood over my face entirely, feeling heat rising to my cheeks. "I—"

"Shall I speak with Ceilail and buy us more time for you to recover?" Nalithor tugged my hood from my grip, his smile replaced with an expression of concern. He didn't seem fazed by my begrudging glare at all.

"I'm fine. Haven't I been asleep for a while anyway?" I sighed as he pulled my hood down completely. "I feel creaky…"

"A day and a half, give or take a few hours," Nalithor replied with a brief nod. "I'm surprised you can already walk on your own. I thought that what you did would have drained more from you. Although…perhaps I'm more surprised that you came looking for me…" He leaned down to sniff at me. "If your magic has returned, you should rid yourself of those women's scents. They are unpleasant."

"Unpleasant?" I sniffed my right sleeve and then looked up, only to find that Nalithor had turned and started walking again. "They said they followed you out of concern, since you won't feed. Were they lying?"

"Concerned?" Nalithor shook his head, sending his braid flailing behind him. "It's hard to believe that *concern* is their reason for following me. Getting them to leave me be was horribly difficult.

"You're certain they didn't trouble you?"

"They're worried that you're either ill, or trying to harm yourself," I stated, falling into step with him. "Like I said, the people in Banayr'e have better manners than the citizens of Dauthrmir thus far. If any of them have a problem with me, other than fear, they haven't made it obvious."

"I'm not ill, and I'm not trying to harm myself." Nalithor shook his head. "Honestly. *That* is what they're thinking? I hope you don't also—"

"I'm not exactly an expert on what makes an Adinvyr tick—especially you." I rolled my eyes. "As long as you're not trying to hurt yourself, that's good enough for me. Otherwise I would have to beat some sense into you."

"I don't think I'm that difficult to figure out." Nalithor arched an eyebrow, glancing down at me. "Don't you think beating sense into me would be difficult? You have only won one of our matches."

"I didn't say I would be successful," I retorted, huffing. "I just...don't show concern well. As far as I could tell, two of the theories those women had sounded like a form of self-harm, so—"

"Two theories?" Nalithor interjected, frowning.

"Suicide was one," I replied with a brief nod, cuddling deeper into my cloaks before continuing, "the second one... They said something about noble and royal Adinvyr being known to cease feeding as a sign of courtship. Both of those options sound like causing unnecessary harm to oneself, and things like that make me see red."

"Well, firstly, I am not ill," Nalithor began with a sigh. "Secondly, the Elders would intervene if I attempted to kill myself—they don't like looking for replacements. Thirdly... I can't deny that some of my kind cease feeding as a display of dedication to the individual they want to court. Personally, I do not believe that is a wise decision.

"Simply put, I haven't been feeding because there are no brothels here for me to drain energy from. Furthermore... I haven't earned the right to feed from *you* in any manner. Now that you're weakened, it would be inappropriate of me to ask. It is considered very rude, in my culture, to ask a warrior to weaken themselves further after being injured or drained of aether."

"Those women also said something about their high concentration of ice-aspected aether in their blood?" I offered, watching as the Adinvyr shook his head. "So, you're just a picky eater?"

"It's quite simple. They both smell *and* taste atrocious." Nalithor laughed, ruffling my curls. "I appreciate your concern, Arianna. However, you are skirting the issue of whether *you* are prepared to travel again so soon. We will be escorting a good fifty people across the Abrantia Valley by ourselves."

"I'd wager we have to take a slow pace anyway, right?" I murmured, thinking. "I'm fine to travel. My main concern is how the two of us will manage to keep them from scattering if, and when, we run into beasts. If we have to set up camp for one or two nights due to the slower pace, we're inviting attacks from the damned things."

"It wouldn't be a problem if Ceilail at least gave us time to contact Dauthrmir," Nalithor remarked, sliding an arm around my shoulders. He shot me a concerned glance. "You're shivering."

"It's *cold* here!" I pointed out. "Ah… Speaking of cold, I'm sorry for my behavior earlier. Those little *shits*—"

"It's fine, Arianna," Nalithor interrupted in a soothing tone, squeezing me. "I'm surprised you're capable of working around your brother and Fraelfnir if you're *that* frightened of light. For what it's worth, the pixies were concerned about you. They didn't mean any harm."

"Darius doesn't exactly use magic much, nor does he exude any light aura to speak of—the pixies do," I mumbled, glancing to the side at Nalithor as he pulled me closer. "I know I said I'm cold, but—"

'We're being followed.' Nalithor's grip tightened. *'Did Ceilail give you the impression that her children may have become violent?'*

'No… It's someone from Banayr'e?' I frowned, reaching into the

shadows nearby.

'You can't sense them?' Nalithor shot me a concerned glance.

'I can barely sense anything *here!'* I huffed. *'It's worse now that Ceilail is free.'*

After a few more paces, Nalithor dispersed into shadows. The sudden disappearance of his warmth made me shiver and hug myself. A few strangled cries followed Nalithor's disappearance. When I turned, I found Nalithor toting a young Devillian male by the back of his coat. Due to Ceilail's corruption I couldn't quite determine the man's race. However, his face turned an interesting shade of dark blue when he spotted me.

"Apparently you have some of the village boys concerned, Arianna," Nalithor spoke conversationally, shaking the Devillian by the back of his coat. "Shall I teach him a lesson for you?"

"No. The sooner we leave, the better," I replied, arching a brow as the Devillian started muttering protests in Draemiran. *'I don't recall doing anything to attract this manner of attention.'*

'Not all *of them find you frightening,'* Nalithor stated, dropping the man haphazardly. "Very well, Arianna. Let's fetch—"

"She can't return to the village!" The young Devillian yelped, scrambling to his feet. He blocked our path, panicking. "The newer citizens don't understand our ways yet! They seek to sacrifice Reiz'tar to Mother Ceilail. They—"

"**Sacrifice?**" Nalithor growled, causing the younger Devillian to whimper. I shuddered, my skin prickling into goosebumps as I watched darkness ripple around Nalithor's form. "I will paint *every single tree* with their blood if anyone so much as—"

"Slaughter isn't what we're here for, remember?" I moved in front of Nalithor and placed a hand on his chest. He shifted his gaze to look down at me, his expression softening a little even as the darkness around him grew thicker and reached for me. "Perhaps it would be best if I leave the forest and wait for you in the plains. I don't want to make the people here more tense than they already are."

"Will you be alright on your own? I don't want to leave you…" Nalithor's darkness wrapped around my legs and torso, pressing against the small of my back.

"I'll be *fine*." I nodded, twitching as his darkness slid across my skin. "Just try not to linger too long, alright? I can't promise that I won't start hunting beasts without you if you take—"

Nalithor leaned down and gave me a firm but brief kiss, stunning me into silence. I simply blinked up at him for a moment. I didn't know what kind of reaction he was looking for, but he seemed satisfied. Nalithor released me, smirking, and moved off in the direction of Banayr'e with the ice-corrupted Devillian in tow.

I sped off in the direction of Ceilail's southwestern border with Abrantia, convinced that my face was scarlet. It seemed like the best way to get my mind off his kiss would be to preoccupy myself with speedy travel through the dense, frosty underbrush. I didn't understand how such a brief kiss could make my pulse race faster than fear ever had.

'He...he's making me hesitant to let my guard down, and *about putting away the Umbral Mage facade.'* I gnawed on my lip while I ran, wincing when I cut myself on one of my fangs. *I'm always "on duty" around him. Or at least I try to act that way. What would happen if I...'*

I shook my head violently and burst out of the Ceilail Forest, into the Abrantia Valley. The warm spring air made me roast within seconds. Cursing, I stripped off the layers of robes and cloaks, then tossed them into a shrizar. I let out a small sigh of relief as the wind made my damp skin grow cool once more. I must have been running harder than I thought if I'd managed to break a sweat while running through the forest of *ice*, of all places.

After switching to robes suitable for travel, I perched on a large rock and yawned, waiting for Nalithor. *'Just great. I'm going to have to share his attention again.'*

Sighing, I tilted my head back and stared up at the stars in an attempt to clear my head of such useless thoughts. I needed to be focused for our journey back to Dauthrmir. It wouldn't do for me to get distracted and miss something stalking us. We needed to protect ourselves *and* the people we were escorting. *'Djialkan isn't here to help refocus me, and* that one *doesn't seem like he would...'*

"You still owe me breakfast after we return," Nalithor commented from somewhere behind me. He slowed to a halt beside my perch and traced his fingers down my spine, his expression soft but indecipherable.

"I haven't forgotten." I laughed, shaking my head. "Think of any brilliant plans for keeping everyone together?"

"Mrifon," Nalithor reminded me, tugging at my curls. "Luckily there are few children among the former captives…and most of them are easily manageable by their parents. However, they are…"

'Scared of me, right?' I rolled my eyes before pulling a portion of my curls up, sliding an ornament with two mrifon into place. *'It's fine, Nalithor, really. That I've been able to find anyone similar to me is already surprising—'*

'It's not *fine,'* Nalithor grumbled, hugging me for a moment before moving away. *'We…should get going. The longer we linger, the more likely it is that beasts will find us. I have contacted Amakiir already—he said that some of his warriors will join us in a few hours to assist.*

'After you've rested, and recovered the remainder of your strength, can I convince you to oversee a few more classes at the academy with me?'

'Ah… Are you sure?' I shot him a curious look and slipped off my perch. *'I don't mind.'*

'Excellent.' Nalithor beamed at me, then turned his attention to the ragged group behind us. *'For now, you take the lead and I'll bring up the rear. By the time we arrive in Amakiir's village, more ships should be waiting for us along the Dauthrmiran Barrier.'*

'How are we going to handle making camp when this lot grows too tired?' I questioned, tracking the Adinvyr as he moved away to inform our wards of the plan.

'I have some supplies in my shrizar for occasions such as this,' Nalithor murmured in thought. *'Amakiir's men are bringing us more. Usually there aren't this many captives in a caravan... That I couldn't get more information out of those* bastards *is upsetting.'*

'You could have let them live longer,' I pointed out with a small smile, taking my place in front. After stretching out the kinks from sitting on the rock, I summoned lightweight armor around myself and a swordbelt.

'Which reminds me...' Nalithor paused, likely addressing someone's concerns. *'Thank you for ending the fool that attacked me from behind and thank you for taking care of me while I recovered, Arianna.'*

'Ah...you're welcome,' I mumbled, feeling my face flush. *'Are you usually so reckless?'*

'Only when I'm confident that my partner will pull their weight.' Nalithor chuckled. *'Everyone is ready to move out when you are, Arianna.'*

After a few deep breaths I managed to calm myself and settled into the proper mindset for our journey. I planned to treat it like an extended hunt even though Nalithor's presence felt so relaxed. Pivoting, I motioned for those nearest to me to begin following me through the high grasses.

After perhaps an hour of silence, Nalithor's presence nudged me again. *'I'm curious, just what sort of state was Sihix in the first time you visited? Djialkan said you were sleepwalking, yet you said the situation was similar.'*

'Djialkan showed you the sickened Angelic runes, yes?' I pursed my lips, playing with a blade of grass as I walked; boredom was slowly beginning to drive me crazy. *'The entirety of the Sihix Forest was covered in those. I was too young to truly understand what they were, but my instincts screamed that they were "wrong." Unlike the runes in Ceilail, the ones in Sihix were fully pitch black and covered every inch of…well, everything.'*

'You have spoken with Sihix itself then, haven't you? As you have with Ceilail?' Nalithor probed.

'No. Sihix was more damaged by the ordeal than Ceilail was,' I replied, a small frown tugging at my lips. The situation struck me as a little strange, to say the least, and I wasn't sure how much I could divulge to Nalithor. *'Corentine and the Guardians have been taking care of Sihix and healing him somewhere. Djialkan has spoken with him personally, but they have kept me away.*

'They're concerned that, because of my affinity with darkness, I might spend too much of my own power healing Sihix.'

'Lari'xan are powerful beings,' Nalithor murmured. *'I would still like to speak with Sihix, but if he's in that poor of shape—'*

'Corentine can act as an intermediary, so long as you filter out her attitude. The same goes for Djialkan,' I interjected dryly. *'You're*

likely going to need to utilize the Sihix Forest in your assault on X'shmir when the time comes anyway. You can pester me for information on that *later. There's too much to show you and doing so while traveling would be foolish.'*

'Very well, I will be patient.' Nalithor chuckled. *'Oh? Did you find a beast, my dear? Your bloodlust is—"*

'Just some small ones.' I grinned, sinking into a crouch. *'I'll take care of them. See if our charges are capable of picking up the pace, will you? I don't like having to worry about the wellbeing of others when I hunt!'*

'Oh? Is that why you seem so averse to having a partner?' Nalithor's tone was a little *too* innocent.

I pulled my swords from their sheathes and rushed through the grass. Too many days had passed since my last hunt.

'I'm not averse to it...' I mumbled, flipping my grip on one of my swords so that I could tear through one of the beasts lengthwise. *'Finding someone I can rely on, let alone trust, is just...difficult. That it's even in the realm of possibility still seems strange to me.'*

Nalithor chuckled again before falling silent, leaving me to focus on the beasts. Despite how nervous he could make me, working him was sounding better and better all the time. However, I wasn't sure how I felt about having to be his *food* if we were to work together. Taking my blood seemed risky, and the other option... Sure, he was nice to look at, but I needed a better reason than that to justify letting him feed off me in such an intimate way.

"Just how many of you are there?!" I demanded, indignant, when I spotted even more beasts slinking through the grass. "Fine. You want to play? Let's play."

END OF BOOK TWO

Thank you for reading!

Also: Please take a moment to leave a review!

Reviews are the lifeblood of any indie author and can make or break the success of a book. It doesn't need to be long, it could be a few words saying what you liked or five things you think could have been done better. Even a sentence or two would mean the world to me and would help me continue to write books in the future.

CONTINUE READING FOR HOW TO CONNECT
WITH THE AUTHOR, UPCOMING RELEASES, AND
MORE!

BOOK TWO GLOSSARY

HONORIFICS

Chrot'zi	The Draemiran form of address for an Astral Mage.
Lyur'zi	The Draemiran form of address for an Umbral Mage.
Reiz'tar	A formal way to address women of high status. It is used similarly to "my lady." Also used when addressing someone whose name is unknown to you, or if it isn't appropriate to speak someone's forename—such as an Empress.
Rely'ric	A formal way to address men of high status. It is used similarly to "my lord." Also used when addressing someone whose name is unknown to you, or if it isn't appropriate to speak someone's forename—such as an Emperor.
Mrirtec	"Young Master" or "Little Master" in the Draemiran tongue.
-jiss	A Draemiran honorific suffix used for

	daughters of royal and imperial families.
-tyir	A gender-neutral Draemiran honorific suffix that is used to formalize addressing someone.
-y'ric	A Draemiran honorific suffix derived from Rely'ric, -y'ric is most often attached to the given name of the person being addressed. Although it is most often used for men of high status, it is not uncommon for people to use –y'ric as a form of address for a man they are courting.
-zir	A Draemiran honorific suffix used for sons of royal and imperial families.
-z'tar	A Draemiran honorific suffix derived from Reiz'tar, -z'tar is most often attached to the given name of the person being addressed. Although it is most often used for women of high status, it is not uncommon for people to use -z'tar as a form of address for a woman they are courting.
	## PLACES
Beshulthien	An empire founded by the patriarch of the

	Vampire race.
Vorpmasia(n)	The Vorpmasian Empire was founded by the Devillian patriarch, Lucifer. Vorpmasia is made up of eleven separate territories, with a central capitol.
Dauthrmir	The capitol of the Vorpmasian Empire.
Draemir	The territory of the Vorpmasian Empire that is overseen by the God and Goddess of Adinvyr.
Gal'edean Ocean	The vast ocean to the east of the Rilzaan Continent, the Gal'edean Ocean is ruled by a variety of sea-faring and aquatic races.
Suthsul Desert	A large desert to the south of the Vorpmasia Empire, and home to the Vunsori—Desert Elves.
V'frul	The Vunsori capital deep within the Suthsul Desert.
X'shmir	A human city-state located on one of Avrirsa's many flying islands. Ruled by the Black Family.

RACES

Adinvyr	A Devillian race with strong ties to sex and sexuality. In order to survive, they must periodically feed on sexual energy which

	they can take from their prey in various forms.
Akor	A Devillian race characterized by their stone-colored range of skin tones and fiery appearance. The Akor have a close relationship with volcanic areas due to their need to drink and bathe in lava.
Imviir	A Devillian race with humanoid torsos and faces but are like a serpent from the waist down. They prefer to live in humid jungles. Imviir possess both fangs and venom like a snake.
Jrachra	A Devillian race that lives and breathes everything arcane. From a young age they paint aether-infused sigils on their bodies. The number of sigils on a Jrachra indicates power and age. The brilliance of the aether indicates status. The color(s) indicate elemental affinity.
Kelsviir	Also known as "Dauthrmiran Elves," the Kelsviir are fiercely loyal to the Vorpmasian Emperor and treat him with the same respect afforded to a race's patriarchal and matriarchal deities.

	Unlike the other Elven races, Kelsviir have skin tones similar to the colors of stones, ranging from pure white like marble to pitch black like obsidian. All tones between are varying shades of grey. Due to the environment and the prevalence of dark aether, they have evolved to have dark sclera like Devillians, and parts of their bodies can contain bioluminescence.
Rylthra	A Devillian race with the characteristics of a fox. Although their faces and bodies are similar to that of Humans and Elves, Rylthra have ears and tails like foxes. Their fur and hair color are sometimes mismatched. Rylthra are capable of shapeshifting into the full form of a fox. The number of tails is indicative of age and power. Those with multiple tails often become priest(esses) or Oracles.
Sizoul	A Devillian race which lives in an isolated,

	northern part of the Suthsul Desert that technically belongs to the Vorpmasian Empire. Sizoul have an appearance similar to that of the Desert Elves, but retain the horns, tails, claws, fangs, and black sclera of the other Devillian races.
	Unlike other Devillians, Sizoul's horns, tails, claws, and eye colors take on the appearance of precious and semi-precious gems.
	While the other Devillian races take interest in war, Sizoul prefer to make and create things.
Sundreht	The shortest of the Devillian races, Sundreht have ears and tails like a cat. Despite their comparatively small stature, Sundreht are one of the more battle-oriented races.
Vampire	A sanguine race created by a twisted god who preyed on a Devillian prince's wish for more power. Despite the prince's desires, Vampires are weaker than Devillians.
Varjior	A race of shapeshifters that can take on

	animal form. Although often confused for Devillian, they are something else entirely.
Vunsori	The proper name for "Desert Elves."

DRAEMIRAN LANGUAGE

shrizar	A Draemiran term that was popularized during the foundation of the Vorpmasian Empire. A "shrizar" refers to the pockets of magic a mage can create and utilize for the storage of items.
fiirzik	A strong alcoholic beverage that is served hot.
varikna	One of the strongest forms of liquor to ever come out of Vorpmasia; even a few sips of this drink is too much for most Humans and Elves.
mrilec	A sweet, wine-like beverage popular among Draemirans. It is a brilliant blue color. One of its primary ingredients is taken from the mrifon tree.
mrifon	A type of tree native to Draemir. It has dark bark with brilliant blue veins of bioluminescence running through it.

	Though "mri" loosely translates to "small," the flowers the tree produces in the spring are the size of dinner plates.
Groslturvir	Draemir's winter festival.
Lari'xan	A Draemiran term than can be translated as Elemental Gods, Local Gods, or Aetherial Gods.
dehsul	A Draemiran curse word that's used in a similar fashion to "fuck!"
jich	A Draemiran curse word that's used in a similar fashion to "shit!"
sh'rlic marnas	A command which roughly translates to "break apart."
throstor	A Draemiran word with combined meanings: "die" and "get out of my sight."

FAE LANGUAGE

Eri'na Jutae, eohim caisa uo	"Eri'na Jutae" a formal manner of address that conveys similar meaning to saying, "my paramour." "eohim caisa uo" is a respectful way of telling someone to put distance between themselves and someone else.

AVAILABLE NOW

Of Astral and Umbral

Beneath the Mists

Deck of Souls

Fateseal

COMING SOON

Of Astral and Umbral

Book 3, Mid-to-Late 2019

Deck of Souls

Fateseal Audiobook, Mid 2019

Book 2, Mid 2019

New Series

Late 2019-Early 2020

ABOUT THE AUTHOR

Bonnie L. Price was born in 1990 and has lived in four different states. At the age of twelve, while living in rural Upstate New York, she turned to writing as a way to entertain herself. Without internet or TV, there was little else to do during the long, cold winters.

What started as a way to amuse herself soon became a passion, and she's been writing ever since.

Want to connect with Bonnie?

FAN GROUP: FACEBOOK.COM/GROUPS/BLP.DEMONDEN

DISCORD: HTTPS://DISCORD.GG/GRUGC2R

AUTHOR PAGE: FACEBOOK.COM/BONNIELPRICEOFFICIAL

TWITTER: HTTPS://TWITTER.COM/BONNIE_L_PRICE

ILLUSTRATION

In love with the cover illustration? Want to see more from the artist? Check out the links below for how to follow her!

LAS-T.DEVIANTART.COM/

LAS-T.ARTSTATION.COM/

FACEBOOK.COM/ThanderLin.Illustration